THE
EIGHTH
CONTINENT

RHETT C. BRUNO
FELIX R. SAVAGE

aethonbooks.com

THE EIGHTH CONTINENT
©2023 RHETT C. BRUNO/FELIX R. SAVAGE

Also in Eight Continent:

THE EIGHTH CONTINENT

MOON 2.0

LUNAR SUPREMACY

Check out the entire series here!

(tap or scan)

PROLOGUE

A soft, relentless throbbing reverberated all around. And the walls amplified it. The same walls trapping him, enclosing his mind in a spiral of terror. Trapped. With the bodies.

Blood pooled on the floor. Even painted the consoles and ceiling in splattery, low-gravity arcs.

Dead eyes stared at him, accusing him of treachery, and worse, neglect.

The stomach-turning stench of death coated his nostrils. He floundered across the floor, avoiding the dead, his gaze fixed on Nick standing at the consoles.

"No! Stop!" His voice was insubstantial beneath the pistons of the Stirling's engines thudding back and forth inside their steel housings.

"I have to turn it off," Nick said.

"No! You'll kill the power to the landers—to everything!"

"There's still the Artemis shuttle." Sweat flattened Nick Morrison's fair hair to his head, his hands visibly shaking over the reactor controls. Tears glistened on his face. But his words... They were like rocks thrown into the quivering air.

Stop him, the dead urged. *We're frightened.*

That was the thing about this place. It allowed the voices of the dead to reach you. Their reproaches were the hardest to bear. But in this case, they weren't telling him anything he didn't know. Everyone was frightened on the moon. The only question was whether they let it show.

Nick was starting to show it, at last. The sight dragged up a vicious satisfaction, even amidst the terror of this death chamber. Nick's refusal to show fear had always irritated him. Now even this stony-faced man was cracking.

"How long have you been on the moon?" The wire cutters hung heavy in his right hand. The handles were tacky with blood.

"Too long," Nick said.

"That's right." He tightened his hold on the wire cutters.

"What do you mean?"

"You're never going home."

The boat scraped over a submerged car's roof, and Nick Morrison pushed off with the Halligan bar before the outboard could foul. Brown water slopped over the gunnel rail.

Ryder Stillman crouched in the prow, peering through the rain with hungry eyes. "Man, look at these houses."

"Why do people still live here?" Nick said. "Why don't they just pack up and leave?"

"'Cause they're rich. Throw enough money at it, fixes everything," Ryder said.

The colonnades and verandahs of palatial homes seemed to float above flooded lawns. Merritt Island was one of the most exclusive neighborhoods in Florida. Of course, that didn't protect it from the weather. Four category 3s in five years, and now Tropical Storm Molly had dumped enough water into Banana River to submerge the whole isthmus.

Nick glanced at the phone strapped to his wrist, checking the app that connected rescuers to people trapped by the floods. "It's this one."

He guided the boat toward a three-story colonial, its hipped roof missing a lot of tiles. Like most houses in the area, it was raised off the ground on stilts with a garage underneath. All the same, water lapped at the downstairs windows and wet curtains flapped around broken glass.

"What a waste. When I strike it rich, I sure ain't gonna live in Hurricane Alley," Ryder said.

"You'd blow it all on something pointless. When *I'm* rich—"

Ryder laughed. "You're never gonna be rich. You don't have what it takes."

Nick compressed his answer into a soundless exhalation. He maneuvered the boat across the submerged front yard, around a fallen palm tree with a child's bicycle caught in its branches. The arched front door stood open, so they wouldn't need the Halligan bar to break it down.

"Harriet Fitzgerald," he read off the app. "Seventy-eight."

He cut the outboard. The current carried the boat into the porch, and they moored it to a column.

The boat belonged to Ryder. He used it for fishing and duck-hunting, when they weren't convoying up and down the East Coast, responding to volunteer calls. Of course, Ryder's motives were far from selfless. Before disembarking, he opened a gun box fastened to the inside of the hull. Nick caught the glint of precious metals from watches and jewelry stirring around as Ryder fished his SIG Sauer P238 out. Ryder locked the gun box and stuck the pistol into his thigh pocket.

It was a sensible precaution. They had surprised looters more than once in storm-flooded neighborhoods. Nick took his dive knife.

They splashed into the house through thigh-deep water, lugging the folding stretcher and first-aid kit, shouting, "Ms. Fitzgerald! Ma'am! Excuse me!"

Their southern politeness never failed. Ryder was a Charleston native. Nick had been born in South Africa, but he'd grown up in North Carolina.

"Ma'am, you there?"

"In here," a weak voice called from the back of the house.

The hall could have hangared a small airplane. A flight of stairs covered in sodden cream carpet curved up to the second floor. Ryder vanished up the stairs. Nick waded into a huge open-plan kitchen and dining room. Ammonia fumes stung his eyes and nose. People always stored toxic cleaning products below the waterline. Never dreaming there might one day *be* a waterline inside their houses, in spite of four straight decades of record temperatures, rising seas, and hurricanes that had obliterated the Florida Keys and the Louisiana bayous.

On a granite countertop sat a slender old woman. Rain beat on the windows at her back. She was aiming a Glock at Nick, and her wrists didn't look all that frail.

Nick raised his hands as best he could while burdened with the stretcher and first-aid kit. "We're here to help." Holding the old woman's eyes, he reached into the breast pocket of his jacket and dangled his Low Country Navy lanyard where she could see it. Of course, there was no reason a bad guy couldn't have gotten himself a lanyard. The proof was upstairs. The old woman relaxed and managed a smile, lowering her gun.

"I'm sorry to be so suspicious," she said. "Some other young men came yesterday. I think it was yesterday..." She suddenly looked incredibly tired. "They took my daughter's computer, the television. Simply deplorable."

"There are some real scumbags out there," Nick said.

Harriet Fitzgerald sounded like a New Englander. You retire to a palace on the Florida coast and the next thing you know, the ocean is in your kitchen and thugs are walking off with your valuables. It must be hard to adjust. Hard to accept that the world's changed since you were a girl. The planet is slowly turning into a steam cooker, and it's only going to get worse. Sea levels were predicted to rise five feet by the end of the century, and humanity was *still* pumping out CO2.

"I didn't think anyone was going to come," Harriet said pathetically. "I called 911, but no one picked up."

"They're overwhelmed, ma'am; forwarded you on to us. So why don't we get you out of here and—"

"Are you a firefighter?" Harriet seemed confused, perhaps on account of what Nick was wearing: black hip-waders and a foul-weather fishing jacket.

"No, ma'am. We're commercial divers—Ryder! Ms. Fitzgerald's in here."

The beefy man splashed into the kitchen, looking pissed. Doubtless the looters Harriet mentioned had already taken all the good stuff.

Nick gave Harriet a drink of Emergen-C. "We work for a company up in Charleston. Drove down when the storm made landfall, so right now, we're volunteers. Can you walk? Are you hurt anywhere?"

"No, I don't think so. You're very kind."

"Just doing what we can, ma'am. Are we ready to go?" Ryder asked.

"I'll carry her," Nick said. Harriet had no injuries that would require the use of the stretcher, and she looked to weigh less than a healthy twelve-year-old.

"Oh, don't make such a fuss. But—" Harriet gripped Nick's arm. "Before we go, I wonder if I could ask a favor. There's something very important to my daughter those young men *didn't* get, that I would just hate to leave behind."

"What exactly?" Nick said, impatient. The app showed a backlog of more than a hundred people awaiting rescue, likely in places more uncomfortable and perilous than Harriet Fitzgerald's two-million-dollar home.

"It's a safe. Just a small one. It's bolted down, I'm afraid, but

I can give you the combination, and you could retrieve the contents—"

Ryder snapped to attention. "No problem, ma'am. Whereabouts is it at?"

"Well, that's the trouble. It's down there." She pointed across the kitchen at a door Nick immediately knew led to the submerged garage and rec room.

2

"We can't go down there," Nick said. "It's flooded."

"Oh. I just thought, as you said you were divers... Well, never mind."

"Sure, we can do it," Ryder said, levelling a stare at Nick. "We got our kit in the boat."

Nick had wanted to be an astronaut when he was a kid. He'd watched the second moon landing in 2026, glued to the TV, breathless with all the wonder a young mind can hold. Those heroic explorers in their pressure suits and gold face-plates had become his role models. He wanted to do something like that, something big and good. But after Nick and his mother moved to America, his grades nose-dived and never recovered. NASA didn't want C students with disciplinary issues. He'd ended up dropping out of UNC and getting his commercial diving license.

The thing was, it *wasn't* second best. He loved the water. Ever since he could remember, nothing could keep him away from puddles, rivers, waterholes, beaches...

And now, catastrophic flood zones.

Their passion for diving was the only thing Nick and Ryder had in common. So, of course they had their kit in the boat.

Not the bulky dive suits, hoses, and air compressors they used on the job. You needed a far bigger boat for all that, and a tender to manage the air supply up top. But they each owned a personal mini scuba kit they'd brought along. And *why*? Why would anyone choose to work for so little money, in an environment so hostile to human life?

Well, in Ryder's case, because you never knew when you'd get the chance to dive into a flooded rec room and steal the contents of a helpless old lady's safe.

In Nick's case, maybe because he knew some day he'd have to stop him.

Out on the porch, Ryder stripped off his jacket, exchanged his waders for flippers, and spat into his dive mask to defog it.

"It's not safe," Nick said.

"Life ain't safe," Ryder said. "You're scared, you stay up here. Just talk to her and keep her calm."

"This isn't like robbing a bank vault. The woman's like eighty years old."

"Hey, man, if you don't want your cut, fine by me."

Nick realized that he fucking hated Ryder Stillman. He opened the boat's other storage box and got out his scuba kit. Ryder gave him a sneering smile and clapped him on the shoulder. He was ten years older than Nick, an inch taller, and built like a Mack truck. Nick was five-eleven, lanky, but stronger than he looked.

They waded back into the kitchen, frog-footed in their flippers. Out of habit, Nick checked that the power was switched off at the mains. They weren't going to get electrocuted in this situation. The grid was down as far inland as Orlando.

After Harriet told them the combination to the safe, they

shuffled down the stairs until the black water closed over their heads.

———

Nick's headlamp illuminated debris bumping against his mask, but not much more. The water was foul with mud, silt, and no doubt toxic chemicals. Nick had dived in worse conditions. You can't be a diver if you can't handle enclosed spaces. Limited visibility. *Traps.*

A child's toy robot drifted in front of him, followed by a Tupperware with tiny components inside. Harriet had said her daughter used the rec room as some kind of workshop.

A strong current pushed against the left side of Nick's body, forcing him to swim into it at an angle. Garage doors open, he figured. Windows likely broken on the other side of the rec room. Water flowing straight through the basement from one inlet of the Banana River into another. He finned vigorously, chasing the fuzzy dot of Ryder's headlamp.

I think it's in the corner, Harriet had said. *Near the scale model on the workbench.*

Ryder's headlamp backed out of the corner nearest the door and headed deeper into the rec room.

Nick followed.

The headlamp light sank toward the floor, and now Nick could see Ryder in his own fuzzy circle of light, reaching for a foot-square safe underneath a built-in workbench heaped with shadows.

A shoal of books engulfed Nick's head, pages fanning out like the frills of tropical fish.

Something entangled his legs. He kicked, getting tangled up worse. Breathing regularly, he doubled over and slashed with his dive knife at sodden yards of rubber and ripstop nylon.

The current struck him hard, shoving him sideways. It tore the knife out of his hand.

Ryder was halfway under the workbench. The current flipped his feet over his head and pushed him across the top.

Glass glinted in Nick's headlamp.

In a confused instant, Nick saw what was on top of the workbench: a three-foot sculpture of what looked like a gallows, protected by a dome of glass, which was now *broken* glass. An industrial robotic arm had fallen on top of it, plunging its claw through the dome. And Ryder was caught on the spear-sharp shards. He was struggling. His mouthpiece had fallen out of his mouth. Bubbles streamed away in the surging current.

The water swept Nick under the workbench. He twisted and hit the wall feet-first. He caught hold of the safe to steady himself and it shifted. It *wasn't* bolted down!

Wrapping his arms around the safe, he kicked off from the wall. Nick pushed the safe across the floor, using it as an anchor so he wouldn't be swept away and pinned against the wall.

Ryder thrashed, face-down on top of the broken glass dome. His regulator trailed free in the water. The bubbles rising from his mouth were tinged red.

Nick thought about going back to help him. An office chair tumbled against him, delivering a shock of pain to his hip and side. He lost his grip on the safe and had to flail wildly to recover it. He didn't look back again. His air hose might get sliced on those shards of glass. The plain fact was, Ryder wasn't worth dying for.

He reached the stairs and heaved the safe onto the first step. The current lost some of its wild strength.

Second step.

He breathed deeply, steadily.

Third step.

The basement door glowed overhead. Nick hauled himself

and the safe through it. His head broke the surface. The water sluicing off his dive mask sparkled prismatically. Unexpected sunshine filled the kitchen.

Harriet stood on the countertop, sunlight pouring through the windows behind her like lemonade. The water surged around her ankles, carrying boxes and cartons newly swept off the kitchen shelves.

"What's happening?" she cried.

Nick spat out his mouthpiece. His jaw ached from gripping it too tightly between his teeth. "Guess another levee broke somewhere. The water might rise more."

"Are you all right?" Harriet eyed the murky water. "Is your friend all right?"

Nick dumped the safe on the kitchen table, which was now half a foot under water. He pushed his dive mask up on top of his head and squinted into the sudden brightness. It happened like this sometimes. The clouds would part, even though it was still raining in fits and splatters.

"He was right behind me," Nick said.

Any diver on the planet would see his situation the same way. It was a risky profession. Risks Ryder had been fully aware of. Nick warned him the rec room probably wasn't safe and he'd gone down anyway. No one would blame Nick for what happened.

The surging water in the kitchen flexed, rising higher. Nick wondered how long he should wait before making a pretense of searching for Ryder.

"You found the safe," Harriet said tremulously.

"Yes, ma'am. Let's get you out to the boat."

Harriet refused to be carried. Nick helped her across the kitchen, one arm wrapped around her thin waist. He couldn't carry the safe at the same time. If she insisted, he would come back for it after he got her safely into the boat. Personally, he didn't give a rat's ass about it.

They'd almost reached the kitchen door when Ryder broke the surface, mouth open, gasping desperately.

Harriet screamed.

Ryder took a staggering step and vomited. He was clutching his left arm. Blood welled through his fingers. He fixed Nick with a glare of hatred that made Nick think of the great white shark he'd once fought off in a North Carolina marina. It'd had nothing in its brain except the desire to kill him.

3

The refugees were being warehoused in a Wumart near the West Cocoa Beach Causeway. When they got there, National Guard helicopters were landing and taking off in the uncertain sunshine. Nick escorted Harriet to the Red Cross tent in the parking lot, which was still mostly dry thanks to its elevation.

"Excuse me, this lady needs to be medevaced. She's dehydrated and in shock." On the way back, Harriet had kept calling Nick "Reed," presumably the name of someone she knew.

As the paramedics took her blood pressure, she turned to him and said with total clarity, "Oh, no! The safe! I must have left it in the boat. After all the trouble you and your friend went to..."

Nick cursed under his breath. Reaching the edge of the water where it'd leveled out, he waded back across the lower parking lot. Turds and garbage eddied around stranded cars. They had tied the boat to a tree near the flooded Pammy's Seafood Shack. Ryder, hunched over, worked on something in the bottom of the boat. Nick approached cautiously.

Ryder looked up from a now opened and empty safe.

"What was in there?" Nick said.

Ryder held up a Ziploc full of papers. Water streaked the outside of the plastic bag, but the papers appeared to be undamaged. "Just this." He tossed it back into the safe, banged it shut, and gave the dial a whirl.

Nick reached over the gunnel and hefted the safe into his arms. "You'd better not have taken anything. She'll know it was you."

"She'll know it was *you*."

Ryder, on their way back, had bandaged his arm himself, using the self-adhesive gauze out of their first-aid kit. Blood was already soaking through the gauze, leaving Rorschach-like drips on Ryder's wet shorts.

"You need to get that stitched up," Nick said.

"You need to shut your fucking mouth."

Ryder came back to the Red Cross tent with him, anyway.

They returned the safe to Harriet. Twittering genteel thanks, she vanished into a helicopter bound for the mainland. There was an hour's wait for a paramedic to see to Ryder's arm. Nick stood outside the tent, thinking about what he was going to have to do next.

The smell of raw sewage steamed up from the water at the edges of the parking lot. The clouds had split for now and retreated to the western horizon, leaving most of the sky blue.

A large star rose in the north. In perfect silence, it shot higher and higher, leaving a contrail twice as wide as an airplane's. With a start, Nick remembered where they were: Space Coast. He'd seen this on a hundred livestreams and videos. He stared, open-mouthed. About thirty seconds after the star had appeared, the noise hit him. It came from all around, as if he were standing next to an invisible railroad with a bullet train passing.

Ryder limped out of the tent, his arm freshly bandaged, and looked up. "The fuck is that?"

"Either a Blue Titan or a SpaceZ Ultra Heavy," Nick said. The rocket itself was too small to see, but its flame glinted at the tip of the contrail. "Probably an Ultra Heavy. Three cores. Thirty-three engines. Fifteen million pounds of thrust. Gotta be a supply run for one of the space stations or the international moon base. Heh—the storm must've cost them a *fortune*. Every time a launch is aborted, they have to drain the liquid fuel tanks and start all over."

"Why do you even know this shit?" Ryder said.

"Look around you. This planet has no future."

"Uh huh." Ryder examined the blister-packed tablets in his fist. "Only two Vicodin. Are you fucking kidding me?"

The thunder of the launch faded below the threshold of hearing. The star lost itself in the sky. Nick struggled with a pang of wistfulness. For the last fifteen years, humans had lived on the moon, conducting research and trialing ISRU technologies—In Situ Resource Utilization. Three separate manned missions to Mars were in the planning stages. But actual colonization—of the moon, Mars, or anywhere else—was as far off as it had been in the 1960s. The roughly one hundred humans in space depended absolutely on resupply flights.

Nick and Ryder headed back to Ryder's pickup, parked near the Wumart building. The other two guys they'd come down with were sitting on Ryder's boat trailer.

Vincent raised his Coors tallboy in greeting. "Causeway's closed," he said.

"Until they know how high the surge is gonna get," Jose said.

The four of them had been staying in a motel on the mainland. Nick's car was there. He'd been planning to get on I-95 and not stop until he reached Charleston.

"Which means we're stuck here?" Ryder said with a smile. "Goddamn."

"What happened to your arm?" Vincent said.

Nick tensed.

"Snagged it on some fucking thing underwater," Ryder said easily.

So that was how he was going to play it.

The two boat owners, Ryder and Vincent, drove down as close as they could get to the improvised mooring. Nick and Jose helped them haul their boats onto the trailers and lock them down. They'd already transferred their loot into their backpacks.

Vincent and Jose were in on Ryder's game. They sold what they stole to a fence in Atlanta for pennies on the dollar.

Nick had taken a cut from time to time, either for holding stuff or just saying nothing. That had been his mistake. He needed the money, but the money was never enough to make it worth it.

He caught Ryder whispering to Vincent as they headed back to the Wumart. Both glanced at Nick with undisguised hostility.

The superstore had become an indoor tent city. There was hardly room to walk between the groups of people camped out on FEMA-supplied tarps. Apart from those stenciled logos, there was no sign that FEMA had ever been there, or ever would be there. The federal government had almost entirely retreated into its metropolitan strongholds. Elsewhere, it was every state for itself, with assistance from volunteer organizations such as the Low Country Navy. Corporations played their part, too, whether they liked it or not. The shelves of the Wumart had been picked nearly clean of edibles and anything else that gave comfort.

Nick, Ryder, Vincent, and Jose found themselves a few square feet of floor space in the toy section; too close to the over-flowing toilets. They sat on the muddy linoleum. Vincent parceled out some jerky and Snickers bars he'd had in his boat. He left Nick for last, and as it turned out, there wasn't any leftover.

"Sorry." He grinned.

Nick shrugged. He wasn't hungry, anyway. His stomach felt like a stone.

4

Night engulfed the Wumart, pierced here and there by flashlights and phone screens. Nick got up on the pretext of going for a leak. He used his phone to light his way to the other side of the store, as far from the other guys as he could get. He sat down in the DIY section, with his folded drysuit between himself and the filthy floor, his back uncomfortably propped against empty shelves.

People quarreled and complained. Children cried. If Ryder came after him, he would be defenseless. His phone was now drained of charge, so he couldn't make an emergency call. The Halligan bar was in the boat. He didn't even have his dive knife. That was $200 ripped right out of his hand.

His gaze roamed the darkness. At the end of the aisle, the backspill from a phone screen gleamed on a few rakes, trowels, and hoes hanging from hooks. Nick moved closer to the display of tools.

Sitting in the dark, he listened to a woman talking on the phone to her family in Orlando. She had diabetes, but was out of insulin. She hung up and lay on the floor, sobbing. Nick opened his backpack and searched it by feel. He wasn't going to find any insulin in there, but maybe he could give her bottled water or something.

His fingers closed on a metal cylinder with a ridge along one side.

Harriet Fitzgerald's Glock.

She'd given it to him to hold, and he'd dropped it in his pack to have his hands free. Then it had slipped her mind, just like the safe.

A sensation of cold revulsion spread from Nick's fingers up his arm. He steeled himself. Taking the Glock out of his pack, he handled it under the cover of darkness, desensitizing himself to its wicked weight. Glocks weren't made with a safety. You just pull the trigger.

Nick didn't know how to remove the magazine, so he'd just have to hope it was loaded. Just have to hope it didn't come to that.

———

He jerked awake.

A cold hard object dug into his neck. He flinched and froze.

"Get the fuck up," Ryder Stillman whispered.

"What do you want?" Nick said, barely moving his lips.

"Just want to talk."

"What about?"

Another jab under his jaw. "About Jesus Christ, our Lord and Savior." Ryder chuckled coldly. "Have some faith in people."

Nick ducked his head and rolled away, hoping to reach the display of tools. Ryder intercepted him with a kick to his face. Cold pain starred into his eyes.

"Now," Ryder said. "Move."

Nick stumbled to his feet. The point of impact on his forehead was hot and cold by turns, pulsing.

Ryder stepped back a pace, pointing the SIG Sauer at Nick's stomach. His twisted grin was just visible in the gauzy grayness of predawn. Ryder must have started to search for him as soon as dawn broke. Nick looked past Ryder. Vincent was coming along the aisle. Jose, the timid one, wasn't there. He wouldn't do anything. He'd keep his trap shut though, just like Nick always had.

"*Walk.*"

Nick carried his backpack by the straps in one hand. It was sagging open, but he hadn't heard the Glock fall out. Maybe he'd left it in the DIY aisle. Ryder prodded him toward the back of the store. They stepped around and over sleeping people. Vincent stopped to ease a phone here, a handbag there, out from under limp hands. He rifled through the bags, took the wallets, and dropped the bags on empty shelves.

Swinging double doors said *Employees Only.* Ryder pushed Nick into the stock area, keeping his pistol in contact with the small of Nick's back. "You don't have any family in this country," he said. "No one's even gonna notice if you disappear."

Ryder was wrong about that. Nick did have family in this country. He'd just never mentioned them to Ryder. The thought of his mother tipped him from numb shock into anger.

"What are you gonna tell Jeff?" he said.

Jeff was their boss at SubSea Solutions, an industry veteran with a hearty grin and no interest in finding out about his employees' shenanigans.

"Why would I tell him anything?"

"He's gonna wonder what happened."

"No, he ain't. You're the type of guy that would quit without saying anything, anyway."

It was brighter back here. A slight breeze carried the smell of the floodwaters into the store. People slept on the floor and the lower warehouse shelves. Ryder tugged the sleeve of his hoodie over his gun hand to hide the SIG Sauer. Vincent lagged behind, consolidating his new haul of loot into his backpack. Nick thought about running, but the aisles were long and straight with no cover, and too many people were in the way.

The loading docks at the back of the store stood open. Beyond a strip of dry asphalt, the floodwaters stretched away, dotted with treetops and roofs, reflecting the dawn with a golden luster. Helicopters were already thudding around in the sky.

"What now?" Nick said.

"Out," Ryder said. "Keep your hands where I can see them."

Nick walked into the sunlight.

A semitrailer was backed up to the next loading dock over.

Ryder turned his head to look for Vincent.

Nick shoved his right hand into the open mouth of his backpack. He fumbled with his scuba kit. The Glock must have fallen out after all.

Ryder whipped around. An outraged shout issued from his mouth. He flowed into a muscular shooting stance. It occurred to Nick to wonder if maybe Ryder had shot anyone before.

Nick dropped to the ground and rolled under the semitrailer, dragging his backpack with him.

The SIG Sauer barked. A bullet hit the side of the trailer with a noise like rattling thunder.

Nick pushed himself farther under the trailer, kicking off from the undercarriage. The asphalt scraped his back. Ryder's legs came into view. The bastard was going to shoot under the truck. He wouldn't miss again.

The Glock slid out of Nick's backpack and skittered on the ground beside his head.

Lying on his side, he grabbed it in both hands, pointed it at Ryder's legs, and pulled the trigger.

Nick dropped the gun, surprised by its recoil. How could such a tiny weapon be so loud?

Gunpowder stung his nose. Chaotic memories prickled at the back of his brain: the dog barking, fists hammering on the front door. He was covering his head with his arms. He picked the Glock up, aimed it with numb hands, then let it droop. The legs of Ryder and Vincent flashed past the side of the semi-trailer. They were running back into the store.

Nick crawled out from under the other side of the trailer and ran.

Voices rose behind him, pissed and confused. He glanced back but saw no one. As he rounded the corner of the Wumart, where the floodwaters had lapped up nearly to the building, he flung the Glock away. It splashed into the brightness and sank without a trace.

The parking lot in front of the building was full of people overflowing from the Red Cross tent, waiting to be medevaced. Nick inserted himself into the chaos. There'd been no response to the gunshots. Well, the police, if there were any here, had better things to do.

He lurked on the periphery of the chopper landing zone, eyes peeled for Ryder, Vincent, and Jose, until, in the middle of the morning, a luxury twin-engined Bell tilt-rotor landed on the glo-tape crosshairs, and a woman got out.

5

She was so lovely, she could have come from another planet.

"Nick Morrison?"

Beside her, Harriet Fitzgerald sat in a wheelchair; she'd been lowered out of the helicopter on the step lift and immediately pointed Nick out.

"That's me," Nick said warily.

"I just wanted to thank you." The woman was about his age, mid-thirties. It showed in the laughter lines around her eyes, and the odd strand of gray in her dark hair. She wouldn't stand out in a crowd, except Nick was a sucker for natural beauty. She wore a loose T-shirt, jeans that showcased her slender legs, and white Adidas that had been pristine thirty seconds ago. Now they were splattered with mud.

A corporate logo was splashed on the side of the helicopter: *Five Stones*. Nick suddenly remembered glimpsing the same logo on the papers inside the Ziploc Ryder had removed from Harriet's safe. His wariness shifted into alarm. There must have been something else in the safe after all. Something valuable. Ryder had stolen it and now these people were looking for it. Nick should have run, even if he had to swim.

"I have to go," he said.

The woman frowned, taken aback. "I just wanted to thank you for rescuing my mother."

Harriet smiled sweetly at Nick from the wheelchair. "*And the safe*," she said. "They didn't let me take it on the helicopter, but I was able to retrieve the contents. As I said, it was very important to my daughter."

"*Mom*," the woman said. "That doesn't matter as long as you're OK. But yes, uh, Nick, thank you for that, too." She smiled. The family resemblance was plain now. The sunlight picked out gold flecks in her hazel eyes.

"Oh, darling, there were two of them, remember. Such gentlemen," Harriet said.

"My colleague. He's uh, around somewhere," Nick said.

A girl of about ten climbed out of the helicopter, followed by a wiry man with Einstein hair, except the hair was dark brown and its owner looked to be in his forties. He was struggling with one end of a case of Poland Spring. Someone inside the Bell lowered the other end down to him. He staggered. Nick crossed to him and took the weight.

"Whoa, careful," the man said. "It's heavy."

Nick could have carried the case by himself, but he matched the man's cautious steps until they found someplace to put it down. People descended swiftly, and without speaking to either of them, ripped off the plastic and took the bottles.

"Storm hit pretty bad this time," the man said, squinting through a pair of $5000 AR sunglasses.

"Yep," Nick said distractedly, trying to figure a casual way to excuse himself.

"You live around here?"

"Er, yeah, Charleston."

"Ouch. I live in Orlando," the man said. "Twenty-five meters above sea level. I keep trying to persuade Charlie to move. But she bought that house for her mom, and it's a ten-minute commute to Cocoa Beach—at least when the causeway isn't underwater."

"The whole of Florida is gonna be underwater by 2080," Nick said, managing to keep a straight face. Did the wealthy really think the coastline was going to back off just because they threw money on a plot of land?

"Ah, true, true. I'm afraid you're right," the man said.

They went back to the helicopter for more cases of Poland Spring. The little girl was taking photographs with a high-end tablet. Her mother—Charlie?—was talking on her phone. There was a lot of water to unload, plus half a dozen camping toilets. Before they finished, Einstein Hair dropped out, his skinny arms not up to the job. He stood in the shadow of the helicopter, checking his email. Nick completed the unloading with the help of the Bell's pilot.

"The toilets were a good idea," Nick said.

"Can thank Aaron for that. Guy thinks of everything," the pilot said.

So, Einstein Hair was Aaron. Nick had thought he might be the mysterious Reed.

"We're going to send the heli back with more supplies later," Charlie said. "And we have space for up to three passengers right now, if there's someone who needs help."

Everyone needed help. Nick's thoughts trailed back to the DIY section. "There was a diabetic woman. She'd run out of insulin." Though he would have no chance of finding her again.

"Insulin," Charlie said into her phone, turning away. "Epi-Pens too, maybe. Asthma inhalers—Oh!" She flashed Nick a smile. "Do *you* want a ride?"

———

In the air, the other two passengers, an old Honduran and her small grandson, looked down at the endless sheet of brown water, the roofs sticking out like neat rows of gravestones, and wept. Harriet Fitzgerald comforted them until she too began crying, in a quiet, polite way.

Champagne leather upholstery cooled Nick's sweat. He took deep breaths. This wasn't about the safe after all. There was nothing missing. There really *hadn't* been anything in there apart from papers. Or else Charlie hadn't noticed that whatever-it-was was missing yet. She and Aaron had simply come on a mission of mercy, combined with Harriet's old-school wish to thank Nick and Ryder in person.

Nick smiled out the window.

Ryder would think he'd vanished into thin air.

But Ryder would guess where Nick was going next. Nick would have to move fast.

Charlie sat on the arm of the seat opposite his. "My mother says you're a climate volunteer? You just travel around helping people out?"

Startled out of his thoughts, Nick said, "Not exactly. Like I said, I'm a diver. But our boss is cool with us taking time off." Jeff had been a good man to work for. Nick was going to miss him. "Sometimes we do post-hurricane reconstruction, too. Welding, roofing, mechanical repairs... It's the same skill set, just in the air instead of in the water."

"Interesting. Quite handy, that. How do you even get to be a diver? What are the qualifications?"

"Helps if you ain't claustrophobic, for one," Nick said.

Charlie laughed, but it didn't reach her eyes. She held her bottom lip between her teeth, looking out of the window at the swollen Indian River. She, too, had just lost everything. She was just trying to distract herself with pointless questions.

"So, what do *you* do?" Nick said.

Charlie brightened. "We're a NewSpace company—you wouldn't have heard of us—but that's why we're located here. Easy access to KSC. I hope NASA moves the whole show sometime before the Eastern Seaboard goes underwater. I doubt it, though."

"I didn't know NASA still existed," Nick said.

"Oh yeah. They maintain the launchpads and run that little space museum off the highway near Cape Canaveral—" Charlie sat a little straighter, waving a hand. "That came out wrong, I'm not exactly being fair to them. JPL still does important work, and Kennedy Space Center is a great resource for the NewSpace cluster here. We even rent their facilities sometimes. But in general, yeah. The 2026 moon landing was their last hurrah."

"At least they went out on a high note."

"You could say that. The whole thing was Apollo all over again, really. Mission accomplished, technological superiority over China established, now what? It was a total waste of money —and the next administration slashed their budget to the bone. They had to sell the freaking Artemis program to ArxaSys—" Charlie smirked. ArxaSys was a well-known NewSpace company, a Boeing spin-off. Nick didn't think she seemed all that broken up about NASA's decline. "Nowadays, they wouldn't even be able to keep the Deep Space Gateway in service without India and Europe kicking in half the budget."

"What about ILI?" Nick said.

"The International Lunar Initiative?" Charlie made a face. "NASA only has like, a one-sixth stake. I guess some people are sore about that. It makes America look like a has-been."

Charlie's daughter glanced up from her tablet. "We're a superpower in decline," she said seriously. "Of course people are sore about that. And climate change just makes it worse." She went back to editing the photographs she'd taken in the

Wumart parking lot. Her top-of-the-line tablet must have cost at least three grand.

"There you have it. Even fourth-graders know the score," Charlie said wryly. "But in the bigger picture, it doesn't really matter if NASA goes out of business, because NewSpace is open for business. How do people get to ILI? On rockets operated by Blue Horizon or SpaceZ, and ArxaSys runs the Artemis shuttles. Even the Russians hitch rides with SpaceZ when Vostochny is closed for repairs. And those are all American companies, like us."

"Someone has to pick up the slack, right?" Aaron said from his spot in the front of the helicopter. He got up and swayed along the aisle, fishing in the pocket of his shorts. "Five Stones." He extended a business card to Nick.

It was made of a stiff gray fabric that felt like spark protection gloves. Laser-engraved in gold, above a telephone number and email address, were the words *Aaron Slater, Chief Visionary Officer, Five Stones Inc.*

"What is this stuff?" Nick said, feeling the gray material. "Fiberglass?"

"*Stone*," Aaron said, flashing a grin. "Basalt fabric, to be precise. Pretty cool, huh? Get in touch if you're interested."

"In basalt?"

"Or just in general," Aaron said vaguely.

The helicopter thundered over the ragged edge of the flood, passing over fields and a waterlogged wildlife preserve. They sank toward northern Orlando. There were cars on the streets. People on the sidewalks. Life was going on.

The men from SubSea Solutions had been staying in a Budget Inn back in West Cocoa, and that was where Nick's car was. It was an ancient Toyota with no self-drive. He'd have to charge his phone so he could get a Lyft back to the motel. His crypto account was on his phone, too, the one he'd set up to receive the transfers from Ryder for holding stolen goods. $3K here. $5K there. It had never been worth it.

The Bell descended toward a cluster of deluxe high-rises overlooking Lake Eola. Swimming pools, walking trails, dog parks. A rooftop helipad offered a cross-eyed grin to the sky. The skids clunked down.

"Thanks for the ride," Nick said. He couldn't bring himself to look Charlie in the eye again.

6

Driving into Charleston at 11 p.m., Nick rolled down the windows. The fragrance of salt water and pluff mud—the deep, sucking sediment of the spartina grass marshes—filled the car. He turned off Calhoun Street and parked outside a crumbling brick apartment building. The street was caked with a cracked layer of mud deposited throughout the peninsula by the last flood.

Nick had come to the city to work on upgrades to Charleston's underground drainage tunnels and pumping stations. He'd taken the job at SubSea Solutions with the expectation there'd be work for years to come. And he'd come to like the city. The weather was comparatively mild, there were technologically reinforced beaches nearby, and the locals exuded a collective, flinty determination to save their city from climate change. What's more, they were all so *nice*. With a few exceptions, such as Ryder Stillman.

He stood for a moment just inside his dark apartment, tasting the air like a fox. A whiff of Thai takeout. Nothing else. No sound apart from the tubercular wheezing of the air conditioner. Satisfied that Ryder hadn't sent anyone to lie in wait, he moved through the living room, packing his stuff into a giant Chinese army kitbag he'd scored while working on seawalls in Singapore.

He didn't have much to take. A few books and electronic oddments. Souvenirs: a beer mug from the Netherlands, a King William tea towel from the UK, a bamboo flute from Bangladesh. Climate change had triggered a boom in the commercial diving industry. He'd spent his twenties knocking around the world, working on seawalls, pumps, and floodgates. The money was never good enough to justify the hardships, so he'd decided it was time to settle down. Live in one place for a while.

A picture of himself with his parents at age six, grinning gap-toothed into the South African sun. In the picture, his father held up a bottle of their own single-tree chardonnay, which had just won a prize. Nick put the picture into his kitbag.

He finished the quick tour of the apartment in the bedroom. Streetlight striped the curves of Ellie's shoulder and her left breast. She was sleeping tangled up in the duvet. She never could sleep without a heap of covers. It made her feel safe, she said.

Nick silently opened drawers and tossed his clothes into the kitbag. Then he gently shook Ellie awake.

"You're back," she said.

"I'm leaving again. You better leave, too."

"Huh? What happened?"

Ellie was a nursing student. She had met Ryder a couple of times and labeled him a killin' redneck, her words. She came from the same kind of people. Little trailer in the big woods, needles on the floor. Her people were *black* rednecks, but the tells were the same. She had one brother who'd escaped to Denver.

Nick explained what happened. "Go visit your brother. You've been talking about doing that."

"I ain't got the money to get out there, sweetheart. And I got my classes."

"You can attend online. Don't worry about the money." Nick took out his phone and transferred $2,000 to her account. That was next month's rent. He wouldn't be needing it, anyway.

"Aw, for real, Nick? You don't got to be that sweet to me." She rubbed her eyes and held out her arms to him. "C'mere."

Her hair, a natural afro, glowed like a nebula in the sodium light. He wanted fiercely to climb into bed with her. But he remembered Ryder hunching over into his shooting stance, and the noise of the bullet drilling a hole in the side of the semi. He picked up her clothes from the floor and put them in her hands. "Get dressed. I don't know how long we have. He could send someone around here any minute."

At the reminder of what Ryder was like, Ellie stopped arguing.

Outside, she hitched her bag onto her shoulder and called a Lyft. Seagulls soared through the dark orange night sky. A car crawled along Calhoun Street, playing grindcore, making Nick twitch.

Ellie looked up at him. "I love you."

"No, you don't," Nick said. He took her hand, but only to turn her phone toward him and make sure she really had input her destination as the airport.

It was true, he thought without self-pity. She didn't love him, and he didn't love her, either. They'd had fun for a while. It could be neither of them knew *how* to love any better than that.

He left the keys to the apartment in the mailbox and got back in his car. Energy flagging, he stopped at a Starbucks drive-thru for a coffee and a thousand-calorie pastry. By 1 a.m. he was on US 17, heading north. Almost twenty-four hours since he'd last slept. The Toyota veered dangerously across the center line. He pulled into a truck stop just across the North Carolina border, tilted the seat back, and closed his eyes.

It was a short but deep and untroubled sleep. Not Jeff, not even Ellie knew where he was going now. Ryder would never be able to track him down.

At eight in the morning, he pulled into a subdivision in Wilmington, North Carolina. Children waiting at the school bus stop stared at him suspiciously. They had been taught to be afraid of strangers, and Nick was a stranger here, although he'd paid the deposit on number 32 and continued to pay off the mortgage, month after month.

He rang the bell.

A leather-faced blonde, with a fixed glow of sadness in her eyes, bulging out of a short nightie, peered past the chain on the door.

"Hi, *Tante* Holly," Nick said. "OK if I crash for a while?"

———

Nick's mother was an Afrikaner. His father had been British. Will Morrison had backpacked through South Africa as a young man and fallen in love with Lydia Adriaanse, or maybe with her family farm. Hailsong Wine Estate was eighty-five hectares of breathtaking natural beauty in the historic Capeland wine region, thirty of those hectares covered with vineyards that dated back to the 1700s.

By 2012, the year Will and Lydia tied the knot, the ruling party had already begun making ominous noises about land redistribution. South Africa's cities were swamped with crime. But nothing could happen in the Capeland, a prime tourist destination that produced some of the world's finest wines. Right?

Right.

After Will's death, Lydia sank into a deep depression. She sold the farm and took Nick to live with her sister in the US. Aunt Holly had married an American, Phil Matthews, a trawl boat captain. The Matthewses had no children and welcomed Nick and Lydia into their home in Engelhard, North Carolina, a tiny Outer Banks fishing community.

Some of Nick's best memories came from that time. Waking up at can't-see-at-night to go out on the boat with Uncle Phil. The sun rising over the sea. The nets coming up dripping, fat with shrimp and bycatch, silver and precious gray gold.

It was bycatch that killed the North Carolina shrimping industry. Trawling had already been in a generational decline; few people had the nerve to pursue such a backbreaking, unreliable way of making a living. New restrictions designed to protect finfish drove the last boats out of business. Phil Matthews took his *Estuary Queen* out one last time. At sunrise, he stood on the foredeck, activated the radio locator beacon, and blew his brains out.

Nick, twenty-three at the time, came back from the Netherlands for the funeral. Holly didn't want to stay in Engelhard, and Lydia didn't care, so he helped them organize the sale of the house and boat. The proceeds just about covered the credit card debt Phil had been hiding from his family in the last years of his life. Nick made up the difference and took out a loan to buy a modest house for his mother and aunt in Alandale, a suburb of Wilmington.

It was not the kind of place where people had swimming pools or walking trails or dog parks. Lydia and Holly had a small forest of weeds that used to be a lawn, and a chronically shy rescue cat.

Nick sat in the kitchen, clacking away at his laptop, while Holly made coffee. She shuffled from sink to counter with an air of begrudging every step.

"I guess you quit again," she said.

"Nah, the job was over," Nick said, schooling himself to remain casual.

They spoke in English. As a child, Nick had spoken English, Afrikaans, a bit of Zulu, and the Xhosa language of the township people who worked in the vineyards, but he had lost most of it.

"Hey! Nick's here," his aunt yelled in Afrikaans.

"Coming," his mother shouted back. She waddled into the kitchen, turned on the television, and sank into the only chair that could support her weight. While Holly still clung to the primping habits of the knockout blonde she'd once been, Lydia had stopped caring about her appearance decades ago. Grubby sweats strained over her stomach and back fat. Her hair stuck out in a frizzy, gray thatch. She smelled as if she bathed in the concentrated essence of the miasma that pervaded the house, a mixture of cat urine, reheated microwave meals, and mold.

She spoke volubly to Holly in Afrikaans and then turned to Nick. "How long are you staying? Chizi won't eat as long as you're here."

Chizi was the cat. It detested Nick. The feeling was mutual.

"Not long," Nick said without looking up from his laptop.

Holly put a cup of coffee down at his elbow. She'd added cream, and no doubt a big pour of sugar, South African style, although he always took his coffee black.

His mother was talking in Afrikaans. Holly listened and then said to Nick, "Your ma is worried you're in trouble again."

Nick sighed. He clicked over to a new website. He was looking for any mention of shots fired at the Wumart in Merritt Island. He still couldn't be sure he hadn't hit Ryder, maybe wounded him. Though his mother and aunt were thinking about an entirely different situation, one that had played out twenty years ago.

"I'm not in trouble," he said.

"That's what you always say." Holly stirred her coffee. "Are you still hanging out with those... what do they call themselves? Crackers?"

"Cracking is over. I haven't seen any of those guys since high school anyway, Holly."

Nick's troubles had worsened when he started high school and gravitated to a group of crackers. What used to be a derogatory term for white people, meant something entirely different in 2028: professional phone crackers. At least, that was how they thought of themselves. Far from being professional, they were actually just a bunch of kids who were good enough at the internet to hack cashless security protocols.

They'd used a method called warshipping. You built warships—jailbroken, souped-up 6G smartphones—and planted them near the checkout at a supermarket. Or a fast-food joint. Or, to Nick's lasting shame, Bob's Live Bait. The warships would listen for phones connecting to the internet and harvest their login information. Password decryption was not a challenge when so many people used "1234" or "PASSWORD." Then the crackers would raid their victims' digital wallets, launder their take through a crypto exchange, and convert it back to USD by buying and selling virtual gold. They were teenagers pulling down thousands a week, thinking they were the shit.

When Nick was seventeen, he'd come home driving a new pickup. Holly, Phil, and Lydia had wrung the truth out of him. And then—while Nick wept and begged for forgiveness—Lydia had called the cops.

Because Nick was underage, he'd got off with community service and a fine. Despite not squealing on his friends, they'd shunned him anyway. Much later he realized he'd been the lucky one. While they graduated to lives of petty crime, or smoked their lives away, Nick rediscovered the will to study and pulled his grades up far enough to get into UNC Durham. But neither Holly nor Lydia ever let him forget about it.

Lydia was talking again. Nick caught the English word "warshipping." He closed his laptop and laid his forearms across it, leaning toward her. "Ma, for your information, warshipping doesn't work anymore. The only reason it worked in the first place was 'cause of a security loophole associated with the 6G rollout. Nowadays, physical specie is where it's at. It's because of the cashless economy. Gold. Platinum. Palladium. Diamonds. *That's* what the pros steal these days."

"Why do you know these things?" Lydia said.

"I read, that's why." Nick went outside to drag the lawn-mower out of the garage. It wasn't working. He drove to Home Depot for a new drive belt, mended the lawnmower, and attacked the weeds.

At lunchtime, Holly brought him a Coke and asked if he could spare a couple hundred dollars for Chizi's veterinary bills.

That night, they sat around the television in the living room, on sagging furniture matted with cat hair.

"You've been here all day. How long is not long?" Lydia asked.

"I don't know yet," Nick said, laptop open on his knees. On the television, a panel of celebrities were discussing the wide-spread belief that the federal government was secretly engaged in geoengineering. Which was obviously untrue. The federal government didn't have the ability to do anything like that.

"Have you started looking for a new job?" Holly asked.

"Yeah, I'm looking."

"Your cousin Brett got promoted to general manager," Lydia said. Brett was the son of Lydia and Holly's only brother. He worked for Anglo-African, one of the biggest mining companies in South Africa. "He runs a whole mine now. Just imagine!"

"That's great," Nick said, hunching a bit lower over his laptop.

"You could ask him for help," Holly said. "I'm sure he would find an opening for you."

"You don't need to worry about that, I'll find something," Nick said.

One tab of his browser was open to the Five Stones website. It was a masterpiece of the NewSpace startup genre. Lots of pretty pictures, very little information. The homepage consisted of infographics about potential resources to be extracted from the moon: water, oxygen, hydrogen, nickel, silicon, basalt—there it was again, *basalt*—and more speculatively, rare earths, platinum-group metals, and helium-3. The About page was nothing but a glossy profile of Aaron Slater, including the nugget that he'd previously been a major rockethead at SpaceZ. He joined SpaceZ in 2038 and left in 2042, right after their IPO, which meant he probably cashed out several hundred million in stock options. Nick's opinion of the guy went up.

Over on the New York Times website, deep in the archives, there was an article headlined "As NewSpace Stocks Fall to Earth, One VC Scores Big." Two years ago, one William Lundgren, a venture capitalist, had made a bundle shorting the stocks of NewSpace companies when they flash-crashed following "the first payload delivery by upstart Five Stones." Nick searched in vain for further details about this "payload delivery." It seemed the NYT writer wasn't fully informed, either.

On a NewSpace fan forum, Nick found a screenshotted announcement that William Lundgren had joined Five Stones as CFO. The date: August 25, 2046. One week after Lundgren's short-selling coup. That looked pretty shady.

A third tab held the results of another search: "Charlie Five Stones." Her real name was Charlotte Fitzgerald. She graduated from the robotics program at Carnegie Mellon in 2036. The second result was a puff piece in the *Boston Globe* about her wedding, also in 2036, to Reed Gottschalk.

Reed. So that was *that* mystery solved.

One more search. "Basalt moon." Approximately six trillion results. The moon was pretty much made of basalt.

"Basalt" plus "moon" plus "Five Stones." Zero results.

Zero.

There was only one way to interpret that. Someone paid to have the results scrubbed.

Nick tried a couple of other search engines and different search strings, but no luck. He'd never been an expert at this stuff, even in his cracking days. His specialty was assembling the warshipping packages, using jeweler's tools and test boards to tinker with devices meant only to be serviced by the manufacturer.

His mother heaved herself out of her armchair. All the prescription meds she took made her sleepy at an early hour.

Passing by Nick's chair, she paused and stroked his hair. "My sweet boy," she said with a heavy-lidded smile. "You look more and more like your father every day."

"Mhm, he does. Will was thirty-six. Nick's about there, yeah?" Holly said.

"Thirty-six this year," Lydia said.

"Thanks for reminding me," Nick said, his knuckles white on his kneecaps, staring at the television.

At midnight in the spare room, he checked his email one more time. Ellie had finally emailed him to confirm she'd arrived in Denver, signing off with a breezy XOXO. He wished her every happiness in life.

Another email appeared. Ryder.

Everyone knows about you motherfucker. You will never work in this industry again. You might also want to know I told Skeletor to watch out for you. You show your face on CCTV anywhere in the lower 48 you're FUCKED. Meditate on that asshole.

"Buy a comma, Stillman," Nick muttered.

He got up and opened the window. The night air bloomed in, still, warm, heavy with the scent of newly mown grass. Nick breathed deeply. Ryder was bullshitting. He hadn't told anyone anything. Actually, he might have talked to Skeletor. The guy was his fence, after all. But it wasn't like Skeletor had access to nationwide security cameras. He was just a smalltime mobster who moved stolen goods through the PGM and gemstone channels. And Nick wasn't about to go into competition with him by starting his own thievery racket.

Nick sat down on the mold-spotted mattress, leaving the window open. One thing Ryder had said was accurate. *You will never work in this industry again.* Nick had been a commercial diver for twelve years. And in a different sense, he'd stopped being a diver when he started helping Ryder steal stuff from flooded houses.

What could he do? What, what?

At four in the morning, reckless with desperation, he typed a new email. To: *aaron@fivestones.com.*

7

Aaron Slater paced up and down in front of a window the size of a cruise ship's prow. In the distance, heat hazed the trees of Cape Canaveral. The Five Stones office occupied the top two floors of an office tower in Cocoa Beach at the north end of Space Coast, on the peninsula's coveted high ground.

Nick sat on a sofa shaped like a cross-section of a nautilus shell. He was trying to focus on Aaron and not Charlie, who perched on another sofa, as fresh as a daisy in a sleeveless white blouse. A muscular Japanese skinhead straddled the arm of the sofa. Aaron had introduced him as Yuta Nakajima, the third co-founder of Five Stones.

Aaron said, "The lunar ISRU challenge has held back space exploration for decades. The moon isn't nearly as rich in volatiles as was once thought, which makes it crucial to innovate *economical* methods of recovering them, as well as any raw materials required by the satellite refurbishment and manned spaceflight markets."

He spoke as if he were on a TedX stage, boosting the already high information content of his sentences with emphatic flourishes of his arms.

"The International Lunar Initiative is now producing 1,900 tonnes of water per year from their mining operation in Shackleton Crater. They use seventy percent of that for the life-support needs of the ILI science team and the crew building the mass driver. They crack the other thirty percent into oxygen to refuel their Artemis landers. *I* say keep the lunar water for human drinking and washing, and maybe hydroponics. Don't waste it on rocket propellant!

"Oxygen is *everywhere* on the moon. We can bake it out of the lunar regolith with a solar roaster! We've already trialed the process at our prototype site. It works. It works. So you have your product right there. But that, right, that still leaves the *other* half of the ISRU challenge, which is getting these resources, the water if you must, the oxygen or whatever, *off* the moon, to where the market is. That means LEO for the most part, although the Deep Space Gateway also consumes 150 tonnes of water annually, and any manned Mars mission would also create significant demand in cislunar orbit, if they ever get off the ground. So that's the issue we're focused on here."

Aaron whirled around and pressed one finger to his lips. "Do you know what a mass driver is?"

"Yeah, basically like a railgun," Nick said.

"Precisely! It's a rail loop along which a payload is accelerated using electromagnets. The lunar mass driver was proposed by NASA in 2025 as a way to lift payloads into lunar orbit. Ten years later, an international team of construction specialists broke ground on the ridge connecting Shackleton and de Gerlache craters. First it was scheduled for completion in 2045, now they're saying 2050—*another* two years. I bet it's more likely to take twenty.

"There's nothing wrong with the design, as such. I mean, if you know how an electromagnet works, you can build a mass driver in your garage. But building anything on the moon is *orders of magnitude* more difficult. They're eight billion dollars in the hole, and they haven't even finished laying the rail loop. Complexity is killing them."

There was a low ripple of laughter from Charlie and Yuta Nakajima.

"It's *killing* them," Aaron repeated, his eyes shining.

Yuta slid forward on the arm of the squashy leather sofa. "We're against complexity. Everyone thinks you have to do the moon with high tech. But every advanced technology you add to your design is just one more thing that can break down. Then you get knock-on effects and systemic collapse. Makes more sense to simplify everything as much as you can. Our motto is *Cruder is Better*. Why build a mass driver when you can do the job better, cheaper, and faster, with a slingshot?"

Nick recalled the Five Stones logo on the side of the Bell tilt-rotor, and in the reception area: a stylized pile of five pebbles and a wiggly line. He now understood that the wiggly line was meant to be a slingshot. "I get it."

"Do you?" Yuta said, sitting back, arms folded.

"Yuta is the mechanical engineer," Charlie said. "And I'm the lead roboticist. Up until now, we've done everything with robots. So you see, we're not totally against high tech."

"We have a working prototype in the Sea of Tranquility," Aaron said, picking up speed again. Back and forth, back and forth, he paced. "We call it the Little Sling—a five-meter slingshot built from lunar basalt."

Basalt. That's the connection. They were using basalt as a construction material. Nick nodded and sipped from his porcelain cup of coffee. Artisan-roasted beans. Black as the devil's heart.

"Here's an actual holo, not an artist's rendering, of pictures taken by our robots at the site."

Aaron swooped at the coffee table and stabbed a button on

the built-in console. A holo clicked into existence above the projector in the middle. Holo projectors were still expensive enough to be rare. Nick had hardly ever seen one in real life. He leaned forward.

The object standing on the coffee table was a slender, black stone pyramid, mounted on a turntable, with a crossbar at the top. One end of the crossbar was thick and short, the other was long—five meters long, in reality, Nick guessed—and thin. The whole thing rotated, sparkling around the edges. A spectral payload shot out of the tip of the long arm and vanished out of the field of projection.

"It looks like..." Nick glanced at Charlie. *Like a gallows.* Like the weird object he'd glimpsed in her rec room, underwater, when Ryder was about to drown.

She nodded. "You must've seen the scale model at my house. I kept it for sentimental reasons. Though I suppose it's ruined now... Well, it doesn't matter."

Aaron switched the projector off. "So that's the Little Sling. It's been up and running since the summer of 2046, launching an average of two hundred tonnes a year into LEO. The concept is proven. The market is there. It's time to scale up. We are building a *Big* Sling, with the capacity to launch *thousands* of tonnes annually. It will bury ILI. *Bury* them."

"How big are you planning for that kind of scale?" Nick said.

Aaron seemed surprised Nick had asked a question. He pointed at him like a teacher calling on a star student. "The arm of the Big Sling will be twenty kilometers long."

"Not meters," Nick said.

"Not meters. *Kilometers.*"

"OK. Wow."

"That's it exactly. This is a *wow* project. And I should probably remind you that you signed a nondisclosure agreement. If you breathe a word about this to anyone, Yuta will come after you with an ice axe."

Nick chuckled. Realizing Aaron was waiting for an acknowledgment, he straightened his face and said, "Yeah, I understand the confidentiality requirement. But—"

"But you're wondering if anyone *needs* thousands of tonnes of lunar resources in LEO. Is the market actually that big? The answer is yes, unquestionably *yes*. Satellite refurbishment and refueling demand alone is worth forty billion a year. And then, further out, we're looking at space-based solar power. Solar collectors in geosynchronous orbit, illuminated ninety-nine percent of the time, transmitting microwave beams to receiving stations on Earth's surface—that will at least *double* LEO demand for silicon and other raw materials, including LOX to power their station-keeping thrusters.

"Obviously, no one's built these things yet. The cost of launching raw materials to orbit has been prohibitive. But the Big Sling is going to change all that. Soon it's going to be possible to construct SBSP arrays for a fraction of the current cost. And I don't need to tell you what massive, cheap solar power could mean for the planet."

"Geoengineering," Nick said with a broad smile.

"And it won't be the government that does it, of course. The partners we're primarily talking with are private companies. They don't want to get cooked or flooded out, either. If we could replace even ten percent of fossil fuel power generation with space-based solar, it would make a *huge* difference."

Charlie and Yuta were nodding, their faces solemn.

"It might slow down global warming enough to save the West Antarctic Ice Sheet."

A doe-eyed secretary poked her head into the conference room. "Bill's here," she said.

"OK, thanks, Melodie," Aaron said.

The door flew open, admitting a silverback gorilla of a man in a ten-thousand-dollar suit. His head appeared to be directly bolted onto his shoulders. He strode across the handcrafted yak-hair carpet like it was a boxing ring. Nick recognized William Lundgren from the photo accompanying the NYT article.

"Gotta steal Aaron for a minute," he said.

"We'll wrap this up later," Aaron said to Nick.

Doe-eyed Melodie escorted him to the balcony of the floor below. Employees in T-shirts and Tevas sat at parasoled tables. Potted trees enlivened the space. There was even a trampoline and a smoothie stand.

Nick ventured to ask for a smoothie, which was smilingly produced for him. He'd skipped breakfast, having driven down from Wilmington overnight. He gulped the honeyed concoction, gazing across the Banana River at Merritt Island. The floodwaters had gone down. A sea breeze cooled the air.

According to Aaron, Five Stones had successfully demonstrated their working prototype, the Little Sling, in the summer of 2046. The share prices of launch stocks had promptly crashed, which made sense. If the Little Sling could throw payloads into LEO for a fraction of the cost of lifting them from Earth, it would gut the business model of every rocket company on the planet. William Lundgren had made a packet shorting their stocks.

Since then, there had been no news about Five Stones. The share prices of SpaceZ and its competitors had recovered, and every mention of Five Stones plus basalt plus moon had been scrubbed off the internet.

Shady. Very shady.

Charlie came out through the sliding doors and waved at Nick. She drew him over to the smokers' corner at the far end of the balcony. "Sorry about that," she said. "They won't be long."

"It's not a problem."

Charlie took a pack of Marlboro Lights from the pocket of her capri pants and lit one. She caught Nick watching and raised her eyebrows. "What?"

"Wouldn't have guessed you were a smoker."

"I smoked in college. Quit when I got pregnant. Picked it up again when I got divorced. Quit *again* because my daughter kept pestering me. So as of now, I'm officially a nonsmoker." She exhaled a stream of smoke and wrinkled her nose charmingly.

That put Reed Gottschalk out of the picture. Nick smiled. "How's Harriet doing?"

Charlie grimaced. "Kind of in shock. Not your fault, of course. You rescued her. But she's mentally a little... you know... in the first place, and the storm—being trapped like that—losing the house... It's a mess. And the insurance company, despite the ridiculous premiums I pay, is trying to pull some Act of God shit on me to get out of paying up. I'm like, Act of God, my ass. This storm was an act of man. *We* are the ones fucking up the planet. *We* are the ones pumping CO_2 into the atmosphere to levels not seen since the Jurassic. What part of *anthropogenic climate change* do you not understand?" She sighed. "Sorry."

"It would be great if that space-based solar-power thing happened."

"Yes. It would be great—*will* be great." Charlie grinned. The sunlight shadowed the valley in the open neck of her blouse. "You've met Aaron. Can you picture something that he wants *not* happening?"

"He does seem kind of unstoppable."

Charlie nodded and gazed across the water with narrowed eyes, dragging on her cigarette. Was she thinking about space-based solar power? About the robots she'd built, hard at work on the moon?

"I shouldn't have bought that house," she said abruptly.

Nick had often felt the same way about the house in Alandale, although there was nothing else he realistically could have done. After staying with Lydia and Holly for two weeks, he'd come to the cold realization he would do anything to be free of them. To be free of the mortgage that followed him around like a hungry dog. Twelve hundred dollars a month. Right now, he had three hundred and eighty-seven, and all his worldly goods were in the back of his car.

Charlie was still talking. "What kind of idiot buys a million-and-a-half-dollar home in a hurricane zone? But my mom couldn't live on her own anymore, and I guess I wanted to make it up to Anna after the divorce. And after our IPO, I had the money." She shrugged. "When you have money, you do stupid things."

"Even when you don't have money, you do stupid things," Nick said.

She laughed. "Point."

Wary of spiking this pleasant intimacy, Nick nevertheless risked the question, "Was it a bad divorce?"

"Kind of. Reed—my ex—is bipolar. It went undiagnosed for a long time. Then when he finally did get diagnosed, it was like, oh, *that's* why…"

"Can be tough. I had an uncle who was bipolar. He never told anyone. After he died, we found his prescription in his wallet. It's possible he wasn't taking his meds at the time."

"What happened?"

"He shot himself."

Charlie flinched.

"Sorry, I wasn't intending to imply anything," Nick said. "There were a lot of other factors, as well."

Credit card debt. The destruction of a way of life that had endured for generations. It wasn't necessary to invoke bipolar disorder to explain Phil Matthews's suicide. But it couldn't have helped, either. Nick still wished he'd been there. He imagined a do-over of that morning on the boat, his uncle confiding in him. Taking out his granddaddy's Magnum—and throwing it into the sea.

"Well, I don't think Reed's going to kill himself," Charlie said. "He's working for some startup out west. He's got a girl-friend who's as fucked up as he is. But honestly—and I know it's a horrible thing to say—I don't think I would even care at this point."

"No. That ain't horrible at all."

Melodie, the receptionist, clip-clopped across the balcony. "Mr. Morrison? Aaron asked me to tell you that he won't be able to meet with you again today. He had to take an important meeting. But we will definitely be in touch. Thank you for coming by."

She waited, smiling, to show Nick to the elevators.

8

The executive suites had their own balcony. Unlike the employee terrace on the floor below, this balcony was furnished with a couple of benches and an abstract metal sculpture. It looked like an explosion in a scrapyard; one which cost Aaron had $80,000. When Charlie entered the conference room, the glass doors to the balcony stood wide. Yuta was outside, sucking on a Victorian-looking vape pipe. The scent of marijuana curled in on the breeze.

Bill Lundgren sat in one of the squashy leather armchairs, glowering at his phone. Aaron sprawled across another armchair, staring at the ceiling, swinging one foot. Five Stones' corporate counsel, Cameron Sulpicio, stood halfway between Bill and Aaron, looking deeply uncomfortable.

"All right," Charlie said. "What the hell is happening?"

"We're about to be investigated for insider trading," Aaron said. "That's what."

Charlie sank into a chair. She'd known this was a possibility. All of them had. Bill took a risk when he shorted those launch stocks. His VC firm was already an investor in Five Stones. And with his early knowledge about the announcement of the Little

Sling's first payload delivery, he'd reaped a nine-figure profit. That was illegal. It tripped the SEC's market surveillance algorithms, leading to threats and warnings from the Division of Enforcement.

Two years had passed, and the danger seemed to recede. But perhaps the danger had actually been stalking them ever since, getting worse the closer they got to starting construction on the Big Sling.

"It's politically motivated," she said, looking at Bill for confirmation. He sank his chin into his collar.

Corporate counsel Cameron said, "No one can prove Bill had prior knowledge of undisclosed materialities. Without a paper trail, they've got nothing."

Aaron tipped his head back, caught Charlie's gaze, and rolled his eyes. They were startup people. Even now. Despite heading a listed company and paying themselves six-figure salaries. Corporate governance and compliance requirements was innovation-stifling BS in their eyes. But they weren't stupid. They'd been careful to leave no paper trail. No phone records. They'd even wiped their own secure email server.

"They won't get anything from me," Bill said. "It's just a fishing expedition."

"They might subpoena me," Aaron said. "Yuta. Charlie."

"And what would they find? Nothing. Right, Charlie?" Bill hooked his avuncular smile at her. "Nothing."

"Of course not," Charlie said. She thought uncomfortably about the safe currently residing in her closet in the furnished condo she was renting in Orlando. She made a private vow to shred its contents the minute she got home.

Two years ago, before they wiped the server, she'd printed every email between herself, Aaron, and Yuta regarding the payload delivery announcement, and the entire email chain relating to Bill's short-selling coup. It *was* illegal, and she'd thought they might need to have the records someday. Thank God Nick and his friend had recovered the safe. She would feel even worse right now if it were sitting in five feet of floodwater in the basement of the Merritt Island house.

Another thought troubled her. What if Nick and his friend opened it and realized what they were looking at...?

No, they couldn't have. They didn't know the combination. Anyway, she felt sure Nick was a good guy. Any friend of his would be a good guy, too. They weren't barracudas in human form like the people in *this* industry.

"Relax, Aaron," she said. "It's going to go away, just like it did before. Right?" She appealed to Bill and Cameron.

"Well..." Cameron said.

"Ninety percent of these investigations end without charges being brought," Bill said.

"We have to accelerate the roadmap to the Big Sling," Aaron said. "Once we're up and running, they won't be able to touch us."

"That doesn't necessarily follow," Cameron said. "It might just make us a bigger target."

Aaron swatted away the objection and swung his legs to the floor. "The biosphere plays in here, too. If we can demonstrate a path to sustainability, we'll be the kings of space. The media doesn't care about launch capabilities, that's too technical for them. They care about human beings on the moon. Give them visuals of a functioning, sustainable, inhabited biosphere, and they'll turn us into the second coming of Neil Armstrong. We'll be too big to prosecute. That's how it works, Cameron. You know that's how it works."

"Weeell..." Cameron said.

Aaron jumped to his feet. "Yuta!"

"What?" Yuta called, from the balcony.

"Can we accelerate the training program? Can we cut it down to six months?"

"Sure. Three months would be enough, actually. They don't need to learn orbital mechanics and fluid dynamics." Yuta took a draw off his vape, a thick cloud momentarily obscuring his face. "If you get people with a background in construction, agriculture, extreme sports—mountaineering, diving, that kind of thing—they're already halfway there."

Aaron banged his fist into his palm. "Then we'll do that. Charlie, habitat construction is on track, right?"

"Yes, but, I'm gonna say this one more time, I don't think it's necessary to send up a human crew. It's all just PR, Aaron. You're talking about risking people's lives for screen share."

"When you build a robot that can climb a seventy-degree slope, I'll agree," Aaron said. "And what about basalt fiber extrusion? Been there, done that, got egg on our faces. Listen, I *love* your robots, Charlie. But there are limits to what telepresence can do. There just are. And besides! Robots aren't nearly as telegenic."

Bill nodded in agreement. "This is the goal. Not a science lab at the end of a highly complex, 250,000-mile supply chain. Not automated infrastructure. *A sustainable biosphere.* This is the goddamn *dream.* And the first people to make it happen—like Aaron said—they'll be the kings of space."

Bill was old school. At sixty, he often spoke about the dry spell before the second moon landing, when it had seemed as if humanity would never return to the moon. He'd grown up on romantic scenarios of space colonization. Dedicated his career and wealth to the NewSpace sector, and saw Five Stones as his best shot to achieve that goal—the telos of the whole industry—before he died.

Aaron, on the other hand, was no romantic. What turned *him* on was winning. But he and Bill fed off each other and egged one another on. Charlie couldn't stand up to their united determination.

"All right," she said. "All right, you've convinced me." She made a face to show she was still unconvinced. "But I want to do the exosuits."

"Fine," Aaron said. "It's a great idea. I'll be interested to see where it goes."

"And I want input into the crew-selection process."

"What about that guy who was here today?" Yuta called from the balcony. "Didn't he say he was a diver?"

Charlie smiled. She'd not hoped for support from Yuta, who rarely noticed people. But his thoughts were running on lunar-appropriate skill sets at the moment, so that detail must have stuck in his mind.

"He's a commercial diver," she said. "Underwater welding and construction. I talked to him; he seems solid."

Charlie had worked in the NewSpace sector ever since she earned her PhD from Carnegie Mellon. The unworldly geek girl with a passion for robotics had long since learned that corporate politics mattered just as much as design excellence. This industry was an absolute shark tank. World-class engineering and technical brains, billions of investment dollars seeking returns, and competing alpha-male egos added up to blood in the water. Charlie had developed self-protective habits. Maybe that was the real reason she'd kept those printouts.

Insurance.

Nick Morrison would be another form of insurance. They had a connection. He was a good guy. Cute, too, but she couldn't let that figure in. If they hired him, he would be *her* guy, not Aaron's or Yuta's.

"We could do a lot worse," she said.

"OK," Aaron said from his desk, already moving on to the next thing. "Tell Melodie to give him a call."

———

Nick drove south along I-95. He didn't know exactly where he was going. Miami, maybe. Half of Vice City was above water and fighting a rearguard action to stay dry. There'd be construction work there. There'd be bars, at least. Find somewhere safe to park. Sleep in his car.

The Toyota rattled like a mariachi band, pushing ninety. Nick barely heard his phone ringing.

Five Stones.

He snatched it up.

"Hello, is this Nick Morrison?"

"Yes."

"This is Melodie from Five Stones. I just called to ask if you're still interested in the job?"

"Yes. God, yes."

Melodie tittered. "I'm glad you're as excited as we are! I've emailed you a packet of information regarding the offer, the terms and conditions, where you'll need to go and what to bring. It's password protected with your own Social Security. I'll just remind you that the material is also covered by our NDA. Check that out and email me the forms. We're delighted you'll be joining us!"

Nick hung up in a daze. He pulled off at the next exit, parked on the shoulder, and checked his email. It hadn't even occurred to him to ask: what *was* the job, anyway?

9

Cruder is Better: An Introduction to the "Big Sling"

1. Project Outline
2. Construction Roadmap & Milestones
3. Biosphere Requirements
4. Personnel Selection, Training, & Compensation
5. Economic Summary

Nick skipped straight to section 4, *Personnel Selection, Training, & Compensation.*

Up to 200 candidates will be recruited for initial training. Nick's excitement cooled a bit. *Through a process of live aptitude testing and self-elimination, 12 individuals will be selected for further training, ultimately resulting in a final crew of 6. The crew will perform primary and secondary construction and assembly of the Big Sling, in addition to biosphere operation and maintenance of robotic and mechanical assets. The selection process will ensure each crew member possesses the appropriate skills and psychological characteristics to perform the job successfully.*

During initial training, candidates will be paid a stipend of $2,000/week, with all travel and living expenses covered. The stipend will increase to $3,000/week during the second phase of training. Compensation for the 6 crew members ultimately selected to work on the moon will be $5,000/week for the duration of their employment, with additional remuneration in the form of a completion bonus, to be calculated using the formula in Section 5, based on the Company's actual earnings during the first year of the Big Sling's operation. See Appendix B for further details.

Two thousand dollars a week, guaranteed, for however long the training lasted.

A guy like Nick, poor in useful connections, couldn't make that much working construction in Miami. Or anywhere.

Except, he guessed, on the moon.

He scrolled to Section 5 and studied the bonus formula. Using the most conservative earnings estimate supplied, he came up with four million dollars per person. Four *million!* Yes. That was a mere half a percent of the profit Five Stones expected to make in one year once the Big Sling began throwing raw materials from the moon into LEO.

No wonder they had such a draconian nondisclosure agreement.

Was that also why they'd scrubbed their digital footprint off the internet? They didn't want any potential competitors catching on?

That didn't exactly make sense, given the splash they'd made two years ago with their working prototype. Nick let the inconsistency go, dazzled by the thought of a multimillion-dollar jackpot.

He could pay off Lydia and Holly's mortgage.

He could buy them a mansion in a gated community for cat lovers.

He'd never have to see them again.

And Ryder Stillman could take a hike off a fucking cliff.

Nick scrolled through the acres of legalese at the bottom of the PDF, and the terms and conditions of the contract included as a separate attachment. He read the words: *I acknowledge that my participation in this training program may involve tests of a person's physical and mental limits, and carries with it the potential for death and/or serious injury... I hereby assume all the risks of participating in this training program, including any risks that may arise from negligence or carelessness on the part of the Company, from dangerous or defective equipment or property owned, maintained, or controlled by the Company, or because of their possible liability without fault...*

It was the same kind of waiver divers had to sign before every job. He signed without hesitation.

He sent the contract back to Melodie, and five minutes later received a reply, this time from Five Stones' HR department, instructing him to proceed in one week's time to Charlotte-Douglas International Airport, bringing clothes suitable for subarctic weather conditions, and anything else he might need for a three-month stay in the wilderness.

10

Nick slumped at a scarred Formica table, wearing fingerless gloves he made from a pair of socks, listening to the wind scream around the Nissen hut where he'd lived for the last ten weeks. In front of him, a computer screen displayed a taunting statement: *The air pressure in your habitat is dropping. Find the cause and fix it.*

The left side of the screen displayed a virtual walkthrough of the hab. Not a schematic. That would have been too easy.

The right side displayed a suite of software tools and a timer: 1:03:46... 1:03:45...

The other five inhabitants of Hut 10 had already finished the problem. They sat at the other end of the long table, talking shit about the training program.

They'd all signed up of their own free will, for $2,000 a week and the chance to go to the moon. They'd all conquered the endurance runs, the outdoor camping ordeals, the map-reading exercises, the mechanical and electronic assembly challenges, even the pop quizzes that felt suspiciously like IQ tests. They'd lasted two and a half months, while other trainees washed out one after another.

If Nick couldn't solve this problem, it would be his turn.

One strike and you're out.

He'd made it this far on raw stamina and his knack for tinkering. Neither quality was any help now.

He bit the dead skin around his fingernails and stared at the screen, trying to see something he hadn't seen in the last three hours.

His anime-style avatar bobbed to and fro in the habitat's work module, in front of the opened hatch cover of the Environment Control and Life Support System (ECLSS). This consisted of the Water Recovery System, Carbon Dioxide Reduction System, and Oxygen Supply System.

When everything was working right, the CDRS and the OSS sat idle. The habitat had a greenhouse module full of plants that ate CO_2 and puffed out oxygen. In combination with the CDRS, this theoretically kept the atmosphere just right for both the plants and the crew. The OSS was more of a backup. Its pressurized oxygen tanks would supply air to the crew if something happened to the plants.

However, in this scenario, there was nothing wrong with the plants. The composition of the atmosphere remained stable. The *pressure* was just falling, on the whim of the bastards who designed the test, and Nick could not work out why.

There couldn't be a leak in the habitat. It was made of solid steel. If there was a hole, you'd know it, because it would have had to be a direct meteorite strike, and they'd all be dead. The only weak points were the seals around the personnel airlock and the vehicle airlock, and he'd checked both of those. No leaks.

He set the virtual OSS to pump out oxygen at the maximum flow rate. The pressure was still dropping. There had to be something wrong with the OSS.

First, he checked the valves. Just like he'd do if it were a commercial air compressor—if you're losing pressure, ten to one it's the valves. But he'd already mouse-clicked the virtual valve seals and the O-rings to replace them. He'd also taken the virtual motor apart and tightened all the internal fasteners. No change.

Next check was the hoses connecting the oxygen tanks. If he actually had the damn thing in front of him, he'd power it down, lather the hoses with hand soap, switch it back on, and wait to see if any bubbles formed. But he didn't have it in front of him. All he had was a screen full of pixels that said the hoses weren't leaking.

Was the problem in the Water Recovery System? Could the condensate drain be clogged, interfering with the intake of the CDRS? Except he'd already checked that.

At the other end of the table, former US Marine Madeline Huxley sat with her elbows on either side of her plate, telling a ghost story. She swore she'd seen the footprints of Sasquatch on their last hike.

Kurtis Dean, an honest-to-God former Army Ranger captain, and the only African-American in Hut 10, chewed on a raw carrot and said calmly, "You're letting it get inside your head, Maddy. Don't be letting it inside your head. Probably just a bear. There ain't no Sasquatches in Patagonia."

"There aren't any bears in Patagonia, either," Maddy said. She was pixie-slight, with cropped blue hair and mousy roots showing. "And who even says we're *in* Patagonia? We could be anywhere."

"Lee saw that Sierran Pekingese sparrow," said Sam Ellis, the FedEx pilot. "That's good enough for me."

"Sierra Patagonian Finch," Lee Yang corrected, relaxed in the bottom bunk of the rack he shared with Nick. Lee was five foot seven, wiry, a bantamweight with a heavyweight brain. He used to work for one of the tech giants in Seattle. After finishing the test before anyone, he'd gone back to his current sci-fi ebook.

"Isn't that what I said?" Sam asked.

"I hate not knowing where I am," Maddy said.

"Bitching about it won't make the time pass any faster." Kurtis bit off another chunk of carrot and chewed loudly, smacking his lips.

Nick stood up and closed his computer. The last thing he saw was the flashing digits of the countdown timer: 00:56:07...

Lee looked up from his ebook. "Finished?"

"Yeah, I'm finished," Nick said.

He went out to the unheated vestibule where their outerwear hung above duckboards wet with snowmelt. He put on his parka, snow pants, and boots, all bought on credit at a Charlotte shopping mall when he thought $2,000 a week would be easy money. He zipped the fur-lined hood over his mouth and nose and left the hut.

The moon was up. Nearly full, it rode high in the pitch-black sky, illuminating the twin mountain peaks to the north. Rounded, snow-covered, one with a flat top—they sure didn't look like the Andes. They could have been mountains on the moon. The terrain was even lunar—lumpy, white, endless.

Only, the moon was up there and Nick was down here. The helicopter would come for him in the morning, like it had for so many others, and take him back to the States, with $20,000 in his bank account and a head full of useless knowledge about lunar geology and biosphere maintenance.

He walked fast, heading for the dark fold in the terrain that was the valley, lined with dwarf pines, which marked the limit of their geographical range. The wind sliced into his face. His hands and feet rapidly got cold despite the exertion of walking through six inches of snow.

On the lip of the valley, he turned for one last look at the hut.

A dark figure pounded toward him, arms pumping.

Sasquatch?

No—too small.

Lee.

"Where are you going?" Lee panted.

"Buenos Aires," Nick said, starting off again.

Lee walked alongside him, puffing white clouds. In real life he ran marathons. He could outlast everyone else on endurance runs. Must have poured on the juice to catch up with Nick.

When he could speak without panting, he said, "Are you really quitting?"

"I couldn't solve the air-pressure problem. If it was real life, we would have been dead by the time I finished checking the valves."

"Oh, my *God*," Lee said. "It wasn't the OSS. It wasn't anything to do with the ECLSS. There was a leak in the personnel module."

"A *leak*?"

"Yup."

"What—the modules are made of *steel*. How do they leak? Was there an actual hole in it? How would that happen?"

"Technically, they aren't made of steel," Lee said. "They're made of pixels. The bastards can punch a hole in them if they want to. Depending on how fast you caught it, you could patch it with Kevlar and do a weld from outside. Eh, you've left it so long, though... You'll probably have to seal that module off and concentrate on bringing the air pressure back up in the other two."

Nick tried to put aside the unlikelihood of a nearly unde-tectable leak in three-quarters of an inch of solid steel. "If it was real life, you could drop something in the air, like a bit of paper, and see if it's pulled in one direction."

"*If it was real life.* You're always saying that. This *is* real life. The tests are real life. Do or die. Succeed or fail. What's not real about that?"

Lee and Nick had started in training together. They were the only candidates originally assigned to Hut 10 who were still here. The rest had washed out and been replaced with people from other huts whose hut-mates had washed out.

"You know, I don't think there were two hundred candidates," Nick said. "That would be $400,000 a week, plus food and expenses. Five Stones can't eat that kind of upfront cost. There were, what, forty people on our flight from Charlotte? That's gotta be all there ever were."

"You're probably right," Lee said, hugging himself. "But it's too fucking cold to be speculating. Let's go back."

"This shit is shady. Five Stones is shady as hell. They're a successful lunar ISRU company pretending to be a vaporware startup. Don't try to tell me they're on the level."

"And? So? That means they don't have money? You saw the Cocoa Beach office. Aaron has a fucking Zeng Fanzhi hanging on the wall. Right or wrong, they have fuck-you money. I don't care where they got it, as long as they give some to me."

Nick snorted.

"Come on. You'll just about have time to enter the answer before your timer expires."

"Why'd you get into this?" Nick asked. "Why not just... stay in Seattle, wait for your stock options to vest?"

"I don't *have* stock options. The tech industry ain't the gold mine you think it is. NewSpace is where the real money is at." Lee shrugged his thin shoulders. "And if it all goes kablooey, no one's gonna miss me. What about you?"

"I've wanted to be an astronaut ever since I was a kid."

"See! Right there. Come on back and fix the stupid leak."

Lee started trudging back the way they had come.

Nick stood where he was and called over the wind, "Why are you helping me?"

Lee looked back. "You helped me repair that robot arm."

"That was easy."

"This was easy for me. Anyway, why shouldn't we help each other? I've been helping Maddy, too."

Nick grinned. "Bet that didn't work for you in grade school, either."

"Screw you. She's got what it takes. Just isn't a software head—like you. Seriously, though, it's idiotic to forbid cooperation. When we get up there—" Lee pointed to the moon— "we're gonna have to cooperate on everything, all the time. Why shouldn't we start now? As long as they don't find out, who cares?"

Nick shivered in the hard wind, looking down into the blackness of the valley. Somewhere down there would be a road with traffic on it. A route back to civilization.

It would be risky. He'd walked out of the hut without any provisions. No water, no compass, no map. He didn't even know for sure what *continent* he was on. But after ten weeks of high-altitude endurance runs and a punishingly healthy diet, he was in the best shape of his life. He'd make it.

Nick balled his fists into stones in his pockets. His heart beat unevenly, triggering a sense of rising panic.

He'd run away from Ryder Stillman. There might be kinder words for it, but none more accurate. He ran all the way to Patagonia ... or wherever this was.

Was he going to run away again?

This is real life.

Shady as hell.

Do or die.

He broke into a run. Heavy-footed in his boots, he galloped through the snow to catch up with Lee.

Lee gave him a judicious nod and pushed back the sleeve of his parka to check his watch. "Twenty minutes left. We'll make it."

They jogged, side by side, with the wind at their backs. The outside light of the hut glowed over a rise like a fragment of the moon fallen to earth.

11

Charlie sat at her desk, frowning at a CAD model of her Gulliver lunar earthmover. The original Gulliver was on the moon, in the Sea of Tranquility. It had done the lion's share of construction on the Little Sling. Gulliver II, her second-generation earthmover, was also on the moon, at the Big Sling site in Amundsen Crater. It was building the habitat where the crew would live. After that, it would help them with their duties.

Problem was, Gulliver wasn't optimized for the specific tasks they would have to perform. Charlie was working on a new version of the excavator, which would be... cruder. And better.

While she glanced back and forth between her CAD and CAM screens, she was also eying the clock. She had to attend a photography exhibition at Anna's school. Anna's photographs of the aftermath of Tropical Storm Molly won a statewide eco-awareness prize. Charlie was proud of her daughter, of course, but she wished she didn't have to go to the exhibition and socialize. Formerly, that would have been Reed's job. Harriet would have gone in Charlie's place, but she had a doctor's appointment. No sugarcoating it: single motherhood sucked. Charlie was fortunate to have money, but that didn't make it any easier for herself or for Anna.

"Charlie!"

Fingernail extensions rattled on Charlie's half-open office door. Rachel Hamilton popped her beaming face in without waiting for an invitation. They'd recently hired Rachel to fill the new-to-Five Stones position of flight director. At present she was coordinating the training program. She and Charlie had hit it off immediately.

"What's up?" Charlie rose, glad of the excuse to go out for a cigarette.

They didn't get that far. Walking through the open-plan office, Rachel lowered her voice to a stage whisper. "Guess what? The final test results just came back. Your sweetie made it through to the final twelve!"

"*Rachel*, he's not my sweetie," Charlie said, unable to keep from smiling. She'd not been wrong to bet on Nick Morrison.

She changed direction and headed upstairs, leaving Rachel standing by the coffee machine.

Aaron was at his desk, poring over the short list of twelve names. He reserved the right to select the final six himself.

"What are you thinking?" Charlie said.

"They're *all* qualified," Aaron said.

"I'm thinking we should give more weight to the mechanical repair tests," Charlie said. "Nick Morrison and Madeline Huxley performed particularly well on those."

"As did Bopha Meng. She'd be the first Cambodian on the moon."

"Yeah, but with regard to skill set diversity—" Charlie's phone buzzed in the pocket of her pants. "Crap." Expecting a text from Anna, she pulled it out.

The lock screen preview of the text displayed an unknown phone number and the enigmatic words: *See attachment.*

She opened the text.

See attachment. This gets sent to the SEC at 9 AM tomorrow. That would be real bad for you. Want to change my mind? Send $10,000 in bitcoin to the following account.

The routing number of a crypto account followed.

Numb, Charlie clicked on the attachment.

It was a photograph of one of her printouts, an email from Aaron to Bill about the payload delivery announcement, sent two days before Bill shorted those stocks and made eighty million dollars.

———

Nick made the second string.

Big fucking deal.

The disappointment stung acutely. Only now that he'd lost the chance to go to the moon did he understand how much he wanted it.

"You gonna ditch?" Lee said. He'd made the second string, too. Along with Maddy and Kurtis.

"Nah," Nick said. "Might as well stick around and get paid for phase two."

"Someone might change their mind. Decide not to go."

"Sam won't change his mind." Their friend Sam Ellis had been named pilot. He had fallen to his knees in the snow and praised God. Then he apologized to those who didn't make it. That was the kind of guy he was.

They disassembled the hut and furniture, and loaded the pieces onto mil-surplus off-road trucks. The last truck was their ride. They sat in the back on their kitbags, a sunburnt, lean, silent group. With numb indifference, Nick watched the snowy ground and the stands of dwarf pines pass. They hit a road that wound downhill.

The air got warmer, tasting ridiculously rich.

Trees lining the road became greener and taller. Some of them were *palm* trees.

They passed a road sign for Hilo.

Nick looked to Lee. "Your Patagonian Sierra Finch was about six thousand kilometers away from home."

The rims of Lee's eyes were red. "There was no finch... I just made it up to stop everyone from bitching about it."

All this time, they had been marooned in the foothills of Mauna Kea, in Hawaii. Remote Patagonia had been an illusion.

Everything in Hilo looked wrong after their months away from civilization. The buildings were ugly, the colors garish, the flashing billboards annoying. The people on the streets, scrolling on their phones as they walked, may as well have been zombies. Traffic set off Nick's fight-or-flight reflex. The only thing that felt right was the plane they boarded at Hilo International, and that didn't last long. All too soon, they had to disembark.

Into a mild winter morning in Houston, Texas.

12

Deep in the world's biggest swimming pool, Nick removed a socket wrench from his utility belt and passed it to the space-suited man floating in front of him. Theo fumbled it. Nick swam down to the bottom of the pool and retrieved the wrench from amongst the cables and umbilicals snaking across the tiles.

This time, Theo managed to grasp the wrench in his EVA glove, but he let go of the mockup rover at the same time and slowly sank to the bottom of the pool, waggling his arms and legs.

Nick sighed into his regulator.

Of all six understudies, Theodor Johansson was easily the clumsiest. A Norwegian national, he was an experienced lunar geologist, but his former career never involved anything more physically challenging than tapping a hammer on rock samples. It was a mystery to Nick how he made it through the first phase of training. But he had, and now here he was in the Neutral Buoyancy Lab, learning to move and work in a spacesuit weighted to simulate, underwater, the one-sixth gravity of the moon.

NASA, strapped for cash, rented out the astronaut training facilities at Johnson Space Center to private companies. Five Stones purchased the full training package for Nick, Theo, and the other understudies, as well as Sam Ellis and the rest of the crew. They'd experienced launch gees on the centrifuge, flown parabolas on a "vomit comet" flight to simulate weightlessness, gone through VR simulations of various disasters, and been fitted for spacesuits.

The six crew members got priority. They only had a week to train in the NBL. It was expensive to rent not only the largest swimming pool in the world, but the NASA technicians and divers who came with it. Five Stones was saving money by subbing in one diver of their own—Nick. He'd spent the last four days submerged for up to six hours at a stretch, breathing nitrox, handing people tools and untangling their umbilicals.

At this rate, he would never get a chance to train in a spacesuit himself.

Not that it mattered.

He waited, finning to hold his position, one bare hand resting on the mockup rover. A jigsaw puzzle of hab modules and other equipment cluttered the bottom of the pool. Everything the crew would use on the moon was here—the habitat, the vehicle airlock, the flexitube connecting them, and the two-person pressurized rover.

Today's task: replacing the suitlocks on the back of the rover. An excruciatingly simple matter of removing bolts, switching out the suitlock assemblies, and bolting them into place.

Of course, everything was more difficult in a spacesuit. Nick remembered his own astonishment, during his fitting, at the sheer complexity and unwieldiness of the NASA-certified pressure suit. Although suits had become lighter and more comfortable since the Apollo era, the basic concept remained the same: you were encased in a stiff, pressurized, human-shaped balloon.

At least it was all in one piece nowadays, as opposed to a separate lower torso and upper torso assembly. Getting into the thing still took a good few minutes, and doing *anything* in those gloves, fighting the air pressure every millimeter of the way, took conscious exertion. As well as dexterity.

The two safety divers assigned to Theo tailed him as he climbed back up the ladder, a man-shaped dirigible hung about with lead weights and blocks of foam. His face, behind the transparent faceplate, was contorted with concentration. He stuck his hand out for the wrench. Nick gave it to him and got the replacement bolts ready, anticipating Theo dropping those, too.

The surface of the gem-blue water, ten meters above their heads, shattered. One of the NASA divers finned down to them. She tapped Nick on the shoulder and pointed up.

He surfaced, spat out his mouthpiece, and gulped cool, chlorine-scented air.

Charlie Fitzgerald stood beneath the massive yellow cranes used to lower the equipment into the water.

———

"How's it going?" she said.

"Oh, you know." Nick used both hands to push his soaked hair back. Charlie wore a pale blue shirtdress and a stylish pair of sunglasses. It was the first time he'd seen her in a dress. The NASA staffers—there were always lots of them around during training sessions—also stared at her.

"Are you getting a chance to use the pool?"

"Not yet," Nick said. "I guess if there's time, I might get a turn in the suit."

"I'll make sure they put you on the roster. Everyone needs training." She hesitated. "I'm sorry you didn't get selected. I was really pulling for you."

"It's OK. I might apply for a job here. Y'know, after."

"Yes. After."

In just three more weeks, the second phase of training would end, the crew would be on their way to the moon, and...

Nick would be back where he started. With a little more money in his bank account, sure. But not enough. Not enough for anything.

"Listen, I wanted to ask you something," Charlie said. "Remember when you rescued my mom? She's doing much better, by the way."

"I'm glad to hear that."

"Yeah. We're back in the house at last. I think that's made a big difference. Anyway, you were with a colleague, I think you said, from your last job?"

The pit of Nick's stomach turned to ice. He held still, hardly breathing.

"He also volunteered with the Low Country Navy? Ryder... Stillman, was it?"

Nick was certain he never told her Ryder's name. Though she could have gotten it from the Low Country Navy organizers. Question was, why had she enquired about him? This was bad. Very bad.

"Yeah. Ryder Stillman. What about him?"

Charlie turned away and looked at the pool, sunglasses masking her eyes. "I was just wondering if you had his contact information."

"I... uh... yeah, sure. I have it."

"If you wouldn't mind? I wanted to get in touch with him. To thank him for his help."

Head spinning, Nick moved to where he dumped his backpack. Towels were spread out on the tiles, catching the runoff from wrinkly orange, deflated spacesuits. Understudies and crew members sat around, waiting for their turn in the pool. Sam Ellis raised his eyebrows at Nick, flicked a glance in Charlie's direction, and smiled. Nick was too distracted to return the smile. This had to be something to do with Merritt Island. Harriet. The safe.

He fished his phone out of his bag and gave Charlie Ryder's phone number, email, and address in Charleston. It now seemed inexplicable he hadn't deleted Ryder from his address book months ago.

"He might not be at that address anymore," he warned Charlie. "Might not even be in Charleston. Divers tend to move on."

And if she wanted to thank Ryder for his help, why hadn't she done it last year? Why now?

"I'll try it anyway. I appreciate it, Nick. Thank you."

Nick picked distractedly at the seam of his rashguard. He needed to tell her that Ryder was dangerous. Then she'd want an explanation. It would all come out.

She would despise him.

"Are you in town for long?" he said.

"Flying back to Florida tonight. Why?"

He needed to have a proper conversation with her, without all these people around. "I was just thinking maybe we could do lunch."

"Oh, no," she said. "I've got a lunch meeting with the JSC people."

"Ah! Yeah, that's totally fine." Nick blushed hotly. What a loser he must sound like. "Maybe next time."

"Yeah. Next time."

Splashes and echoes filled the air. Theo's time was up. They were bringing him to the surface on the crew lift.

"Well, I should get back to work," Nick said. He sat on the edge of the pool, put on his scuba harness and adjusted his mask. As he slid into the cold water, he felt that she was still watching him.

13

It wasn't Nick, Charlie decided.

He'd plainly been dumbfounded when she asked for Ryder Stillman's contact information out of the blue. Anyway, he'd been living in a fishbowl administered by Five Stones for the last six months, half that time with no internet. It would have been physically impossible for him to have sent the first blackmail threat. Even the second one. And his reaction today suggested he didn't know a thing about it.

Charlie was uncomfortable trusting her instincts like this. She was a logical thinker. And it annoyed her that logic wouldn't help her get out of this nightmare.

During her meeting with the JSC robotics people, she researched Ryder Stillman on her phone. As expected, she got nowhere. The man was a ghost. Two kinds of people typically had no or very little digital footprint: the rich and criminals. Not that those were mutually exclusive categories. The sheer paucity of information about Ryder Stillman suggested he was the latter.

Hardly something she wasn't already aware of.

He never signed his texts, and he used a different phone number and crypto address every time.

All the same, she was now sure it was him.

On the day the first text arrived, she'd confronted her mother. "Mom, you didn't... I don't know... tell those guys the combination to the safe, did you?"

Harriet had scrunched up her face, trying to remember. It broke Charlie's heart to see her struggling with her memory. She was about to say, *"Never mind, it doesn't matter,"* when Harriet said suddenly, "Yes, darling, I did. I remember now. I thought they might need to get into it because it was bolted to the floor."

"It *wasn't* bolted to the floor."

"Well... you said you were going to, so..."

"I never got around to it."

That's what happened. Harriet couldn't always remember people's names, but she remembered the combination without getting a single number wrong. Ryder Stillman opened the safe and photographed every document it contained.

Charlie wasn't absolutely sure that photographs, as opposed to originals, would be admissible as evidence in the SEC's investigation. But she was too frightened of giving herself away to research it online. She couldn't afford to chance it. Admissible or not, if Ryder followed through on his threats, the SEC would know for damn sure that Aaron and Bill were guilty of insider trading. They'd transition into full Rottweiler mode, and they would find out the truth.

All of them—Aaron, Yuta, Bill, and Charlie herself—might go to jail.

Anna, who had already lost her father to bipolar disorder and divorce, might lose her mother as well.

It was unthinkable.

Charlie paid Ryder what he asked for. $10,000 the first time. $9,000 the second time. $15,000. $8,000...

The amounts were so small and various, she almost thought he was asking for however much he needed to pay his bills.

This could go on forever.

But *she* couldn't go on forever.

She was losing sleep. Losing focus at work. She was overseeing the construction of her new robot, Woombat, a dedicated lunar excavator. Her twenty-five-year-old assistant had caught potential component interference in Woombat's sensor array. *That* was embarrassing, and it happened because Charlie's mind wasn't on the job.

Even when she was with Anna, she wasn't really with her. She was thinking about Ryder Stillman and trying to think up some way of getting rid of him for good.

She was still thinking about it when her flight landed at Orlando International, and she walked out of baggage claim into a Dior-scented hug from Rachel Hamilton.

"Thanks for coming to pick me up," Charlie said. "I hit the rosé a bit too hard on the plane."

"Oh, that's a shame," Rachel said. "I was hoping you were up for a drink at Q."

Charlie was.

They sat on the thirty-fourth-floor balcony of Q Lounge, with a cool breeze ruffling the ficus in the planters, and drank chardonnay from South Africa. In winter, Florida was actually pleasant. The lights of central Orlando gleamed through the dark trees below. An electrojazz quintet played, and Rachel unloaded about her ex.

Like Charlie, she was divorced, and that's where the similarities stopped. Rachel's ex worked at SpaceZ, which was where Rachel had worked, until Five Stones lured her away with better benefits. NewSpace was a small incestuous industry, populated by, in Rachel's words, the "highest concentration of weirdos outside of a UFOlogy conference." She described the embarrassing lengths her ex had gone in an attempt to get her to sleep with him again.

"You're not listening, are you, Charlie?"

"Hm? Yes. Of course I am," Charlie said.

"No, you're not. I know that look. *You're* thinking about your *sweetie.*"

Charlie laughed ruefully. True, she had been thinking about Nick—at least, in terms of his connection to Ryder Stillman—but no one could describe the general tenor of her thoughts as romantic.

"Did you get to see him in Texas?"

"Only for about five minutes." Charlie hesitated. "Rachel, I-I wanted to ask you something..."

Rachel leaned forward. Her bony face, lit from below by the windproof votive candle in the middle of the table, appeared distorted and greedy for some salacious confession.

"Do you have any idea where I could get a gun?"

Rachel's eyes popped wide. She sat back. "A *gun?* Charlie, is there something I need to know about?"

"No, it's just that I—"

"Is Reed back? Has he been harassing you?"

Reed was many things, but he wasn't violent. Charlie had enough self-respect not to use him as an excuse. "No, it's just for security in general. We were robbed after Molly, and my mother doesn't feel safe anymore. And to be honest... I don't either. I was just thinking, if I had a gun, I would be able to sleep better."

"Guns are more likely to be used *against* you," Rachel said, quoting the same argument that had been used to make it impossible for private citizens to purchase guns in the US.

Legally, anyway.

Charlie sighed and drained her wineglass. "Well, it was just a thought. Probably a dumb one."

"Do you even know how to shoot?"

"No. I mean... It can't be that hard."

"It isn't. I shot a handgun once. There's nothing to it, really," Rachel said, leaning back over the table. "If you really want to buy one, I might be able to ask my brother."

"You have a brother?"

"Yeah. He's in law enforcement."

"That would be great," Charlie said.

Why didn't she feel any better? Her feelings were getting mixed up and murky. She shouldn't be going down this road. Violence never solved anything. She hoped Rachel's brother turned out to be a dead end. She'd drunk too much, that's all.

Head buzzing, she visualized Nick Morrison's bright, yet guarded, eyes. She wished she'd had the courage to talk to him about Ryder's blackmail demands. But then he would know Five Stones had something to hide...

Damn. Damn, damn.

Well, she'd see him at the launch.

14

The upper rim of the sun rested on the sea. Warm, dusty wind gusted over the bleachers outside the south entrance to Cape Canaveral Air Force Station, bearing the taint of rocket fuel. The basso throb of engines carried from Launch Complex 40. A little less than two miles away, the nose of a SpaceZ Ultra Heavy glittered above the trees.

T-minus 1 minute...

Nick sat at the top of the bleachers with the other understudies, drinking Bloody Marys from a thermos Maddy brought along.

The bleachers teemed with bloggers, vloggers, and even a cable television crew.

———

"Hi, I'm here at Cape Canaveral for the launch of the first private-sector manned mission to the moon since Biorocketix in 2033. Fifteen years ago, the Biorocketix expedition ended tragically when equipment failures compromised the company's lunar habitat. But lunar startup Five Stones is confident they have learned from the past. Five Stones CEO, Aaron Slater, is here with me to discuss the challenges that lie ahead for his crew. Aaron?"

"Thanks, Cynthia. Well, the first challenge is getting there. As you can see, the Ultra Heavy is going to launch in a tri-core configuration with two solid fuel boosters. Once it reaches LEO, the boosters will be jettisoned, and Tranquility 12 will rendezvous with the SkyStation orbital depot—"

"And SpaceZ owns SkyStation, isn't that right?"

"That's right. We have a very close partnership with them."

"In fact, you used to work there."

"In the not-so-distant past, yes. SkyStation will fill the rocket's tanks with LOX and fuel, which for the Ultra Heavy is liquid hydrogen. It's quite sufficient to get it to the moon *and* back. This is a *reusable* moon rocket, which has been a great source of cost efficiencies for us, as we've repeatedly used the Ultra Heavy to deliver our assets to the lunar surface."

"This is your twelfth mission to the moon, but the first crewed mission."

"That's why we've named it *Tranquility 12*. The previous missions delivered everything the crew will need, as well as materials and equipment—"

"If I could just interrupt, why *Tranquility*? Your landing site is near the lunar south pole, right? And the Sea of Tranquility is on the equator."

"Yes. The south pole actually offers better launch trajectories toward Earth. Our working prototype was built in the Sea of Tranquility, and the name just sort of stuck."

"Right, your working prototype. You made quite the splash two years ago when the Little Sling, as it's called, first went into action. There was chatter about a tie-up with SpaceZ to deliver raw materials from the moon to SkyStation, but that never materialized. Since then, you've been very quiet. What happened?"

"We were unable to achieve the utilization ratio for the Little Sling that we hoped for. In essence, we couldn't guarantee deliveries with an acceptable level of reliability. As a result, that agreement never came to fruition.

"However, the Little Sling *is* operating, and we're providing spot deliveries of basalt to LEO for our customers, who include SpaceZ. So, yes, it works—it *works*. The missing piece is real-time human input during construction and operation. That's why we're sending up a human crew at this time, with the additional goal of demonstrating a biosphere that will utilize regenerative life-support hardware and a plant-based atmosphere-management system to make our presence on the moon truly sustainable."

"That's wonderful. Thank you very much for talking with me, Aaron. I'm Cynthia Honeywell, at Cape Canaveral, and we'll be back with updates on this story in the coming hours."

———

"Dumb bitch," Aaron said to Yuta and Charlie, shucking off the blazer he unwillingly wore for the interview, and slugging water. "She didn't even follow up on the change of site."

"*Better launch trajectories from the south pole,*" Yuta mocked. "So very convincing."

"I know, I know. I had to say *something*."

Charlie rolled her eyes.

"It's fine. They don't give a shit about the Big Sling. All they care about is warm bodies in space. And if we pull this off, we'll be *untouchable*." Aaron drank more water. He'd been sweating under the TV crew's lights. "Jesus, I wish we didn't have to let them all in. Couldn't we just have *stayed* in stealth mode?"

"Not if you want to distract them from the insider trading investigation," Charlie said dryly.

The media attention was unnerving for her, too. Five Stones had retreated from the public eye shortly after their initial payload delivery announcement. It became obvious to the team there were issues with the Little Sling and the associated oxygen plant, which would preclude the regular deliveries of oxygen to lunar orbit and LEO. They very thing their investors and customers, primarily SpaceZ, had hoped for. They tried for almost a year to fix the problems remotely before giving up and shifting to the crewed-mission template.

Two weeks ago, they canceled their digital-scrubbing contract and re-emerged dramatically with the Tranquility 12 launch announcement. The mission concept had electrified the whole NewSpace community. Even normies were paying attention. Aaron was right, of course, about the PR value of a human crew. Of all the mentions sleeting across Charlie's phone screen, hardly any contained the string "SEC investigation."

T-minus 30 seconds...

She checked the livestream. Six and a half million people watching. Holy shit.

———

T-minus 15 seconds...

Wisps of steam drifted up from the base of Tranquility 12, white in the floodlights bathing the launchpad.

T-minus 10...

On board the rocket, the crew sat in two rows of three, strapped into their couches. Sam Ellis, the pilot, monitored the prelaunch metrics on the touchscreens in front of him. There was a little talking. Some nervous laughter. Mostly they sat in awed silence, no doubt struggling to grasp the audacity of what they were about to do: *leave Earth* for the first time.

———

5. 4. 3. 2. 1.

Liftoff.

Clouds boiled up from LC40, momentarily obscuring the Ultra Heavy and the strongback that supported it. The world's most powerful rocket engines shook the air so loudly, the vibrations reached out for miles around. Everyone in the bleachers jumped to their feet, mouths stretched open in cheers that no one could hear.

Tranquility 12 howled into the sky on a jet of flame and smoke.

The noise faded.

The rocket curved away into the upper atmosphere.

Hearing returned.

People bent over their phone screens, following the feed from the onboard cameras.

Fifty miles above the surface of Earth, travelling at Mach 10, the rocket's main engines cut out.

"MECO complete," the speakers boomed. Seconds later, the onboard feed showed the solid fuel boosters separating from Tranquility 12, arching back into the atmosphere. They would fire again on reentry and land in the crosshairs of the cameras still trained on LC40.

"Tranquility 12 has reached orbital altitude."

More cheers flooded the stands. The livestream switched to a split screen, showing the onboard feed–engine bells, exhaust jetting out, Earth below—and the internal feed from the crew cabin. Sam Ellis, visibly floating above his couch, though still strapped in, flashed a grin and gave the camera a thumbs-up.

A white flash blanked out the external feed.

Murmurs rose from the crowd.

Sam Ellis's grin vanished. He lunged for his touchscreen.

All at once, every screen in the bleachers went blank.

"Oh my God!" shrieked someone who would be identified, in the millions of replays to follow, as Sam's girlfriend. "Oh my *God! What's happening?*"

"We have lost communications with Tranquility 12," the speakers said. "Attempting to reestablish communication now."

Sam's girlfriend stopped screaming. Someone else began crying. Faces swiveled to the dark sky, waiting. And waiting.

———

It was Aaron who made the announcement. Standing in a blaze of TV lights, voice breaking, he said, "We have confirmation from SkyStation, as well as Ground Control. Tranquility 12 has been lost with all hands."

———

While every other camera zoomed in on Aaron's reaction to the disaster, one intrepid vlogger turned his lens to the top of the bleachers. He filmed a clip, which later went viral, of the understudies hugging each other and weeping.

Only one of them stood apart. Nick Morrison stared at the sky, his mouth open, hands balled at his sides. Microexpression analysis—a tool now commonly available on video streaming sites—revealed that he was feeling not grief, but anger.

———

COCOA BEACH, Florida—March 12, 2049—Leading lunar ISRU innovator Five Stones Inc. has announced the results of its investigation, conducted jointly with SpaceZ Inc., into the loss of the Tranquility 12 rocket on March 2. The companies determined the cause of the rocket's failure to be a space-debris strike

...

15

"Space debris, my ass," Lee whispered to Nick.

They were seated in the event room at SpaceZ's Florida campus. The two companies had called a news conference when it became clear a press release wasn't going to satisfy the industry's demand for a postmortem. All eyes were on Aaron, who spoke with uncharacteristic restraint.

Nick, Lee, Kurtis, Maddy, Theo, and Fenella sat in the first row of seats, wearing their Five Stones flight suits. Black-framed pictures of the six dead crew hung at the back of the stage. Nick had only to raise his eyes to see the face of Sam Ellis, radiating excitement, wearing the same flight suit he wore now. *See you on the moon, bro.* Those had been Sam's last words to Nick. It turned out his girlfriend was pregnant. That baby would be fatherless because Five Stones and SpaceZ fucked up.

Lee writhed in his seat. "Bullshit," he chanted under his breath. "This is such bullshit."

"*Quiet,*" Nick said. "Later."

After the investigators concluded their presentation, while the media milled around in hopes of getting one-on-ones with the executives, Aaron went to take a leak. Nick and Lee followed.

Fortunately for them, Aaron disdained the plebeian toilets behind the event room. He headed upstairs to one of the unisex executive cubicles. The hall was empty. Nick took several running steps and caught up with Aaron. He pushed into the cubicle before the door could close and wedged his shoulder against the sensor. Lee crowded in with them. Nick moved off the sensor so the door could close and set his back to it.

"Hey," Aaron said. "I need to take a leak."

"Go ahead," Lee said.

"What the hell?" Aaron's thin face flushed. "Is this some homo thing?"

"Nope," Nick said. "We just want to talk."

"What about?"

Aaron was crossing his legs urgently. Nick said, "Go ahead. Wouldn't want you to piss your ten-thousand-dollar pants."

Aaron held out for a few seconds more before he unzipped and urinated. He flushed the toilet and turned to wash his hands. The sink was a Zen depression in a granite slab that also held a bowl of water lilies, a stack of fresh towels, a charging stand, and a fan of industry publications. The top one carried the headline *Five Stones Announces 2nd Crewed Launch Following Tragedy.*

Aaron met Nick's eyes in the antique oval mirror. "Well?" he said sharply.

Lee stepped forward. "Space debris, huh? To be blunt, that's B as in bull, S as in shit. Every piece of debris in orbit larger than ten centimeters is tracked by ground-based radar *and* detectors on SkyStation, not to mention the Aurora and Tiangong II space stations. *And* Tranquility 12 had its own in situ detectors. You seriously saying all those failed at once? Bullshit, Aaron. Six of our friends are dead, and we want to know why."

"It was space debris," Aaron said. "You saw the video."

Everyone had seen the video. It didn't tell them much. It was a long-distance capture from SkyStation. Fifty kilometers out from rendezvous, the fuzzy, computer-enhanced Tranquility 12 bucked like something had stung it, and begun to spout a thin jet of liquid hydrogen from its fuel tank. It immediately lost trim and began to tumble, too fast for either Sam Ellis or the computer to null out its spin. Within the space of fifteen seconds, the engines sputtered out, and Tranquility 12 plunged back into the atmosphere, burning like a meteor.

No debris from the rocket had been recovered.

The investigators could say anything they wanted to, as long as it was consistent with the video evidence. And that could be easily managed.

"Ever heard of deepfakes?" Lee said. "How do we know the video is even real?"

"For fuck's sake," Aaron said. "What are you trying to say? Space debris is a real problem. That's why we need better on-orbit satellite refurbishment facilities, so even more junk doesn't end up in LEO—you know what, I'm out of here."

He juked past Lee. Nick stood firm with his back to the door. Aaron glared at him, pink with anger.

"Fake debris is a real problem, too," Nick suggested.

Fake debris was the term of art for tiny kinetic missiles with cold-gas propulsion thrusters and guidance chips. More than one quiet, nasty skirmish had been fought in orbit between countries using fake debris to take out each other's satellites. Detectors were useless against such attacks, because fake debris could suddenly change course after the algos already decided it was harmless.

"Yeah, no," Aaron said. "As we stated in the analysis, the rate of LOX venting points to an impactor at least thirty centimeters in diameter, and that's larger than any of the known fake debris models. If you make these things too big, they get noticed. Now get out of my way."

"Aurora is a military space station," Nick said. "I'm sure they've got something larger than thirty centimeters in their armory."

"You've been spending too much time on the internet," Aaron said dismissively. "Aurora has nothing to do with the military. It's purely commercial. And besides, they're one of our customers."

"Have you got any enemies, Aaron?" Lee said. "Is there anyone in the industry who wants Five Stones to fail?"

Aaron loosed a loud, angry laugh at Lee. "Wrong question. The right question is, who *doesn't?*"

"Including SpaceZ?" Nick said.

"No, Sean is cool," Aaron said. "He wants to get to Mars and needs the Big Sling's launch capacity to refuel his big fucking rockets in lunar orbit. If we fail, he fails, too."

"I don't care about Mars," Lee said. "Here's what I care about. This mission just got a lot riskier." He tugged at the collar of his flight suit. Today, they had mission patches on their chests flashing *Tranquility 13*. "If you want us to go up there, we also might mysteriously find ourselves in the wrong place at the wrong time." Aaron started to argue. Lee spoke over him. "Bearing that risk in mind, we want hazard pay. How much you think would be good, Nick?"

They'd already rehearsed this part. "Five million," Nick said.

"Not enough," Lee said. "I'm thinking ten."

Aaron shouted, "Jesus! You've got four million dollars coming to you, *minimum*. Isn't that enough?"

His voice was loud. Nick reached over and turned on the hand dryer. Hot air roared.

"No, Aaron," Lee said over the noise. "Given what just

happened, it *isn't* enough. Tell you what. We'll take eight mil— double the original completion bonus—and call it good."

"To be paid to our heirs," Nick said. "In the event of space debris strikes or other *accidents*."

"This is extortion," Aaron said, in a comically prissy tone. He reached for his pants pocket. Nick had been waiting for that. He lunged, grabbed Aaron's wrist, and twisted. Aaron yelped. Nick plunged his hand into the pocket and yanked Aaron's phone out. He put it into his own pocket, and only then did he let go. Aaron stared at him with hatred, nursing his slightly reddened wrist.

"Fuck you," Aaron said. "You're fired."

"Nice try," Lee said. "You've already told the whole world that Tranquility 13 is launching on the twenty-fourth. That's just one, short little week from today. I don't know what the big hurry is. You could at least do a *real* investigation first. But whatever. You can't replace us within a week."

"Are the rest of the crew in on this?" Aaron demanded.

They weren't. They accepted the space debris story at face value. Nick and Lee kept quiet about their suspicions; morale was bad enough as it was. Plus, they figured their chances would be better if they weren't asking for *forty* million dollars.

"Just the two of us," Nick said. "You still can't replace us inside a week."

"Oh yeah?" Aaron said. "There are thousands of guys who would jump at this opportunity."

"Could be," Lee said. "But they haven't trained for six months. They haven't been fitted for spacesuits. They haven't memorized every last *fucking* detail of the Big Sling construction procedures. And you haven't vetted them down to the toenails."

Aaron scowled. "I obviously could have vetted you two better."

Lee started to smile. He obviously thought they'd won, or were almost there. He had no experience of dealing with sharks in human form. Nick had. Aaron wasn't beaten yet.

Nick spoke over Lee, staring into Aaron's face, giving his gravelly South-African-Southern drawl full play. "If you vetted me, you know about my juvenile conviction for theft. The court records are sealed, so let me tell you a little more about that. When I was in high school, I used to run with a crew of crackers."

Aaron's face twitched in recognition. He didn't need the cracking scam explained to him.

"The top dawg of our crew, guy named Remy, couple of years older than me, he was a genius. He figured out how to exploit the 6G rollout loophole before Google or Amazon even knew it was there. That guy's brain, oh man. He was making six figures at the age of eighteen. Where do you think he is now?"

"Working for Google?" Aaron said.

"Nope," Nick said. "He's doing twenty to life for digital account compromise. He's in a federal penitentiary, Aaron, and I put him there."

The last part wasn't true. At seventeen, Nick was too proud to squeal on his friends. Remy the cracker king had gotten busted years later for a ransomware scheme. But in another sense, Nick *had* put him in jail, because if he'd said something when they were in high school, maybe Remy would have changed his ways before it was too late. Anyway, the story sounded good. Aaron's eyes widened; he nervously touched the knot of his necktie.

"Do you want to go to jail, Aaron?" Nick said. "I know you're already being investigated for insider trading. You'll probably beat the rap on that. The cool kids always do. But it could get a lot worse for you." He leaned closer to Aaron. Aaron leaned away. "Milo Campbell," Nick said.

"He signed the waiver," Aaron said.

Milo Campbell had been one of their original hut-mates. He suffered a heart attack during training. "We have four eyewitnesses who can testify that Kurtis made him go out on that run even though he wasn't feeling well," Nick said. "And we can also testify there was no electronic defibrillator device in the hut, and it took the helicopter eight hours to arrive. His death was *avoidable*. Any responsible company would have avoided it. How are you gonna feel when you're standing in court, facing manslaughter charges, with your company in ruins, because you were too tight to pay the entirely reasonable hazard bonus we're asking for?"

"All right, all right! Seven million each."

"Done," Lee started.

"No," Nick said. "Ten. In crypto."

"On completion."

"Now."

"I don't fucking have it *now*! We had to move the Tranquility 13 launch up by six weeks and convert it to a crewed flight. We had to replace all the cargo that burned up with Tranquility 12. And need I mention the lawyers. The space debris conclusion limits our financial liability, but we're still on the hook for fuel and launch-related costs. Cash is tight, understand?"

Nick thought that was probably the truth. "Fine. On completion."

Lee took out his phone. He'd recorded the entire conversation, as he now made clear to Aaron. They got Aaron to electronically sign the contract they'd drawn up, guaranteeing each of them an extra $6,000,000 on top of their bonus. On completion.

When that was done, Nick returned Aaron's phone. They

hung back in the hall and watched him stomp down the stairs ahead of them.

"That was fucking awesome." Lee's grin was incandescent. "You scared *me* for a minute there, Morrison."

Nick shrugged and bobbed his head. He felt slightly giddy. He hadn't really thought they could pull it off. He considered, with adrenaline-tinged detachment, what this meant: Aaron definitely had a guilty conscience. He wouldn't have agreed to pay up otherwise.

They returned to the event room. It was still crowded. Charlie stood by the buffet table, chatting and laughing like she was having the time of her life. Nick sheered away before she could spot him. He didn't feel like talking to her at the moment.

He followed Lee out to the minibus. The night smelled of melted blacktop. The planet was burning up.

———

Beneath the planet-shaped LED chandeliers, Charlie spoke with the SpaceZ electronics guys about semiconductor radiation-hardness testing. These chumps were nowhere near matching the lifetime performances she achieved on the moon with her robots. Half-listening to their competitive bluster, she twirled her champagne flute in her fingers. Whose bright idea had it been to provide *champagne* for an occasion like this?

In all probability, the catering defaults hadn't even been reviewed. It was the NewSpace way of doing things. Always the champagne, the exotic fruits and seafood, the robot waiters and live musicians. Always everyone acting like everyone else was their best friend in the entire fucking world.

Where was Nick? She'd seen the other astronauts leave. Charlie scanned the crowd again.

The chandeliers circled on their rails, imitating the motion of the planets around the sun. Aaron plunged toward her, ignoring the bloggers and tech journalists who tried to get his attention. His necktie was askew. Her first thought was that he'd had too much to drink.

"Gotta steal Charlie," he said, clicking a smile on and off at the SpaceZ guys. His hand on her elbow steered her out to the back of the building.

Yuta was already there, toying with his replica Butz-Choquin vape pipe. There was an ashtray in the shape of the Death Star for SpaceZ's resident smokers. Charlie lit up.

"Those fuckers," Aaron said. His voice trembled. He wasn't drunk. He was nearly too angry to speak.

"What fuckers?" Yuta said.

"Morrison and Yang. Those *fuckers* just basically accused us of destroying Tranquility 12 *ourselves*."

Charlie brought her free hand to her forehead and ground the heel of her palm into her eyes. "My God. How ironic is that."

"Yeah," Aaron said. "They also wanted to know why we're in such a hurry to launch Tranquility 13."

"What did you tell them?"

"Nothing." Aaron's face changed. Seconds later, Charlie was half-asphyxiated by cologne. Sean Radek, the CEO of SpaceZ, ambled up to them.

Sean had mentored Aaron, made him rich, and continued to support his vision after Aaron went out on his own. He'd seen the potential of the Big Sling when it was just a sketch on a napkin. He now looked forward to monopolizing the Big Sling's launch capacity when it went into operation. The loss of Tranquility 12, however, had shaken his faith in Five Stones.

"I'm worried about the landing conditions in Amundsen," he complained. "We're pushing the safety envelope."

Aaron smiled broadly. "I have total faith in your rockets, Sean. After all, I designed them myself."

"Six fatalities. I hate fatalities."

"It's the business we're in."

"Regardless, I don't want any more. Why can't you wait until next month?"

Aaron's smile vanished. "Because it might happen again," he said brutally.

Sean winced. "Upgrade your goddamn IT security."

16

The on-pad elevator carried Nick and the others up through a morning as close to perfect as Florida could offer. They rose past the orange block letters painted on the side of the rocket: *TRANQUILITY 13*.

"Unlucky thirteen," Maddy said.

"Quit that," Kurtis said.

Nick looked down at the technicians dashing around the launchpad, then out across the Atlantic. Heat hazed the distance. Seagulls circled. He wondered if this would be his last sight of Earth. In that moment... he didn't want to go after all. Then the elevator reached the airlock in the crew capsule, and it was too late.

Inside the crew cabin, they sat in two rows of three. Nick was in the left front couch, next to Kurtis, who'd been named pilot. Though it didn't mean much. The rocket would be operated by the computers and the technicians at SpaceZ mission control. Kurtis wasn't expected to do any flying. And if the need arose, it wouldn't help, anyway. Certainly hadn't helped Sam and the others.

To make up for their lack of control, SpaceZ provided a

wealth of data. The touchscreens in front of each couch displayed graphs of engine status, cabin pressurization, and a hundred other things, including individual telemetry from the biosensors in their flight suits.

Nick regularized his breathing as if he were on a dive. He took satisfaction in watching his heart rate drop to a cool sixty beats per minute and his other stress indicators level off.

4. 3. 2. 1.

Liftoff.

Tranquility 13 safely reached orbit. Then they experienced a delay.

———

Due to a technical complication, it took a day and a half for the rocket to dock with SkyStation, instead of the planned four hours. While the crew grew antsy, the mission controllers reassured them—if it could be called a reassurance—that this kind of thing happened all the time. On-orbit fueling was still a technology in its infancy. Hiccups were to be expected.

Sure enough, in the end, the docking maneuver was completed successfully. Both craft tiptoed forward, running their ullage motors, while SkyStation fed Tranquility 13 the LH2 and LOX that had previously been reserved for Tranquility 12.

Thirty-seven hours late, Tranquility 13 burned out of orbit, bound for the moon.

"We came this close to aborting," Kurtis said, holding up his thumb and forefinger. As mission commander, he got updates that no one else did, and seemed to relish doling them out to the rest of the crew.

"Why?" Fenella Khan said. Fenella was a British-Pakistani

mountaineer. She had a blunt manner and never shied away from asking questions that started with *why*.

"A technical issue related to the heat radiation capability of the spacecraft," Kurtis said.

"Oh, the hydrolox thing," Lee said.

"Why don't *you* go ahead and explain it," Kurtis said irritably.

Lee shrugged. "It's not that big a deal. SpaceZ uses hydrolox engines because hydrogen can *theoretically* be produced in bulk on the moon. When really, ILI already produces a lot of it, they just haven't got the capacity to safely store it. Which is the point. Liquid hydrogen is dangerous shit. Really dangerous. And we're carrying enough of it for the return flight to LEO. That's why SpaceZ always lands their spacecraft in the dark, to make triply sure the LH_2 doesn't heat up. But since we had that delightfully exhilarating delay, our landing site might end up being sunlit."

"So?" Fenella said impatiently.

"We might go boom," Lee said. He laughed. "Seriously though, we won't. The cryocooling system is rated for ambient heat exposure up to 150 degrees Celsius, and if that fails, the valves would safely vent the LH_2 to vacuum."

All this time they were floating in the cabin's upper compartment, having received the green light to leave their couches. Nick pushed off from the ceiling with his fingertips and turned in the air. The floor became the ceiling—and then the wall—and then the floor again. A touch of queasiness hit him.

He'd expected to be a "good astronaut." After all, he never got seasick, and he'd enjoyed the brief bursts of microgravity on their suborbital training flights. But he found it difficult to adjust to living in free fall.

His whole body felt unpleasantly loose and uncontrolled.

He was constipated. His feet were cold. His sinuses were blocked up. Whenever he tried to sleep, strapped into his couch, he would startle awake, thinking he was falling. And if he did manage to drift off, he would be woken again by flashes of bright light. They'd been warned about this: particles of cosmic radiation zipped right through the craft, and some of them intersected with human eyeballs. Despite the flashes having a rational explanation, they were still eerie and unsettling.

None of the others seemed to be having any trouble sleeping or keeping their tasteless prepackaged meals down. Nick dragged himself through his make-work tasks, but he felt increasingly isolated from the rest of the crew. Even Lee was in high spirits now that the danger of space debris lay behind them.

Nick, on the other hand, was hyper-focused on the real dangers ahead. The moon was the single most dangerous place for humanity this side of Mars. Only the thought of the $10 million coming to him kept Nick from begging Mission Control to take him back home.

After two long days, Tranquility 13 dropped into orbit around the moon. The cabin had three real windows, each scarcely bigger than a dinner plate. The crew took turns pressing their noses to the heatproof glass. Craters stared up like blind eyes. Mountains fringed the maria, gray and white, aggressively stark. Nick shivered. It was like observing a dead sea bed —acidified, bleached, lifeless—through glass instead of water.

The moon seemed to slowly rotate onto its side as Tranquility 13 hurtled to the apogee of its lunar orbit and executed a plane change to enter a polar orbit.

Rushing over the south pole, they saw the pinprick lights of ILI on the rim of Shackleton Crater. On the far side of the moon, the Chinese lunar base was a candle burning in Von Karman Crater. At the north pole, the Russian base twinkled in

Peary Crater. Then it was time to strap in for their deorbit burn. The rocket swung around to point its engine bells in its direction of travel. For the first time since they left Earth orbit, all three cores fired.

Their headlong flight over the lunar surface slowed, little by little, the ground creeping closer. They cruised across the Sea of Serenity at Mach 4. Composite radar picked out the Apollo 11 landing site, now almost a century old. Near it, the Little Sling stood on top of Mount Marilyn. The screen flashed: *Hello!* Charlie's robots on site at the Little Sling had been programmed to welcome them. Nick smiled.

The Little Sling vanished over the horizon. Tranquility 13 dipped toward the mountainous South Pole-Aitken Basin. Inky shadows cupped the hills and puddled inside crater rims.

Slower.

Lower.

Tranquility 13 crossed the northern rim of Amundsen Crater less than a kilometer up. It was nearly noon on a lunar summer day. Only a sliver of the crater floor, below the southeastern rim, lay in darkness. The central peak, 1,500 meters high, cast a mere fingernail of shadow at the northern edge of its base. That was their destination. The screens pinpointed their designated landing site—*right* on the dark side of the line between sun and shadow.

"Cutting it close," Kurtis grunted.

"Abort?" Lee said with gallows humor.

Kurtis laughed and lifted his hands in the air, reminding them he wasn't controlling anything.

With the same computer-controlled grace as before, Tranquility 13 heeled over, its engines now pointing downward, slowing the rocket's descent.

From above, the surface of the moon looked hard as stone. It was anything but. The dust coating the floor of the crater lay several inches deep. Fountains of dust spurted up from Tranquility 13's engine plumes, white in the sunlight, invisible in the shadow. The rocket seemed to be dropping into an explosion sheared in half by the terminator. Dust engulfed its 115-meter height. The windows turned gray and then black.

The aft fins thudded onto lunar bedrock.

Nick sagged in his couch. They were back in gravity. One-sixth of Earth gravity, weak but real. It felt great.

Aaron popped up on their screens, yelling, "Congratulations, guys!"

The camera pulled back to a view of the entire Five Stones workforce gathered at the office in Cocoa Beach. Applause and cheers crackled into the silent crew cabin. Champagne corks flew. Nick ran his tongue around the parched inside of his mouth.

"Thanks, Aaron," Kurtis said. "It's a pleasure to be here at last."

"I hate to spoil your big moment," Aaron said, sobering. "But you've got to move fast. We don't want to excessively stress the rocket's cryocooling systems."

"What did I say? I completely called it," Lee said.

The Five Stones office vanished. In its place appeared a pudgy SpaceZ flight controller, surrounded by people talking urgently into headsets. "T-13, we're gonna have to ask you to haul ass. We have determined you're too close to the terminator for comfort. You'll need to disembark yourselves and your cargo and clear the area within a turnaround time of three hours. In view of this, we would like you to utilize the emergency disembarkation apparatus. Get moving on that now, please. We'll be right here if you need assistance."

17

Nick sprang up from his couch—higher than he intended in the low gravity—and nearly bumped his head on the ceiling. He'd have to watch that. He dropped through the hatch into the lower deck of the crew capsule and wrestled the emergency disembarkation apparatus out of its storage webbing. Fenella was there. She helped him maneuver it up through the hatch.

On the upper deck, Kurtis hunched in his couch, nodding along to Mission Control's detailed instructions for unloading the cargo. Lee perched on his right, working the surface comms, electronically talking to their rover. An ESA castoff modified by Charlie, the rover had landed a few months back at the Five Stones base camp. It could navigate autonomously over the lunar terrain using satellite navigation and sun tracking. It would arrive shortly to pick up their cargo.

Theo waited by the airlock. "Hurry up!"

Nick manhandled the EDA over to the airlock while Fenella went back to help Maddy haul their personal belongings and light cargo out of the lower deck. Nick and Theo undertook the protracted task of donning their spacesuits. They closed their rear entry ports and visually checked each other's seals.

"Looking good," Nick said over the suit radio. With his stiff, gloved forefinger, he keyed in the code to open the airlock.

The airlock chamber was large enough to hold them and the EDA. It opened at the other end to a disorientingly strange vista. Total darkness, 110 meters up. A few feet away, a sparkling mist hung suspended in the vacuum, blotting out the view of the crater Nick had expected. He looked up—the sky was there, all right. Stars. Blurry. He looked down. The pilot lights around the rim of the airlock revealed that the sleeves of his orange spacesuit had already turned salmon gray.

"The *dust*," he said.

"Who cares about that?" Theo's voice was taut with fear. "Deploy the EDA."

"Yeah, let's do this."

They held out the rectangular package, twisted the release lever, and let it go.

One hundred and ten meters down.

The original plan had been for them to rappel from the airlock, carrying the light cargo on their backs.

That was a scrub. It would take too long. Hence the EDA.

As it fell through the darkness, the spring-loaded package automatically snapped open. It hit the ground twelve seconds later, fully unfolded into a sturdy, three-by-three-meter-square safety net. At least that's what it was meant to do. Nick unclipped the powerful halogen light inside the airlock chamber and pointed it down. The light reflected off the opaque haze of dust, completely obscuring the net, making it impossible to know if it had deployed properly or not.

"All right," Mission Control said in his helmet. "The dust hasn't had time to settle. You can't jump into the net if you can't see it. Someone has to rappel down and attach a line."

"I'll do it," Nick said. Mission Control carried on speaking throughout the three-second round-trip signal lag. By that time, Nick had already shaken out one of the lines coiled inside the airlock chamber, attached it to his belt tether, and begun to walk down the side of the rocket. Theo stayed in the airlock, fiddling with the light.

The airlock dwindled to a lighthouse beam in the fog.

Descending, Nick ignored whatever Mission Control was saying. He concentrated on the rope. His feet. His breath.

Kurtis broke in. "Nick. Nick, are you listening? Our cryocooling system has failed."

"Failed?"

"That's what they're saying. Get this: the venting valves on the LH2 tank have *also* failed."

"Shit."

"Yeah."

"What's that do to our timeframe?"

"They're saying we got an hour to unload everything and clear the area. You down yet?"

Nick tried to judge how far he'd descended.

In the minutes since he started his climb, sunlight had engulfed the top of the rocket's nose cone.

He reached down and unclipped his line so it could run freely through the carabiner. Then he jumped.

Twisting in the darkness, he fell long enough to feel afraid. Then he hit the safety net with his right shoulder and hip. He rebounded, limbs thrashing, and fell again.

"You down?" Kurtis repeated urgently.

Nick scrambled to the side of the net and climbed off. He stumbled in an invisible dent on the crater floor. "Shit, fuck, yeah."

"Well, that ain't quite 'One small step for a man,' but it'll do," Kurtis said. Nick laughed at the unexpected flash of humor from Kurtis, not known for cracking jokes. "Secure your line, big guy, make sure the net is stable and illuminate it. We're gonna start sending stuff down."

What they did was throw stuff at him. Package after package bounced on the net, rebounded lazily, and settled into the glow from Nick's headlamp. He scrambled around, piling things on the ground beside the net. After a few minutes, Theo descended on the line that Nick had fixed, in cautious jerks and halts, and helped.

By the time they got all the cargo situated, sunlight had swallowed the nose cone and the crew capsule. It reflected off the faceplates of the remaining crew as they emerged from the airlock and descended, one by one, on the line.

Nick sat on a pile of cargo, getting his breath back. The pressure suit made every movement an exertion. His ears popped every time he moved. Sweat soaked the thin T-shirt and long johns he wore underneath, stinging the raw places at the backs of his knees and the insides of his elbows where the suit's joints rubbed. "Where's the rover?" he said.

"Coming," Lee said. He backed into the sunlight, dragging a case of tools, scuffling up more dust.

"Start unloading the heavy cargo," Kurtis said. His head-lamp bobbed in long arcs towards the base of Tranquility 13.

The rocket had several cargo bays at its base, arranged in a ring around the engine nozzles. The bays held sixty tonnes of consumables and equipment, including the Woombat excavator. Kurtis, Theo, and Nick shuffled around in the five-foot gap below the base of the rocket, releasing the latches and dumping packages wrapped in thermal foil onto the ground. One package tore on a jagged rock and came apart in Nick's hands. Pieces of flatpack furniture slid everywhere.

"Leave it," Kurtis said.

A bow wave of dust heralded the rover's arrival. A fat, six-wheeled capsule, top-heavy with solar panels and antennas, towed a string of three flatbed utility trailers. It breasted a low upheaval ridge to the west and skidded down the slope.

The top half of the rocket was now in full sunlight.

Nick dragged furiously on a package. The foil tore.

The rover trundled into the splotch of shadow still protecting Tranquility 13. The crew began to pile the cargo onto the trailers.

"It's not gonna all fit," Lee said.

"Of course it isn't," Kurtis said. "The rover was supposed to make two trips."

Mission Control broke in. "Guys, you're down to ten minutes of safe operating time. If everything isn't going to fit on the rover assembly, just drag it out of the vicinity of the space-craft for now."

Aaron came back on the radio. "I'm going to give you the barcodes of the absolutely essential shit. Ready?"

Nick unsnapped his tablet from the strap on his chest. Dust coated its screen. When he wiped it with his glove, scratches turned the ruggedized glass smoky, making the display hard to read. He moved among the packages under the rocket, stooping and jumping to locate the barcodes. Fenella did the same.

"You need that," Aaron said. "Yeah, you need that. Christ! Yeah, definitely take that, it's the Woombat."

Nick started to drag the motorbike-sized package toward the rover. The other four stood on the flatbeds, tossing ropes to and fro, tying the cargo down.

"Clear the area!" SpaceZ interrupted. "You're out of time. Clear the area!"

Nick kept on dragging the Woombat. Charlie and her team had built it in marathon mode to replace the one lost on Tranquility 12. Every screw and circuit represented their love for the moon.

Step. Jerk. Step. Jerk.

On Earth it would have weighed half a tonne. He felt like one of those stunt strongmen towing a monster truck. Fenella passed him, bowed double beneath a package bigger than she was.

"Nick! Fenella!" Kurtis yelled. "Fucking leave it!"

Steel tanks could withstand a lot of pressure. Nick didn't believe the rocket was going to explode the minute the sun touched the housing. Even if the cryocooling system was FUBAR, and the valves were offline, it would still take a while for the hydrogen to get hot enough to blow the fuel tank. They still had time.

Step. Jerk. Step. Jerk.

"Leave it! That's an order!"

Nick straightened up. Sweat trickled into his eyes. Kurtis, a neckless salmon-gray humanoid, stood on the back of the last flatbed, gesturing angrily at him. Then the rover began to move away, taking Kurtis and the others with it.

Nick ran. Canting his body forward, bouncing in clumsy long strides, he caught up with the rover, which was not moving much above a walking pace, and hauled himself aboard the second flatbed.

"They're trying to troubleshoot the cryocooling system," Lee said, sitting on top of a mountain of packages. "Apparently it's a software issue."

The rover toddled across the crater floor and began to ascend the ridge to the west. Packages spilled off the overloaded trailers. The crew jumped off to catch them before they tumbled all the way back down the slope.

From up here, Nick could see over the wake of dust they left on the crater floor. Tranquility 13 now stood in full sunlight. Abandoned packages lay scattered at the base of the rocket. And nothing was happening.

"I want to go back and drag that stuff clear," he said.

"No," Kurtis said.

"You guys stay here. I'll do it." Nick looked around for Fenella. He figured she would come with him.

"I said no." Kurtis loomed down the slope, pointing at Nick. "Mission Control says *no!*"

Nick gazed up at Kurtis's blank, gold faceplate. Kurtis had been an Army Ranger. Completed two tours in Brazil before quitting in search of more extreme challenges. His life had gone right. Nick's life had gone wrong. He could not fix it by saving a couple more packages.

"Ten-four," he said, and climbed back onto the flatbed.

The rest of the way up the ridge, they took turns riding on the trailers and walking behind. At the top, Nick looked back at Tranquility 13. They *would* have had time to retrieve the rest of the cargo.

"Yup, it's a software issue," said Lee, still talking to Mission Control. "They've found the problem. Let's hope—"

"Take cover," Mission Control interrupted. "Take cover *now!*"

Pale orange flame spurted from Tranquility 13's engine nozzles. Geysers of smoke and dust shot out to the sides.

Nick ducked behind the rover, pulling Fenella with him.

Particles of ejecta, accelerated to orbital velocities, hit the trailer and cargo like microscopic hailstones. Tiny geysers of dust puffed up from the ground. Nick peered around the rover.

Amid the haze, Tranquility 13's fiery exhaust plume beat down on the lunar surface, charring the cargo left at its base. Shock waves flung scorched packages tumbling out of the smoke, spilling their burning contents.

The rocket rose off the ground. The crew watched in silence. Up it went, up and up, until it was just a bright speck in the black sky. Then it was gone.

"Well, fuck… They didn't tell me they were going to do *that*," Lee said.

The flames licking over the scorched cargo packages flickered and died in the vacuum.

"The cargo," Fenella said. "They burned it up!"

"They thought the rocket was going to explode," Theo said. "That would have been worse."

"But it didn't," Maddy said.

"The cargo might not all be burned up," Nick said. "We could go back—"

"No," Kurtis said. "We need to move. We have limited air in our suits. The spare O_2 bottles are back there. We were supposed to top up after unloading, now we can't do that. And it's another fifteen klicks to camp."

18

The central peak of Amundsen Crater, half again as high as Table Mountain in South Africa, had been formed by the same prehistoric meteor that created the crater itself. The impact turned the rock to liquid. In the center of the crater, the magma had rebounded with such force, it spiked 1.5 kilometers above the crater floor. This jagged, triangular massif loomed over them, lit white by the sun, as they trudged west around its base.

Once they were over the wrinkle ridge, the landing site was hidden from them. The terrain ahead was flat. The base of the mountain broke from the plain like a steep wall, and the rover's outbound tracks hugged it, curving to the south.

Pale gray rock. Black sky. No color anywhere apart from their own spacesuits and the Five Stones logo on the rover. Nothing moved except the rover and themselves. Nick began to feel the lifelessness of the place as an oppressive force. Like a hurricane moving in.

"Cheer up, guys," said Mission Control. SpaceZ had gone off the air after Tranquility 13's emergency launch, but Five Stones was still with them. The rover had an uplink to the Five Stones comms satellite in orbit. Its satellite dish was flexible enough to run voice communications via VHF, and data and images via Ka-band frequencies. "This is kind of awful to say, but in the final analysis, it was only stuff." The voice of Rachel Hamilton, the flight director, was so perky it made Nick's teeth hurt. "I'm looking at your suit telemetry, and everyone checks out OK. Better than OK, actually. Your vital signs are beautiful."

"Where's Aaron?" Maddy said.

"Well, it's three a.m. here," Rachel said.

Nick could guess what she wasn't saying. The emergency launch must have started a public relations dumpster fire. Aaron would be too busy to babysit the crew. Nick didn't mind. He was good with not talking to that guy right now—scratch that —*ever* again.

Lee was less restrained. "Well, Rachel, here's what you tell him from me. Losing one sixty-million-dollar hunk of hardware looks like an accident, but losing two looks like carelessness."

"Tranquility 13 is fine," Rachel said. "It's orbiting around the shadowed side of the moon. They just needed more time to fix the cryocooling system. They expect to return the rocket safely to Earth."

"What about returning *us* safely to Earth?"

Rachel laughed, displaying empathy. No one else did.

"The space-debris story isn't gonna fly this time. Guess it was a software issue, huh? Do yourselves a favor and pick a different story. I'm a damn coder. I've got some idea of the redundancy built into these systems. What *really* happened?"

Rachel shifted smoothly into corporate-mouthpiece mode. "I have to ask you not to make that type of comment, Lee. At the present time, responsibility has not been admitted by either Five Stones or SpaceZ. We aren't making any public statements regarding the cause of the incident until the software failure—and, yes, it *was* a software failure—has been comprehensively analyzed. So please refrain from speculation."

"Oh, all *right* then. That's just super peachy convenient for everyone, isn't it?" Lee said.

He was walking beside the rover, ahead of Nick. Kurtis was ahead of both of them. Kurtis turned back and grabbed Lee by the shoulders, making him stumble. Lee bumped into the side of the moving rover and let out a yelp. Kurtis shook him. "Shut. The fuck. Up." He'd switched to the ground channel, not the channel that uplinked to the satellite. "We need to focus on staying alive out here. Ain't gonna do a damn bit of good to start throwing accusations around. *Got it?*"

"Yeah, I got it," Lee muttered.

Nick felt bad for him. But Kurtis had a point. They needed to focus on their immediate survival needs. They were on the *moon*.

That sense of oppressive isolation hit him again, like a punching bag on the backswing. Rolling with it, he turned and walked backward, looking back the way they'd come. A mess of shadowed dimples marked their trail, stretching into the distance.

He left the others and walked at an angle up the slope alongside their route, hoping to get a view of their destination.

Nick saw something else.

Ahead of them, the rover's outbound tracks wound south around the base of the mountain.

About half a kilometer away, *another* set of ruts emerged from an irregular depression and joined them, heading in the same direction they were now.

Beyond that point, the tracks were all jumbled up, suggesting that multiple trips had been made.

"Nick, get back down here," Kurtis said.

"Has the rover made any sorties to the southwest?" Nick said, pointing.

"Why?" Theo said.

"Just wondering."

"No," Rachel said. Nick had thoughtlessly defaulted to the uplink channel. "The rover's only job is servicing the crew's transport needs. It hasn't gone anywhere apart from scouting out its route to the landing site. That's also to conserve its solar batteries and avoid drawing down fuel cell power during the lunar night. Why do you ask?"

"No reason," Nick said. He descended the slope to rejoin the others, slipping on loose shale, bringing down a small avalanche of pebbles and dust.

When they passed the rim of the depression, he got a better look at the other set of wheel ruts. His boots scuffed them over at the point where they merged with the Five Stones rover's tracks. X-shaped dimples in the dust, rather than Vs. A *different* rover?

The International Lunar Initiative was only 150 kilometers southwest of here, on the connecting ridge between Shackleton and de Gerlache craters. Could ILI have visited the Five Stones site for some reason?

Well, so what if they had? It wasn't as if the moon *belonged* to anyone. There was no such thing as trespassing up here.

They walked on. As far as Nick could tell, no one else noticed the second set of wheel ruts. They were all too focused on getting to their destination.

The monotony of the landscape dulled the senses and extinguished thought. The dwindling air supply readout in Nick's HUD urged speed, but the rover plodded on at seven kph. And it was all the crew could do to keep up, forced as they were to adopt the lunar gait of long low bounds, which tested little-used muscles. Theo and Maddy ended up riding on the trailers while the others slogged along on foot.

At last they rounded a spur of rock that jutted out from the southern slope like a cat's claw. A welcome mat of color splashed the plain ahead.

The Five Stones base camp was spread out at the foot of the mountain. The weary procession passed through the construction zone. Above the heaps of slag and discarded trial castings towered a "Dailir" rocket, one of the SpaceZ workhorses that had carried Five Stones' robotic advance troops to the moon. The robots had unloaded this particular rocket, turned it upside down, and converted it into a basalt furnace. Its empty fuel tank served as a crucible. Parabolic solar collectors attached to the sides concentrated the sunlight into heat, which melted the crucible's contents.

Close to the furnace stood the spring-loader that fed it. Yuta Nakajima had reimagined the simple concept of a coiled spring as a loader system for the furnace. A cylindrical cradle pivoted in a heavy frame, with a plunger powered by a memory-metal spring at one end. In the cradle rested an empty canister whose bottom could slide up and down.

Charlie's robots flocked toward the rover to help unload the cargo. There were ten cat-sized, networked Bob robots, which handled tasks requiring climbing. Their master, Spiffy II, was a large metal kangaroo whose deft forelimbs could tie knots and rewire circuits. Gulliver II, a half-tonne earthmover, lurked in the background.

Nick ignored them all, stumbling toward the habitat.

Air. Water. Shelter. *Life*, in a giant tin can.

It looked just like the hab at the bottom of the pool in the Neutral Buoyancy Laboratory, except it was brightly lit by the sun. It consisted of three steel cylinders, each one thirty meters long and three meters in diameter. Like the furnace, these started out as the housings of Dailir rockets. The robots unloaded them, laid them down on their sides, cut the fuel tanks out, and riveted the housings into a pressurized volume of six-hundred-plus cubic meters, in the shape of a T with an extra-long crossbar.

At one end of the crossbar, a flexible tube snaked from the end of the habitat to the vehicle airlock. This was a shed-sized structure with a hatch on one side, to which the rover could seal its own pressure hatch.

At the other end of the crossbar, a personnel airlock was built into the side of the cylinder. It was painted in cheerful shades of orange and blue, slightly faded by its eight-month soaking in cosmic rays.

Theo got there first, with Fenella right behind him.

"Go ahead, guys," Kurtis said.

A simple lever actuated an internal gearbox to open the hatch. Theo and Fenella, in their dust-caked suits, went in. The hatch closed.

Theo kept up a running commentary: "We're in... The air is fine... I am removing my suit. Moving into the common area now—and seriously, be careful not to bump your heads on these ceilings. Overall, I give it five stars. This desirable lunar residence can be yours for the low, low price of just $20,000 a day!" The relief of reaching safety made even Lee laugh at the lame joke.

Fenella joined the conversation. "I've removed my suit and am off to inspect the greenhouse."

The crossbar of the habitat would be their living area. It was salami-sliced into bedrooms, storage space, a workshop, laboratory, bathroom, kitchen, and a common room. The upright of the T was their greenhouse. Several months ago, after the hab was pressurized, a dedicated aeroponics robot had planted crops in moisture-controlled tanks—wheat, sweet potatoes, kale, tomatoes, lettuce, spinach, marrows, and anything else successfully grown in urban aeroponics farms on Earth.

During training, Nick had spent hours watching the livestream from the greenhouse. Nothing ever happened except when the robot glided to and fro, adjusting the humidity, temperature, and nutrient mixes of the tanks. Maybe that was why the feed was so soothing.

Now he pictured the plants standing tall in their trays, and felt an intense craving. A few minutes from now he could be biting into a juicy cucumber or chomping a handful of lettuce leaves. Saliva filled his mouth, salty and shocking.

"Theo! Come in here," Fenella yelled. "Look at this."

"Fenella, what's up?" Kurtis asked.

"I'm in the greenhouse," Fenella said. "It looks like there's some kind of a... a problem..."

"*Herregud!*" Theo exclaimed.

"*What?*"

"The plants," Fenella said grimly. "They're all gone."

19

"Unload what we've got of the cargo and inventory it," Kurtis said. He'd told Nick, Lee, and Maddy not to go inside until Theo and Fenella ran exhaustive checks on the habitat's life-support systems. Mission Control's best theory was that a problem with the air supply had killed the plants.

Though Nick wanted to get in there and assess the situation for himself, Kurtis was right. It was more important than ever to know exactly what they'd managed to salvage from Tranquility 13.

It turned out to be easier to make a list of what they *didn't* have.

The spare vehicle airlock and its spaceframe.

The sandbags they were supposed to use to shield the habitat.

Replacement solar panels.

Extra seeds for the greenhouse.

Most of the furniture.

Spare parts and patches for their spacesuits.

Spare parts for the rover.

Extra charcoal filters for the trace-contaminant control system.

The parabolic solar collector frame for the oxygen plant.

Nick's and Maddy's personal kitbags.

And the biggest blow: the Woombat excavator for the Big Sling construction project. But that was irrelevant to their life-support needs, which was all anyone cared about at the moment. After eking out another sustained burst of physical activity, they were all far gone into exhaustion. Nick had drunk every drop of the electrolyte-infused water in the reservoir built into his suit. His HUD told him he was down to less than an hour of breathing time.

"Let's review airlock procedure," Kurtis said imperturbably. Nick let out a controlled sigh. "During normal operations, we'll not be using the personnel airlock, to avoid dust contamination of the scrubbers and the inside of the hab. We'll be exclusively using the vehicle airlock. Only reason we're walking in through the personnel airlock today is to get the indoor cargo in, but we still need to minimize the number of cycles and the resulting contamination.

"First, we'll move the packages into the chamber, where Fenella and Theo will unwrap them and then return the wrapping foil to us. Lee and Maddy will enter the hab together with the final packages. After that, Nick and myself will hook up all four of your suits into the suit charging assembly, and then enter the hab via the vehicle airlock. Questions?" Kurtis was already moving away to pick up the most important package of all, the giant steel jerrycan containing five hundred gallons of potable water.

Fifty minutes later, Nick flopped backward into the rover's dim interior. He dragged his legs out of the suit port and lay in a fetal position, inhaling big gasps of the canned air inside the rover. It tasted better than a Coke on a hot day.

Kurtis stepped over him and shouldered into the vehicle airlock, which was now sealed to the hatch on the rover's side. LEDs cast a sickly sheen on his dark skin. A pungent smell of body odor filled the chamber. Nick figured some of it was coming from himself.

The other end of the chamber opened, admitting a blast of air colder than you'd ever want your house to be. Fenella and Theo had confirmed the atmosphere was breathable. Oxygen was slightly high at 24%, but the partial pressure was what counted. With pressurization slightly under one atmosphere, they wouldn't experience any oxygen toxicity.

He and Kurtis crawled on all fours along the flexitube and emerged into the end compartment of the crossbar, meant to be the workshop. And lo and behold, the interior partitions hadn't been completed. That would be the package that came apart in Nick's hands back at the landing site. Through the steel frames where the partitions were supposed to go, he could see all the way down to the pressure door at the end of the cylinder. It was a bare tunnel, empty of furniture, interrupted only by modular fixtures and the freestanding toilet and shower cubicles.

Kurtis headed straight into the toilet where he pissed like a horse. There was no soundproofing whatsoever.

Nick bounded along the cylinder, careful not to bump his head. As Theo had said, the ceilings were uncomfortably low. There was storage space above them. Nick glanced up at the lightweight plasterboard and thought about tearing it down to use for partitions. Walls mattered more than overhead storage.

He cranked the lever of the pressure door and ducked into the middle of the T, where the greenhouse module met the crossbar at a ninety-degree angle. This three-by-three-meter area had pressure doors on three sides, all of which stood open. Maddy, Lee, Fenella, and Theo, in their sweaty T-shirts and long underwear, sat on the floor, huddled around Lee's laptop.

"The thing I just don't get," said Rachel, on the screen, "is we aren't seeing any of this on our cameras. Everything looks fine."

"I suggest you have a look at the cameras," Lee said. "There are literally dozens of ways a security camera feed can be looped or deepfaked."

Nick stepped around them and went into the greenhouse. Warmer, moist air enveloped him. Along the whole length of the cylinder, aeroponics racks stood head-high. Aeroponics differed from hydroponics, in that the roots of the plants were suspended in chambers filled with a fine mist of water, nutrients, and oxygen. It used only half as much water as hydroponics, making it the perfect technology for a moon farm.

Images of lush leafy greens, juicy berries, and ripe heads of wheat were still fresh in Nick's mind. The reality was crushing. Fenella had exaggerated: not *all* the plants were gone. Only about half. The trays they'd been in, with their attached grow lights, were gone, too, leaving long gaps on the racks.

The remaining trays appeared to have suffered the devastation of a storm or tornado. Many plants had been roughly torn from them, exposing the cloth medium. Leaves and stalks littered the floor.

Nick picked up a spinach leaf. It was wilted, but not yet rotten. Whatever happened, it hadn't been long ago.

A rust-spotted steel monster lurched out from behind the end of the racks and charged up the center aisle, straight at him.

Nick shied aside, lost his balance in the low gravity, and caught himself on the nearest rack. A tray clattered to the floor and he bit back a cry. It was only the gardening robot.

Greenfinger, as it was called, looked a lot like Charlie's "Spiffy" construction robot: a metal kangaroo with a cylindrical belly and agile forearms. Greenfinger, however, had wheels instead of recurved legs. Rust dappled its housing due to the moist atmosphere in the greenhouse, and its axles squeaked. It maneuvered around Nick as if he were part of the furniture, and stopped at a tray that still held some drooping tomato plants. With the steel claw on the end of one robotic arm, it carefully pinched off a couple of unwanted leaves.

Nick reached past the robot and picked a surviving tomato. Greenfinger did not react to his movement. He popped the tomato into his mouth. It was flavorful and juicy, and it was the last one.

Maddy came into the greenhouse, glaring at the robot. "Maybe *that* did it. Its algorithms went wild. It screwed up the pH of the tanks, messed with the grow lights—"

"And stole half the trays?" Nick said.

"Yeah. I don't know." She shivered. "I'm starting to think we're cursed."

"Don't be silly."

"It could have been a demon."

Nick thought about that other set of rover tracks. No demon left *those* in the lunar dust. "If it was a demon, how'd it get here?"

"With us, of course," Maddy said. "They attach to people."

"If so, it beat us here." Nick showed her the wilted leaves on the floor. "This happened before we got here. Probably before we landed."

Lee came in. He scowled at the empty trays. "The cameras were hacked. Mission Control says they're still showing a loop of normal activity." He stood under the nearest of the cameras affixed to the ceiling, eyeballed it, then looked around. "I need something to stand on."

Nick found a broom and started sweeping up. "Just jump. We're on the moon, you know."

Lee chuckled. He launched into a standing jump, snatched at the camera, and pulled it off the ceiling.

"What are you doing?" Maddy said.

Lee tossed her the camera, trailing loose wires. "See if you can find any spyware in there."

"I'm not the IT expert."

"I'll give you a hint. It's *all* spyware." Lee pulled another camera down. "Now that we're here, we can monitor the plants ourselves. And I don't know about you, but I don't want those clowns at Mission Control monitoring *me*."

"Kurtis is never gonna let you take down the cameras in the other modules," Maddy said.

"That's fine by me. As long as we have one place where we can talk freely." Lee pulled down a third and fourth camera.

"The robot has optical sensors, too," Nick said.

"Yes, yes, now that's a thought. That would be a lot harder to hack. It probably doesn't dump its sensor data to the uplink unless it's specifically requested." Lee eyed Greenfinger, which had retreated to its sentinel post at the end of the cylinder. "Wonder if I could get in there..."

"No, man. Don't even think about it," Nick said. "You might break it, and we still need it."

"What for? We don't have any plants."

Nick leaned his broom against a rack. He beckoned Lee over to a tray that still held the bruised, snapped-off stems of squash vines. "The plants are gone, but the roots are still healthy. They'll grow back. Same for this tray of kale and some of the other crops. And look here." Lee and Maddy followed him to the storage corner near the door, where he'd found the broom. Secateurs and collapsible stakes hung from hooks. A large, heavy box on the floor opened to the common security code. Nick lifted the lid. Inside were spare LED grow lights, plastic bottles of nutrient solutions, and several vacuum-packed packages of seeds. "We can replant."

Lee grabbed the seed packages. "Strawberries. *Bamboo?*"

"There were supposed to be two more boxes like this," Nick said. "Hey, it's better than nothing. I'll start by planting the strawberries. They're pretty forgiving, and they grow fast."

Maddy frowned at him. "I didn't know you knew this stuff. You never mentioned it in training."

"Yup, grew up on a farm," Nick said.

"I thought it was a shrimp boat."

"Before that."

"Nick!" Fenella stood in the doorway of the greenhouse. "Kurtis wants us to go back to the landing site and see if we can salvage anything."

20

Barefoot, wearing a retro sweatband around his forehead, Aaron pounded along Satellite Beach with the high-kneed gait of a habitual jogger. Beside him ran Sean Radek of SpaceZ. Charlie wasn't running. Her idea of exercise was wielding an electric screwdriver. She'd also complained it was too hot to run outdoors, even though the sun had barely risen. That was why they had the beach to themselves.

She rode on the golf cart instead, which followed the two CEOs at a discreet distance. The driver was a heavyset Eastern European man, wearing AR glasses and a suspiciously loose T-shirt. Sean was, or thought he was, important enough to need a bodyguard.

Sparkling waves scalloped the sand. The golf cart bumped over regularly spaced ridges, which betrayed the presence of geotextile bags underneath the sand, buried there to resist erosion. Seabirds shrilled. Charlie watched the tracks the men's feet left in the sand, and thought about the ways in which sand was like and unlike moondust. Sand had larger grains. It was sticky only when wet. And it couldn't kill you.

She was too far away to hear what Aaron and Sean were

saying. But when Sean stopped dead, pointed angrily at Aaron, and swung around and stomped to the golf cart, it was clear the conversation had ended.

He flung over his shoulder at Aaron, "Go to hell, and take your chick botter with you!"

Charlie slid off the golf cart. Without a glance at her, Sean jumped on. The golf cart drove away, heading for the nearest of the wooden ramps that led up to the dunes.

"*Botter*," Charlie said. *Chick*, fine, that was just a fact. But she was offended by *botter*—that meant a hobbyist. And her robots were the best on the moon.

"He's just jealous," Aaron said, wiping his face with the tail of his T-shirt.

"What did you say to him?"

"I told him I was going to sue him into the ground."

"Was that smart?" Charlie said neutrally.

"His share price is crashing. Can't blame space debris this time. Their software. Their fuckup."

"Our cargo. My robots. Our crew."

"They're going to make us whole. Cameron thinks we have a solid case."

"Yeah, but how long is that going to take?"

Aaron started to jog back along the beach. Groaning, Charlie ran to keep up with him.

"Sean tried to threaten me," Aaron grunted. "Said he can prove that Bill knew about our payload announcement in advance. Threatened to go to the SEC. I called his bluff. He doesn't have anything. Just hearsay after the fact. But it might be a good idea to wait until after the investigation before we take them to court. Just in case."

"Slow down, for Pete's sake." Charlie dropped back to a walk. Her guilty secret throbbed like a bruise. Sean Radek only had hearsay, but Ryder Stillman had actual proof of Bill and

Aaron's malfeasance. Another demand had arrived yesterday, for $21,000.

The toe of her sneaker pressed through the sand and squeaked on rubbery geotextile. She stopped and kicked away the sand, exposing a patch of the bag. The technology solution underpinning this beach was coming to the surface. "I saw these bags being laid down," she said. "Anna was fascinated with the dredger. Guess they don't last forever."

"When was that?"

"Three years ago."

That had been Five Stones' lowest point. Before the completion of the Little Sling, when Bill was putting the thumbscrews to them to produce a return on his initial investment, Aaron, Yuta, and Charlie had foregone compensation for a while. They'd been so broke, Charlie had to frequent the local Catholic church's food pantry. She rarely reflected on those dark days. It seemed unreal, like a nightmare, in comparison to her comfortable life nowadays. But now, fear returned.

"Aaron," she said cautiously, "are we going to be broke again?"

Her bank account was bleeding money into Ryder Stillman's serial crypto accounts. She'd paid him close to a hundred thousand dollars already. She couldn't keep this up. She was going to have to ask Rachel if she'd heard anything back from her brother, who was in law enforcement, about buying a gun.

"No, of course we're not going to be broke," Aaron scoffed. "We're gonna beat the SEC thing. And when we win our case against SpaceZ, Sean will have to pay all our legal costs *and* recompense us for the loss of the cargo. We might even be able to hang T-12 on him. I can't wait."

"The crew can't wait, either," Charlie said.

Aaron veered toward the dunes. When Charlie caught up with him, he was using his fitness tracker to summon his Tesla.

They emerged onto Highway A1A, on the other side of the condo strip, as the muscly electric vehicle glided to a halt on the shoulder. Charlie settled into the passenger seat. Classical music was playing. The pine-scented AC cooled her sweat.

"I've done the math," Aaron said. "They have enough packaged rations to last ninety days. That's assuming they can't get any calories out of the greenhouse. But that's an unnecessarily pessimistic assumption. I reviewed the situation with Nick Morrison. He's taken charge of the greenhouse, which I'm not entirely happy about, but fuck it, he seems to know what he's doing. They should be able to achieve at least thirty, forty percent of expected production. That extends their survivability window for quite some time."

Charlie shook her head. She had spent a good fraction of the night doing the math herself. "I'm more concerned about oxygen. We assumed a conservative baseline of five kg of plant growth per day, which would have been achievable at seventy-five percent of production, with an emphasis on staple crops. The numbers ring out needing fifteen kg of growth per day to get up to full sustainability. Anything less, and we're supplementing with the OSS. And those backup tanks aren't going to last forever. Based on twenty percent greenhouse production, they've got a survivability window of eighty days, max."

"You're forgetting about the oxygen plant," Aaron said.

"I didn't factor that in, because there is no oxygen plant. And there isn't gonna be one anytime soon. They lost the frame for the solar array."

"Then they can make a new frame. They still have the mirrors."

"And to do *that* they have to make it out of something. I think they need to start the bamboo."

"No ulterior agenda there at all," Aaron said.

"No," Charlie snapped. "In fact, I do *not* have an ulterior agenda. I'm just concerned about keeping these people alive. That has to be our priority, don't you think?"

In his silence, she heard the truth: *Aaron* was the one with an ulterior agenda. The six people on the moon were no more to him than tools to achieve his goal. But by putting them there, he'd created complications none of them foresaw.

The creases at the corners of his eyes deepened as he stared out at the early traffic. Had those creases even been there before last night?

"I'm still mystified about the greenhouse cameras," Charlie said, offering an olive branch.

"Lee Yang removed them," Aaron said. "Without permission."

"That's not what I'm talking about!" Her short-lived conciliatory mood evaporated. "How did the cameras get looped? Who did it? *When* did they do it?"

"I think you have to face the fact that Greenfinger malfunctioned," Aaron said. "It could be something as simple as a sensor failure—"

"Greenfinger did not malfunction. Even if she did, she didn't make the trays disappear into thin air. And she didn't hack the cameras! So, who did?"

"I don't know," Aaron said, and turned up the Rachmaninoff.

21

To make the crew feel more at home, the lights in the habitat had been set to automatically dim and brighten on a twenty-four-hour cycle. In the industrial glare of an LED dawn, while everyone else was still asleep, Nick sat in the bedroom he claimed—the salami-slice of the personnel module nearest to the center of the hab—between his improvised walls.

Kurtis had prevented him from tearing down the ceiling panels, but Nick had found some big sheets of rubberized Kevlar in one of the cargo packages and taped those to the circumferential hoops. It gave him some privacy. His knees were drawn up, elbows rested on his kneecaps. His hands were a ball of knuckles pressed against his mouth. He breathed in and out in harsh gusts.

Mission Control had promised a resupply flight within six weeks. Nick had gotten the impression they would say whatever it took to pacify the crew. Rachel Hamilton's relentlessly warm and reassuring manner reminded him of a hostage negotiator in a movie.

That put the crew in the role of hostage-takers. But what

hostages did they have? What could they use as leverage to make sure the resupply flight happened on schedule?

Like everyone in space, they were utterly dependent on Earth. He'd known that all along, of course. But now the sheer helplessness of their situation forced itself upon him like a rip current. He bent his forehead against his fists.

The lights brightened some more. After a while he unfolded himself from the floor and went to have breakfast with Fenella. Vacuum-packed chicken stew, six hundred calories per serving.

They set out after breakfast in the rover, with a single trailer attached. As he drove around the Cat's Claw, Nick broke the silence. "I don't think their calorie estimates are realistic."

"Yeah," Fenella said. "Eighteen hundred calories a day? You've got to be kidding me."

Relieved he wasn't the only one thinking about it, Nick turned to face her. "When I was diving, I used to eat three Egg McMuffins for breakfast. Lunch? A six-pack. For dinner, I got out my portable deep fryer. That's a great invention. I used to hook it up in our motel room and toss in whatever I found in the supermarket—steak, chopped potatoes, veggies. Chocolate bars."

"That is *so* gross."

"You gotta try it." His stomach growled just thinking about those deep-fried Snickers bars. "Point is, it probably came out to four thousand calories a day, and we were *still* hungry."

Fenella nodded. "When I was climbing, I had to force myself to eat. You don't think about it when you're up there, but you gotta stuff yourself just so you don't lose too much weight." She looked out at their murky, green-tinted view of the crater floor. The front end of the rover was one big bubble of tinted, reinforced glass. It made the moon look like the bottom of the sea. "This isn't Everest. But in a way, it kind of *is*."

"What other mountains did you climb?"

"All of them! I did the Seven Summits. I've climbed on every continent except Antarctica." She chuckled. "I couldn't get a permit for Mount Vinson, so I figured this was a good alternative."

"Which one was your favorite?"

"Might surprise you, but it wasn't one of the biggies. You ever hear of Ein Fara?"

"Not a clue—where's that?"

"Israel. I know, I know, a Muslim climbing in Israel? But climbers don't care about that stuff. Anyway, Ein Fara is *beautiful*. It's a canyon with a very balancey cliff at the northern end, where actual monks live. They're all cozy in this cave on the cliff. They invited me in for tea... Now I'm getting all misty-eyed."

"It sounds great."

"I've got some pictures. I'll show you when we get back."

Half an hour into their drive, they approached the depression where Nick had seen the other rover tracks yesterday. The tracks were almost invisible through the rover's heavily tinted windshield, but on the dash screen, with its panoramic view, Nick saw *more* sets of tracks overlapping the first ones. It looked as if the mystery rover made another trip since yesterday. Was he imagining things? The rover's air-circulation fans thrummed.

Fenella was leaning back, arms folded, eyes closed, breathing deeply, a smile on her lips. Perhaps she was dreaming of Ein Fara.

He woke her when they neared the landing site.

"Look at that."

"Bloody hell. What *is* that?"

"Looks like a rover."

Not a demon. Not a dream. It stood in the middle of the scorched, reflective scar where Tranquility 13's engines had fused the lunar regolith into glass. Four-axled, it looked like a fully armored military tactical truck, easily twice the size of their own rover. It had once been white, but moondust had abraded off most of its paint, leaving an arctic-camouflage look. Nick could just make out the ILI logo on the side. Its titanium treads had a crisscross pattern that would leave Xs in the moondust.

"Hello?" he said, leaning to the radio. He waited. "Hello?"

The other rover did not answer.

Nick parked near it, but not too near. He and Fenella wriggled through the suitlocks into their spacesuits. They waited for the automated locking mechanism to verify their seals, and pressed the complicated series of levers to detach the suits from the rover. Nick jumped off the rear step. His breath sighed in the silence of his helmet.

"Hello, Rachel?" he said on the uplink channel. "There's an ILI rover at our landing site. Can you see it?"

"This is Rachel's day off," said the voice of Jason Bloch, Rachel's deputy. "Yeah, I see it. Neat truck, huh?"

"What's it doing here?"

"I dunno. I could call Luxembourg and ask."

ILI was headquartered in Luxembourg. It would probably take forever to get anyone who knew something on the phone.

"Don't bother," Nick said.

Sunlight bathed the plain. Darkness puddled at the foot of the peak. The cargo—the reason they were here—lay scattered over a surprisingly wide area. The lighter things had been physically blown aside by the thrust of the departing rocket's engines. Nick bent and picked up a steel rod, which he recognized as part of the spaceframe for the spare vehicle airlock.

He walked in the direction of the other rover and stopped to prod at a charred, crushed lump the size of a double bed. "I think this was our rations."

Fenella stood near the terminator. "Is that moving?"

"What?"

She pointed at a piece of wrapping foil that lay half in, half out of the shadow. It twitched, as if wind lifted it. Then it vanished into the darkness.

Moments later, a person in a bubble-helmeted, dust-gray spacesuit shuffled backward into the sunlight, dragging the foil with its ends knotted in their glove. It looked lumpy, as if it were being used as a makeshift bag. Another spacesuited person followed, carrying a satellite dish with a bent, dangling receiver. Nick recognized the spare for their own rover. His fingers tensed on the steel rod.

"Hey!" he said. "That's not your stuff."

A faint squelch of noise came from his suit radio. The strangers set down their loads. They both had an unknown logo on their chests. Even obscured by the dust that coated their spacesuits, it was definitely not the ILI logo. Judging by their heights, one was a man, one a woman. The woman flashed numbers with her fingers. Nick noticed that the palms of her gloves were tattered and patched. The numbers were an FM frequency. Still holding onto the steel rod, he retuned his suit radio.

"Hi," a female voice said. "You must be the new kids."

22

"Who are you?" Nick said.

"I'm Kat. This is Trig."

"Heyup," Trig said. He sounded Australian. "Welcome to the moon. How was your trip?"

"Everything went beautifully until we were forced to abandon half our cargo, with the results you see," Fenella said. "I'm Fenella Khan and this is Nick Morrison. We're part of the Five Stones mission, obviously. And you are...?"

Trig pointed in the direction of the other rover. "ILI. We heard you had a rough landing. Came to see if we could help."

"Seen a construction robot?" Nick wished he could see their faces. "About this big."

"Nah, nothing that big," Kat said. "Everything's crushed. Charred. Sheared apart. You can see for yourselves." She lifted one end of her makeshift foil bag and jerked it so the foil fell open, revealing a trove of mechanical and electronic components, more or less scorched. "We were just trying to find anything that might be in working order, so we could return it to you."

"That's real neighborly of you," Nick said. His Southern

sarcasm was as subtle as spiked lemonade, and it went right over their heads.

"Now that you're here, there are ninety-one human beings on the moon, counting the Chinks and the Russkies," Kat said. "We have to stick together. Help each other out."

"Yeah," Nick said. He wandered off to examine the other charred lumps spread out around the landing site. He identified the sandbags—they came apart in his gloves, disintegrating into black dust—and the package of suit spares and parts, now fused into a Rubik's Cube of melted plastic.

Mission Control spoke up, startling him. "Hi, Nick, this is Jason again. Can you get us some pictures of the damaged cargo?"

Nick clenched his teeth together. He breathed in, then out again. "Can't you see it?"

"Yeah, but we'd like some close-ups."

Nick turned so his helmet camera was pointing at Fenella, Kat, and Trig. "Do you know anything about these two? They said their names were Kat and Trig. I think I've got that right."

"Hold on," Jason said. A few moments later he said, "Right, yup, this looks like them. Katniss Reyes and Trigger McLean. They're on the ILI personnel roster. They're not NASA, ESA, or JAXA, though. They're employed by something called ArxaSys Lunar. That probably means they work on the mass driver."

"Isn't that the company that runs the Artemis shuttles?"

"Same company, different division," Jason said. "These guys are probably making minimum wage. The mass driver is eight years behind schedule and two billion dollars over budget, but it isn't because ILI is overpaying for labor. They're just trying to do too much in a very challenging environment."

"Cruder is better, right?"

"You got it."

"OK," Nick said. "Point me to what you want pictures of."

Jason coached him through a tour of the landing site. There was still no sign of the Woombat. Nick eyed the ILI rover's sample-return hatch. The Woombat was too big to have fit through there.

"Maybe it got sheared apart by the pressure waves in the exhaust," Jason said. "You could be walking over the pieces without realizing it."

"Yeah, maybe," Nick said. "Anything else you need?"

"Nope, that's it."

"Hope the pictures help with the insurance."

Jason chuckled. "They're for our lawsuit against SpaceZ."

"I guess I saw that one coming."

"It's gonna be brutal."

Nick walked back to Fenella and the pair from ILI. He retuned his radio to their frequency and caught Kat in the middle of saying: "—find anything?"

"Nothing worth taking," Nick said.

"Well, doesn't that just suck," Kat said. "These rocket boys send up bleeding-edge tech that doesn't work right, and we're left picking up the pieces."

"Thanks for this stuff, anyway," Fenella said, lifting the makeshift foil sack. She had the broken satellite dish in the crook of her other arm.

"No problem. If you need anything, let us know. We're right over there." Kat sliced a hand in the direction of the south pole.

There was a short silence.

"It's quite a long way, isn't it?" Fenella said.

"Hundred klicks as the crow flies, hundred fifty with the terrain," Trig said. "We made it in ten hours."

"And you're fine getting back?" Fenella sounded concerned. "You've got enough power, air..."

Both of the contractors laughed. "We could stay out for a week in this baby," Kat said. "It's a mobile outpost. The geeks use it to do science in the outlying craters. Got an onboard lab and everything."

Nick said, "Ever been up this way before?"

There was another pause.

"Once. Before you came," Kat said.

"When was that?"

"Oh, God, months ago."

"That's right," Trig said. "Five Stones asked us to make a scouting trip to your location before they finalized their choice of site."

Nick raised his eyebrows. He hadn't been aware of any contact between Five Stones and ILI. He'd wondered why the Big Sling site was so close to the ILI base. Especially when they literally had the whole moon to choose from. After all, the Little Sling was way up near the equator. It had been explained to him that there were certain topological requirements that had to be met. The Big Sling required a 1,500-meter elevation, and at least 1 km of ground clearance all the way out to 20 km from the hub. Amundsen Crater, with its prodigious central peak and 120-km diameter, met those criteria. No other craters on the near side of the moon did.

Trig was still talking. "We came up here and checked it out, reported back. They decided to go with this site anyway."

"How do you mean?" Nick said.

"Not enough light. Where you're at, you're only illuminated for thirty-five percent of a lunation. Means you only got solar power less than half the month. A little more at this time of year."

"We're set up to deal with that," Fenella said.

"Are you set up to deal with the *dust*?" Trig scraped a glove down his forearm. Moondust drizzled off his sleeve. The finest particles stayed suspended, following his hand, statically charged.

"The dust is what we're here for," Nick said, and he laughed. Kat and Trig laughed, too.

"Good luck," they said.

Nick walked away. Fenella followed, carrying the foil bundle and satellite dish. When they moved around behind their rover, out of sight of the other two, Nick pulled the stuff away from her and dropped it to the ground. "We don't need that junk."

"*They* were going to take it."

Kat and Trig stood beside their own rover. Kat lifted her hand and waved.

Inside the Five Stones rover, Nick hung his arms over the steering yoke, staring out the windshield, whistling through his teeth.

"What are we waiting for?" Fenella said.

"They're waiting for us to leave."

"And you're what, waiting for *them* to leave?" Fenella rolled her eyes.

"Yeah."

"They were going to take our stuff," Fenella said. "But like you said, there's nothing worth taking. Let's just leave them to it."

Nick let out a surprised laugh. He started the engine. "I thought they might have put the Woombat through their sample return hatch. But it's not wide enough to fit it."

"They might have taken the suit spares. Their suits looked pretty beat up. Although it's odd that ILI wouldn't just give them new ones."

"No, I found the spares. They're a write-off." Nick swung the rover in a ponderous half circle. Kat and Trig stayed standing beside their rover as the Five Stones rover pulled away.

"They don't actually work for ILI," Fenella said. "They're contractors."

"I know. I asked Jason. Did you...?"

"I asked *them*. The girl, Kat, was all too happy to vent about their working conditions. Trying rather too hard to establish a rapport, if you ask me. Deflecting attention from their suspicious activities."

Nick chuckled. "You don't miss a trick, do you?"

Fenella smiled briefly. "I suppose not. Once bitten, twice shy, I guess. There's a lot of this sort of thing in the Everest community."

"This sort of thing?"

"Heh... I've seen climbers step over a corpse without breaking stride. Accredited guides ignore cries for help from people who are clearly in distress, just because they aren't in their own party. I once had my spare oxygen canisters stolen out of my tent at fourteen thousand feet."

Nick raised his eyebrows. "Seriously? Bastards."

"Yeah. But people still go. Mallory said he climbed Everest because it's there. We have to be here for the same reason." Fenella touched the dash screen. "Because it's here. Because we're human. Because this is what we do."

But that *wasn't* why they were here. They had a specific, limited mission: build the Big Sling. And time was ticking by.

23

Fenella stared at the dash screen. "What the hell are they doing?"

The rover had just rounded the Cat's Claw. Three orange-gray insects inched up the nearly sheer cliff above the construction zone, each one dangling a length of orange rope.

"Looks like they're getting started," Nick said.

"They're nuts!" Fenella punched the comms. "Kurtis, can you tell me what those morons are doing on the cliff?"

Kurtis sounded out of breath when he came on the radio. "Who you calling a moron?"

The highest of the three spacesuits took one hand off the rock and waved to the rover. It was Kurtis.

"This view is something else," he said.

Fenella said, "If you fall, you'll kill yourselves. Why didn't you wait for me?"

"We're on a tight schedule," Kurtis grunted.

He was referring to the same thing Trig had mentioned—the limited availability of sunlight at base camp. They'd landed just before lunar noon, but soon the darkness would return. In fact,

Nick could see the oncoming shadow of the crater wall in the distance, creeping across the plain like a black tide.

"That's no excuse to skimp on basic safety precautions," Fenella said. This was her area of special expertise. Nick supposed she felt the right, or even the duty, to come on strong. "First of all, three people, three ropes, no belay? No. Just no."

"Relax. We're fixing the ropes as we go," Kurtis said.

"Yeah, no. *One* person goes up first to fix the rope. When it's secure, the others can ascend. I can't believe you don't know this stuff."

"I'm not a mountaineer," Kurtis grunted. "I'm just a guy trying to get a job done."

"Come down, all of you, and I'll go up and fix the ropes." Fenella moved aft toward the suitlocks. "And be careful, for God's sake. Most falls happen during descents—No, actually, wait. We salvaged the EDA yesterday, didn't we? I'll set that up at the bottom of the cliff, and Nick and I will act as your spotters, just in case some moron comes off the face." Fenella winked at Nick. She might see the funny side, but Nick was pretty sure Kurtis didn't.

Nick parked in the construction zone. Fenella climbed through the suitlock into her suit. The rover jolted slightly as she jumped down from the rear step.

"Go ahead. I'll be there in a minute," Nick said.

Fenella jogged to the hab to fetch the EDA. Nick rose to get into his suit.

"No, you gotta help Theo," Kurtis said over the radio. "Sit tight. He's coming out to you."

"Ten-four." Nick sighed.

Alone in the rover, he scratched his scalp and drank from his thermos of Gatorade. He thought about food again. The climbers were going to be hungry when they came down. How long would it take before Kurtis admitted 1,800 calories wasn't enough to sustain them?

Theo hopped onto the rear step. "Let's go," he said, pounding a glove on the back of the rover.

"Where to?"

"The quarry."

Nick started the rover. Fenella was dragging the EDA near the foot of the cliff. The three climbers were descending in floaty jerks. Nick swung the rover east, heading out into the plain.

Charlie's robots had swept the area around the base camp clear of dust, leaving the light-gray rock exposed. Two hundred meters out from the foot of the mountain, the rover crossed into the darker sea of dust that covered the crater floor. The quarry was plainly visible. It wasn't an actual quarry; just a dusty place, no more or less dusty than anywhere else. In a haze of electro-statically suspended particles, a dinged-up yellow midget earth-mover trundled back and forth.

They'd lost the Woombat, but they still had Gulliver. The tough little earthmover had done the lion's share of the construction work on the habitat and basalt furnace. It was presently pushing what looked like a steamroller attachment back and forth across the dust. This was lunar quarrying. No need to break up the regolith when millions of years of meteorite impacts had done it for you.

The steamroller attachment was covered with a sheath of fuzzy gray basalt fabric, similar to fiberglass insulation, which picked up the dust. The Woombat had a more advanced collection system, which used an electrostatic levitation field to suck up the finest dust particles. With the Woombat gone, they were stuck with the same method Five Stones had pioneered when they built the Little Sling: roll, sift, collect.

For the Big Sling they needed more basalt. A hundred times

more basalt. Human labor would have to supplement robotic labor. This would have been the case even if they still had the Woombat. Since they didn't, they'd just have to work harder.

"Let's go," Theo said. "There should be a couple of hand rollers over there."

Nick exited the rover. They tramped through the dust to the collection frame. Gulliver got there at the same time. It plunged its roller attachment, which was so thickly coated with dust it looked like a gray marshmallow, into the slot of the collection frame. Mechanical brushes moved along the roller, dislodging the dust into a funnel that led to a sieve at the bottom. The finest particles fell through the sieve into the collection canister. The larger ones stayed on top and got tipped out of the back of the frame, onto a growing slag heap.

Theo squatted and dipped his glove into the collection tub. It came out coated with dust, as if with gray flour. "These are some high-quality fines. See how sticky they are? Can thank being bombarded by meteors and heavy cosmic ray neutrons for that. They're the strongest basalt particles on the moon." He let his handful of dust run through the fingers of his glove. "This is exactly what we need for casting the hub and the sling arm."

A sudden memory struck Nick: his father squatting between the cabernet sauvignon bushes, running soil through his fingers in exactly the same way.

"You're going to shred your gloves doing that," Nick said.

He picked up one of the hand rollers that lay beside the collection frame. It was like a giant's paint roller, weighing no more than a hoe in the lunar gravity. He found an area the earthmover hadn't yet quarried, and began to push the roller along the ground, learning as he went how hard to lean on it, striking a balance between forward motion and sufficient pressure to pick up the dust.

Many wine growers had gone all in on robotics to cut down

on labor costs. In South Africa, however, labor remained relatively cheap. Nick's father had joined the countervailing movement toward low tech. In keeping with the historical aesthetic of Hailsong, he'd reintroduced walking ploughs pulled by draft horses. The horses had a much lighter impact than a tractor, resulting in better soil and better wine.

It took skill to wind between the rows, taking out the weeds without damaging the roots of the vines. Nick remembered walking behind his father, or Midas Ngidi, his father's right-hand man, surrounded by the smells of horse farts, crushed weeds, and sun-warmed earth. Midas used to sing a Zulu working song as he guided the plough along: "Shosholoza, shosholoza..."

Nick leant into the roller, pushing it faster, farther, out into the plain. When no more dust would stick to the basalt-fiber sheath, he delivered his harvest to the collection frame. Then he went back for more.

While Nick and Theo worked, Fenella was climbing. She'd taken the end of the rope up with her that would haul the winch they intended to emplace on the top of the peak. Nick listened to her commentary and watched her for as long as she was in view. The first, nearly sheer face, she said, was the most technical part. After that the mountain sloped like a pyramid, and it was more of a scramble. An hour after she began her climb, she vanished over the top of a crag several hundred meters above the ground.

The canister was full. Nick and Theo levered it out of the frame and replaced it with an empty one. They put the lid on the full canister, which now massed a quarter of a tonne, rolled it over to the rover, and lifted it onto the trailer.

"*Herregud,*" Theo said, leaning on the trailer. "There has to be a better way to do this."

Nick gulped water from the nozzle in his helmet—it was

like the drinking nozzle in a hamster cage—and stretched out his lower back and hamstrings as best he could in his spacesuit.

A cry of elation crackled into his helmet.

"I'm up!"

Nick straightened. An orange speck stood in the sunlight on the summit of the peak. Though Fenella was more than a mile away, he could make out her arms raised in triumph.

He toggled his radio. "Add another summit to your résumé."

"That was actually embarrassingly easy." Fenella laughed breathlessly. "You can walk the last half a klick. The radar imaging was dead-on."

"Congratulations," Kurtis said gruffly. "Guess you know that's a triple record? First ever free climb of a crater peak, and *highest* free climb, *and* first climb by a woman on the moon."

"I know! And it just occurred to me, but no human being has ever before stood where I'm standing now. I can't even put this feeling into words. It's just... incredible. Incredible."

The rest of the crew joined in a round of congratulations. Then Kurtis reminded Fenella to fix the rope she'd carried up the peak, so that it could be used to haul up a heavier cable and then the all-important winch.

"Yeah, yeah," Fenella said. "Let me just catch my breath."

The climb hadn't been quite as easy as she was pretending, Nick guessed. It really was an astounding feat. Sure, the lunar gravity helped, but at the same time, the clumsy gloves and boots of the spacesuit made every move an order of magnitude more difficult. Fenella had also had to lug a bag of active cam devices to fix the rope, jamming them into any crack that would hold.

Without showing any fear or hesitation, she'd climbed up past the point of commitment, past the point where the EDA could save her if she fell, up pitch-black crevices and over sunlit overhangs, until all that was left was to make it to the top. She deserved a moment to savor her accomplishment.

Kurtis, however, was thinking about their construction schedule. He and the others sent up the cable and then the winch package. They all heard Fenella's breath juddering in and out as she drilled holes in the peak to secure the winch.

"The summit is perfect," she said more than once. "It's so flat, we'll hardly have to level it." And, "This is a dream come true."

The collection canister was full again. Theo sat beside the frame, taking a break. Nick stooped to lever the tub out of the frame.

Fenella screamed.

Nick dropped the canister back into the frame. He sprang backward, staggering in a half circle.

The little orange speck was falling.

It slid and bumped from one rocky outcropping to the next. Fenella wasn't attached to the rope. She must have unclipped in order to move around more freely on the summit.

"Grab hold of something," Nick yelled. "Anything!" He unconsciously clenched his fists.

"The EDA!" Kurtis yelled. "Get it under her!"

For a moment, Fenella seemed to succeed in arresting her fall. She swung by one glove. Five voices shouted encouragement: hang in there! You can do it! Hold on! Don't let go!

The friction between glove and rock failed. Fenella slid down again, bumping faster and faster until her momentum carried her off the top of that first, steep cliff.

They heard her screaming all the way to the ground.

24

Nick ran up to the others. They were stooping over Fenella, who lay where she'd fallen, several meters out from the base of the cliff, twenty meters from the EDA. It couldn't have saved her anyway. She'd fallen from too great a height. Nick had been listening to the others talk all the way back from the quarry, so he already knew she was dead. He pushed between Maddy and Kurtis to see for himself.

She lay facedown. Her suit was deflated, a shriveled, orange-gray layer of shrink-wrap outlining her body. Nick took hold of her hip and shoulder. Kurtis grabbed his arm. Nick struck his glove away and rolled Fenella onto her back.

Her faceplate was intact. But inside, her face was unnaturally dark. Her tongue and eyeballs protruded.

"Oh my God," Maddy said. She swiftly turned away.

"You'll need to remove her suit," Rachel at Mission Control said over the comms from Earth.

"Are you fucking joking?" Nick exploded.

"Do it before the sunlight heats up the remains too much," Rachel continued before Nick's voice could reach Earth. "The lungs will already have emptied, but there'll still be gases trapped in the internal body cavities. Heat would speed up the putrefaction process, and that wouldn't be pretty." The crew received these words with a tense silence. "I'm not joking. I'm telling you to implement the procedure for dealing with a fatality. You need to salvage her suit."

Lee lifted one of Fenella's arms. "There isn't much to salvage."

It was true. The forearms and gloves of her suit were shredded from her futile attempts to grab the mountain. Razor edges of rock had ripped the external Kevlar layer and breached the inner pressure garment.

"The undamaged material can be used for patches, and the helmet electronics might also be reusable," Rachel said.

"These suits are crap, anyway," Lee said.

Kurtis turned Fenella over again and fumbled with her rear entry port.

"They're the same ones ILI uses," Rachel said.

"So?" Lee said.

Kurtis said, "Pipe down, Lee. You're right, the suits are a joke. A mission specialist at KSC told me, your first suit malfunction is when you really become an astronaut. But that ain't what killed her. She died of falling off that mountain, so if you need to take it out on something, go kick a fucking rock."

The rear entry port opened. Kurtis reached in.

"Jeez... Someone help me," he said.

———

Nick stumbled into his bedroom. He sat on his sleeping bag and rubbed his face. In the blackness behind his eyelids, he saw the dry red mist of blood boiling away in the vacuum.

They'd carried out Mission Control's orders to remove Fenella's spacesuit. It turned out they had body bags in storage.

They'd stuffed her into one. Maddy had wanted to bury her properly, whatever that meant on the moon. Kurtis had insisted on waiting for guidance from Mission Control. For the time being, she was lying behind the hab, a state of affairs that seemed more horrible, somehow, than any other alternative. Nick had been told to pack up her belongings.

He stripped off his sweat-soaked underclothes. The cold prickled his skin. He put on his sweatpants, hoodie, and indoor shoes, and padded down their makeshift hall. The others had followed his example and hung various things up as walls and curtains. Nick ducked past Fenella's sparkly Indian shawl and began to fold her clothes into her kitbag.

Near her sleeping bag sat a holocube, a fad from a few years back. The four-inch cube displayed a selection of 3D pictures inside. Nick swiped through images of Fenella with her climbing buddies on top of various mountains, including Everest. He remembered what she'd said about climbers behaving badly. There was no evidence of that in these pictures, just uncomplicated joy.

He glanced around and slipped the holocube into the pocket of his hoodie. She was gone, anyway. She no longer needed it.

On his way back through his own room, he stashed it in his kitbag.

"Done," he said when he joined the others in the kitchen.

"We got guidance on her personal belongings," Kurtis said. "Put them in overhead storage. The body bag goes out in the shed." The shed was an outdoor storage area where the spares and tools for robot maintenance were kept, as well as the kit they would need to assemble payloads, if they ever completed the Big Sling.

"I'll do it later," Nick said. He got his mug out of the sterilizer. He still had a few hundred calories left for today. He scooped cream of mushroom soup mix into the mug, added water, and put it in the microwave.

The kitchen was the only room in the hab that actually felt like a room. Located at the inner end of the personnel module, it had the microwave, a sink, counters, and a table. No chairs, but they had brought in a couple of storage boxes to use as benches. Theo sat on one of these, staring into a cup of hot water flavored with instant coffee. Maddy sat on the counter beside the microwave. Kurtis leaned against the wall.

"Where's Lee?" Nick said.

"Somewhere," Kurtis said. "He takes things too hard. Lets shit get inside his head."

No risk of that happening to you, Nick thought. *There's no room for anything inside your head except your massive ego.* For an instant he thought he'd spoken aloud. But he hadn't. The microwave beeped. He took out his soup.

"I am telling you," Maddy said. "We're cursed."

"That's the kind of superstitious BS I would expect from a Marine," Kurtis said. "She slipped. That's all. She just... slipped."

"Or something pushed her," Maddy said.

"I don't believe in ghosts. Especially not on the damn moon."

"Do you believe in *anything,* Kurtis?"

"I believe in myself," Kurtis said. "I believe in this team."

Nick drank his soup in two swallows and escaped to the greenhouse. He still had a lot of tidying up to do in here before he got started on planting.

The air was drier now. The smell of decay had faded to the faint fragrance of leaf mold in winter. Greenfinger sat inert in a corner, arm awkwardly poised with a clump of leaves hanging from one claw. Nick had turned the robot off in a small, but pointed statement of control, equivalent to Lee's removal of the security cameras.

Water had collected in the bottoms of the aeroponics trays. Nick picked them up one at a time and tipped the water into the graywater trap. It fell out in wobbly masses that gradually broke up into streams. He removed the cloth growing medium from the trays and cleaned each rectangle as best he could. He put the cloths to soak in pH-balanced water. Then he sat on the floor to mix nutrient solutions for strawberries and bamboo.

Bamboo?

Not many calories in that.

But Rachel had told Nick to plant all the seeds they had, adding that it was a direct request from Charlie. She'd not explained why, but Nick thought he knew. It wasn't for food. Bamboo grows *fast*. It would supplement the oxygen content of the atmosphere quicker than any other crop.

The pressure door wheezed and thudded. Lee came in. "They think the shredding on the arms of her suit happened on the way down. But what if it happened on the way up?"

Nick raised his head. "Then she wouldn't have reached the summit."

"If the first tear was small enough, she might not've even noticed it. Oxygen deprivation affects cognition."

"I know." Nick had experienced it himself once, during a dive, when his air compressor failed and his tender wasn't paying attention. "It makes you disoriented. You have trouble thinking. Forget what you said a minute ago. But if she was suffering from hypoxia, she would have fallen earlier."

"Maybe the breach occurred on the summit, while she was installing the winch."

"Then why didn't she say anything about it?"

Lee shrugged. Nick remembered again what Fenella had said about Everest climbers. They would sometimes ignore cries of distress. Had Fenella ignored a cry of distress... from her own body?

"But the suit telemetry," he said. "Her HUD would have warned her if there was a problem."

"Yeah," Lee said. "According to Mission Control, her biofeedback was fine. Elevated heart rate, sure, she's climbing a mountain. But she displayed no signs of respiratory distress." He squatted down, picked up a bottle of nutrient solution, and turned it to look at the label. "Maybe her suit wasn't reporting telemetry correctly. In that case, she might not have been aware of the breach until she went into hypoxia."

"*That's* a scary thought."

"Here's a scarier one." Lee put the bottle down. "What if her telemetry was deliberately altered to give false readings?"

"All right, now you're just being paranoid."

"Gotta think of all the possibilities."

"Who would have done that?" Nick stared at Lee, trying to work out if he was for real. No trace of humor showed on Lee's face.

"Mission Control, of course. Think about it. She did her job. She climbed the peak. That's what she was here for. After the job was finished?" Lee snapped his fingers. "*Whoops.* Too bad, so sad. More air and calories for the rest of us."

Nick flushed. He'd already worked out how many extra calories they'd each be able to consume, splitting Fenella's allotment five ways. "That's crazy."

"Is it, though?" Lee said.

"If they want to get rid of anyone, it's you and me."

"Maybe, but I'm the IT guy, and it looks like you're the greenhouse guy, as well as construction. Neither of us is dispensable. *At the moment.*" Lee produced a rigid smile. "If I were you, though, I wouldn't let Kurtis do maintenance on your suit."

"Oh, come *on*. He's a dickhead. He's not a—a..." *Murderer.* Nick couldn't bring himself to say the word out loud.

Lee ambled away down the central aisle, peering at the trays Nick had emptied and cleaned. "Well, maybe it's just me. Maddy pointed out that when all you've got is coding skills, everything looks like a software issue. I have to admit that's a fair point. I'm predisposed to look for a software glitch whenever something goes wrong. On the other hand, it could have been a hardware glitch. Semiconductor radiation testing is still more of an art than a science. Too many cosmic particles zipping through your chip package, and those expensive rad-hardened SoCs are toast... Maybe that's what happened."

"Do they use the same type of chips in rocket fuel cryocooling systems?" Nick said.

Lee pointed at him. "That's what I'm saying. *Exactly.*"

The timer on Nick's tablet trilled. The growing medium had finished soaking. He got up and started to transfer the saturated rectangles of hemp back into the trays. "By the way, we met our neighbors at the landing site this morning."

"Huh? Kurtis didn't mention that."

"He told me not to say anything." Amidst the horror and sadness of Fenella's death, Nick had forgotten about their encounter with Katniss Reyes and Trigger McLean. Now it came back to him vividly. While he fitted tiny peat blocks into holes in the hemp rectangles, he described the episode to Lee. "They admitted they came up here before. Said it was months ago, but they could have been lying. And there's nothing to stop them from getting in. The personnel airlock opens with a simple lever. Nothing to stop 'em from busting in here and taking our plants."

"It's possible, I guess," Lee said, frowning.

"It's the only thing that makes sense."

"Yeah, but you're forgetting about the cameras. How did

those clowns loop them without getting caught out by Mission Control? How did they not even get caught on the external cameras?"

"You're the IT guy, you tell me."

Lee rubbed the patchy black stubble he'd begun to grow. "They'd have to be really good. Better than me, and that's a high bar. Not that there *aren't* hackers better than me—It's just, if we're assuming all these incidents are connected, they'd have to break into the systems of SpaceZ *and* Five Stones. I don't know anything about SpaceZ, but I've poked around the system here, and although I hate to admit it, they've got best-in-class network encryption. I can't really see anyone gaining unauthorized access. That's why I've been assuming it was an insider who... who did everything."

"Well, maybe they had inside help," Nick said.

"Could be. Which puts us back to square one: why would anyone at Five Stones want to wreck the biosphere? It's *their* 'game-changing photosynthetically-closed-cycle lunar sustainability concept.'" Lee had reached the end of the module. He flicked Greenfinger's housing with a fingernail. "I'd really like to know what you saw," he said to the robot. "I'm very tempted to take you apart and see if I can extract your memory."

"Nuh-uh," Nick said. He instinctively moved to head Lee off from Greenfinger, as if he might take a screwdriver to the robot on the spot.

"Well, you're not going to use her anymore, are you?" Lee lifted the power switch cover and turned Greenfinger on.

"I might. You never know." The mangled clump of leaves in the robot's claw caught Nick's eye. He pulled one free. "No way."

"What?"

Nick held out the leaf, laughing despite himself. "Seen something like this anywhere before?"

Lee stared at the seven-pointed leaf. Then he grabbed it and sniffed it. "My highly trained senses tell me this came off a healthy, fully grown cannabis plant."

"That's what it looks like."

"Hot damn. They were growing hemp in here?"

"You *can* use it to make fabric."

"Not this stuff. This is high-THC weed."

"Could've gotten mixed up." Nick slapped Greenfinger's housing lightly. "Smoke 'em if you've got 'em, baby." He pried the other leaves out of the robot's claw and moved toward the compost bin.

"Hey! What are you doing?" Lee caught Nick's arm as he was about to drop the leaves into the compost. "Don't do that!"

"Why not?"

"Maddy has to see this."

While Lee was gone, Nick emptied the compost onto the floor. He'd swept up without looking very closely at *what* he was sweeping up. Now he discovered, amongst the torn leaves and stems, several more marijuana leaves, as well as a fuzzy, frondy *Cannabis indica* seedhead. That *definitely* hadn't been on the manifest.

Lee and Maddy burst in, giggling like teenagers. Maddy grabbed the leaves and wafted them under her nose. "Oh my, oh my. That is some premium bud."

"Yep, and I'm going to throw it away now," Nick said.

She whisked the leaves out of his reach. "Oh, hell no. I'm going to dry these and smoke them."

"Damn straight," Lee said. "We're going to germinate those seeds, Maddy. Get our own little supply going."

"Are you serious?" Nick said. He didn't think Lee really wanted to grow cannabis. He just wanted to cheer Maddy up.

"Oh, *yeah*," Maddy said. "I'll do it myself. It'll give me an excuse to hang out in here. Take my mind off things." Her eyes darkened, and reflected in them were pinpoints of red light.

He turned around. The red lights were Greenfinger's pilot lights. The robot was powered on and staring at them. He went and turned it off.

25

"There's something I want you to look at," Charlie said to Yuta, standing behind him.

The three giant monitors on Yuta's desk were alive with simulations of the central peak in Amundsen Crater, the winch, and the hub of the Big Sling. The crew was on schedule to finish casting the hub today. Yuta was working out the best way for them to haul it up to the top of the peak, without breaking the five-meter pyramid of solid basalt in the process.

"Gotta run the winch cable through the eye at the top of the hub," he muttered. "So *da, soshite,* use the menhir method to stand it upright in the rotation collar." He bit the end of his vape pipe.

"Yuta! Can you come to my office for a minute?"

"Is it about the heat batteries? I'm a little worried about excavating pits on the summit. I'm thinking it would be better to dig caves lower down on the slopes. We would get less sunlight but more structural stability."

"No," Charlie said. "We need to keep the heat batteries as close to the hub as possible. And I don't want the crew working on the slopes, anyway."

"Fenella fell from the summit." Yuta's eyes squeezed into slits for a moment.

"She may have been suffering from hypoxia. We'll probably never know," Charlie said. "But that's what I mean. Working on the summit is dangerous, and working on the slopes is even more dangerous. Which brings me to my point."

"Huh?"

Charlie grabbed a handful of the shoulder of Yuta's T-shirt. She hauled him, complaining, to his feet and pushed him across the fifteenth floor. It was eleven o'clock at night. No one was left in the open-plan seating area except for a couple of IR people monitoring the slow decline of Five Stones stock on the Asian exchanges.

The internal windows of Mission Control glared brightly. The controllers were working around the clock, babysitting the crew and managing the streams of data from the moon.

As Charlie and Yuta passed the Mission Control room, Rachel came out, her handbag over her shoulder. "I'm heading home," she said, stifling a yawn. Her eyes flicked to Charlie's hand, which still grasped a wad of Yuta's T-shirt.

Charlie dropped her hand. Feeling awkward, she said, "Everything OK up there?" She knew it was a dumb remark. Everything was *not* OK on the moon. They'd lost a crew member. The surviving crew were short on food and oxygen. And hanging over it all was the catastrophe in the greenhouse.

"Well, no one died today," Rachel said. "So there's that."

"Ha ha, yeah."

"The bright spot, I guess, is the media hasn't found out about the greenhouse thing. Data security for the win."

Following the advice of Sean Radek of SpaceZ—although Aaron would never admit it—Aaron had sprung for a data security upgrade. They'd completed the shift to the expensive new system before the crew arrived on the moon. Data security,

Charlie knew, was only as strong as the people who had access to it. What Rachel really meant was that her people were trustworthy. The Five Stones ship had no leaks.

That's what Rachel thought, anyway.

Feeling her smile droop, Charlie said, "Well, we should have a drink tomorrow."

"Yeah. Maybe we can even persuade Yuta to join us!"

"I have to work," Yuta said.

"He can't really be this boring," Rachel said. "Is he seriously this boring?"

"Oh, no," Charlie said grimly. "He's a party animal under the skin."

Rachel giggled. "Well, see you tomorrow." She teetered off to the elevators on her high heels.

Charlie dragged Yuta into her office. She sat him down in her chair and clicked PLAY.

A wide-angle video filled the screen. The time bar at the bottom gave the information that it was thirteen minutes long. It showed the greenhouse, seen from Greenfinger's position at the end of the module. Lee Yang and Nick Morrison stood in front of the robot.

"*I might. You never know*," Nick said. Then he reached past the robot's optical sensor, to the clump of leaves in its gripper. "*No way*."

"What's this?" Yuta said.

Charlie paused the video. "They turned Greenfinger off last month, as I'm sure you remember. Nick was instructed to switch her on again, but he claimed the power switch wasn't working, which is obviously not true. The day after that, they switched her on for thirteen minutes." Charlie bit her lip, annoyed with herself. "I'd stopped checking for updates after they switched her off. I mean, what's the point? She's powered down. This has been sitting in her internal memory the whole time."

She started the video again.

On the screen, Nick held out a seven-pointed leaf. He was laughing. Charlie had never heard him laugh on Earth. It was a spontaneous, happy sound. It gave her a mournful feeling to hear it from 360,000 kilometers away. "*Seen something like this anywhere before?*"

Lee grabbed the leaf and held it to his nose. "*My highly trained senses tell me this came off a healthy, fully grown cannabis plant.*"

Charlie moved around to stand in front of Yuta, whose gaze was riveted to the screen. "You're so busted," she said.

Yuta sagged in her chair, arms hanging limply over the ergonomic armrests. "It's not illegal," he said to the ceiling.

"And that makes it OK? I could kill you. I honestly could."

"You knew…"

"And now they know, too." She sighed in exasperation. "Why is it so hard for you and Aaron to grasp that these people are *just* as smart as we are? If they haven't connected the dots yet, they will soon."

Yuta said nothing for a minute. On the screen, Nick emptied the compost onto the floor and picked out several more cannabis leaves. He stared at them, shaking his head, with a goofy smile on his face. Charlie's heart ached for him.

"They don't deserve this," she said.

"I'm not trying to defend it," Yuta said, toying nervously with his vape pipe.

"You're not sorry. You're just sorry you fucked up."

"I'm just pointing out that no one here, *or* up there, has done anything illegal. So even if the crew connect the dots, so what?"

"So what? So *what?*"

"They can't even tell anyone." Yuta offered her a smile that was probably meant to be reassuring. "We control the comms satellite."

Charlie knocked his vape pipe out of his hand. It fell on the carpet and she kicked it under her bookshelves.

"Hey, that's my replica 1875 Butz-Choquin," Yuta said.

"I can't find the footage of the break-in. What happened to that footage?"

"Aaron probably deleted it."

"Yeah, I bet he did." There were two separate streams of data from the moon. One came from the hab and rover systems. The other came from Charlie's robots. Stupidly, she hadn't kept a copy of the footage from the hab cameras, but she had everything from the robots archived on her own cloud drive. Aaron couldn't have gotten to that. She breathed out. "Yuta, why don't you go home?"

"Why don't *you* go home?" Yuta countered. "Don't you need to be with Anna?"

She did. Only, Anna would already have gone to bed, after reading and watching TV with her grandmother. Anna understood that there were five people on the moon whose lives depended on her mother. That was how Charlie explained her long hours.

"*You* go home," she said savagely.

Watching him leave, she figured he would go straight to Aaron. He'd either go to Aaron's condo or phone him on the way back to his own apartment.

She used to think she and Yuta were a team. That was still true in terms of the technology. Yuta's Cruder is Better engineering concepts and Charlie's cutting-edge robots meshed into a harmonious whole. They got shit done like no one else.

But in terms of office politics, which signified the overall strategic direction of the company, Charlie had lately come to realize she was the odd one out. Yuta and Aaron were conspiring without her. They hadn't even fessed up about the break-in straightaway, leaving her to pull her hair out until she finally hounded the truth out of them.

I knew you would freak, Aaron had said at the time.

I'm not freaking.

It's OK. It's all gonna be OK. Besides, we had to grow the cannabis. That was non-optional. Otherwise, we would have lost the Big Sling before we even started building it.

And now we're going to lose it anyway.

No, we aren't. We made a deal with them.

Right. The *goddamn* deal.

God, she was sick of it.

She dropped into her chair. The video had ended. On the screen flickered the last frozen image of Nick reaching out to turn Greenfinger off.

26

Yuta drove home.

Since he left Japan, he'd lived in many different places, including his car during Five Stones' dark days. His home now was a studio apartment ten minutes from the office. "Studio" was misleading: the apartment was a single room, but the room took up the whole fourth floor of a building overlooking Manatee Cove Golf Course. Most of the other tenants were retirees. That didn't bother Yuta. He'd installed a green wall, floor-to-ceiling windows, a slate floor, and a bed that levitated off its circular platform on rare-earth magnets. He liked space. He liked openness and simplicity. Conflict and complexity gave him stomachaches.

His stomach hurt right now from the showdown with Charlie. He rubbed his gut, wincing, as he kicked off his shoes and padded into the dark apartment.

The shower was running.

The bathroom was a freestanding glass enclosure at one side of the room. Through its barely frosted sides, the faint light from the golf course outlined a slim female form. Water streamed from masses of long hair.

Rachel had beat him here.

Yuta undressed and got into the shower with her. She gave him a wet kiss and massaged his shoulders with soapy hands. "You look stressed."

"Yeah, a bit."

"What did Charlie want?"

"She doesn't suspect anything," Yuta said. He felt confident that no one at the office guessed about their relationship. He wasn't sure exactly why Rachel was so hot on keeping it a secret —she was divorced, after all, free to see whoever she liked—but it suited him this way, too. This way it was *simple*.

"No, what was she so pissed about?"

Yuta winced at the memory. "She found some sensor footage from Greenfinger. Looks like the crew found out about the export crop."

"Uh-oh."

"It's not a big deal." He didn't want to talk about it. She was lithe and lovely, her skin glistening. He ran his hands over her waist, down to her shapely rear end. "So... I'm boring, am I?"

"Oh, heavens, no," Rachel breathed into his neck. "You're not boring at all."

They made love in the shower. Afterward, they dried off and sprawled side by side on the big circular bed, in a cloud of marijuana vapor.

Rachel circled back to the thing with Charlie. "Did she find out about the break-in, too?"

"She already knew about that. We had to tell her."

"She can be pretty persistent."

Yuta chuckled and drew on his second-best pipe. "Yeah." He was vaping the same strain of cannabis he selected to grow on the moon, a genetically modified La Bomba that was easy to clone. The knots in his stomach loosened. "Honestly, I don't think it's a big problem. I mean, the crew still don't know who took the plants. And even if they do find out, so what? They can't do anything about it."

He knew he shouldn't be talking about this stuff. Rachel wasn't supposed to know anything about the break-in. Let alone about the deal.

Except Yuta was up to his neck in corporate machinations that would destroy billions of dollars in wealth for some people, and create billions of dollars in wealth for others, while shaping the future of space exploration for decades to come. Machinations that had already killed seven people.

He had to talk to *someone*.

"Maybe you should just tell them," Rachel suggested. "They might understand."

"About the deal?" Yuta laughed. "Aaron would kill me."

The only people cleared to know about the deal were him, Aaron, Bill, Charlie, and Cameron. He laid his cheek on Rachel's breast. Her long limbs, outflung on the rumpled sheets, glowed like moonlight.

"I don't think you need to be so scared of Aaron," she said.

Yuta raised his head indignantly. "I'm not scared of him."

"What do you call it, then?"

He didn't know what to call it, not in English, anyway. He owed Aaron everything. Yuta had a PhD in engineering, but his twin obsessions with preindustrial technology and the moon made him practically unemployable. He'd bummed around the world for years, climbing mountains and designing megastructures that would never be built... until he met Aaron Slater. Aaron turned Yuta's quirky philosophy of Cruder is Better into a workable lunar ISRU plan. He'd put together a company to implement it, lured Charlie away from a lunar prospecting startup, and given Yuta money to build things on the moon.

Not *enough* money. There was never enough money. But the deal would change that.

Soon, they'd be billionaires, and then Yuta would be able to do all the *other* things he dreamed of. Spinning torus habitats. A new point-to-point lunar transportation system. A large-scale lunar solar installation. Things that would change the face of the moon. Change the future of humanity... Save the planet.

It all depended on Aaron.

And the deal.

"The deal has to go through," he said. "Aaron's concerned that if the crew knew about it, they might be demotivated. We can't tell them."

"Because the Big Sling has to get built," Rachel said, wrinkling her nose. Yuta knew she was not a fan of the Big Sling. It lacked the science-fictional pizazz of, say, ILI's mass driver. But she wasn't an engineer.

"That's right," he said. "It has to get built."

"No matter what."

"No matter what."

"Even if *more* people die?"

"Yeah... Even if more people die." Pain twisted Yuta's stomach again. He pulled her closer.

27

Evening was coming on. Shadows crept across the crater floor. The crew were nearing the end of their second lunation. In Earth terms, they had been here two months. The hub of the Big Sling, newly installed, cast its own finger of shadow across the summit of the central peak. Near the hub, in the parking-lot-sized area they'd levelled with the help of the Bob robots, Kurtis and Maddy worked with jackhammers, excavating the pits for the heat batteries, which would power the sling's rotation.

Down in the construction zone, Nick heaved yet another canister of moondust off the rover's trailer. One step after another, he rolled it to the spring-loader that fed the furnace.

Left foot. Right foot. Left foot.

His body was one big ache. But they hadn't yet made quota for the day, and since Nick had set the quotas himself, he couldn't exactly slack off. In addition, Theo had begged off quarrying for the last two days straight, on the pretext that he needed to work on the oxygen plant.

Nick's new job was fiber extrusion. With the hub success-fully installed, it was time to cast the sling arm. This would also be made of basalt—basalt *fibers*. When extruded from a bushing, the stone became flexible enough to weave into fabric. They would use these fibers to weave a sling arm twenty kilometers long, which could throw tens of tonnes into lunar orbit, or LEO, for the cost of a sandwich.

Sandwiches.

Hamburgers.

Deep-fried Snickers bars...

Visions of real food, high-calorie food, and lots of it, filled Nick's mind as he wearily rolled and kicked the tub into the cradle of the spring-loader. He resisted the impulse to brush the dust off his gloves. The dust wouldn't *come* off, and the friction would only further abrade the palms of the gloves. Already the Kevlar had almost worn through. Nick had never forgotten Lee's fears about faulty suit telemetry. He inspected his gloves, and the suit's lower legs and joints, every night, looking for thin places. He patched any weak spots before they could fray.

Spiffy the robot was manning the spring-loader. At Nick's verbal command, she tilted the cradle upward. Her optical sensors observed the distance to the furnace, and her CPU decided, with greater accuracy than any human could manage, what angle to stabilize the cradle at. She removed the lid of the canister, then threw the switch to heat up the memory-metal spring. It extended, pushing the canister's bottom up inside the canister with propulsive force. Nick picked the lid up and turned back to the trailer.

In the corner of his eye, the moondust shot out of the canister in a coherent jet, straight into the funnel on top of the furnace. No air—no scattering. Only a few grains drifted to the ground. The rest trickled down into the crucible.

During the lunar day now ending, the parabolic solar collectors on the furnace had heated the crucible to 1,400 degrees. Melted into magma, the basalt fines separated into pure basalt and silica, better known as glass. The molten glass floated on top; the larger particles of basalt sank to the bottom of the crucible.

There were taps on the sides of the furnace to release the magma for large casting projects. That was how they'd cast the hub of the Big Sling. During the eighteen-day lunar night that followed, they dumped the leftover melt, closed the taps, and installed a bushing at the bottom of the furnace. When the sun heated the furnace up again, they'd been ready to begin fiber extrusion.

Right away they produced several bobbins of fiber that passed Yuta's evenness, tensile strength, and strain resistance tests. They had celebrated.

And then the breakages started.

The last few days, they weren't even getting a dozen meters before the fibers snapped in the winding machine. No one could work out why.

While Nick unloaded the rest of the canisters from the rover, Theo worked at his oxygen plant, a smaller furnace known as a solar roaster, located right at the foot of the cliff. It still wasn't operational. One of the items lost in the *Tranquility* 13 emergency launch two months ago, had been the frame for the parabolic solar collectors. Theo was trying to fashion a new one from lengths of bamboo. He cursed in Norwegian as the whole thing fell apart in his hands again.

"That's never going to work," Nick called to him.

"There's a long history of using wood in space," Theo said. "Three of the Ranger probes were made of balsa wood. And China sometimes uses oak tiles as heat shields."

"Yeah, if you're trying to get the stuff to char up on re-entry, I suppose it might be a good idea."

Theo sighed, left the mess around the oxygen plant, and joined Nick. He stood half in and half out of the basalt furnace's shadow, watching the glossy black threads ooze out of the bushing. Pushed out of the crucible by gravity, the fibers cooled radiatively in the vacuum, and the solar-powered winding machine next to the furnace reeled them onto big bobbins.

As Nick rolled the last canister up to the spring-loader, another fiber snapped. The bobbin it had been winding onto spun wildly, the loose end whipping around. Theo lunged to catch it.

"If you're here, I'm going back out," Nick said.

"Go ahead," Theo said, removing the problem bobbin from the machine. "I'm seriously starting to think Maddy's right: there's a demon doing its best to piss us off."

Nick took a deep breath, mustering his strength, and hauled himself onto the trailer with the empty canisters. The rover jounced into motion. All the way out to the quarry, he lay on his back, gazing at Earth. It was a blob of blue-and-white Play-Doh caught on the northern crater rim. Soon it would set.

1.5 kilometers from camp, the rover stopped by the collection frame. Nick slid to the ground and got back to work.

Having harvested all the sticky fines near the camp, he was now quarrying the crater floor farther away. From this distance, the camp was a mere sprinkling of litter at the foot of the cliff. But even out here, Nick wasn't alone. The radio brought his crewmates into the inside of his helmet. Kurtis and Maddy were sniping at each other on top of the peak. Today they were arguing about food. Maddy was convinced someone was stealing rations from the common storage area. Kurtis told her she was wrong. Maddy then segued to the topic of the resupply flight: when was it coming?

Never, Nick thought.

Five Stones was in the process—a very expensive process—of suing their principal launch provider. SpaceZ wouldn't be offering them any more discount moon flights anytime soon.

The two companies were playing chicken, with the Big Sling crew stuck in the middle.

He leaned on the handle of his roller, pushing it faster.

Kurtis and Maddy broke off their quarrel when Yuta unexpectedly called in from Earth to talk to Theo. It was unusual to hear directly from any of the Five Stones executives. This meant the breakages problem was really serious.

"It's a quality-control issue," Yuta said.

"Sounds about right," Theo said.

Nick had developed a method of working one-on-one with the earthmover. The robot didn't have a tight turning arc. It left unraked strips of dust in between its furrows. Nick would walk those strips with his hand roller, picking up the dust it left behind. They'd pass each other halfway along the furrows. When he was feeling good, he'd race the machine, like his father and Midas Ngidi used to race each other with the walking ploughs, back and forth along the rows of vines.

"*Shosholoza, shosholoza,*" he sang under his breath. "*Ku lezontaba, stimela si qhamuka...*" He'd forgotten all his Zulu, but Midas's working song stayed with him. *Working, working, working in the sun...*

"Speed of extrusion is the enemy of quality, beyond a certain rate," Yuta said. "If you're flinging the fines into the nozzle too fast, you'll get a deeper melt in the crucible. That means higher hydrostatic pressure and faster extrusion. The fibers might not be getting enough time to cool before they hit the winding machine."

Nick leaned into the roller at an angle and skimmed it around the turn. The earthmover bore down on him, heading the other way. It blinked its headlamps before trundling past. It didn't always do the blinking thing. Nick thought maybe Charlie had programmed that as an intermittent reward to encourage him to compete with the machine.

He'd come to see the machine as an extension of Charlie herself, helpful but uncommunicative.

"On the other hand," Yuta said, "the extrusion speed issue might be tangential."

"Oh," Theo said.

"Try slowing it down. If you're still getting breakages, I think it's a purity issue. The molten glass floats on top of the melt, right? The basalt sinks down. You drain off the glass with the taps."

"But if we're extruding too fast, the molten glass might make it all the way down to the bushing before liquid separation occurs," Theo said eagerly.

"*Shosholoza, shosholoza,*" Nick grunted. Way ahead of him, the earthmover made the turn and started back. The field of light where they worked was still large, but the terminator in the distance was coming on, a line of blackness like a wall. Another three days and they'd be working in the dark again. His boots skimmed over the ground. Sweat prickled his face and neck. It pooled in the crooks of his elbows and around his groin. His ears popped.

"No," Yuta said. "I'm trying to say it might have nothing to do with the extrusion speed. Maybe there's just *too much glass* in the melt. If your fines have too many glassy particles mixed in with the basalt, liquid separation is going to be incomplete even if you slow it way down. Getting glass in the fibers causes breakages. I've looked at your pictures of the broken ends, and that could be what's happening."

"Can you put all that in an email?" Kurtis interrupted.

"Sure," Yuta said. "I'll try to figure out the maximum acceptable percentage of glassy particles. But honestly, any is too much."

"What's the solution?" Maddy said.

"The solution?" Yuta laughed despairingly. "There isn't

one. We have no way of controlling the quality of the fines."

"We were fine until a couple of days ago," Theo said. "Zero breakages, tensile strength in excess of requirements—"

"But you're mining different areas all the time, right?" Yuta said. "You probably hit an area with a higher percentage of glassy particles in the dust."

"That means we need to identify those batches of dust before we fling them into the melt," Kurtis said. "How do we do that?"

"You can't," Yuta said. "Not until the melt is already poisoned. And then the only thing you can do is dump it and start again. You're basically throwing darts in the dark."

Nick kicked up a jet of dust. It looked the same as yesterday's dust and last month's dust. He certainly couldn't tell if there was too much glass in it.

"If the stakeholders find out, we're fucked," Yuta said. "Don't say anything to anyone."

"How would we even do that?" Maddy interrupted. "You read all our emails, anyway. You *censor* them. I wrote my mom about how I can't sleep, but she didn't mention it in her reply. That's totally unlike her."

"Nobody is censoring anything," Yuta said warily.

"Yes, you are. I tested it. I wrote to my boyfriend, *The company is censoring our communications. Tell the media.* He never even got back to me."

"Maybe he just dumped your whiny ass," Kurtis murmured.

Nick had also emailed Ellie in Denver, but received no answer. The recollection drained his energy. He leaned on the handle of the roller, using his body weight to push it along. The earthmover approached him, coming the other way. Nick was walking toward the low sun, so the earthmover was just a square black shadow with two headlamps in the middle.

Blink at me, Charlie, he thought. *Twice for yes, once for no.*

Are you censoring our emails?

"Did you even tell anyone Fenella died?" Maddy demanded. "My mom didn't mention that, either. There was nothing about it in that sucky little news digest Mission Control sends up."

"We put out a press release," Yuta said. He sounded tired. "I'll memo Mission Control to send you a copy. Kurtis? Nick? Lee? Do you have anything to add?"

Sweat trickled into Nick's eyes. He blinked twice. *They're keeping secrets from us, Charlie. We're going to run out of food in less than a month. I don't think the resupply flight is ever coming. And I don't think they announced Fenella's death, either. It would have scared the stakeholders.*

"No one?" Yuta said. "Wonderful. For now, just try reducing the extrusion rate. We'll see if that helps."

Vertigo clawed into Nick's brain. He slumped over the handle of the roller and collapsed. Inertia trumped lunar gravity. He tumbled into the earthmover's path.

The roller attachment loomed over him like a gray wall. Dust sifted off its leading curve onto his faceplate and his left arm.

He expected the earthmover to stop automatically. It was programmed to halt whenever a large obstacle was in its way.

It didn't.

The roller bumped over his arm.

Panic gave him a burst of strength. He rolled, jerking his arm out from under the roller. The movement spun him around and he kicked out with his left leg, trying to push off from the side of the earthmover. Instead, his foot went into the gap between its first and second axles.

The deep treads of the wheels caught on his suit, hauling his foot off the ground and crushing it against the chassis.

A few minutes later, the machine finally stopped.

28

Nick woke up in his room. It was dark. He felt hungover, dry-mouthed. He sat up. Then he tried to stand up.

His scream brought Maddy, with Kurtis behind her.

The ceiling light flickered on. Nick was lying in the middle of a forest of IV stands. His flailing had knocked a couple of them over. Maddy set them up again and checked the lines going into the backs of his hands, the side of his neck, and his right foot.

Nick strained his neck to see his left foot. It was blue, yellow, and purple, and swollen to twice its normal size.

"We're power-washing you," Maddy said with the ghost of a smile. She replaced one of the IV bags with a new one. "The fluid doesn't flow like it would on Earth. That's why the multiple sites. We tried pumping the fluid, but you kept moving around and messing up the weights."

Kurtis knelt beside Nick's sleeping bag. "You've got a compound fracture in your foot. Advice was to not put a cast on it until the swelling goes down. Theo set the fracture, at least, and taped it up. Lucky you were out cold at the time, because there isn't that much morphine on the moon."

Kurtis smiled, and Nick dredged up a chuckle. His sleeping bag felt softer than usual. He explored with his fingers. There were two others layered underneath it. Two of his crewmates had given up their own sleeping bags to make him more comfortable. His eyes prickled. He recognized that he was in a weakened state, both emotionally and physically. "Thanks, guys."

"You passed out from heat exhaustion," Kurtis said. "Do you remember that?"

"*Heat exhaustion?*"

"You got confused, dizzy, then collapsed. Right? I had the same thing happen to a bunch of my guys in Brazil. I used to tell them, the sun don't care how tough you think you are. Respect that motherfucker and stay hydrated."

"Now I feel stupid," Nick said.

"Everyone makes mistakes," Kurtis said. "Don't let it get inside your head."

"You really ought to feel lucky," Maddy said.

Nick's mind was clearing. He reassembled the accident in his memory. "The earthmover didn't stop."

"Oh, it stopped," Maddy said. "After it dragged you halfway across the quarry."

"Its optical sensors were fucked up," Kurtis said. "So many scratches on the lenses it couldn't see a thing. And you fell in its blind spot below the main camera. It just didn't see you in time." He rose. "We need those spare parts, bad. I'm gonna get after Mission Control again. They gotta send that resupply flight. I'm not fucking around." He went out.

Maddy said, "Lee feels terrible. He should have caught it."

"Caught what?"

"The degradation of the optical sensors. He didn't realize how bad it was because the earthmover was doing its thing, right? Back and forth and back and forth. But that was all inertial navigation. If he'd actually gone out there and inspected it, he would have seen what a mess the sensors were. It's just... he hasn't been outside since Fenella died."

"Sure he has."

"Nope. Not once."

Nick thought back. She was right.

Maybe that made Lee smarter than Nick, who'd worked ten and twelve-hour shifts in the sun, on starvation rations, until he keeled over.

Tiredness swamped him. He lay back and closed his eyes. "It's not Lee's fault. It's on me." Afterimages of the ceiling fixture swam across his eyelids. "I'm out there with the earth-mover every day. *I* should have inspected the damn sensors."

"Well, no one's out there with it now," Maddy said. "Dust mining's on hold."

Nick opened his eyes. "Just because I fucked up—"

"You didn't fuck up. It's the fiber breakages issue. Nothing's working, and it's going to be night in another few hours." Maddy's expression darkened. She braced her hands on her thighs and stood. "They just dumped the last melt and shut the furnace down."

"Maddy, wait—"

"I can't stay by your bedside, much as I might like to. I'm on shift. We're going up to the summit. At least we can finish the heat batteries, and then they want us to move ahead with the payload spring-loader."

———

Nick got up.

The IV stands were adjustable, with claws at the top to support the lines. He took one and padded the claw with a spare sweatshirt. It made an acceptable crutch. He hung the other IV bags on the same stand and hop-limped along the hall. In the noisy silence of the air-circulation fans and the wastewater cycling—slosh-*slosh*, slosh-*slosh*, like a washing machine running around the clock—his uneven footsteps echoed from one end of the hab to the other. It sounded like no one else was home.

He headed for the greenhouse, worried about his plants. He'd been out of it for thirty hours, according to Maddy, and none of the others were up to speed on the aeroponics procedures. The moisture and nutrient levels had to be checked, and often adjusted, twice a day, every day.

To his surprise and relief, everything looked good. His forest of bamboo stood tall, rustling in the fans, breathing lovely, lovely oxygen into the air. The tips of the stalks almost reached the ceiling. This was his second crop—he'd soon have to harvest it again and add to his pile of bamboo poles in the work module. Maybe Theo could use them for the solar collector frame. It *might* work, if Theo wasn't such a klutz.

Nick moved farther into the greenhouse and checked on his kale. The plants were tall and bushy, replete with vitamin C, vitamin A, and B12. Microgravity was a leafy vegetable's best friend. The wheat, too, was coming along. Nick pinched a small green head of grain. He estimated it would be ready to eat in another two weeks. His hopes were hanging on the wheat. Man cannot live by bread alone, but he can at least survive on it for a while.

He limped over to the strawberries and peeked under their leaves. No fruit.

"That's gotta hurt," Lee said.

Nick turned, carefully, putting his weight on the IV stand crutch. Lee sat in the corner behind the storage cabinets with his laptop on his knees. The red end of a strawberry poked out of his mouth. He chewed and swallowed. His lips were stained crimson.

Nick pointed at him. "How many strawberries have you eaten?"

"All of them," Lee said.

"What about everyone else?"

"Never mind the strawberries," Lee said. "Can you really walk on that?"

"I'm walking on painkillers. Those were *our* strawberries."

"We can eat the bamboo."

"What?"

"Never tried bamboo shoots? They're pretty tasty with soy sauce. Gotta boil 'em first."

"We need the bamboo for the solar collector frame."

"Well, we got enough of it. I looked after the plants while you were laid up."

"Did you add nutrient solution to the water tanks?"

"Shit, no. Was I supposed to?"

"Yeah. I'd better do that." Nick started to shuffle back to the workbench, still pissed at Lee for eating the strawberries.

"Do it later. I found something you'll want to see."

"Oh yeah?"

Lee stood up. Wiping his mouth, he set his laptop on the workbench, which Nick had made from his plentiful supply of bamboo. That was what had given Theo the idea.

Nick leaned on his crutch, looking over Lee's shoulder. Lee smelled disturbingly rank. Water was at a premium here, so they had to combine showers with laundry. You stood on your dirty clothes and swished them around with your feet while hustling to wash your hair and body in three minutes or less. And the water pressure was a joke. Nick never felt as if he was really getting clean. Lee's thin fingers danced over the keyboard, bits of strawberry beneath his fingernails.

"I shouldn't really say I *found* this." Although Lee's body odor was rancid, his breath smelled sweetly of strawberries. "It was sent to you." He opened Nick's email.

"Hey! How did you get into my account?"

"I'm just that good." Lee winked. "No, I saw you typing in your password. *Hailsong*; what's that?"

"Have you been reading *everyone's* email?"

It occurred, unpleasantly, to Nick that Lee might be responsible for the disappearing email situation. Maddy had accused Five Stones of censoring them. But maybe it was Lee...

No. Lee had nothing to gain by concealing the truth about their difficulties.

"I don't know everyone's password," Lee said, somewhat huffily. "And I haven't been reading yours, either. I just checked your account because you were out of it. Thought you might've received something important, and lo and behold, you had."

He clicked on an email from Charlie.

Nick shoved him away from the laptop and greedily perused it.

But it was a disappointment. It consisted of only a few bland lines—hey, how are you doing—and several photographs: Charlie's daughter, Anna, licking an ice cream cone, and three pictures of Anna and Harriet in the garden of their house on Merritt Island.

"Is she *trying* to torture me?" Nick said.

"Not whatsoever. Watch this." Lee right-clicked the first photograph and brought up a window full of code. He typed at virtuoso speed. A new window appeared. A different photograph began to materialize, one line of pixels at a time.

"It's called steganography," Lee said. "Hiding one image inside another one. I wrote a simple Python algorithm to unmerge the images."

Nick's gaze was glued to the screen. "How did you know this was there?"

"Look at what she says here: *Check out the goodness in these pictures!* Doesn't that suggest something to you? It does to me. Anyway, I was bored, so I gave it a whirl."

The hidden photograph appeared in full.

It was a slightly blurry still shot of the greenhouse, taken from about waist height. A lush garden of crops sprouted from racks fully loaded with trays. The date stamp said *March 27, 2049.*

"The day before we got here," Nick breathed.

"Yup," Lee said. "I figure it's extracted from the robot footage." They both glanced at Greenfinger quietly rusting at the end of the module. "I *knew* that robot must have seen something." Lee typed again. "Wait for it. The other pictures are even better. Or, you might say, worse."

29

In the second image, two people had entered the greenhouse.

In the third, they were picking up entire trays complete with their contents, putting the covers on, and stacking them on a dolly.

Lee zoomed in. "There's our cannabis."

"I wondered why I never saw it on the livestream," Nick said. The cannabis had been grown on the lowest shelf of the racks, out of view of the security cameras. The raiders had taken all of it.

In the fourth image, the pair grabbed motion-blurred handfuls of spinach, lettuce, and zucchini out of the remaining trays and stuffed them into bags.

Nick's jaw hurt from gritting his teeth. "Go back up." The faces of the thieves could be seen most clearly in the third image. One was male, one female. He dabbed a fingernail on the woman's face. Pale, pinched lips, square jaw. "This could be our friend from the landing site, Katniss Reyes."

"What about this guy?" Lee hovered the pointer over the other thief, a large man who looked Polynesian, with a face like a car crash.

"Probably the other one," Nick said. "Trigger McLean."

He focused on the timestamp. Only six hours had elapsed between the burglary and the Five Stones crew's arrival.

"They stole the plants and headed home," he said, thinking aloud. "But before they got there, they heard about the Tranquility 13 incident, and turned around to see if they could pick up anything else useful from the wreck." Nick groaned. "They must have had the plants in their rover the whole time! We were *this* close to catching them in the act! No wonder they acted twitchy."

"That's how I figure it," Lee said. "But the interesting part is what's happening now."

"How do you mean?"

"Charlie sent you these pictures. Why did she do that? There's only one possible explanation. She knows we weren't told about the burglary, but she suddenly decided we need to know about it after all. What changed?"

Nick shrugged. As heartening as Charlie's gesture was, it was equally crushing to realize she must've known all along that the crew were being lied to, yet had said nothing.

"She's going behind their backs," Lee said. "That's why the encryption. She's broken ranks."

"Doesn't help us much," Nick muttered.

"It's confirmation. Evidence. It'll help to prove our case against them."

Nick stared at him. "We're not going to have a chance to make a case against them, Lee. We have eighteen days of rations left. That means someone has to die. And then someone else, and someone else again. When the last person tightens the last rivet on the Big Sling, the robots will take over and start sending up payloads. A happy ending for the stakeholders."

A slow red-lipped smile broke across Lee's face. "Nice to know you've finally come around to my point of view."

"Yeah, well... I nearly got killed."

"You were lucky."

"That's what Maddy said." Nick shifted his weight on his crutch. *Could* it be true that he'd been meant to be the next casualty? He was still weak from his ordeal. He started to lower himself to the floor. Lee caught his elbow and helped him sit down with his injured foot awkwardly sticking out in front of him.

"If my suit had been breached, I'd be dead..." Nick rested his head on one hand. "That's where I got lucky. The earthmover's been operating out there in the dust so long, its treads are worn right down. There weren't any sharp edges or right angles that could've torn the suit. It just crushed my foot." He smiled with one side of his mouth. "Moondust saved my life."

"Stay where you are," Lee said. He opened one of the storage boxes under the workbench and took out a dehydrated applesauce box. Nick's mouth watered, but when Lee opened the box, it was the fragrance of marijuana that wafted out. The box contained dried leaves. Lee and Maddy had followed through on their plan to raise a new supply of weed from the seeds left behind by the thieves. "It's Maddy's, really," Lee said. "But I don't think she'd begrudge you a few hits."

"I'm good, man," Nick said.

"For the pain."

"I'll stick to OxyContin."

"Have it your own way." Lee picked a small pipe out of the box and packed its bowl with crumbly dried leaves. "Maddy made this out of parts. It's got a heating coil in the bottom." He inhaled, fiddled with the pipe, tried again. "She says it's the only thing that helps her sleep." He exhaled a thin stream of smoke.

"Yeah, she mentioned she's having trouble sleeping," Nick said.

Was Lee sinking into paranoia? He'd voluntarily jailed

himself inside the hab, and now he was self-medicating with pot.

"The nights are tough for everyone," Lee said, eking another hit out of the DIY pipe.

Could Nick himself be sinking into paranoia? After all, he had no actual proof the earthmover tried to murder him, and strong proof that it had been an accident. Why would he have been targeted, anyway? Without him, dust mining would grind to a halt. Without him, the wheat would die.

He suddenly heard his mother's voice on the day they drove through the mist-shrouded vineyards for the last time. *Your father used to say this place would die without him. We'll see.*

Will Morrison had been right. A few short years after his death, Hailsong Wine Estates had gone back to wasteland, except for one end of the chardonnay slopes, which had become a slum. Nick used to count the expanding numbers of prefab shacks on Google Earth until he got too bitter about it. There was nothing to go back to, even if he could go back.

His mother had sold the farm to the neighboring township, where Midas Ngidi lived, for $1.3 million. At the time, it had seemed like a lot of money. Nick was a teenager before he realized how dramatically Lydia allowed herself to be ripped off. The farm had been worth $30 million, at least, not counting the intangible value of the Hailsong name. The Morrisons—and the Adriaanses who came before them—had been robbed.

That, of course, was the point. *We can rob you in broad daylight and there's nothing you can do about it.*

Consider yourselves lucky you didn't get killed, too.

I got lucky.

We all got lucky.

If I'd been killed, the wheat would die.

He derailed his runaway thoughts by dragging himself over to the storage box. "I think each of us should share our expertise with at least one other person... So, look. Here's the nutrient solution for the kale. Here's the wheat, the strawberries, bamboo. I premixed them in bulk and noted the amounts on the sides of the bottles. I'll jot down the temperature, moisture, and light requirements and put that on the trays." He smiled at Lee. "Now you tell me how to do what *you're* working on."

"Oh, Jesus," Lee said. "Right now, I'm working on the fiber breakages issue."

"Do you have any ideas?"

"No. But I know the right question to ask. How do we characterize the fines *before* we pour them into the furnace? That's the problem. All I have to do is solve it."

"Ha! Good luck with that." Nick finished adding the nutrient solutions to the water tanks, and turned to leave the greenhouse.

"Where are you going?"

"Back to bed."

———

The next time he woke up, he went to the workshop. Although his spacesuit hadn't been breached, the outer cover of his left boot had been torn in a couple of places. With no spares, he'd have to patch it.

His suit lay on the workbench like a shriveled, orange-gray corpse. Whoever brought it in tried to clean off the dust first, but you never could get *all* the dust off. Sparkling eddies rose off the suit every time Nick touched it. He'd positioned a fan behind his shoulder to blow the dust away from him, but it didn't do much good. His sinuses burned, even though he'd tied a cut-up T-shirt over his mouth and nose, and he coughed continually.

It was worst in here, but the dust situation in the habitat was getting worse in general. Every time they brought a suit or a tool in from outside, the dust that came in with it stayed. The blades of the circulation fans turned black and furry every few days, and the sharp-edged particles were degrading the CO_2 filters in the ECLSS. Nick hated to think about what they were doing to the crew's lungs. He held his breath and applied the electric sander to the area he needed to patch.

It occurred to him as he worked that Lee might have another reason for lurking in the greenhouse. Nothing from outside ever went in *there*. The whole hab shared a single air-circulation system, but in the greenhouse, there were that many more filters and fans between you and the dust.

Lee planned to survive.

Nick did, too.

He cut a patch from Fenella's suit. If his suit looked like a corpse, hers looked like a partially eaten corpse, lying under the workbench. Nick once felt revulsion at the thought of cannibalizing a suit that someone had died in. Now it was just useful material. He applied epoxy to the patch and positioned it on his left boot cover.

"The Camptown ladies sing this song, doo dah, doo dah. Camptown racetrack's five miles long, oh, doo dah day."

"Shut *up*, Kurtis. Do you hear me inflicting my perverted folk fetish on you?"

"Perverted Folk Fetish would be a good name for a band," said Theo's voice.

Kurtis, Maddy, and Theo were back. Nick left his patch to dry and looked out of the workshop.

"Going to run all night, going to run all day," Kurtis sang, stripping off right there in the hall—something he was always doing, without regard for Maddy—and grabbing clean clothes from the laundry line, which ran the length of the module.

"You're in a good mood," Nick said.

"I bet my money on the bobtail mare, somebody bet on the

bay." Kurtis had a tuneful baritone voice. Nick hadn't heard him singing in weeks.

"You fix the fiber breakages issue?"

"Nope," Kurtis said. "You eat yet?"

"No."

"Come on and join us."

In the kitchen, Kurtis dispensed ration packets with a lavish hand. "Here's two for you, and two for you. Who wants the last blueberry pudding?"

"That's Lee's favorite," Maddy said.

"Well, I ain't going to save it for him." Kurtis tore open the blueberry pudding and rehydrated it. "Blue is the color of my true love's hair..." He grinned at Maddy, whose blue-tipped hair had grown down to her shoulders. She threw a rag at him. It floated like a feather in the lunar gravity.

"All right, spill it," Nick said, smiling. "Is it somebody's birthday?"

"Nope."

"What, then? They schedule the resupply flight?"

Kurtis, Theo, and Maddy looked at one another and laughed.

"There isn't *going* to be a resupply flight," Maddy said.

"That situation's been clarified," Kurtis said. "Mission Control told me today in strictest confidence—to which I say, fuck that—the company is not in a financial position to resupply us at the present time. Remember the insider trading thing? The SEC is seeking an injunction. They're looking at a mega-millions fine. Rachel says they got no proof, but I don't know about that. Anyway, there's no money, honey. We're on our own."

"Well then, we're fucked," Nick said.

"Not quite." The microwave beeped. Kurtis opened a packet of rehydrated pasta Bolognese and squeezed an oily, bloody-looking hunk into his mouth. "Aaron's done a deal with ILI," he said, grinning with tomato-colored teeth. "They're going to front us whatever we need. Food and everything else— spares, patches, electronic components, hydrogen for the fuel cells. Shit, they got *everything* down there."

Nick grinned. "Seriously? Well that's pretty fucking fantastic!"

"Right?" Theo was smiling so widely, he looked a little insane. He did a Cossack skip, clapping his heels together.

"When's it coming?" Nick said.

"No, dummy," Maddy said. "We have to go pick it up."

Kurtis pointed at Nick. "We, as in you. You can't work outside with that foot, anyway."

"And me," Maddy said. "Zippa-dee-doo-da-day, I get to get away from Kurtis for a while."

30

In preparation for the drive to ILI, Nick and Kurtis gave the rover an overhaul. The fuel cell was still good for a couple hundred hours of driving time, but the pressurized interior wasn't meant to support trips of more than a few hours. They took four spare oxygen cylinders and connected them to the reactant tanks over the rover's wheels, which also provided the rover's air.

"Y'all *better* make it back safely," Kurtis said.

Nick was lying on his back under the rover, tightening the cylinder valves one crank of the wrench at a time. His left foot throbbed. The swelling had mostly gone down, but squeezing the foot into his boot had been awful. "We will," he said.

"Just be aware of the political realities." Kurtis's headlamp bobbed. Night had swallowed the foot of the mountain. Kurtis crouched in an awkward position, holding the tank in place.

"What political realities?"

"ILI, man. They aren't doing this out of the goodness of their hearts. They hate our guts."

Thinking back to what Kat and Trig had done, Nick figured that was true. He wondered if he should tell Kurtis about it.

"When we get the Big Sling built—"

With the fiber breakages issue still unsolved, it felt more like *if*, but Nick didn't interrupt.

"The day we throw our first payload into orbit, their mass driver will be obsolete. Twelve billion bucks down the crapper. Bunch of people out of a job. Bonfire of the government contractors."

"Why did they even agree to help us out, then?"

Kurtis snorted. "It's like when an American citizen gets their ass in trouble overseas. Government gotta step in. They got no choice. What I'm saying, they'll likely give you the food, but they might try to dick you on the spares and components, anything related to the job. Just be aware of that."

Nick hesitated. He turned the wrench another crank. "There's something *you* should be aware of."

"What?"

"Tell you later." They were using the ground channel, but Nick didn't feel confident the suit radios were truly private. For all they knew, there might be recording devices in the helmet electronics. Lee wanted to take Fenella's helmet apart and see what was in there, but Kurtis had said no. They might need it intact for spares. They had no other source of spares, unless Nick and Maddy brought some back from ILI.

Inside, Nick drew Kurtis into the greenhouse. Lee was in there, standing at the workbench, scowling at his computer. "Lee, I'm gonna show Kurtis that email."

Lee scowled even more ferociously, but didn't object. Nick opened his email and showed Kurtis the decrypted pictures of the greenhouse burglary.

"Oh man," Kurtis said. "Oh, man. These people."

"Yeah, figure it's like you said. They want to stop the Big Sling from getting built. They sabotaged our hab before we even got here."

Kurtis looked up from the screen. "Well, this gruesome twosome, they're contractors, right? They ain't actually working for ILI. Whereas it was ILI that promised us the supplies. Maybe their bosses found out about this shit, slapped them down, and now they're trying to make it up to us." He sighed heavily. "Just be careful. Be *really* careful."

Lee said, "Maybe Maddy shouldn't go."

Kurtis laughed. "Don't let her hear you saying that. She can look after herself better than... better than any guy." It was clear he had been going to say *better than you.*

Lee's face clenched. Nick mindlessly scrolled the pictures up and down, trying to think of some way to defuse the tension between them.

Kurtis stabbed the screen. "Hey, what's that?" He'd seen the cannabis plants.

Nick tensed, expecting a rant.

Instead, Kurtis laughed out loud. "So *this* is where she's getting it. I thought she just brought a massive stash with her. I was like, how did you get that past security?"

"It helps her sleep," Lee said with trembling defiance.

"It better. Sure stinks the place up."

Later, as Nick came out of his room, he saw Maddy and Kurtis coming out of Kurtis's room together. He wondered if Kurtis had been giving Maddy a lecture about her weed habit. But both were smiling.

"Thanks, Kurtis," Maddy said, lifting the rucksack she carried. It was a battered camouflage item with Army patches on, which Kurtis treated like a favorite teddy bear. Nick was surprised he was lending it to her. But Maddy had lost her own kitbag in the Tranquility 13 incident. "I'll look after it."

They went out to the rover and got rolling.

Dust jetted up from the treads, sparkling in the cone of light from the headlamps as they pierced the dark.

31

Charlie ordered a mojito. The sun was only a handsbreadth above the Atlantic. Aaron's idea of brunch was more like breakfast. But it *was* the weekend, even if it didn't feel like it.

There had ceased to be any practical difference between weekends and weekdays at Five Stones. The crew on the moon didn't get to take weekends off, nor did Mission Control, and by extension, neither did the executives. However, unlike the others, Charlie had a life outside the company. She had a daughter.

When Aaron asked her to come in early on Sunday, she'd exploded. "What am I supposed to do with Anna?"

"Can't your mother look after her?"

"She goes to Mass."

"Oh, weird," Aaron said.

"She's Catholic. What's weird is that you think that's weird."

"Why don't you bring the kid with you?"

Now Anna ordered a grilled cheese sandwich and sat holding up her tablet, looking at the world through its screen, turning this way and that in her chair to take pictures of fishermen and surfers.

The Pieradise Tavern, on the end of Cocoa Beach Pier, had always been a favorite haunt of the Five Stones gang. The Big Sling had been born here, while Charlie and Yuta traded cocktail napkins back and forth in delirious excitement. This morning, Yuta wasn't present. Charlie suspected he'd begged off to avoid conflict. Bill's slumped posture, and the way Aaron relentlessly shredded a coaster, told her conflict in some form was coming.

What she wasn't prepared for was Aaron sticking his phone in her face before their food had even arrived, showing her an email.

Her email to Nick.

"What?" Charlie said, trying to bluff it out. "I'm not allowed to write to them?"

"How dumb do you think I am?" Aaron said. The rims of his nostrils were white with anger. He tapped up another window, showcasing the pictures she'd steganographically encrypted in her email.

"Uh-huh," Charlie said, hyperaware of Anna photographing seabirds while undoubtedly listening to every word. Anger bubbled up. How low could Aaron go—confronting her in front of her child so she couldn't defend herself without terrifying Anna?

"Yeah, I sent those," she said carefully. "I thought they deserved to know what they're going to be walking into."

She'd hit on the idea of secretly sending the pictures when Aaron decided to have the crew seek assistance from ILI. From the very same people who plundered the Five Stones habitat in the first place.

All right, so ArxaSys Lunar wasn't ILI. It wasn't even Arxa-Sys. But Charlie had no great confidence that the ILI base management could rein the contractors in. They obviously hadn't been doing it so far.

Bill grunted into his martini. "I don't like it either, Charlie. But we have no other options."

They honestly didn't. They'd approached the Russians about buying space on one of their flights, but the Russians refused, for geopolitical reasons, to land in Amundsen Crater or anywhere near it. They wanted way too much money, anyway. Blue Horizon, SpaceZ's main competitor, had at first said they would do it, only to later double their asking price, probably at Sean Radek's instigation.

Aaron tossed his phone on the table. Having shredded his own coaster, he grabbed Charlie's coaster and started to tear it up. "I really wish you hadn't stirred the pot. I'd feel better if they didn't know who was responsible for the break-in... Don't get me wrong, I have every confidence in Nick and Maddy to carry out their mission successfully." The shower of recycled paper shreds on the table said something different. "They'll do the right thing. The smart thing."

"And what is that, exactly?" Charlie said.

"They'll do what they have to do to get the stuff they need," Aaron said.

"It's all about survival," Bill said. He was due in New York tomorrow to give a deposition in civil court, where he would lie his ass off, gambling that the SEC had no documentary evidence against him.

And maybe they didn't. Charlie sure knew who did. A text bubble flashed through her mind: *$100,000 or your CEO goes to jail.*

"Yes, it's all about survival." She leaned toward Aaron. "You're setting them up—"

To die. She bit back the words because of Anna, and

because a smiling waitress just brought their food. Charlie had ordered a croque monsieur. The smell sickened her.

"That's where you got it wrong. The fact is, Charlie, the *fact is* the whole goddamn world is ganging up on us because they know what we have might actually work!"

The waitress backed away, startled.

Anna's eyes were wide. "How is the world ganging up on us?"

"Not the whole world, sweetie," Charlie said. "Just Big Space."

"And the industrial-defense complex," Aaron said.

"And the SEC," Bill said. Charlie and Aaron nodded. They all knew the insider trading investigation was politically motivated.

Anna looked from one of the adults to another. "Mom." She pulled Charlie closer so she could whisper to her. "Are we going to be broke again?"

A lump rose in Charlie's throat. Anna still remembered those awful months of scavenging, hitchhiking, sweltering without A/C, and, once or twice, dumpster-diving. The experience had left a permanent scar on her young soul.

"No, sweetie," she said with all the conviction she could muster. "We're not going to be broke again."

$100,000 or your CEO goes to jail.

The wording of the message said Ryder had been tracking the SEC investigation. He must have decided now was the moment to sting her for the big bucks.

She couldn't give him $100,000. Not when there was the mortgage, Anna's school fees, Harriet's neurologist...

She sipped her mojito, willing herself to be calm.

She had shilly-shallied long enough. It was time to deal with Ryder Stillman once and for all.

32

The route computed for them by Mission Control led across the floor of Amundsen Crater and up the crater's southwestern rim. This must have been the same way Katniss Reyes and Trigger McLean had come. A stretch of the rim had slumped into a rocky rampart. It was navigable, but only just. By the time the rover reached the top, Nick was sweating with tension, his neck and back stiff from hunching over the steering yoke, straining to see out through the scuffed concave circle of the windshield.

Maddy had slept through the whole climb, curled up on the floor behind the seats with her head pillowed on Kurtis's rucksack. Apparently, her insomnia didn't bother her outside the habitat.

Nick turned the steering over to the AI and got up, wincing when he put his weight on his left foot. Careful not to wake Maddy, he stretched his back, swigged water, and gazed out at the new landscape dimly visible through the windshield. They were two kilometers above the crater floor. Up here, the sun was still shining. There was the central peak in the distance, stabbing up out of the crater's shadows. Ahead of the rover, rounded folds of rock undulated to the west and north. The landscape to the south dropped away into darkness.

Until now, he'd only seen the inside of Amundsen Crater. The moon was bigger than he properly understood.

They only had to travel across 150 kilometers of it, but the rover's slow speed made it feel like so much more. Kat and Trig claimed to have made the trip in ten hours. Either they'd been bullshitting, or their rover could go faster. That seemed probable. The Five Stones rover wasn't a mobile outpost, just a glorified suitlock. Nick and Maddy bumped along, rarely achieving a speed of more than ten kph, circling north around the rim of Amundsen Crater. They needed to go south, but the terrain constrained them to an indirect, zigzagging route. It was a good thing they'd brought those extra oxygen cylinders.

A connecting ridge branching off to the west took them around Faustini Crater. From the rim of Faustini, the ground dropped steeply into a permanent abyss of darkness. Sun never reached the floor of this crater. It had been mapped by radar, but ILI had only just begun to explore it physically with robots. Temperatures were so cold down there that fuel cells froze. And if the rover's wheels slipped, that was where they'd end up. Likely in pieces.

The crater was several kilometers deep. The rim was reasonably level and wider than a ten-lane highway, but to Nick it felt like a narrow ledge. He didn't relax his white-knuckled grip on the steering yoke until they were safely past Faustini, into the intercrater highlands surrounding the south pole.

"Why don't you let the computer take over?" Maddy yawned.

Nick was tired and anxious. He snapped, "Remember the earthmover? That's why."

"I don't think you should pay too much attention to what Lee says."

"Just because he's paranoid doesn't mean he's wrong."

"Doesn't make him right, either. You really need to relax, save your strength."

"What other explanation is there?"

"The obvious one," Maddy said. "Fenella slipped. You passed out from heat exhaustion. The cryocooling system on Tranquility 13 failed. The moon is *dangerous*."

"And space debris hit Tranquility 12?"

Maddy was quiet for a moment. "Yeah... That one's a bit harder to swallow."

"All in all, I feel safer driving."

"All right then, *I'll* drive," Maddy said. "You get some sleep."

When Nick woke up, the noises around him were different. Softer. The suspension was no longer rocking him gently up and down. The rover had stopped.

Maddy sat in the driver's seat, cursing at the diagnostics.

"What happened?" Nick scrambled to his feet.

"Dust."

"No way, really? I don't believe it," Nick said.

She didn't smile. "Stupid particles probably shorted out the drive motor and the circuit breaker tripped. I can't get it to reboot."

"Shit, don't reboot it yet." Nick rubbed sleep out of his eyes. "We'll have to blow the dust out of the electrical distribution box."

"I was afraid you were going to say that."

Nick reached past her and called up the life-support telemetry. "How long ago did it short out?"

"Five minutes?"

Nick sat back, arms folded, doing mental calculations, like he used to do on dives.

"Let's get this done," Maddy said, moving toward the suitlocks.

"Wait."

"For what? The only thing we've got that'll blow the dust out of the distro box is one of the oxygen cylinders. We can use one of them and still make it."

"Yeah, but look," Nick said. "We're sitting in the sunlight." Pale green light slanted through the windshield over the controls and his lower body. "The short must have heated up the drive motor. How hot, I don't know, but it's going to take a while to cool radiatively. If we shoot oxygen in there while it's at ignition temperature—"

"Boom." Maddy retreated from the suitlock.

"Exactly. Big boom."

"How long can we afford to sit here waiting for it to cool down, and still have enough oxygen to get there?"

"Don't know that, either. How far out are we?"

"Thirty klicks."

They waited as long as they dared. While they waited, they talked. Maddy told Nick stories from her days in the Marines and her subsequent career as a bodyguard. She swore she'd seen a ghost in the hallway of an old hotel in Riyadh. Nick told her about the commercial diving industry and hair-raising underwater accidents he'd seen or been in.

He didn't bring up the human slugs who populated the diving industry, such as Ryder Stillman. Nor mention stealing valuables while pretending to be a climate volunteer. There was likely stuff she wasn't telling him, too, but the conversation made him feel better about her. She might be an infuriating mixture of superstition and reckless insouciance, but he was happy to have her along.

When they could wait no longer, they got into their suits and went out.

The rover stood on a scarp, winding like a diamond road through a sea of darkness. An archipelago of hills, sanded to the bone by the solar wind, rose from the night in the north. The sun, directly behind them, elongated Nick's and Maddy's shadows to grotesque proportions. They were the only moving things in the entire landscape, and for a breathless moment, Nick felt their presence here to be sacrilegious. He understood for the first time that the moon was a glorious thing in its own right. A celestial work of art. And perhaps, like any other wonder of nature—a coral reef, a rainforest, a glacier—it should not be messed with.

He stood for a moment longer, drinking in the unexpected stark beauty of the landscape. Then he crawled under the rover to remove one of the oxygen cylinders.

"I don't think it's cooled down enough yet," Maddy yelped.

Nick knelt, awkwardly angling the cylinder's nozzle at the inside of the electrical distribution box. If he shot oxygen into it, and it turned out to be hot enough to ignite the gas, the engine would blow up. Even if he survived the explosion, they would both be stranded here forever. The stakes could not be higher.

The sense of detachment stemming from his belated appreciation of the moon's beauty had worn off. Only the math of survival mattered.

"Maybe it's cooled down, maybe it hasn't," he said. "We can't wait any longer or we won't have enough air to get there."

He shut his eyes and opened the valve.

33

"Oh my God! Oh—ha ha!" Maddy said.

Dust jetted out of the box. No fireball.

"That's our good luck used up for a while." Nick played the jet over the components for another few seconds and then closed the valve to save what oxygen remained.

They wearily climbed back into the rover—which started without complaint.

———

In the fifteenth hour of their journey, the rover climbed onto the rim of Shackleton Crater. Situated right on top of the south pole, the small circular crater hosted ILI's exploratory water-mining operations. There was no evidence of human activity to be seen from up here. They circled the crater on a sunlit ridge lapped on both sides by chthonic darkness. Earth had sunk below the horizon. Nick watched the rover's oxygen reserves, chewing on the side of a thumbnail.

West of Shackleton, their route dipped into darkness. The rover swayed through valleys submerged in night, engine straining on the steeper slopes. It seemed to be getting colder inside the cabin. Nick broke the silence. "Cruder really is better."

"How do you mean?"

"Try opening up the distro box of your car back home. We were able to fix that short because this rover is as simple as a kid's toy."

"Dude, it's got an AI and a satellite uplink."

"Yeah, but you know what I mean. You can get under the hood and fix the engine. And if it breaks down again, we'll fix it again."

"That's right. We'll fix it again," Maddy said.

They relapsed into tense silence, waiting for the engine to latch up and stop.

———

Twenty hours and seven minutes after Nick and Maddy left base camp, Earth dawned again on the northern horizon. A shining hilltop rose out of the darkness ahead. One of the famous "Peaks of Eternal Light" scattered around the south pole, this was the highest point of the broken ridge connecting Shackleton and de Gerlache craters. It was in the sun for 85% of each lunation. On the knobby crown of the hill, solar arrays on ten-meter masts rose from a cluster of equipment, drinking the light.

"Hey there," a relaxed, antipodean voice said over the radio. "You made it. C'mon in."

"Shit, that's him," Nick said.

"Who?"

"Trigger McLean. I'm almost sure that's his voice." Nick was rigid, his fight-or-flight reflex engaged. "What's he doing here?"

"What do you mean? He works here, doesn't he?"

"He *should* be on probation. Something. They should have sent them both back to Earth."

"It's not all that easy to send people back to Earth," Maddy said dryly. "Anyway, what do we know? Maybe he is on probation." She jabbed a finger at the oxygen reserves. They were into the red. "We're literally gonna die if these folks don't help us. *Talk* to him."

Nick took a deep breath and pressed transmit. "Hey, good to see you again, man."

As he spoke, he actually did see Trig. On the top of the hill, a skeleton buggy stood below the solar masts. The buggy's driver stood up on his vehicle, straddling the flimsy bucket seat, waving to them. "Keep going past the oxygen plant," Trig said. "I'll catch up."

The buggy skimmed down the hill, taking flight on the bumps, and plunged into the darkness. Nick kept driving, as instructed, toward a constellation of colored lights speckling the dark side of the hill. Closer up, a snarl of radiator fins, pipes, and industrial-sized tanks loomed into the rover's headlights. People in spacesuits were working at outdoor consoles that looked like they'd been borrowed from the 1960s. Another buggy with a dump trailer loaded rubble into a giant hopper. ILI's oxygen-recovery technology might be dated, but the scale of their operations made Theo's half-built solar roaster look like a backyard prepper project.

"High-ice-content regolith in, water out," Trig spoke in the bored, skeptical tone of a teacher showing visitors around a failing high school. Nick relaxed a bit. "We crack the water into hydrogen and oxygen with electrolysis. The plant also refines aluminum, iron, and silicon from lunar ore."

"It's a good thing Theo isn't here," Maddy whispered.

Nick nodded. What madness of ambition had convinced Aaron that he could compete with these people?

"Keep going straight ahead," Trig said.

They broke into sunlight. Trig's buggy rolled alongside the rover. It was light and maneuverable, like an oversized go-kart. Trig took one glove off the joystick and pointed. "That's our landing site."

About two kilometers away, an Artemis lander stood in the sun behind a semicircular regolith berm. It looked like the obese big sister of Apollo. It was being refueled from a toylike tanker. Another manned buggy towed a utility trailer away, toward a cluster of smaller landers standing on splayed legs farther along the ridge.

"And that's where we live."

The landers presided over a jigsaw of berms of piled-up regolith. Construction materials littered the ground beyond them. The terrain had been levelled around the habitat complex and for some distance along the ridge to the north, which connected the rims of Shackleton Crater and de Gerlache Crater—like a vast expanse of cobblestones.

"Microwave sintering?" Nick said.

"Yeah. We melt the regolith with a portable microwave beam source, then let it reharden," Trig said. "Lotta work, but it helps to eliminate dust. Landing pad is sintered, too."

The Five Stones crew had been planning to use the same technique on the Big Sling platform, but that was only an area of a hundred square meters.

In the distance, an earthmover plunged through contrails of dust, continuing the work of grading and levelling the ridge. A metallic pipe ran north along the ridge toward de Gerlache Crater.

"That's the mass driver," Trig said. Now he sounded smug, conscious of the scale of ILI's ambitions.

"We're low on oxygen," Nick said sharply. "Where's the vehicle lock?" Scanning the habitat area, he didn't see a free-standing vehicle airlock like they had at home.

"Over there," Trig said. "See the trailer-looking thing?" It was backed up to one of the landers. It was three times the size of the Five Stones vehicle airlock. Nick had taken it for a storage container. "But you can't use it. Park over here."

The buggy led the way to the nearer end of the jigsaw of joined-up berms. The berms were regolith shields for inflatable habitats, Nick reckoned. They looked ramshackle and unfinished, like everything on the moon. The shielding was a good idea, though. He wanted to do something similar at home if he ever got a spare moment. Radiation was a constant worry, and he did not have confidence in Five Stones' assertion that the hab was sufficiently shielded by its insulation.

They slithered into their suits and left the rover. The pain in Nick's foot immediately devoured his thoughts. Maddy swung her upper body around. "What's that?" she said, pointing.

A hundred meters from the hab complex, in the opposite direction from the landing site, two rectangular wings of silver stretched out from an upright truss the height of a three-story building. Nick had taken the structure for another solar installation. On second look, those weren't solar panels. They were radiator vanes.

"That? That's the reactor," Trig said.

A man in a battered, gray ILI spacesuit ducked out of the personnel airlock. He spoke in a tired, but authoritative voice. "Thanks, Trig. I'll take it from here." He turned toward Nick and Maddy. "Welcome to the International Lunar Initiative. Come in, come in."

34

Nick and Maddy followed the ILI man into the personnel airlock. While the chamber cycled, the man introduced himself as Dr. David Hofstadter.

"Wow, the cold traps guy? It's an honor." Maddy said.

Nick had heard of Dr. Hofstadter. A Nobel Prize–winning geophysicist, he'd led the first-ever manned expedition into the permanently shadowed region of Shackleton Crater. A lesser mortal would have retired to a highly paid professorship after that, but Dr. Hofstadter returned to the moon, using his fame to shake loose more funding for research into lunar volatiles. He was a living legend. But Nick's foot was hurting too much for him to say anything flattering, or even polite. He was grateful Maddy continued to engage Dr. Hofstadter in conversation.

The airlock opened on a tunnel-shaped room. Twenty empty spacesuits sagged along the walls like weary soldiers. Several more lay on workbenches. The suits were gray with dust, and so was the air. If the Five Stones habitat had a problem with dust contamination, this place had it twenty times worse. Nick started coughing as soon as his seals were opened. He didn't care—he just wanted out of his suit. His foot had swelled up again during their drive. It was agony.

While he sat on the floor, alternating careful tugs on his left boot with deep breaths to manage the pain, Maddy and Dr. Hofstadter wriggled out of their own suits. Maddy coughed herself red in the face, one hand clamped over her mouth and nose.

Dr. Hofstadter gave her a sympathetic smile. "Gene Cernan, one of the Apollo 17 astronauts, said 'Dust is probably one of our greatest inhibitors to a nominal operation on the moon. I think we can overcome other physiological or physical or mechanical problems, except dust.' He was prescient."

"Wasn't Gene Cernan the guy who read Genesis over the radio?" Nick had finally gotten his suit off. He stood up, leaning on his new crutch. He'd brought the crutch in with him, as Maddy had brought Kurtis's rucksack, using the sample hatch to get them out of the rover. It wasn't ideal, as it meant dust clung to the crutch and rucksack. But that hardly seemed to matter in here.

"No, that was the crew of Apollo 8," Dr. Hofstadter said. "Bill Anders, Jim Lovell, and Frank Borman."

Dr. Hofstadter stared at Nick's crutch. Nick was rather proud of it, having made it himself using more of his endless supply of bamboo. Now, however, he felt embarrassed by its DIY vibe. He started to explain about his foot.

Dr. Hofstadter interrupted him. "Yes, of course. I was sorry to hear about your accident... and your other losses."

Nick finally mastered his pain and exhaustion sufficiently to get Hofstadter into focus. The renowned geophysicist was short, compact, graying. His intense green eyes belied his weary manner.

Hofstadter's voice rasped like a two-pack-a-day smoker's.

"Anyway, we can definitely get you fixed up. Not a problem. This way, this way."

At the end of the room was a pressure door. They entered a chamber fitted with boxy units on telescopic robot arms. They stood on boot prints marked on the floor, and the units whirred slowly from their heads to their feet, sucking at clothes and hair, like vacuum cleaners. "The dust is partly composed of metallic minerals, so it's magnetic," Dr. Hofstadter yelled over the noise. "There are magnets inside the suction units that help to suck it in and trap it in filters."

"Sick!" Maddy yelled back, grinning as her hair was sucked flat over one side of her face.

Adhesive rollers followed the suction units, nuzzling up and down their bodies. When they emerged out the other end of the decontamination chamber, Nick could still taste the gunpowder tang of moondust. The system didn't really work.

"This is the geology laboratory," Dr. Hofstadter said. A woman working at a computer greeted them. "Cynthia's studying moonquakes. Did you know the moon undergoes seismic events, just like Earth? Of course, most of them are scarcely detectable. It takes sophisticated instruments to pick them up."

Nick rubbed a finger along the housing of a spectrometer. It came away grubby with dust.

They followed Dr. Hofstadter through the mazelike habitat. It'd clearly been expanded over the years in a haphazard fashion, with additional modules being bolted on wherever they'd fit. Pressure hatches and sometimes flexitubes connected the low-ceilinged, cramped inflatables. Nick had subconsciously been expecting space, light, warmth, comfort, and amenities commensurate with ILI's vast budget. In fact, the base was more like a cross between a Rubik's Cube and a submarine. Partitions carved the inflatables into smaller work and living areas, all crammed with computer equipment, dingy old furniture, and people. People, people.

Nick found his mouth was dry, and he had a sensation of pressure in his chest. Without realizing it, he'd gotten out of the habit of seeing humans he did not know. He felt like an Amazonian tribesman dropped into the middle of a city. He'd felt the same way after they came down from Mauna Kea, only now it was worse. The ceilings were low, the walls concave, the noise of life-support machinery carried through the habitat, and everywhere there was dust.

Dr. Hofstadter introduced some of his colleagues in passing. "Ajay is a radio astronomer... Sarah's working on the mineral composition of crater central peaks. Ah, here we are. How's it going, Priya?"

They arrived in a module that was obviously the ILI clinic. Battered medical devices surrounded an examination table. Boxes of supplies overflowed from cots. A solidly built Indian woman looked up from her computer.

"Priya's our doctor," Dr. Hofstadter explained. "Priya, this is Nick Morrison, the guy with the foot injury."

"We'll do an X-ray," Priya said. Her voice had a Hindi lilt, but it was empty of warmth. "How are you feeling, Nick? Any pain right now?"

Sweat plastered Nick's hair to his forehead. His leg throbbed all the way up to his hip. Dr. Hofstadter had set a brisk pace as they moved through the hab. "I'm surviving, thanks. We're actually just here to pick up the supplies."

"The supplies?" Dr. Hofstadter echoed.

"Yeah. The food and suit spares and stuff," Maddy said.

"Food? Suit spares? ...*Stuff*?" Dr. Hofstadter seemed genuinely bemused.

"Their outpost is criminally underequipped, Dave," Priya said, as if the pair from Five Stones weren't standing right there.

"There ought to be a law against sending people to the moon without adequate prep and equipment."

Nick and Maddy had agreed not to mention the theft of plants from the Five Stones greenhouse unless the ILI people brought it up first. "Our supply situation was impacted by the Tranquility 13 incident," Nick said. "I'm sure you heard about that."

"Yes, of course," Dr. Hofstadter said. "It was the cryocooling systems, wasn't it?"

"That's what they said, yeah."

"Destroyed half of our supplies," Maddy said.

"You've had very bad luck, I understand that," Dr. Hofstadter said. "But I'm afraid we really can't spare you anything. Our supply drops are designed to meet the needs of our own teams."

"It costs $200,000 to land one kilogram on the moon," Priya said. Nick knew that figure well. The Little Sling had already shaved twenty percent off it. The Big Sling would halve it again. *If* they ever got it finished.

"Our company is going to pay you back, as far as I understand," Nick said. "Is there some problem with that?"

Dr. Hofstadter shook his head, suddenly less authoritative, just a scientist harassed by responsibilities that had nothing to do with his work. "I don't understand. All I was told is that someone had an injury. We agreed to offer you medical support. Nothing was said about giving you—giving you *stuff*."

"We talked with your base manager," Maddy said, her voice rising. "Yangsook?" They'd actually emailed, not talked. There was no protocol for radio communications between Shackleton and Amundsen craters, so they had to email via Earth. "She said you would have everything ready for us to pick up when we got here."

"Uh huh, uh huh." Dr. Hofstadter dragged his hands

through his graying hair. "I'll see if I can track her down and find out what's going on. In the meantime, let Priya have a look at your foot. She's very good."

Maddy followed Dr. Hofstadter out of sight around the privacy partition that closed off the clinic. Nick started after them, accidentally put his weight on his left foot, and nearly blacked out.

"I think you should let me examine that foot," Priya said dryly.

Nick submitted to an X-ray. The silence of the coffin-like cubicle was welcome after the noisy hab. He thought about Dr. Hofstadter's befuddled reaction. The geophysicist had been genuinely blindsided. Someone misrepresented Nick and Maddy's mission to him.

Nick's doubts about Kurtis—recently dormant—swirled back into his mind. Had Kurtis been lying about his email exchange with the ILI base manager? Nick had seen the emails, but that didn't mean they were real. Yangsook.k@il-i.gov could be anyone. She might not even exist. If Kurtis invented the whole thing—or *Aaron* had invented the whole thing—what could possibly be the purpose of it? Why send Nick and Maddy all this way on a wild-goose chase?

The answer came to him.

To get rid of them.

The X-ray cubicle hinged open. Nick climbed out.

Priya glared at her screen, where the X-ray of Nick's foot was displayed. "Fractures of the first and second metatarsals," she said. "Normally, an elastic dressing would give enough support for healing, as the other metatarsals act as splints. But there's significant displacement, probably because you walked on it. I'm going to recommend reduction, followed by casting."

"Reduction?"

"I'll need to set the bones. I'll give you a local anesthetic. How long have you been up here?"

"Eleven weeks."

"Then your bones are still in pretty good shape. The fractures should heal as quickly as they would on Earth."

"How long have *you* been up here?"

"One month, but it's my third time on the moon." Priya prepared a shot, frowning in concentration.

"How long do you guys usually stay?" Nick could taste the dust in the back of his throat. Feel it on his eyeballs. The first ILI outpost—a NASA outpost, at that time—had been planted here almost thirty years ago, and all they'd done since then was expand it, adding modules and infrastructure contributed by various national space agencies. The inhabitants were basically breathing a thirty-year accumulation of tracked-in dust. He didn't see how anyone could survive here for long.

"The scientists and support personnel, like me, stay for six weeks to two months. Most people are ready to go home after that. Aren't you?" Priya smiled crookedly at him.

Nick smiled back. "I was wondering about the ArxaSys Lunar contractors."

"Oh, them." Priya's smile vanished. "We don't see much of them. The science track and the ISRU track are separate. It's an artificial distinction, in some ways, but it protects the integrity of the science."

"But ISRU *is* science," Nick said.

"No, it isn't. It's engineering," Priya said crisply.

Nick backtracked. "I was just wondering how long the contractors stay? On average?"

Priya rolled her eyes. "As long as they like. Some of them have been up here for years."

"Really?"

"It's up to them. If they want to renew their contracts, they do. The private sector doesn't give a damn about bone density loss, radiation risks, or any other kind of risks, apparently. Well, you would know all about that." She uncapped her syringe. "Roll up your pant leg."

"I think I'll skip the shot," Nick said.

"Scared of needles?"

"No, it's just..." He shook his head.

She sighed in exasperation. "If I don't give you the shot, it's going to hurt."

"I can deal."

She threw the syringe into the medical waste bin. "Last of the bloody tough guys. What is it about the moon that attracts idiots like you?"

Nick forced a laugh. "I guess it's the biggest challenge there is."

"Yeah. That's one pattern. Then there're the ones who come up here to get away from something."

Nick instantly thought of Maddy, though he didn't know why. "Yeah."

"And then there's a few people, not many, thank God, like Dave. He *loves* it up here."

Nick flinched. The corner of his mouth twisted in the opposite of a smile.

Priya studied him cynically. "You, too, huh?"

The intercrater highlands popped back into his mind. The arid splendor of the landscape. The silence. The near-holy sense of solitude. He said—defensively, uncertainly: "Well, it's beautiful up here."

"Beautiful. That's what you think?" Without warning, she grabbed his foot and twisted.

35

Maddy came back while Nick was adjusting the fit of his new cast. Priya had printed it on the spot from lightweight plastic. Bungee cords ran through little holes in the top of the cast, like shoelaces.

"Look," Nick said. He stood up, arms outspread.

Setting the bones had hurt more than breaking them in the first place, but he could feel the difference inside his foot—a sense of rightness where there had been an inflamed mass of wrongness before.

Priya rolled her eyes. "Don't walk on it—though I don't know why I bother, you will anyway. Do you want pain medication? No, of course you don't. Get out of here."

Maddy slid her arm through Nick's elbow and dragged him away. In a low voice, she said, "Yangsook doesn't know anything about it. She never got our emails. She's talking to Luxembourg now, but what do you want to bet they don't know anything about it, either?"

Nick remembered his conclusions in the silence of the X-ray cubicle. "Kurtis set us up."

"Or Aaron did."

"Yeah." Kurtis could have easily been Aaron's unwitting dupe. On the other hand, there was an advantage for Kurtis in sending Nick and Maddy to ILI. Two less mouths to feed. "Could be the rover was *meant* to break down. We were never supposed to get here at all."

"Jesus, you have a twisted mind."

"Am I wrong?"

"You're wrong about Kurtis, anyway. He guessed the situation was hinky. We talked about it before we left."

"I know—"

"No, he talked to *me* about it."

Suddenly, Nick remembered Maddy coming out of Kurtis's room. He'd thought she was just borrowing his rucksack—the same rucksack she now clutched to her chest as they squeezed around the partitions.

"Yup. He figured there was a chance they'd back out of the deal or find some excuse to not give us anything. He said if that happens, just take what we need."

"Just *take* it?"

"Right." Maddy's cheeks were flushed. Her eyes flicked from right to left. She was patrolling through the ILI hab as if it were hostile jungle. Her left arm held the rucksack, and her right hand was free to punch, jab, or snatch.

"We can't just *take* shit," Nick said.

"Why not?"

"Because... because there's about fifty of them and two of us." Nick offered the most obvious practical objection, since she'd clearly already dismissed the moral ones. And who was he to object to stealing on moral grounds, anyway?

"Not about numbers out here," Maddy said. "It's about who wants it more."

"Maybe. But here's the other problem. We've had the grand tour of this place." They were presently edging through a module half filled with fish tanks. A man and a woman tended the dimly lit aquariums, chatting in Italian. Fish mouthed at the glass. "Where's the stuff? Have you seen anything that looks like ration packages? Or suit spares? Electronic components? We can't take it if we can't find it."

"Um. Point," Maddy said.

"There you are." Dr. Hofstadter rejoined them. "I can't understand how this happened. There has to be some explanation."

"I'm sure there is," Nick said.

"We've requested clarification from Earth. But I can't promise immediate answers. Everything we do here has to be signed off on by seventeen government agencies in eight countries. Things sometimes—sometimes slip through the cracks."

"I understand," Nick said.

"I'm sorry we can't be of more help. You're welcome to stay here until they get back to us," Dr. Hofstadter said.

Maddy's fingers dug into Nick's arm. Nick shook her off. "Can we just top up the fuel cell of our rover? We were into the red when we got here. If you can't spare us some oxygen, at least, you're gonna be stuck with us for good." He tried to smile.

"Oxygen? That shouldn't be a problem. No, we can certainly do that."

"And water and food for the drive back?" Maddy pressed. Nick knew she was hoping to find out where the rations were stored.

"Well, you'll have to talk to Joe about that." They were back in the geology lab. "And here he is."

A lean, scruffy man stared into an electron microscope. He might have been an Arab or an Italian, or Israeli, or South American. He had thick eyebrows, an air of intent concentration, and on his right cheek a scar of the type that was attractive to women.

221

"Joe, these are our visitors from Five Stones," Dr. Hofstadter said. "This is Joe Massad, the ArxaSys Lunar project manager."

Joe looked up and smiled broadly. The scar twisted. "Might have found an iridium-rich meteor."

"Where?" Dr. Hofstadter said.

"Halfway to Sverdrup." Joe named a crater fifty kilometers to the north on the far side of the moon. "If it's a big one, we might need both rovers to bring it back home."

"Do what you have to do."

"We will." Joe shut down his machine and removed the sample. Puzzled by the odd vibe of hostility between Joe and Dr. Hofstadter, Nick looked from one man to the other and back again. "Anyway," Joe said, "what can I do for you guys?" Nick explained. "LOX? Not a problem. We're drowning in the stuff."

"I'll let you know if we hear from Earth," Dr. Hofstadter said.

They passed through the decontamination module again. "This system doesn't really work." Joe sighed. He had a slight, unplaceable accent. "Which are your suits?"

"The ones with all the patches," Nick said.

Joe laughed. "My patches are more badass than your patches." He showed them a suit with a shield and spear logo on the chest, which Nick now recognized as the ArxaSys logo, and a strip of epoxy-bonded Kevlar across one side of the faceplate. It matched up with the scar on Joe's cheek. "I did that while I was out on a rover run. Fixed it on the spot with duct tape."

They went back out into the stark landscape of sunlight and shadows. To Nick it was a relief after the crowded conditions, the noise, and the bad air inside the hab complex.

"Wesley! Come in. Where you at, man?" Joe said.

"Yo," a voice crackled over the radio. "I'm at the plant."

"Can you take these guys' machine up there and top it off?"

"Roger that."

Joe extended a glove in Nick and Maddy's direction. "If you don't mind me saying so, the both of you have got to be wiped out. Come and hang with us while Wez takes care of your machine." He did a Count Chocula voice. "Ve haff cookies."

Joe seemed friendly, it was just... he worked for ArxaSys Lunar. Nick started to decline the invitation, but Maddy spoke first. "Sure, that sounds amazing. Lead on," she said, with the same bubbly verve she'd shown to Dr. Hofstadter when she thought *he* had what she wanted.

Nick gritted his teeth and braced his crutch in the armpit of his suit. He hadn't had much trouble getting the suit on over the cast, as it was paper-thin and custom-fitted to the contours of his foot. The suit's compression, on the other hand, was not kind. He limped after Joe and Maddy around the perimeter of the hab complex. Dust wept from the sides of the regolith berms. A buggy crawled out of the distance with people clinging like fat gray bugs to its frame.

The nearest of the repurposed landers hulked over them. From its airlock, high above the ground, sprouted a rigid structure like a fully enclosed flight of air stairs. The stairs ended in the vehicle airlock Trig pointed out to them earlier. It was a pressurized module, mounted on treads, with a suit port on either side and a vehicle docking hatch at the end.

"Trig said we couldn't use this," Maddy said.

"The mobile vehicle docking assembly?" Joe said. "He probably thought it wouldn't work with your machine. ESA never put that model into production. Who'd you get to make it for you? Toyota? Yeah. They changed the hatch specs after that."

The buggy they'd seen earlier bumped up to the mobile vehicle docking assembly. The rider and passengers spilled off. They greeted Joe in American, British, Australian, and non-native accents. The chatter on the public channel could for the first time be matched to visible human beings, even though the construction workers were all indistinguishable inside their dust-colored suits and scratched, gold faceplates. One of them came up to Nick, Maddy, and Joe.

"How'd it work out? Did they give you anything?"

Nick recognized Katniss Reyes's voice. "No. Not even a drink of water," he said.

36

"They're assholes," Kat said. Her faceplate stared blankly at Nick and Maddy, reflecting their own helmets. "Maybe I'm being too harsh. They're *tourists*. Do their six weeks and go back to Earth."

"How long have you been here?" Nick asked.

"I'm in the one-year club," she said. "But some people have been here three, four years."

"Guilty as charged," Joe said.

"You aren't concerned about radiation?" Nick said.

"The landers are shielded," Joe said. "If a big solar flare hits, we'd shelter in the reactor room."

They were close enough to the radiator vanes of the reactor to see that the base of the vertical truss supporting them was a solid dome. An airlock pimpled out from it. Someone stood outside, operating the hatch. Nick had the impression—nothing more than an intuition at this distance—that it was Trig. Joe gently grasped his elbow and urged him into the shadow of the MVDA. Their suits mated to the suitlocks with soft sighs.

Inside, the air smelled of chemical outgassing, but it was amazingly free from dust. They climbed the stairs into the lower module of the lander. It would have held cargo when the lander was in operation. Now it contained folding chairs, cots, and a table stocked with snack bars and drinks. Defaced motivational posters and a TV hung on the wall. The gaudy graphics of the news broadcast playing on the screen looked unnatural and slightly sickening. Nick glanced away. The off-duty contractors talked quietly, standing in front of the vents, cooling down and wolfing high-calorie snacks.

"This is about a thousand times nicer than the ILI hab," Maddy murmured.

"No kidding," Nick whispered. "I would have assumed it would be the other way round."

"Me too."

A young woman came in, shaking out red hair that almost reached her waist. "You can go on upstairs." Nick matched Kat's features with the indistinct face in Charlie's pictures of the greenhouse raid. She was prettier in person, but too thin, giving an impression of restless, strung-out hyperactivity.

Joe joined them in the upper module of the lander and lowered a hatch, sealing the module off from the noise of the communal break room below. He dropped onto a sofa in front of a low coffee table. Nick and Maddy sat opposite him.

Originally the lander's crew cabin, this module was bisected by a partition. This half appeared to be an office. As well as two sofas and the coffee table, it held an L-shaped desk with a four-monitor computer setup, an ancient radio comms console, a giant e-paper screen covered with memos and to-do lists, and a small galley. Kat went to the hot water dispenser. "Coffee?"

"Coffee?" Maddy said. "You're joking, right? Actual, freaking *coffee*? I think I love you."

"It's just instant," Kat said.

"Bring it on," Maddy said. "If I was offered a choice

between a cup of Nescafé and a trip back to Earth right now, the rocket would have to leave without me."

Joe laughed. "Kindred soul here."

"You might have heard we're short of supplies," Nick said, watching Kat's back. "Coffee is just one thing we're out of."

"I heard," Kat said, without turning around.

"Yeah, the Tranquility 13 thing," Joe said. "That was ridiculous. SpaceZ used to be an innovative company. They've commoditized moon delivery; now they're just a cheap company. Best wishes to your CEO. I hear he's going to sue the pants off them."

"That's right," Nick said. He accepted a mug of coffee from Kat and thanked her. The mug was the same style as the ones they had at Five Stones, with a lid and a little spout to drink out of. He held it up, looking at the ArxaSys logo on the side. "What kind of a company is ArxaSys Lunar? ILI doesn't make much noise about using contractors on the mass driver."

"That's not all we do," Joe said. "We fix things when they break down. Operate the oxygen plant. The mining robots. Maintain the habs. Service the Artemis shuttles. There isn't much we *don't* do, right, Kat? What else... The reactor, we operate the reactor—Basically, without us, everyone dies."

At the Five Stones base, they were all responsible for everything, with a limited amount of specialization naturally arising. Here, with ten times the number of people—most of them on short stays—it made sense that a semipermanent crew of professionals would have responsibility for infrastructure and operations.

"What kind of reactor do you have?" he said. "I didn't know you had one at all."

"ILI isn't *completely* stupid," Joe said with a grin. "The usual suspects would be up in arms. Nuclear power on the moon! They're imagining Fukushima. What we have is a small

Surface Fission Power System, about the size of a compact car. Generates four hundred kilowatts, with the option to scale up to six hundred KW. It's safer than falling off a buggy."

Nick caught Kat flinching. It was a quick shiver, as if her whole face and body had been wrenched sideways by an unseen hand. Just as quickly, her face returned to normal. She sat beside Joe, cradling her mug, hunched over her knees, her gaze roving over Nick and Maddy with an intense, opaque scrutiny that didn't quite read as hostile.

"It's all about image with ILI," Joe continued. "They have to make everything look good for the stakeholders. The public. Eight different governments, God save us. ArxaSys is in the same position. It's a big multinational with a specialized lunar surface operations subsidiary. They're under less pressure from the public, but the cost-cutting mentality is psychopathic. Every single kilo of cargo mass has to get signed off on by three different budget oversight committees, and if there's any conflict, ILI wins. Every time.

"You saw my suit. I've had an application in for a replacement for more than a year. The knee joints of Kat's suit keep locking up. My demolitions guy, Evan, his glasses broke and he had to mend them with duct tape, yet the scientists have their disposable contact lenses specially shipped up. We get stiffed on our basic calorie needs because someone needs a new fucking seismometer. That's where their priorities are at." Joe's dark gray eyes gripped Nick's gaze with palpable intensity. He was one of those people who sucked all the oxygen out of a room. "If I didn't look out for my crew, we would literally be starving."

"That's kind of the position we're in," Nick said quietly.

Joe sat back and flung his arm along the back of the couch, behind Kat's shoulder. Shrewdly, he said, "Dave gave you the runaround, huh?"

"You got it."

"What'd he say?"

"Don't know anything, never heard anything, must've slipped through the cracks. Yangsook said the same."

"I would guess that no one ever contacted them from your end," Joe said. "The whole thing... I dunno, it just doesn't sound kosher to me. You know how much it costs to ship one kilogram to the moon?"

"Two hundred thousand dollars," Maddy said in a tone that implied they'd been given the speech.

"And we were just supposed to *give* you, what, a couple tonnes of rations and electronics?"

"And suit spares," Maddy said.

"Ha! If we had any suit spares, I wouldn't be walking around with a cracked faceplate. My point is, if Aaron doesn't have the dough to buy a flight from a launch provider, I don't think he has the dough to go shopping here, either."

Nick said, "You know him?"

"Aaron? I met him about ten years ago, when he was still at SpaceZ. I could tell he was going places. Could also tell he was the kind of guy who'd do... this."

"Do what?" Maddy said.

Joe grimaced. "Better to ask for forgiveness than permission, right?" He jolted forward, half rising with the momentum of the movement. It was so sudden, Nick flinched despite himself. "He send you here to raid us? Is that it?" Joe yelled.

Nick glanced at Maddy, willing her silent. "No. Jeez. If we'd been sent here to raid you, would they send the guy with the broken foot?"

"Deflect suspicion," Joe said. "Win sympathy."

"Right. I can tell you're *so* sorry for us," Nick said. "You've already told us you don't give a shit about anyone except your own crew."

Joe remained immobile, considering Nick with his intense

gray eyes. Then he smiled. "If I came off like an asshole, I apologize."

Kat suddenly giggled. The reaction seemed so out of place, Nick stared at her. She'd locked her hands around her elbows and was swaying slightly back and forth. The image came to him of a Cape Cobra under the table in the kitchen, swaying back and forth, its flat head level with the three-year-old Nick's eyes. His mother had killed it with a cast-iron frying pan. He repressed a shudder.

"I *like* what you guys are doing," Joe said earnestly. "The Big Sling is revolutionary. It's a stake through the heart of the standard lunar narrative. Way overdue. So Aaron got out over his skis? It was bound to happen. The whole industry—the whole *world* is against him. But you shouldn't have to pay for it." He sprang to his feet. "What do you need? We'll hook you up."

Nick stayed sitting. "You don't need to talk to Dr. Hofstadter?"

"Nope," Joe said, already moving toward the hatch.

Nick held Maddy back as the ArxaSys Lunar pair descended the ladder ahead of them. "Don't say anything," he whispered. "Let's just get the stuff and get out of here. Don't fuck it up."

"Where are our *fucking plants*?" she whispered back.

"I was gonna bring it up, but maybe not." Kat scared him, although he didn't know exactly why. "Let's just see what they're gonna give us."

37

From the break room below Joe's office, they crossed via mated docking hatches to another of the landers. This one was an open-plan office. Shaggy, bearded contractors leaned around their screens to shoot wisecracks at the visitors.

Joe swooped down on one man who was eating a sandwich. "Sharing is caring," he said. He tore a second sandwich in half and gave it to Nick and Maddy. Nick sniffed.

"Bread?"

"We get the mix in our shipments. You just rehydrate it and put it in the machine."

Nick took a bite. He pulled out a scrap of green from the rehydrated egg salad filling. Fresh lettuce.

"Vic, Andy, Maria, Jean-Paul," Joe yelled. "Need some help carrying stuff."

Four people rose and followed Joe, Nick, and Maddy through to the lower module of the next lander. It was a warehouse. Boxes and sacks of consumables and spare parts filled the room to overflowing.

"So *this* is where it's all at," Maddy whispered.

Nick wondered why Joe complained about shortages. It looked like the contractors had everything.

"Wez recharged your rover," Joe said. "We'll bring that down to the MVDA, and the guys'll help you load this stuff onto your trailer." He pointed at boxes. The contractors began carrying them back the way they'd come. "Hamburger mix, egg powder, milk powder, soy cereal—That'll keep you going. Want some of the bread mix? You might be able to bake it in the microwave, even if it might come out kind of flat. Anything else?"

"Components," Nick said. "ASICs, image sensors, motion sensors, display driver ICs. Displays of whatever size you can spare. Lenses. Saw blades. Engine controllers. CO_2 filters. Epoxy. Rope. O-rings..."

Joe was already shaking his head. "That stuff is in high demand, man. Sorry."

"Guess you need it."

"That's right," Joe said, his gaze cool.

"All right."

"You're thinking I'm holding out on you because you're the competition. The Big Sling's gonna put us out of a job."

"It's not personal," Nick said.

"No, no, man, let me finish. First of all, I don't believe in competition on the moon. We're all in this together. Second of all, I admit I was kind of pissed when I first heard about the Big Sling. After all the years put into our project. All that money down the hole.

"But the more I think about it, the more I like the idea. If you can cut the cost of lunar launches by ninety percent, like Aaron says—fucking go for it! Then we wouldn't be in this situation to start with. And looking further out, it's essential if colonization is ever going to happen. *Both* halves of your project are essential. Affordable lunar launch and a sustainable biosphere.

What you're actually working on over there is a roadmap to colonization."

"Colonization," said Maria, a stout dark girl carrying a crate on one shoulder. "Now that's a word I haven't heard for a while." All the contractors laughed.

Joe shrugged ruefully. "I'm big on colonization. Isn't that the whole *point*?"

"Guess it is," Nick said. Again, he recalled the intercrater highlands, hills carved by the solar wind into curves as delicate as a Michelangelo. He felt a hopeless yearning for something he couldn't put into words.

"The moon's got everything we need," Joe said. "Except this stuff." He waved at the Aladdin's cave of supplies around them. "*Carbon.* Fortunately, there's more CO in the bottom of Shackleton Crater than there is water. Heck, that's been known going all the way back to the LCROSS mission. It's trapped in the ice-rich regolith and we've been letting it boil off, but that's just crazy. We should be capturing it and using it to make plastics. Ever heard of the Fischer-Tropsch process? We've built an experimental F-T reactor. That's where my iridium-rich meteor comes in."

"Right, I was wondering about that," Nick said.

"I'm not especially interested in iridium per se, but an asteroid rich in iridium probably has some cerium along for the ride. We won't know for sure until we haul it home and test it. But that's the theory. And cerium can be used as a catalyst in the Fischer-Tropsch process."

Nick laughed. "And they say ISRU isn't science."

"Right? God, I get sick of hearing that. These people act like they have a monopoly on the moon, but their narrative is stuck in the twentieth century. Water, water, water. That's *all* Dave talks about. The Mars crowd are obsessed with water, too. Water is *everywhere*! We should be focusing on carbon. Nickel.

Rare earth elements. Helium-3 is a potential high-value export in the future." Nick opened his mouth but Joe spoke first. "I know what you're thinking, but don't. Helium-3 fusion is never going to happen, but it does have other uses. Radioisotope diagnostics. Radiation detectors. And it's a *waste product* of melting lunar rock. You guys are extracting He-3 every day. You just need to capture it and centrifuge it."

"You should be running this place," Nick said.

Joe gave him a closed-lipped smile. "There are a lot of dead bodies littering the halls of electrometallurgy, organic chemistry, even geophysics. Perfectly good processes that were killed off by the search for something newer and sexier. Fischer-Tropsch got dumped when synthetic diesel went out of style. But on the moon, even losers can dance."

While they were talking, Maddy had wandered into the middle of the warehouse module. She peered up at the closed hatch at the top of the ladder leading to the upper module. "What's up there?"

"Nothing," Joe said.

"It just dripped on me." Maddy rubbed her fingers over her forehead. "Something's leaking."

"Kat's up there. She'll take care of it," Joe said.

"Oh, perfect. I want to talk with her, anyway." Maddy started up the ladder.

All the contractors made a concerted movement toward her. The man named Vic got there first. "Come down off of there, honey."

Halfway up the ladder, hugging Kurtis's rucksack with one arm, Maddy said, "Why? Is there something up there we're not supposed to see?"

The hatch whirred open and Kat looked down. Her head and shoulders were framed by a softly lit aureole of green dapples.

Maddy sprang up the last few rungs and pushed Kat out of the way. Both women vanished into the greenish brightness.

Nick moved as fast as he could. Joe beat him to the ladder. Nick climbed up after him, crutch tucked under one arm, in a succession of one-armed pull-ups. Someone grabbed at his ankle. He kicked them away and boosted himself into the upper module.

The aeroponics trays from the Five Stones greenhouse carpeted the floor. Grow lights filled the module with a fairytale radiance that started from the floor and tangled the shadows of hoses drooping from the ceiling. One of the hoses was leaking; water puddled on the floor. Each tray sprouted lush crops. Blueberries, tomatoes, salad greens, marrows, dwarf wheat, runner beans. Cannabis.

Nick blundered across the module, pausing to roll a leaf between his fingers here, check a moisture readout there.

Kat stood with her back to the wall, her thin arms folded across her chest. Maddy faced her, one hand bunched in the fabric of the rucksack, calling her a fucking bitch and a liar.

"OK, OK," Joe said.

"You accused us of coming to raid you. *You* raided *us*!"

Nick spun around at a noise. Trigger McLean was climbing into the module.

Trig kicked the hatch shut behind him. "You're going for a long walk off a short pier, mate." He lumbered toward Nick, hands loosely fisted. His face looked like a three-car pileup.

"Wait, wait, wait. Everyone, cool down. Cool down!" Joe said.

"Fuck you," Maddy spat.

Nick expected Trig to make a move. He reversed his grip on his crutch. It wasn't much of a weapon, but it was all he had.

"Let's knock 'em off, Joe," Trig grunted, keeping his distance, watching Nick and Maddy with slitted eyes.

"It's not *their* fault," Joe said. "They don't even know about the deal."

"What deal?" Maddy said.

"Aaron's deal with ILI."

"Well, one of you really needs to start talking!" Nick said.

Joe nodded somberly. "We don't know all the details, either—"

"Yes, we do," Kat interrupted, eyes gleaming. "They probably told you that Five Stones is going to sell the Big Sling's launch capacity on the open market, right? *Wrong.* ILI has bought it all up in advance."

"What for?" Maddy said.

Joe shot Kat a quelling look. She hesitated and then said, "So this place can start paying for itself, of course. That's what the mass driver was supposed to do. But your technology is better."

"Cruder... but better," Joe murmured.

"What's in it for Five Stones?" Maddy said. "Money, I guess."

"That's right," Kat said. "ILI offered them a deal they couldn't refuse."

"Also keeps them viable," Joe murmured. "Don't forget ILI is a *government* agency."

"Why can't Five Stones even scrape together enough cash to send us a resupply flight?" Nick said.

"Payable on completion," Joe said. "Doh. I think they gave them a small down payment."

Kat giggled. "SpaceZ, Blue Horizon, High Frontier, Near Earth Resources, all those guys are gonna be shut out. They think they're going to get cheap oxygen for interplanetary missions. They're wrong. You can see why Aaron is keeping it quiet, can't you? If this got out, he would have *no* friends left."

"How come you guys know about it?" Nick said.

"We operate ILI's comms," Joe said. "They had to get Dave's buy-in, so we saw those emails."

"If you can read all their emails, what happened to our emails to Yangsook?" Maddy said.

"We keep telling you," Kat said. "There *weren't* any. No one emailed anyone from your end, except about his foot."

"Oh, whatever," Maddy said. "Just give us our plants back."

"Let it go, Maddy," Nick said.

If she pissed Joe and his crew off beyond the point of no return, they wouldn't get anything. Nick didn't trust the contractors, either, but at least they had to stay on good terms with them. There was no help to be had on the moon apart from what was right here, and they might need help again in the future.

"They keep the plants," he said. "They give us supplies in exchange. That's fair enough—"

"Fuck that," Maddy said. Her hand came out of the folds of Kurtis's rucksack holding a gun. She pointed it at Joe's chest. "I'm a United States Marine. Don't think for one *fucking* second I don't know how to use this. We clear?"

38

Joe stood frozen. The leaky hose dripped. Trig's mouth hung open. Kat's face twitched.

"You're giving the fucking plants back," Maddy said. She swung to point her gun at Trig. "You, big guy. Start packing up the trays."

Nick's heart hammered. His mind was blank. Images dropped into it like stones falling into water. Ryder Stillman's SIG Sauer nudging the skin of his neck. The grit of a Florida parking lot scraping his knees and forearms. The weight of Harriet Fitzgerald's Glock. The oil-scented heat under the semi-trailer. The kick. The fear. A long black pistol in long brown hands inching around the kitchen door. Thunder echoing through the farmhouse, across the parking lot, through his head, across the years, blasting through his whole life like a bullet through sheetrock.

He crossed to Maddy in two swift steps, wrapped his left arm around her shoulders, and closed his right hand over the barrel of the gun. She hadn't expected that. He twisted the gun toward his own body, bending her right wrist backward. She let go and he elbowed her away. She stumbled and went to her hands and knees on top of a tray of spinach. The gun settled into Nick's grip with uncanny familiarity. It was a Glock, identical to the one he'd flung into the floodwaters outside the Wumart, except it had an extended grip and trigger guard.

"Everyone, relax," he said, pointing it at the floor. "We're leaving."

"How the *hell* did you smuggle a gun up to the moon?" Joe said.

"It belongs to our mission commander." Maddy picked herself up. "He lent it to me because he had a feeling you guys would turn out to be assholes."

Nick's hands were trembling. When Maddy scrambled toward him, he brusquely waved her back with the gun. He was afraid she would shoot someone. He wouldn't, so it was safer for him to have it.

"Damn, man," Joe said.

"Have your guys finished loading the supplies into our rover?" Nick barked.

"Yeah, but—"

"And the components I asked for! Tell them to load that shit, too. Everything you can spare, and everything you can't." He remembered the blue sparks of an underwater cutting torch spreading through floodwaters in Georgia. Florida. New Jersey. Louisiana. Safe doors falling open. The dim gleam of gold bars. *Heck, it's illegal to possess this much physical specie, anyway. If the government found this, they'd confiscate it. We're just doing their job for them.* He heard Ryder cackling in his mind. "None of this shit is yours, anyway. It belongs to the government. The *governments.*"

Joe cast him an unreadable look and went to the top of the ladder. He yelled down for the contractors to load a bunch of robot repair kits. That sounded like the right kind of thing. If it wasn't, there was nothing Nick could do about it. He kept the gun trained on Kat because he figured Joe valued her. They were almost certainly sleeping together. As for Trig, he wouldn't lift a finger without Joe's say-so.

"We shouldn't be fighting like this," Joe said. "Think about the long term. If we're ever gonna make a place of our own up here..."

The words plucked with unexpected force at Nick. *A place of his own.* A place where he could be alone. Right now, that sounded better than ten million dollars.

"Save it," he said. "I'm gonna do my job, get paid, and go home. And no one's gonna stop me."

"Go home? Go *home?*" Joe was laughing. "Oh, man. They're never gonna let you go home. Don't you know that?"

Maddy made a lunge at Nick. She chopped the side of her hand down on his left wrist. His fingers sprang open in an involuntary reflex. She snatched the gun back. "Now load the motherfucking plants!" she shouted.

"Fucking stop it!" Nick shouted. His wrist stung, making him angry. "The trays won't all fit in our rover, anyway!"

Her eyes darted. He saw her realizing he was right. "What the fuck ever. Cover my six and get your crutch." She shouted at Joe, "You guys go down the ladder first."

Maddy kept Kat in front of her as they moved through the landers. The Glock was never more than six inches from the younger woman's back. Nick shuffled behind them, holding his crutch like a stave, jabbing the end in the direction of the shocked faces that lined the modules.

Joe followed them down the stairs into the cold, gusty belly of the MVDA. Kat twisted her head around and looked back, her face a white diamond of fear.

Maddy prodded her shoulder blade with the Glock. "Nick, make sure everything's on the rover. I'll stay here until you give me the all clear."

Nick reflected that she would be in danger. Even though the rover was docked with the MVDA, she would have to turn her back on the contractors in order to clamber through the docking hatch. But after what Kat told them, he didn't think any of the contractors, even Trig, really wanted to hurt the Five Stones crew. Their outrage was emotional and political, directed against their own organization, which had thrown them under the bus in the name of cutting costs.

He limped to the suitlocks. During the flurry of action, he'd walked on his left foot without noticing it. Now it hurt abominably. He turned to Joe and asked quietly, "Why did you say they're never gonna let us go home?"

"Oh," Joe said. "In exec-speak, you're a depreciating asset. That's why they let us renew our contracts ad infinitum. It's cheaper than training and sending up someone new. Also—" he smiled, convulsing his scar— "this way, they don't have to pay you."

Nick got into his suit. Leaning on the MVDA and then the rover, he limped around the back of the trailer, surveying the boxes and crates efficiently stacked and tied down with bungee webbing. He couldn't tell exactly what was there, but one crate said *Mining Robot Change Kits (All Models)*. It would have to do.

He removed Maddy's suit from the MVDA, dragged it to the rover and plugged it into one of the suitlocks. Climbing onto the rear step of the rover, he sealed his own suit to the other lock. *Click, hiss, beep.* He fell backward into the cabin. Light streamed in through the docking hatch from the MVDA.

"Looks good," he shouted.

Shadows bulged and jittered. There was a thump, a feminine cry, and then Maddy somersaulted into the rover, immediately whisking around on her knees to seal the hatch.

"What happened?" Nick said.

"Bitch tried to grab my gun." She was still holding it as she plunged into the passenger seat. "No damage done. Just drive, *drive!* You got my suit, right?"

"Yes."

"Then *what* are we waiting for?"

The headlamps pinioned someone in an ILI spacesuit. He or she was gesticulating at the rover. Nick frantically stabbed the channel seeker.

"—*take* that! We need it!"

"Here we go again," Nick said.

"I gave it to them," Joe said. "You got a problem with that, Dave?"

The name cued recognition of Dr. Hofstadter's voice. It was now thick and distorted with anger, and most likely fear. "How are you going to account for the missing items?"

"I'll say you used them," Joe said.

Three ArxaSys Lunar suits dropped off the MVDA, landed on their feet, and circled around into the rover's headlamps. They surrounded Dr. Hofstadter.

"*We* used all that?" Dr. Hofstadter gestured at the Five Stones rover and its trailer. "As if we had the chance! You barely give us enough food to stay alive—"

"Complain, complain," Joe said. "If you're not happy, go back to Earth. No one's stopping you."

One of the spacesuits turned to face the rover. "Get moving, mates," Trig said. "Sunshine here is getting out of the way." He threw an arm around Dr. Hofstadter's chest and dragged him out of the rover's path.

Nick punched the throttle. The rover, dragging the trailer, strained into motion. Nick swerved in a half circle, passing close to the radiator vanes of the power plant, and drove back toward the solar installation. The shoulder of the peak of eternal light hid the altercation behind them. Nick touched the radio, silencing Dr. Hofstadter's feeble protests.

"Wow," Maddy said. Her eyes were round. The gun lay forgotten on her lap. "Sounds like someone is in charge back there, and it is so *not* Dr. Hofstadter."

"Makes sense when you think about it."

"Yeah? How's that?"

Behind them, the radiator vanes caught the sun. "Joe literally has his finger on the nuclear button." *You should be running this place.* Nick had said it as a joke. And Joe said something back about dead bodies.

"But he doesn't have a gun," Maddy said, rallying. She picked up the Glock, pushed the magazine release, and dropped the bullets into her palm. She shook them like dice with a satisfied smirk. "That'll teach them to fuck with the US Marine Corps."

Nick erupted. "I've never seen anything that *stupid* in my life. What were you thinking? Were you even thinking at all? You pulled a fucking *gun* on them! You could have killed someone! Could have gotten us killed!" He turned from the controls and made a grab for the now-unloaded Glock.

Maddy snatched it out of his reach and jammed the flat of her other hand against his chest, pushing him away. "*You're* the stupid one! The last thing on earth I expected was that my own backup would jump me! Seriously, the hell? What was the big idea? If this was the Corps, I would make you get out of this rover and *walk* home!"

"Are you still in the Corps, Maddy?"

"The fuck?"

"Are you working for the government? You here to make sure we don't screw up Aaron's deal with ILI?"

Sheer incredulity wiped the anger off Maddy's face. "That is so absurd I don't even know how to respond."

"Yes or no?"

"If I was working for the government, I'm not doing a very good job, am I?"

Nick laughed. "True." After a second, Maddy laughed, too.

"That's exactly what I thought about Kurtis at first," she said. "I thought he was still working for Uncle Sam in some capacity. He's totally the spy type. Always the clean-cut, right-stuff one, am I right? He isn't, though. What you see really is what you get with him. He quit. And I—I quit, too."

"Why?"

Maddy stared out the windshield. They were bumping around the rim of Shackleton Crater. She squeezed her fistful of bullets with a noise like teeth clicking. "I killed someone."

"I thought that's what they paid you to do."

"Ha... No. I killed someone I wasn't supposed to."

"Who?"

"My commanding officer. *God*, that bitch." She glared at Nick. "This is just between us, got it? They told her folks she died in action. But they suspected what really happened, so I was out with a dishonorable. That's why I couldn't find anything else apart from personal protection for the rich and paranoid. Until this."

Nick was silent for a moment. "All we need now is to find out that Lee and Theo are in the pay of the Russians."

Maddy let out a whoop. Nick hadn't thought it was that funny, but now laughter bubbled up in his chest. They both laughed until tears came.

"Actually, Lee is a little shady," Maddy said, calming down. "He used to dabble in hacking."

"Seriously? Black-hat stuff?"

"I'm not sure. His job was in like, data security, antivirus stuff, so he naturally kind of scootched over to the dark side. I really don't understand that stuff."

"Makes sense," Nick said, thinking of Lee's expertise in steganography. He was a little surprised Lee had opened up about his past, not to Nick, but to Maddy. He'd probably been trying to impress her. "What about Theo, then? The Norwegian mafia?"

They laughed some more, until Maddy said, "What about you, Nick? What's your dark secret?"

"Don't have one," Nick said.

"Oh, come on."

"I told you about my fun times in the diving industry. That's as dark as it gets. Sorry."

Maddy's nostrils flared. Pettishly, she said, "Well, you don't have any experience with guns, anyway. The way you were holding that piece, you would have been more likely to kill someone than I was."

———

High in the intercrater highlands, the rover bumped along a ridge between two lakes of darkness, following its own outbound tracks. Maddy slept. Nick leaned his elbows on the steering yoke, his hands locked in front of his mouth. The arid, serene landscape was a cathedral in basalt, olivine, and ilmenite, commanding awe and respect. But the thoughts crawling through Nick's mind were filthy things.

This way, they don't have to pay you.

39

Joe dragged Kat to the reactor. The nearer of the twenty-meter radiator vanes hung overhead like a guillotine blade. Their boots tracked dust onto the Mylar apron that covered the ground to lower the sink temperature of the vacuum.

Dr. Hofstadter followed them at a distance. "You had no right to give them that stuff!"

"I wouldn't have had to, if *you'd* given it to them," Joe said.

"I thought you wouldn't like it," Dr. Hofstadter said gruffly.

Joe smiled at that. Kat sensed his distraction and tried to jerk away. Joe stumbled, recovered, and tightened his grip on the arm of her suit.

"How are we going to replace everything?" Dr. Hofstadter moaned.

"*You'll* contact Earth," Joe said. "Tell them to leave some of the scientific instruments out of the next launch and send us food and basic parts instead. This would also be a good time for them to send that printer."

He'd been angling for a new 3D printer for more than a year. He wanted to start printing components from regolith. Luxembourg refused to play ball. 3D printing wasn't cutting-edge science, and they didn't buy Joe's fancy justifications for why he needed to do it at scale. Even requesting the printer was risky. But at the rate events were moving, it was a risk he needed to take.

So was this.

The truss towered above them. He pulled Kat into the airlock and sealed the chamber. Air jetted out of the vents. Kat gripped him by the shoulders and stretched up so their face-plates touched.

"We should have killed them!" she shrieked. She wasn't using the radio. The layers of gold and polycarbonate plastic conducted sound through their helmets. Her voice reached Joe's ears as a muffled buzz. "Why didn't you let Trig kill them?"

He bent his head, grinding their faceplates together. "Do you think I'm some kind of monster?"

"They saw too much!"

"Whose fault was that? Why did you open the hatch?"

"I just wanted to see—"

"And then you told them about the deal? What made you think *that* was a good idea?"

Kat's voice was still distant and muffled, and her faceplate opaque, but her jerky movements betrayed near-hysteria. "I wanted to see how they would react. It would have been good to know if *they* know about—"

"They sure as shit do now."

"I thought we were going to kill them, so it wouldn't matter, anyway!"

Joe pushed her away. He chin-pressed his radio on. "I have nothing to say to you. Think about what you did, and let me know when you're sorry."

He levered the other end of the airlock open. The reactor room yawned below. It was a circular cavern sunk into the regolith, walled with sheet aluminum; the airlock opened onto a catwalk seven meters above the floor. A blunt concrete cylinder, the cap of the reactor's radiation shield, stuck up from one side of the room. The core was buried even deeper underground.

From the reactor cap, pipes ran across the floor, carrying superheated sodium-potassium to the twin Stirling converters that occupied most of the floor space. Even with his helmet on, the hum of their vibration reached him and the basso throb of the coolant pumps rose up through his boots into his chest. A feeling of loneliness, regret... *terror,* began to grip him.

He shoved Kat out onto the catwalk. She clawed at his arms. "Please. No. *Please—*"

Joe pried her off and slammed the hatch. Three minutes later he was back out on the surface, breathing heavily.

Dr. Hofstadter was still there.

"Would you fucking go away," Joe shouted at him.

He gazed out along the connecting ridge that stretched to de Gerlache crater, letting the stillness and serenity of the lunar landscape stabilize his emotions. He'd fallen in love with the moon at first sight. The barren, timeless solitude of these hills reminded him of the landscape of his early childhood: the desert in eastern Israel that used to be the shore of the Dead Sea.

Joe had never seen the Dead Sea itself. By the time of his earliest memories, it had dried up into a mud puddle, leaving salt flats baked white by the Middle Eastern sun. The vanished sea haunted Joe's family like the ghost of a murdered ancestor. His mother, an Israeli, inherited a guesthouse that used to overlook the healing waters. When the Dead Sea dried up, their livelihood dried up with it.

Joe had known nothing about this as a small child. He'd played contentedly in the empty parking lot of the guesthouse and pretended to drive an abandoned bus, its back wheels trapped in a sinkhole. To him, the desert was beautiful.

So was the moon. The ridge before him had been levelled

and graded by machinery, shaped for human purposes. It was no longer untouched. Yet he now knew the landscape of his early memories had *also* been shaped by humanity. Climate change had doomed the Dead Sea, and the Israeli and Jordanian governments failed, culpably, to build the Red-Dead Sea canal that might have saved it.

Human concupiscence was killing Earth. Human ingenuity, in contrast, was bringing the moon alive. The earthmovers toiling in the distance could not spoil the lunar landscape—there was nothing *to* spoil. They were improving it for future generations.

On the horizon, at klick three of the mass driver rail loop, a slight upswelling of brightness marked Mount Hope, the hill through which they were presently cutting a tunnel. The tunnel was half a kilometer long so far, and wider than the rail loop required, with a couple of side tunnels that appeared on no blueprints and were invisible to radar. Joe had been allowed to name the hill himself because it looked so insignificant to the bean counters on Earth. They'd interpreted his choice of "Mount Hope" as Israeli humor. They were wrong. *Mount Hope*. He meant it.

But the tunnel wouldn't be enough by itself. There were so many moving parts. So many factors to take into account and balance against each other. And now there were two more: Maddy Huxley and Nick Morrison.

At least Kat hadn't told them everything about the deal. Maddy's violent intervention cut her off before she got to the heart of it, the part that really mattered. The whole thing was still frustrating. Joe had been planning to lie to them, to get them on his side. Now that hope was gone. He'd just have to hope they didn't work the rest out for themselves.

He remembered Nick's eyes above the gun. It had been unnerving the way the guy flipped. Maddy—he'd figured her all along for the type who might go off on you. But Nick, no. His pleasant, polite demeanor was a mask. You couldn't tell what he was thinking. That made him dangerous. Joe should know.

"In my opinion," Dr. Hofstadter said tremulously, "you might actually be a sociopath."

Joe looked around. Dr. Hofstadter's headlamp bobbed in the shadow of the truss. "Are you *still* there?"

Dr. Hofstadter was a factor he'd analyzed, stress-tested, and operationalized as long as eighteen months ago, when the famous scientist arrived for his second stint as the field director of ILI.

"You ought to be psychologically evaluated," Dr. Hofstadter insisted, perhaps kidding himself he was doing Joe some good. "Let Priya give you some tests."

"I took one of those online tests once," Joe said. "I'm not a sociopath. Sorry to disappoint you. Anyway, I passed all the psych evaluations in ArxaSys Lunar's training program." Those things were so easy to game.

"So did Kat," Dr. Hofstadter said.

Joe started toward him, boots scuffing up linear jets of dust. "Do you want to go check on the reactor, too? Huh?"

Dr. Hofstadter's headlamp bobbed away through the darkness. A moment later, he reappeared in the sunlight, running for the termite-mound maze of the ILI hab. Joe snorted. He worried about a lot of things, but Dr. Hofstadter wasn't one of them. The man's occasional fits of defiance didn't make him any less a coward. The other twenty-five scientists currently residing at ILI were also cowards. Even better, they were terminally oblivious. And that suited Joe just fine.

40

Joe watched Hofstadter running clumsily back to the hab complex. Halfway there, he crossed paths with someone coming the other way. The lumbering gait, more frog than grasshopper, suggested he'd run into Trig. Joe's guess was confirmed when Trig pretended to lunge at Dr. Hofstadter, who veered out of his way.

Trig yelled after him, "What have I ever done to you?"

"What indeed?" Joe muttered.

"We never *have* done anything to them," Trig said. He had a police record in New Zealand, where he'd done jail time for growing industrial quantities of weed. As Dr. Hofstadter obliquely pointed out, ArxaSys Lunar's screening procedures did not select perfect people. Still, Trig had an animal quickness of mind. He knew when Joe was making a dig at him—in this case, for threatening Nick Morrison. That had been unnecessary and damaging, part of a pattern of gratuitous meanness directed all too often at the scientists who were, for the time being, their meal ticket.

Joe knew precisely how far it was safe to go at any given moment.

Concoct air-quality survey results indicating the landers were affected by outgassing from the plastics used in the cargo modules, to the extent they were unsafe for long-term inhabitation—thus ensuring the contractors, whose lives were of comparatively little value, would be assigned to live in them?

Yes. With that move, he'd cornered the best habitat on the moon for his crew and saved them from respiratory infections and pulmonary silicosis. The dust in the ILI hab complex was a known problem, but nearly all the tourists went home before it could start to tell on them.

Propose and implement a central depot for supplies in one of the landers, to save precious space in the hab complex?

Yes. ILI loved centralized distribution systems. They'd failed to red-flag the fact that only a single airstair connected the hab complex with the last of the landers in the chain.

Sneak a keystroke-logger onto ILI's computers, ensuring Joe could read every email they exchanged with Earth?

Yes. Kat had done that for him. She'd served time on Earth, too. She freelanced for some of the most notorious cash-mining collectives, specializing in bot armies. Capturing a few scientists' passwords was child's play for her.

Wreck the Five Stones greenhouse and steal their crops?

No, no! Fuck no!

Whatever Joe had thought when Kat ran her mouth about the deal—however irked he'd been when Trig issued his death threats—it was nothing to how he'd felt two months ago, when they pulled *that* stunt.

It could have ruined everything.

Still might.

He remembered the shocking sight of the rover packed to the ceiling with trays that blotted out the interior lights, the unaccustomed taste of moisture in the air, the earthy smell of plants. The stupid grins on Kat's and Trig's faces.

When they saw how angry he was, they'd tried to justify it.

You said we need to move faster now.

We're going to have to grow our own food in the long run.

ILI is never gonna give us aeroponics.

How else were we going to get what we need?

"Not like this," Joe repeated aloud what he'd said to them then. "Not like *this*!"

It had been, of course, impossible to take the stuff *back*. He was forced to make the best of it. Fine. Clear out one of the storage modules, set up water hoses. Have at it. Trig had his weed farming experience. He knew all about moisture levels and pH ratios. The plants flourished and everyone ate salad. Morale skyrocketed. Joe had taken the credit, but he'd known all along there would be repercussions, no matter what Yuta said.

"When were you thinking of letting her out?" Trig stood diffidently in the sunlight, smoothing one boot over the ground.

The crack in Joe's faceplate ran straight through the time display portion of his HUD, making it unusable. He had a rugged old NASA wristwatch, left behind by some astronaut years ago, duct-taped to the arm of his suit. He checked it. Seven minutes since he'd closed the airlock. "Not yet."

"It wasn't her fault, though," Trig said. The anxiety in his voice betrayed that he was less concerned about Kat than he was about incurring punishment himself.

Joe let him sweat. He gazed at the eastern horizon, where a dump truck crawled toward the oxygen plant, loaded with anorthosite dust from the valley to the east of the plateau.

"It was those two fuckwits. *They—*"

"They handled themselves better than you did. I was extremely impressed by the girl. Fucking terrified at the time, yeah. But impressed. And the guy? Intelligent. Very intelligent."

Trig snorted.

"I know his type. The more he doesn't say, the more he's

thinking. In fact, I expect he's putting the pieces together right now."

"Shoulda knocked them off," Trig muttered.

"And I suppose you'd like to explain to Luxembourg why they came to see us, and then vanished?"

"Right. No. Sorry, boss. I was just thinking—"

"Well, don't." Joe was the one who thought about things. He did not want Trig or anyone else thinking too much. It would be bad for morale. "I'm rotating you out to the tunnel. I want to know if we're really going to break through by the end of the month. And make sure they're double-checking all the wiring work, especially on the motion sensors. Take one of the rovers and pack for a week!" he called after Trig as the big man turned away, clearly relieved to escape punishment.

Trig turned back. "Don't leave her in there too long."

"Stop *worrying*," Joe said, putting a tolerant smile into his voice.

He watched two more minutes pass on his wristwatch. He radioed the office to make sure they could free up a rover for Trig. They could. They all understood the importance of completing the tunnel as soon as possible.

"Good work," Joe said. "Stay frosty." He waited two more minutes. Smoothed down the edge of a patch on his sleeve that had begun to lift. He thought about his parents and his sister, back on Earth.

Then he let Kat out.

She burst out of the airlock on her hands and knees, screaming. The banter on the public channel fell away into a hush. Kat kept screaming, clawing at her helmet as if trying to remove it. Finding that it would not come off, she sprang to her feet and started to run.

Joe caught up with her in three strides. He wrapped his

arms around her from behind, pinning her arms to her sides. "It's all right. Kat, it's all right. You're safe."

She fought him.

"It's OK, everyone," Joe said breathlessly. "I've got her." He held on until her struggles slackened. Then he wrapped one arm around her back and supported her.

She cried all the way back. He knew this only because of the way her shoulders shook. She'd turned her suit radio off—a sign she'd regained her senses. By the time they reached the landers and reunited, suitless, in the MVDA, her sobs had dwindled to sniffles. Her face was blotchy red. Clumped eyelashes framed wet blue pools of shock. She gripped his hand, nails digging in, and pulled him up the stairs.

They climbed into the office and shut the hatch. On the other side of the partition was their bedroom. Kat's brassiere landed on the chess set. Joe's pants knocked over the handcrafted glass vase full of origami flowers. They fell onto the air mattress.

"I'm sorry," Joe said. "I'm *sorry*."

"Do me."

"I'm so sorry."

"*Fuck me.*"

Sweat dripped off Joe's face and landed on Kat's, adding fresh wet streaks to her cheeks. He found himself thinking about the mass driver. When the tunnel was completed, there would be no reason not to turn the power on and prepare to fire test loads. ILI had been waiting eighteen years for that milestone.

There had been so many setbacks, delays, and fuckups. For years it had looked—*still* looked to most people—as if the thing would never get finished. Even back when Joe was working for the Israel Space Agency, he'd heard the whispers: Chinese malware. Russian sabotage. Mysterious accidents. *Spooky shit.*

Joe was not the kind of person to be fazed by any of that.

He'd thrown himself into the project 200%. Worked sixteen-hour shifts out in the dark, troubleshooting and redesigning the construction processes until the crew, for the first time, really knew what they were meant to be doing.

Then he moved back into a more managerial role.

A more *central* role.

A role with greater potential than he himself—despite his love for the moon—had initially conceived of.

It had been Kat who noticed the possibilities first.

Dave walks around like he runs this place, she'd said. *But who REALLY runs this place?*

Joe had answered flippantly, *Probably the Department of Defense. Possibly the CIA. I've never quite worked it out.*

No, no, honey. YOU do.

With those two words she'd opened the door to the future. And it had been her skills—drastically undervalued by ArxaSys Lunar, which sold her to ILI as a mere computer technician—that made it possible for them to get this close to achieving their dream of colonization.

Without her, he wouldn't be here.

Without her, he wouldn't succeed at the balancing act that lay ahead.

"I love you." He sprawled across her, depleted. The breeze from the vents cooled the sweat on his back and made the origami flowers on the floor tremble like real ones.

"Love ya," she said hoarsely. "You asshole."

Joe chuckled. She pinched his flank none too gently. He rolled onto his back, teased a lock of her long red hair from under her shoulder, and watched it drift slowly down. "I sent Trig out to see how the guys are getting on."

"As if it matters anymore." Her voice was bitter.

"But it *does* matter. It matters more than ever."

"Huh. All the finest, cutting-edge technology in the world,

and we're getting leapfrogged by a company with technology out of the Old Testament."

"Cruder is Better," Joe said, echoing Yuta Nakajima's catchphrase.

He ran his fingers over the hollow of her waist, the sharp ridge of her hipbone. He often compared the beauty of her slender body to lunar terrain, a notion she laughed at. But now he thought about the irreducible crudity of the act they just performed—the squelching noises, the sticky body fluids, the fingers clawing at skin, and the procreative purpose—as remote as it was from both their minds—that forced their bodies together.

Human nature *was* crude. The contractors were expected to live chaste and productive lives, but that was wishful thinking. Joe knew of at least five other couples on his crew; he turned a blind eye except when their romantic quarrels spilled into public. They brought their human crudeness to the moon. And that was how they would conquer it: with full-spectrum humanity, unhindered by artificial regulations.

"They *have* to get the Big Sling built," he muttered.

"But will they?"

Joe pictured Nick Morrison's stony, watchful face. "They *will* if they can."

Nick would put the pieces together. He would discover the hidden heart of Five Stones' deal with ILI.

Maybe that wasn't such a bad thing.

If he did figure out the truth, he would realize there was only one way he was ever going home.

41

Nick sat in the kitchen on a crate of dehydrated hamburger mix, loosening the cast on his foot. Kurtis watched in silence. Theo and Maddy were carrying in the last boxes of supplies from the rover.

"I'm extremely disappointed, Morrison," Kurtis said. "Extremely." He gave it a beat. "You seriously mean to tell me you forgot the *beer?*"

Kurtis laughed uproariously. So did the others. A mood of elation filled the hab.

"We could *brew* beer," Theo said. "Actually, it would be grain alcohol." He opened the bread mix crate. "There's yeast in here. All one has to do is mash some grain, ferment it, and—"

"Hell no," Nick said. "You're not getting my wheat for any unlicensed brewing experiments." He glanced at the green-house door. It was closed. "Has Lee been looking after the plants?"

"Assume so," Kurtis said. "He shut himself up in there ever since you left."

"Get off that crate," Maddy said. "I'm making hamburgers."

Nick hobbled up to the greenhouse door. He tried it. It was locked from the inside. "Lee!"

"What?" Lee's voice crackled from the intercom beside the door.

"What are you doing in there?"

"Working."

Nick hesitated and put on a fake-hearty voice. "We're ba-ack!"

"Did you get the stuff?"

"Most of it. Everything except the suit spares."

"Good," Lee said. "I won't have to eat your bamboo. Just slide a few Ho Hos and Hershey bars under the door."

Nick looked back into the kitchen. Maddy and Kurtis were arguing about the right way to shape hamburgers: flat or fat? Theo was whipping up smoothies with powdered milk. "We're having a party. Come on out and join us."

"Maybe later. I have to work."

"On what?"

"We still have a fiber breakages issue, you know."

Kurtis called, "Yo, Nick! You bring back any potentiometers? The mad Norwegian scientist thinks he can build a hot plate."

Nick and Theo delved into the boxes of *Mining Robot Change Kits* (*All Models*). They found potentiometers, as well as circuit boards, servomotors, insulation, lubricant, ball bearings, haptics controllers, batteries, battery clips and wiring, and entire preassembled grippers and drill attachments. Some of it would be useful as spares for the Five Stones robots. The other stuff; well, they'd find some use for it. Starting with a hot plate to fry hamburgers.

The hastily assembled contraption worked—almost too well. Fat sputtered on long lunar trajectories, smoke hazed the air, and Maddy burnt her hand. Nick mixed up some bread dough and made rubbery tortillas. They sat on the floor and stuffed themselves. Nick thought of Lee locked away in obsessive communion with his computer.

They needed to talk.

Just not now. Not right now.

He'd almost forgotten what it felt like to have enough—in fact, too much—to eat. A dim, ironical gratitude to the ArxaSys Lunar contractors was firmly in place. Full and tired, he sprawled back on his elbows and listened to Maddy's second or third rehash of the confrontation.

"And then she said the same thing Yangsook said, that there were no emails. They've set it up so they can read all ILI's emails. There was nothing about our supplies. Rachel asked Dr. Hofstadter if they could treat Nick's foot. That was it; nothing else. You were right, Kurtis. You were never really emailing with them at all. We got set up."

"I knew it." Kurtis sighed. "Man, I knew it."

"Knew what?" Theo said. "*Who* set us up?"

"Aaron, of course," Kurtis said. "It's his responsibility to keep us alive. And they're one civil court ruling away from financial meltdown."

"Kat said they're expecting mucho moolah from ILI," Nick noted. "When they complete the Big Sling."

"Right, so they have to get it finished. Which means they have to keep us alive. I guess this was the only way Aaron could think of to do that." Kurtis's earlier lighthearted mood had been replaced by a brooding frown.

"And perhaps this is the way he can escape legal responsibility if there are consequences from Maddy brandishing a gun around," Theo said.

Kurtis squinted at him. "That, too, I guess."

"Hey, whatever, it worked," Maddy said.

"And it was completely unnecessary," Nick said. He

hadn't quite forgiven Maddy for her reckless behavior. "They were going to give us most of the stuff we needed, anyway."

"Not the spare parts," Maddy said.

"Still not sure it was worth pissing them off," Nick said. How badly they'd damaged their relationship with the ArxaSys Lunar contractors was a dark unknown. Either way, Joe Massad was an enemy he didn't want.

"It was *you* who robbed them of the spare parts at gunpoint," Maddy said.

"Hey," Kurtis said easily, "if you didn't get that shit, we wouldn't have a hot plate to fry our hamburgers. It's all good, Maddy."

Maddy sighed. "Whatever. Let me give you your piece back before I forget."

She went to fetch Kurtis's rucksack. On her way out of the room, she accidentally kicked Nick's outstretched left ankle. He stifled a strained groan.

"Ohhh, my God, sorry. Did I give baby an ouchie?" She kissed her fingers and patted the kiss onto Nick's ankle, finishing with an almost painful squeeze.

"She's still mad at me," Nick said.

"No, she ain't," Kurtis said. "You're cool, Nick. Don't let it get inside your head."

Nick moved the rubble of their meal to make a safer place to sprawl against the wall. "Kurtis?"

"Speak on, pardner."

"Did you get permission to bring that gun up here?"

"I was wondering the same thing," Theo said.

Maddy's footsteps returned. She stood in the doorway, hands on her hips. Kurtis's rucksack, with the Glock inside, dangled from one sinewy wrist.

Kurtis glanced swiftly at her. Then he said, "Sure did.

Aaron himself told me it would be a good idea to have firepower available to the mission commander."

"Why?" Nick said.

Kurtis looked straight into his eyes. "In case there was any trouble."

Maddy skidded Kurtis's rucksack carelessly across the floor to him and squatted to dig in the crates. "Who's up for dessert?"

———

Nick lay on the floor while the others continued to talk. His legs were splayed carelessly, his head pillowed on a sack of soy protein powder. He appeared half-asleep. In reality, every nerve thrummed. He was acutely aware of the distance—no more than a meter and a half—between the rucksack, lying behind the relaxed, laughing Kurtis, and his own right hand.

Kurtis: *In case anyone causes trouble.*

Aaron: *This is the dawn of a new era in space. The moon is the key to the future.*

Joe Massad: *They're never gonna let you go home.*

The other three were discussing movies.

Nick got up and returned to the door of the greenhouse. "Lee," he said impatiently into the intercom, shoving on the lever that opened the door.

It moved and he stepped inside.

The lights had dimmed throughout the hab, marking their scheduled transition from artificial day into night. Here, too, the ceiling fixtures glowed a sultry orange, but the grow lights bathed the plants in the UV of a summer day. In the shivering shadows of the bamboo forest, Lee sat at the workbench, hunched over his laptop. He'd also brought in the electron microscope from the workshop. Nick reached past Lee and wiped his fingers on the bench near the microscope. Gritty.

"I thought you didn't want any dust in here," he said.

"I'm *working*."

Nick turned away and cocked his head to peer up at the tops of the bamboo plants. Some of them had begun to bend over against the ceiling. He would have to harvest again. It was a pain in the ass doing it with shears. What he wouldn't give for a machete. He went to the corner where the tools hung.

"It was Monopoly money all along," he said.

"What was?" Lee asked without looking up from his screen.

"Ten million dollars. It was Monopoly money. Aaron knew he'd never have to pay us."

"He *signed*. That contract is legally valid and would stand up in court."

"Not if we're not there to take him to court." The shears weren't hanging on the wall. Nick knelt to search the storage box. "They're not planning for us to ever go home."

"You got the supplies, didn't you?" Finally, Lee's voice had the sharper edge that meant he was paying attention.

"Yeah. My math gives us another three months at 2,500 calories a day. Should be just enough time to finish the Big Sling."

"*If* we can solve this breakages issue," Lee said. "Which I've actually cracked. All I have to do is see if my solution works."

Nick dragged the storage box out from the wall. Then pushed it back. "Lee, where are the shears? You seen them?"

He rose up from his haunches. Lee was sitting facing Nick's way on the workbench stool. His smile did not reach his eyes. He reached, deliberately, onto the shelf above the workbench. "Here they are," he said, holding out the shears. Orange light gleamed on the blades.

Nick scrutinized him for a moment. Took the shears by the handles. "You keep the door locked, man. Why do you—"

"I have to go to the toilet sometimes."

Nick squatted and began to hack through the tallest stem of bamboo. Lee came and stood beside him. Nick forced the shears through the tough fibers. The stem slowly toppled. Lee caught it.

With his arms full of leaves, he said, "I'm *frightened*, OK?"

"Maddy said you used to be a hacker."

"She told you that?"

"Yup. Did you hack Kurtis's email?"

"*What?*"

"He thinks it was Aaron. Was it you?"

"I—no, I couldn't do anything like that. The mail program uses 1024-bit encryption. I could disable the server, but that would kill everything, ingoing and outgoing." With a flicker of humor, Lee added, "And *Kurtis* isn't dumb enough to let me see him typing his password."

"There's such a thing as keystroke loggers."

"I would never do *that*," Lee said. "That's totally unethical."

Nick started on the next stem. "What did you do, then? Back on Earth?"

"Stupid shit," Lee said, in a confessional rush. "Climate activism. DDoSing the banks. Defacing corporate websites. Like, you know, replacing their graphics with doomer memes. Real, real smart for someone working for a big corporation. That's actually how I got fired."

Nick smiled crookedly. "We sure are a fine, morally upstanding crew."

"Oh, come on. You, Theo, Kurtis—"

"Yeah. Kurtis, not so much."

He told Lee about the Glock. Maddy's flamboyant hostage-taking stunt in the ArxaSys Lunar hab. And Kurtis's words to Nick: *Just in case there's any trouble.*

Lee rubbed both hands over his stubble. It had graduated into being a quasi-beard, patchy on his cheeks. His mustache had grown in stringy. Lee looked—and smelled—like a homeless Confucian scholar.

"They're really not planning to ever send us home, huh?" he said.

"Follow the money," Nick said bitterly.

He'd intuited something like this on their very first day, after the Tranquility 13 incident, and promptly dismissed his own fears. Well, suppressed them into nervous tics and nightmares. He'd *run away* from the truth. He scissored the shears viciously on a stem, barely denting it.

"These fucking things are blunt."

"It costs too much to build the Big Sling," Lee said. "It costs more than they have. Especially after the Tranquility 12 disaster. They're tapped out. But Aaron doesn't give up. He *never* gives up. Decides to cut costs. Instead of a return flight for six... one Glock nine-millimeter." Lee let out an explosive laugh. "Kurtis probably thinks there'll be a return flight just for him. Boy, I'd like to see his face when Spiffy lets the air out of his suit with a screwdriver."

"Charlie might do something to help us." Nick spoke indifferently, not wanting to pin his hopes on Charlie. She might be a little more sympathetic to the crew than the rest of them, but that was a low bar. He went back to the storage box and found the whetstone. He sat down and began to pass it along the blades of the shears.

"We don't need her help."

Lee spoke with such force that Nick looked up.

"I'm going to *make* them bring us home."

"Yeah? How you plan on doing that?"

Lee grabbed Nick's shoulders and dragged him to his feet. He pushed him toward the door, still holding the shears and whetstone. "Out. I gotta work."

"Lee—"

"I need to concentrate! Out! I'll tell you when I finish."

————

Nick saw the smoke before he smelled it. Wispy gray threads curled toward the vents. He'd *known* the hot plate was dangerous. He plunged into the kitchen. "Something's on fire—"

Maddy looked up and laughed. The smell registered: skunky, sweet. Theo held out a blunt rolled from the thin page of a hardcopy instruction manual. "Please. Would you like to try?"

Nick waved the thick, smelly smoke away with the hand not holding the shears.

Kurtis's eyes were fried-egg yellow. He took the blunt. "I do not approve of drug use. Not one, itty-bitty, little bit. I should go back to Tennessee, get a job driving a school bus." He dragged on the blunt and broke into coughs. Maddy knelt behind him, driving her hard little fists into his shoulder muscles.

Nick went to his room. He snatched up his headphones, plugged them into his laptop, and thought about Charlie. Her square capable hands. Slender legs. The concentric rings of green, brown, and gold that you could see in her eyes under sunlight. A glimpse of bra strap. Soft flesh swelling out of a lacy white cup... Physical longing shivered through him like pain.

He put his favorite hard rock playlist on repeat and sat whetting the shears until the blades were sharp enough to cut silk.

42

Charlie pulled up outside Rachel's cute little house in Rockledge and shooed Anna out of the car. She parked on the street while Anna rang the bell. "Biankini! Biankini!"

Rachel's labradoodle shot out of the house. Anna rough-housed on the lawn with the furry bundle of energy. The women drank white wine on the patio.

"I should get her a dog," Charlie said. "Biankini's about the only thing that can pry her away from that tablet."

"Charlie, do you really have the bandwidth for a dog?"

Charlie sighed. "No."

The SEC had filed a formal claim against Bill and Aaron in the 5th US District Court. It was not looking good for Five Stones. If they lost, Bill would have to pay back the millions he made shorting stocks... money that had long since been ploughed into robots and rockets and crew training... Plus additional penalties of up to $500 million *and* legal fees.

What was in it for the bastards? They'd already forced Five Stones to sign that goddamn deal with ILI, yet the wheels kept on grinding. A line came to Charlie's mind: the future is a federal judge's loafer stamping on your face, forever.

And a cruder counterpoint: $60,000 or *I send everything to the Feds.*

Ryder Stillman's evidence would slam shut the case against Five Stones, rendering them all broke again.

"Why'd you sell your car?" Rachel said, eyeing the basic-model Chery at the curb.

Charlie hunched her shoulders. "I'm so stressed." The patio pavement flashed white in the sun, like lunar regolith. "I *knew* the supply run was going to go wonky."

"They got all the supplies..."

"Apart from the suit spares, yeah. But it's not clear exactly what happened while they were over there. Dr. Hofstadter called Luxembourg to ask what it was all about." They knew this from Aaron's contacts at ILI. "Then, a couple of hours later, he reported Nick and Maddy went away *without* any supplies! Yet we know they got the supplies. Why did he lie about it?"

Rachel poured more wine. It was a rare morning off for her. Charlie didn't actually have a morning off. She'd invented a conference with Anna's therapist. She put her hand over her glass.

"Maybe he didn't want to admit that Nick and Maddy seized the supplies at gunpoint."

Charlie groaned softly. "That has to be the worst idea Aaron's ever come up with."

"Yet it apparently worked."

On the lawn, Anna threw a chewed-up frisbee for the labradoodle.

"I don't think the rules are the same on the moon," Rachel said. "Ethics, you know. That's civilization. Up there, there's no civilization. There's just people."

"All the same, if Dr. Hofstadter got robbed at gunpoint, you would think he'd report it."

"Too proud?" Rachel shrugged. "Too scared?"

"Or it really didn't happen. Nick and Maddy *said* they were given everything they needed freely."

"Maybe *they're* lying."

There was a bug floating in Charlie's wineglass. She fished it out with one finger. "I don't think they would lie to us."

"Why not? After all, we're lying to them about the deal."

Charlie frowned. Rachel didn't know about the deal. Only five people did: Aaron, Yuta, Bill, Cameron, and Charlie herself. "What?"

Rachel's mouth tensed. She tucked a strand of hair behind her ear and the glass baubles of her earrings tinkled. "More wine? I just heard Aaron and Yuta talking about some kind of deal. It sounded like it was a deep dark secret. I thought... what's it all about, anyway?"

Charlie grimaced. "Just some financial thing, I think." And now she was lying to her best friend. This goddamn industry. She stood up. "I think Anna's been out in the sun long enough. Anna! Baby!" Her daughter's face was pink and damp. "Let's take Biankini inside."

She could picture how it might've happened. Aaron and Yuta discussing the deal in Yuta's office on the fourteenth floor; door open; Rachel walking by. *Dumb.* Aaron was slipping. The thought filled Charlie with terror of a peculiar timbre, cold and centering, different from any of the other fears that haunted her.

In the split-level living room, Biankini flopped on the floor, tongue hanging out. Anna drifted over to Rachel's glassworking equipment set up on a trestle table in the corner.

"I haven't touched that stuff in so long, there are probably spiders living inside my kiln." Rachel sighed.

"How does this work?"

"I'll show you..."

Aaron was slipping. Charlie stood by the patio windows, turning the thought over in her mind. He was making mistakes. Well, how would he *not* be? There was a lot weighing on him. Those five people in Amundsen Crater. They were with him night and day. Aaron *did* have a conscience, despite what most people thought. He knew in his heart he shouldn't have done the deal.

Shouldn't have done it.

Oh, God, I wish we hadn't done it.

Rachel showed Anna some glass beads she made a while ago, and invited Anna to string them. "You could make a necklace, a keychain, windchimes." Her voice was as cheerful as ever, but when she joined Charlie by the windows, lines of strain bracketed her mouth.

Charlie's phone buzzed.

Well? Have you got it? She didn't need to look at the text to know what it said.

"It's a nice color," Rachel said, finding the only good thing that could possibly be said about Charlie's new car.

"It's a secondhand piece of crap," Charlie said. "But I had to sell my Volvo because..."

"Because?"

"Because some asshole is blackmailing me." She dragged out her phone and showed Rachel the latest texts. "He's still holding out for $60K."

"Charlie! What—Who *is* this lowlife?"

"Some guy named Ryder Stillman."

"Who?"

"Nobody. A nobody who's managed to get his hands on some of our confidential documents."

"How long has this been going on?"

"Months." Charlie's eyes prickled. It was such a relief to tell someone at last. Anna, on the other side of the room, bent over the beads, the nape of her neck pink and vulnerable. Charlie lowered her voice to a whisper. "I've given him all my money. Everything I can scrape together."

"Charlie, you have to go to the police."

"And have the whole world find out about..."

The deal.

She couldn't say it. Rachel seemed to read the desperation in her eyes. "Yeah. I get it. Wow."

"I'm not giving him any more money. I can't. I don't *have* any more."

"You're going to call his bluff."

"Basically. Yeah."

"And you think he might turn dangerous."

"It's possible."

"Now I get it. *This* is why you need—"

"Insurance." Charlie dragged the back of her hand across her eyes. "I need insurance."

They went into Rachel's bedroom. Rachel closed the door and dug among the shoeboxes on the floor of her closet.

"*How* many pairs of shoes do you have?" Charlie joked nervously.

"Not enough," Rachel said. "There is no such thing as enough shoes." She laid a Fluevog box on the bed and opened it. Folds of stained terrycloth wrapped a black semiautomatic. It was smaller than Charlie expected. She touched it with a cringing fingertip.

"It's a Beretta .380," Rachel said. "Ammo's in the box."

"How—how much was it?"

"Less than a pair of Louboutins," Rachel said. "Don't worry about it. This one's on me. Besides, my brother set up the buy."

"Please thank him from me."

"I will."

"Mom?" Anna burst into the room. Charlie slammed the lid onto the shoebox. "Look what I made."

"It's beautiful, honey!" Charlie said. "Just beautiful."

43

Nick walked over the chardonnay slopes with Midas Ngidi. Small hard grapes hung on the vines like clusters of green bullets. Midas carried an armload of broken trellises. "Look," he said, gesturing at the misty hills. "What do you see?"

"Rain," Nick said. The fine droplets tasted sweet on his lips. "Our vineyards."

"Uh huh," Midas said. "That's because you have white attitude."

"Hey!" Something jabbed at Nick's ribs.

He sat up, rolling away in the same motion, cringing from the shadowy figure stooping over him.

"It works!" Lee grinned like a jack-o'-lantern. "I've got it! It works!"

"Jesus, you scared me." Nick's mouth was as dry as moondust. He glanced around for the shears. Lee had kicked them heedlessly aside.

"My method for characterizing the fines—I gotta tell Kurtis."

"Everyone's asleep."

"Feh! They're gonna wanna hear this." Lee flung open the makeshift curtain-door of Kurtis's room.

On the floor, two sleeping bags, unzipped. On the sleeping bags, two figures, one pale, one dark, loosely intertwined in slumber. Both were naked. Maddy's head rested on Kurtis's pectoral muscle; her mouth curved in the unconscious smile of a cat. Kurtis snored quietly. The smell of marijuana still hung in the air.

Nick flinched back, automatically averting his eyes.

Lee croaked, "Maddy?" His eyes bugged out with astonishment.

Nick tried to drag him away. At the same time, Maddy woke up. She laughed at Lee's expression.

"Lee, come *on*," Nick said. "Leave them alone."

Lee's mouth worked, but no sound came out. He seemed shrunken.

Kurtis woke up and firmly closed the curtain. Nick urged Lee into the kitchen and made some instant coffee. After a while, Kurtis and Maddy, now appropriately dressed, joined them.

"Lee has something to tell you," Nick said, staring levelly at Kurtis. Now that the first shock of horrified amusement had worn off, he found he was angry at Kurtis. As mission commander, he should have known better.

"Hey, what are you looking at him for?" Maddy said. "Don't *I* get any credit for getting stoned and sleeping with the ugliest woop on the moon?" She chuckled and peered at their mugs. "Where's my coffee?"

Nick realized that he was plenty angry at Maddy, too. "Make it yourself."

"Whoa. Attitude." She grabbed two sachets of coffee, one for herself and one for Kurtis.

274

"I do *not* appreciate you disrespecting my privacy like that," Kurtis ground out, glowering at Lee.

Theo wandered into the kitchen, yawning. "Why's everyone awake?"

For an instant there was silence. Then Lee scraped up a smile. "Guess what? I've cracked the fiber breakages issue."

"No way!"

"Yes way. Get a load of this, my friends..."

Lee's method turned out to involve image processing. He'd taken samples of moondust from different areas of the crater, photographed them, applied filters, and ran the filtered images through a program he'd written himself. Comparing the results with samples of the dust from the bad melts, which they knew to be glass-rich, he refined the program until it could reliably detect silicon dioxide content down to a tenth of a percent.

"Motherfucker," Kurtis breathed, his anger forgotten. "You're the man, Lee."

"It wasn't that difficult," Lee said modestly.

"Yes, it was," Theo said. "This is a perennial topic of science. No one has previously developed a method of analyzing moondust in situ. This is a breakthrough with wide applications!"

"I can also detect iron, platinum, magnesium, and calcium," Lee said.

"You see? And it only requires a camera and computer!"

"How'll this work?" Nick said. "We go out there with a camera, take pictures of the dust, send the pictures to you..."

"Precisely," Lee said. "From there I'll analyze them and tell you if it's a good area to quarry. Use the Nikon, and *please* don't get the lens scratched. That could mess with the analysis."

"Well, shit, let's go," Kurtis said. "If this works, we got a lot of lost time to make up."

Five days later, lunar dawn lit the solar collectors of the basalt furnace. Nick, Kurtis, and Theo stood below in the dark, watching the first droplets of their new melt ooze out of the bushing. The droplets stretched into perfectly straight, glossy strings. They touched the spools of the winding machine. Kurtis ceremoniously punched the button to start the machine spinning.

Round it went. Kurtis counted the clicks out loud. "Twenty meters... thirty meters..."

"You're killing me," Nick said, laughing.

"Let's go and have lunch," Theo said.

They went into the hab. Nick hardly tasted his soy-egg-and-kale microwave muffins. They went back out.

"Four hundred meters!"

"I'll add more fines into the melt," Theo said.

That evening, Maddy called down from the peak, where she was installing the conduits of the heat batteries. "Well? You guys have been quiet for a while. What's going on? Is it still working?"

"Wait," Nick said. "Wait..."

The winding machine clicked around. Each of the six spools carried a bulge of shiny black fibers, which still only took up a small percentage of the spools' depth.

Click.

"Two kilometers!" Kurtis exulted. "If we can get to two, we can get to twenty. I would now like everyone to join me in a round of applause for Lee. HOORAH!"

"Guys," Rachel said plaintively, from Earth. "Care to share what you're doing?"

It was 4 a.m. on Earth. Aaron came on the radio within half an hour. Lee, Nick, and Kurtis were sitting around the radio console in the work module of the hab. Maddy and Theo were out tending the furnace.

"This is incredible," Aaron said. "I thought we were fucked. You've saved our asses, Lee! Huge, huge congrats."

"The fibers still might break at klick nineteen," Lee said.

"They won't, as long as you keep characterizing each batch before you shoot it into the funnel. How does the program work?" Aaron sounded euphoric. "I gotta know."

The hab console had no video functionality, yet Nick could sense Aaron's tense anticipation.

"Wellll," Lee said.

"We've got a patentable discovery here," Aaron went on. "This, in and of itself, is worth *millions*. Maybe hundreds of millions when you think about licensing revenue streams. Send us the code and I'll get a patent application started."

"No," Lee said.

"*No?*" Kurtis echoed, staring at Lee.

"That sounded like *no*," Aaron said, 360,000 kilometers away.

"It's my discovery. If anyone's filing a patent on it, I am."

Lee folded his arms. Nick studied him with admiration.

"You can't do that," Aaron said. "Any intellectual property generated during the course of the mission belongs to Five Stones. It's in your contract."

"And we have *such* a lot of respect for contracts around here," Lee said. "Here's my offer. I'll give you the code... once we're all safely back on Earth."

Three seconds passed. Kurtis scowled and worried his fingernails.

"Stop fucking around," Aaron said. "Do you have any idea of the financial status of the company at the moment? If you don't give us the code, you might not ever get home."

There it was. He'd said it. Nick met Lee's eyes. Lee nodded significantly.

"I'm sure you can find some way to stay liquid," he said. "Sell the helicopter. Sell your Tesla. Anyway, you're not getting the code until all five of us are safely back on Earth."

Kurtis lurched at Lee. Lee snatched up his laptop and hurried away along the module.

"That's my bottom line," he shouted over his shoulder. "Take it or leave it."

The door of the greenhouse whirred and thumped. When Kurtis tried it, yelling at Lee not to be stupid, it wouldn't open.

44

The mission control room at the Five Stones office was barely bigger than a two-man tent. Ferocious air-conditioning cooled the computers. Aaron prowled around and around the cramped space. He grabbed a back scratcher and swung it lightly at the wall. "We *need* that code!"

Yuta sat at Rachel's desk, wearing her headset. They'd kicked Rachel, Jason, and Isioma out for the time being. Rachel leaned against the other side of the soundproof glass partition, drinking coffee. She caught Yuta's eye, lifted her cup, and mouthed: *Get you some?* Yuta shook his head. The knot in his stomach felt like a bundle of knives.

"If we get that code, we can turn lemons into lemonade," Aaron said. "Our shares are cratering. The bears are piling in. They all think the share price is gonna fall through the floor when the SEC rules against us. This is the *perfect* time to go long our own stock. Bill could buy it through one of his offshore investment vehicles. Then we leak the patent application for Lee's algorithm. Everyone will know what that's worth as soon as they see the abstract. Kaboom! The stock spikes. We'll make a *killing*."

Yuta moved the cursor around on Rachel's screen. "What would Cameron say?"

"He'd ramble on about compliance in his usual dick-brained fashion," Aaron said.

"He'd say this is why the SEC went after us in the first place."

"No, it isn't," Aaron said. "Insider trading? Ha! Everyone does it. They went after us to make sure we signed the deal."

The deal. The *damn* deal. Yuta drew invisible orbital trajectories on the screen. Earth to LEO. Moon to LEO. Moon to Earth. *Kaboom.*

"This could be our chance to get out of it."

Yuta looked up sharply, unsure if Aaron had really said that. He'd been the one pushing the deal all along, despite knowing what it meant.

"If we get that code, we won't need their money." Aaron whirled to a stop behind Yuta. He reached over his shoulder with the back scratcher and tapped the keyboard. "Call your friend at ILI."

"He isn't my friend."

"He sure as heck isn't mine. Call him and ask if he can exert some pressure."

———

Joe sprawled on the couch in his office, contemplating the Falkbeer Counter-Gambit. After a hard day in the tunnels, he often relaxed by playing chess. The chess pieces were cast on the first run of their homemade Fischer-Tropsch reactor, made of heavy, greasy-feeling plastic you could dent with your fingernail. The board was a piece of sheet aluminum with alternate squares anodized.

No one at ILI was good enough to give him a game. Sometimes he played over the radio with the Russian commander in Peary Crater. When Mikhail was busy, Joe played the computer. He had it set up next to the chessboard right now, running Deep Blue 3000. It opened with the King's Gambit.

The computer was also the unofficial comms center for ArxaSys Lunar.

"Why in the heck would I help you steal this guy's code?" he said to it.

He picked up a pawn and moved it two spaces into the center. He entered his move into the computer, which responded by taking his queen's pawn. Kat moved the computer's piece for it.

"Come on, Joe," Yuta said distantly. "You owe me."

They were speaking on a scrambled VoIP transmission. Kat had set it up so the ArxaSys Lunar contractors could make and receive calls over their internet connection without the knowledge of the pinheads in Luxembourg, much less the famous geophysicist next door.

"Oh, *I* owe *you*," Joe said, rolling his eyes. The computer moved out a knight. Joe moved his queen back a single square.

He'd known Yuta since his climbing days. They'd met in the Alps when Yuta was preparing to scale the Matterhorn without fixed ropes or modern crampons. Joe had been intrigued by Yuta's obsession with preindustrial technologies. At that time, Yuta was just an unemployed engineer taking out his frustration on mountains. The magic hadn't happened until he met Aaron Slater.

By that time, Joe had been at the Israel Space Agency, working on orbital mechanics. He'd followed Yuta's career from a distance, and vice versa, as it turned out. They didn't get in touch again until Joe was on the moon, when he learned the designer of the Big Sling was none other than Yuta Nakajima.

So he had someone he could call up to yell at.

"I hooked you up," Yuta reminded him.

"And very nice bud it is," Kat smirked. She touched a lighter to the bowl of a silicone pipe, inhaled, and passed it to Joe. He had to admit he admired Five Stones for growing marijuana on the moon. No other company would even have thought of it.

When Joe called Yuta to rage at him about the Big Sling, Yuta had responded with a bribe. If Joe would refrain from driving up to Amundsen Crater and smashing the Five Stones robots with crowbars—something Joe actually threatened to do amidst his anger and disappointment—Yuta would hook them up. Adding cannabis to the list of crops to be grown in the Five Stones greenhouse would be a cinch. The gardening robot would raise and harvest the weed and place it in the airlock. The contractors could drive up every so often to collect it.

Like many habitual stoners, Yuta thought good weed made everyone happy. Joe didn't see it that way, but he understood what this could mean for his crew. ILI was completely dry. It was a no-smoking, no-vaping zone. ILI's inhuman clean-living policy even extended to a ban on synthetic opioids. Joe had people in chronic pain who were struggling by with Tylenol. People coping with repetitive stress injuries and plain old stress. He'd body-bagged a suicide not that long ago. A supply of cannabis could literally be a lifesaver for the contractors.

And so it had turned out. Morale improved by an order of magnitude.

Joe had known all along that when the Five Stones crew arrived, the supply would dry up. That prompted another trade with Yuta. They'd agreed that the ArxaSys Lunar contractors would go and pick up the cannabis plants before the Five Stones crew got there.

Joe dispatched Kat and Trig to Amundsen Crater.

And the numbskulls had taken everything else, as well.

Joe frowned at the chessboard. "You promised you'd cover

up for us," he said to Yuta. He took responsibility for the green-house burglary, even though he hadn't sanctioned it.

"We did," Yuta said.

"Well, they found out anyway."

"That wasn't us. It was Charlie."

"Charlie, huh?"

"Our head of robotics."

"Yeah, I know who she is." Joe made a mental note: *Charlie. A risk factor.*

"They might have figured it out by themselves anyway," Yuta crackled. "Some of them are pretty smart."

"No shit. They're even smarter than you think they are." He captured one of the computer's pawns, opening his queen's rank up to put the enemy king in her line of fire. *Check.*

"That's why we need this code," Yuta said. He was begin-ning to sound desperate. "You helped us before!"

"It was a *trade*," Joe said patiently. "I gave you a piece of seriously valuable information in exchange for those plants. And as far as I can see, you haven't done anything with it."

"There's nothing we *can* do," Yuta said. "There's no one we can turn to. Except you."

Joe attacked. "And you think I'm going to help you, because... why, exactly? Because you made a pathetic attempt to buy us off? Like a few ounces of weed could make up for losing our jobs? Our *future*? Sorry, Yuta. I don't want to be harsh, but you're a tool. You sold out, got ass-fucked, and now you're crying to me. Get real. I have exactly zero interest in helping you. There isn't anything you can do for me this time. And there isn't anything you can do *to* me, either. That's the advantage of being on the moon."

"We'll cut you in," Yuta offered.

"Oh, Yuta, don't you understand I have no interest in money? There's nothing to buy and sell up here." Joe leaned closer to the computer microphone. "On the moon, we're *free*. Oh, and by the way, Aaron, I know you're listening. Go fuck yourself."

He ended the call. Kat patted her hands together in applause.

Free.

That was the moon's great revelation, which it offered, in time, to everyone with eyes to see. *Up here, we're free.* It'd come to Joe; to Kat and Trig; it'd come at various times to all the long-staying contractors.

Now Joe just had to hope it would come to Nick Morrison and his friends as well.

It sounded as if this computer guy, Lee Yang, was getting there, anyway.

Free.

Bishop, knight, castle. Checkmate in twelve moves.

"Good game," Kat said. She didn't understand the first thing about chess. Her bright gaze rested on the pieces like a magpie considering birdseed.

Joe picked up the computer's toppled king. It was pale gray, whereas his own pieces were a few shades darker. The Fischer-Tropsch reactor didn't do black and white. Only shades of gray. "I should have asked him how the Big Sling is coming along."

"Why?. We've got their satellite images." Kat had put together a Ka-band monitoring device that allowed them to read all the traffic to and from the Five Stones communications satel-lite. It was mostly encrypted, but that presented no obstacle to her. "We can see them cranking out those basalt fibers in real time."

"Yeah... Something we don't want Yuta and Aaron to know. It would have seemed more natural to ask." He shook his head.

Kat jumped across the table in a graceful lunar frog-hop.

She squatted next to Joe. "Don't worry about them. Money makes people dumb. The crew, on the other hand..."

"Yeah. They're going to either find out the truth about Aaron's deal with ILI, or work it out for themselves."

"And what'll they do then?"

"Either they do the smart thing, or..." Joe left the thought unfinished. He swept the chess pieces off the board, into the box.

———

Yuta took off the headset. "That crashed and burned harder than I expected."

"What an asshole," Aaron said.

"Let's go to Washington."

"*No.*"

"Please."

Aaron whirled around. "NO!"

Yuta pushed back from Rachel's desk. He stumbled out of the room and hurried to the toilet before he threw up.

45

"We need more fines," Theo said. "*Much* more fines."

"Tell me about it," Nick said.

They were sitting in the rover, eating lunch. Outside, Gulliver continued to plough back and forth across the latest area that Lee's algorithm deemed safe to quarry. Nick and Theo had been pushing the hand rollers all morning. They just couldn't keep up with the pace of demand from the furnace.

"If we don't keep the melt deep enough, we'll get inhomogeneities again," Theo fretted.

"What do you suggest? Clone ourselves?"

"Make Lee come out and help," Theo said, and promptly rolled his eyes. "No, stupid me. Cloning ourselves would be easier."

Nick snickered. He chewed on his sandwich—rubber tortilla, with a filling of rehydrated scrambled egg and hamburger crumbles. He'd been experimenting with various methods of tortilla-making to distract himself from the painful tension in the hab.

Lee flatly refused to come out of the greenhouse, for fear of Kurtis stealing his code and transmitting it to Mission Control.

Kurtis, thwarted, had been losing his calm, periodically banging on the greenhouse door and screaming at Lee. It fell to Nick to slip Lee food when Kurtis and Maddy were both out. And worst of all, Nick was cut off from his plants. Lee was toiling away doing the bare minimum in there, while Nick labored out here in his dusty exile.

Unfortunately, Theo was right. They needed more fines. Extruding the twenty-kilometer fibers had started at lunar dawn, and had to finish by lunar sunset. If not, the melt would harden into a lump of stone, and the fibers would snap. They had three more days and were behind schedule.

"Tell you what," he said. "I'll go look for the Woombat again."

"The Woombat? It was destroyed in the T-13 incident!"

"I don't see how it would have been. When we were over there, I actually thought those ArxaSys Lunar punks took it. But when I got an up-close look at their rover, the hatch isn't large enough to fit anything that big. Maybe it just got blown aside by the exhaust plume and it's still there."

"It is too heavy to be blown aside," Theo objected.

"I know. But it can't hurt to go and have a look."

Nick thought if he could find the Woombat, and it turned out to be in working order, that would cheer everyone up.

"You just want a break from this boring as crap work," Theo said with a small smile.

Nick didn't return the smile. "If I wanted a break, I would say so. This isn't a break, it's getting shit done."

The oblique accusation of laziness stung, in part because he did crave a break. No, not exactly that. He wanted to get away from these fucking people for a little while.

He shooed Theo out of the rover, radioed Kurtis to say where he was going, and drove away from the quarry.

Kurtis exploded in anger. Why did Nick think he could just

head off on a joyride without asking permission first? What was the point, anyway?

"To stop you from fucking bitching at us all the time," Nick yelled, and turned off the radio.

He drove north around the Cat's Claw, breathing deeply, trying to cool down. The lowering sun dug craters in his path, which turned out to be shallow dimples. The shadows on the moon were deceptive. On Earth, if there was a pool of shadow in the bottom of a depression, you'd think it was really deep. Here, it might only be a couple of inches. The same went in reverse for boulders and hummocks. They looked higher than they were, and often appeared to bulge where they didn't. More tricks of the shadows.

Soon he drove into the vast shadow of the peak. While the construction zone was in sunlight, the opposite side of the peak naturally lay in darkness. The rover's headlamps dug into the night, and Nick sank into a semi-trance that skirted his memories of South Africa.

His father used to take him on drives at night. Said it was important for Nick to know their land in all weathers and at all times. Identify animal calls; be aware when the antelope were migrating; recognize which snakes had poisonous bites; know how to find your way in the dark. Looking back now, Nick thought the night drives had been an escape for Will Morrison from the dangers that increasingly haunted his family and his business. The bushveld was *less* dangerous than the world of men.

He reached the landing site, parked, turned off the headlamps.

We'll get out here, Nick, and walk.

It wasn't true that you couldn't see in the dark on the moon. Earth, low down on the crater rim, and the stars in the sky provided enough of a backscatter to see by. You just had to let your eyes adjust.

He turned off his helmet lamp. When he could see, he walked away from the rover in slow bounds.

He had an idea of where to search. Near the cliff, in the area which had lain in darkness last time he was here. Nick hadn't searched there at all. And there were numerous boulders lying on the crater floor, which could conceal—or *be*—a Woombat in damaged, scorched thermal packaging.

He looked back. The rover was a paler, easily identifiable silhouette in the dark.

I'm cold, Dad.

Walk faster, it'll warm you up.

A trail through the scrubby woods on the edge of the vineyards. The smell of moist autumn earth. The deafening noise of cicadas, blending with the sound of the river ahead, now louder, now fainter.

Where?

There!

A huge tortoise, sitting right on the trail. Nick's father took a photograph, elated. He had a fondness for tortoises. In some ways he resembled them: hunker down, pull in your head, don't move until it's gone.

Where?

Rocks. Dust and more rocks.

Keep going.

Nick roamed along the foot of the cliff, kicking boulders. Kinda dumb to try this at night. He was getting hot and out of breath. His foot was hurting again. And even out here, he wasn't alone. He remembered Fenella squatting on the plain, painstakingly picking up little pieces of trash.

Fenella, the moon's first victim. Was it the moon that killed her? Or human beings? Either way, Five Stones bore the responsibility.

He wiped his faceplate. It only smeared the dust around.

Fuck this. I'm going back.

He turned, and couldn't see the rover.

46

Nick had wandered too far, and was lost on the crater floor.

No worries, just use the radio direction finder.

Except he'd turned the rover's radio off.

Dark gray dust. Paler gray boulders.

He walked, straining his eyes. Looking at the plain and not the oxygen reserve indicator in his HUD.

Listen!

What, Dad?

His father gripped his arm. *It's close. Oh my God, Nick. Hear that?*

A sound like a motorbike engine turning over. Low, harsh, weirdly purposeful.

The rumble of an indigenous leopard, rarely seen or heard on the Hailsong estate.

Even the cicadas seemed to quiet at the menacing noise.

His father was enraptured. Nick was petrified.

I think we'd better go back.

Yeah, Dad, let's.

If only he *could* go back.

Running.

Don't stop.

No one'll help anyway. They'll say it was just an accident.

Run.

His boots thudded on the lunar rock. Dust jetted up. Boulders loomed at deceptive distances. His panic resonated across the years. The only thing missing was his father beside him.

Ow, Dad, my foot, I've hurt my foot—

OK, Nick. Slow down. Do you need me to carry you?

No. I can walk.

Slowly then.

Behind them, the motorbike engine turned over, revving in the depths of the woods.

Do you know, it was really interesting to see that tortoise. He must have been feeling pretty groggy. His father was trying to distract him from the pain in his foot, from his fear. *It's almost winter. You know where tortoises go in the winter, right?*

Yeah, Dad. They bury themselves underground.

That's right.

They bury themselves... underground.

Nick switched on his headlamp. His eyes ached in the sudden light. He looked back at the dust he kicked up during his wild sprint. It rose in straight lines and then fell back to the ground. He remembered the mountainous geysers of dust Tranquility 13 created when it landed... and again when it took off.

Swinging the other way, his headlamp caught a hummock he remembered from his outbound walk. It looked too big, so he'd passed it by. But that could be a deceptive effect of the shadows... and the fact it was covered with dust.

*Buried... under *dust*.*

He bounded up to the hummock and dashed his glove over its side. Dust sheeted off.

Thermal foil packaging glinted.

He pulled at the foil until it tore, revealing the shiny metal snout of the Woombat.

And there, not a hundred meters away, stood the rover, pale and curvaceous. He didn't know how he could've missed it.

———

Back at base camp, Kurtis was waiting for him, primed to deliver a military-grade blast of invective. As Nick had hoped, his mood softened when he saw the Woombat.

Their mood of excitement did not last long. Once the blackened foil was off, the damaged housing of the Woombat's processing unit was revealed. It wasn't working. The exhaust plume must've fried components inside.

The Woombat lay inert in the construction zone, while Spiffy, serving as Charlie's eyes and hands, removed the housing.

"Try rewiring the connections to this circuit board," Charlie said. She'd come on the radio as soon as they informed Mission Control that the Woombat had been found. "If the circuit board itself is damaged, it's hopeless. Let's hope it's just the wiring."

Her voice sent a complex shiver of emotion through Nick. He poked with a universal tool at the partially melted tangle of wires. Shadow surrounded the construction zone, like a black sea lapping at a shrinking island. Nick thought of the warm waters of the Atlantic. Floodwater rushing through a drowned basement. *Get out, get out now.*

"Guess it isn't the wiring," he said forty minutes later.

"Guess not... Damn," Charlie said.

"I have an idea."

Nick went into the hab, taking the fried PCB with him. This board wasn't like the ones Charlie used in Gulliver, Spiffy, or the Bobs. It was larger, with a different arrangement of components. He scraped melted solder off the board with a fingernail. He recalled seeing one like this before.

He dug in the box of *Mining Robot Change Kits* (*All Models*).

"What's that?" Charlie said. He was in the workshop, so she could see him on the interior cameras and talk to him from the intercom.

"Stuff we got from ILI." Nick remembered the moment when he pointed Kurtis's Glock at Joe Massad and yelled at him to give them spare parts. Five Stones had made him do that. *Charlie* had made him do it. He said shortly, "Most of it doesn't work with our equipment. But this board..."

He found what he'd been looking for and held it up to the camera.

"Isn't it the same as this one?"

"Bring it closer to the camera... yeah, it's the same! Nick, that should work."

"Why did you use a different board in the Woombat?"

"I didn't originally," she said. "But after the first Woombat was lost in the T-12 disaster, I had to build another one in two weeks flat, if you recall. I wasn't able to get the same custom board I used before. Had to reach out to a different supplier. Don't worry though, this one's just as good; it's got all the same functionality. I just had to tweak the software to incorporate it into the design."

"But why *this* one?"

"What do you mean?"

Obscured by blackened solder on the damaged board, the ILI logo stood out legibly on the replacement.

"It's an ILI component," Nick said. "Why'd they help you out? We're the competition."

He remembered what Katniss Reyes had said. *Aaron struck a deal with ILI.* He'd scarcely thought about it since. What did he care who got to buy the Big Sling's launch capacity? Only now, he started wondering if there was more to the deal. Something Kat hadn't mentioned. Something Charlie wasn't telling him.

"Listen, space-hardened printed circuit boards for robots aren't exactly off-the-shelf products," Charlie said. "There was nowhere else I could reach out to in the limited timeframe I was working with."

She hadn't answered the question.

"Now why don't you get out there and bring the Woombat into the workshop?" Her voice had grown sharp. Cold. "You'll want to do the soldering inside."

"Yes, ma'am," Nick murmured.

Climbing back into his suit, that leopard growling in the night came back to him. He'd been frightened. Even his father had been frightened. They'd run. They'd run headlong in the wrong direction. Back to the car, back home... The real danger wasn't and never had been the leopard.

It was other people.

―――――

The rejuvenated Woombat's labors in the quarry got them across the thirty-kilometer line before dark. As lunar night fell, they began to braid the fibers into a twenty-kilometer tube. They had a braiding machine; it ran off the hab's fuel cell, so they could use it in the dark, but the drive gears required frequent de-dusting, and someone always had to be standing by to stop the machine when it jammed.

Now and then, Lee shouted at them from the greenhouse. "Who killed Fenella?"

"Ignore him," Kurtis said.

"Who destroyed Tranquility 12?"

"This is driving me *crazy*," Maddy said.

"Lee," Theo said. "Lee, please. We're your friends."

"Who hacked Tranquility 13's cryocooling system?"

The braiding machine's bobbins chattered soundlessly in the vacuum. The sling arm grew.

47

Joe was planning his sortie in search of that iridium-rich meteor when he got a call from Wez.

"You gotta come out to the tunnel."

"What's happening?"

"*Now.*"

Joe pulled Kat off her duties. They got into the second rover and drove out along the ridge, following the mass driver track. As they went, Joe explained to Kat what Wez had told him.

Dr. Hofstadter and Priya Nataraj, the ILI doctor, were out at the tunnel. They were not supposed to be there. They did not have the use of a rover—Joe only let the scientists use the rovers for verified scientific expeditions. They must have walked all the way. He had not thought they would ever do that.

Mount Hope filled the rover's windshield. Ahead, the mass driver track ran into a jagged black hole in the hillside. Cabling streamed out, leading to the cluster of antennas hidden beneath lunar camouflage netting on top of the hill, including Kat's illegal Ka-band dish. The tunnel had enough clearance for the rover. Joe drove slowly in, past the gleaming hoops of tens of thousands of electromagnets. He permitted himself a pang of regret. The mass driver could've been great, if only he had been given time to complete it.

Of course, part of the reason progress had not been faster was because the crew spent half their time working on the tunnel.

The other rover blocked the way. It was parked outside the mouth of a side tunnel. Power lines ran from its chassis into the side tunnel—the crew were using the rover's fuel cell to drive their power tools, excavating the rooms and halls of what they were already calling Hab3.

Right now, however, Wez and his assistants stood outside the airlock on the opposite side of the tunnel, staring at it helplessly.

"They're in there," Wez said. "They got in while we were busy working."

"Right," Joe said.

"I never thought they'd come all the way out here."

"Me either." Joe contemplated the Hab2 airlock. It had been meant as a replacement for the dangerously degraded personnel airlock of the hab complex. Now it was the entrance to Hab2, a mirror image of the hab under construction on the other side of the tunnel. His crew had welded the airlock into the side-tunnel mouth, riveting the rim flanges to the aluminum liner of the hab. The digital display above the hatch indicated that it was operational. "Come on, let's get this over with," he said to Kat.

They went in.

Hab2 was already complete and partly furnished. The aluminum coating of the rock walls gave the rooms and halls a stark retro aesthetic. The air was cold enough that they could see their breath. Two suits, belonging to Hofstadter and Nataraj, lay in the vestibule, shedding dust. The sight irritated Joe. He wanted to keep Hab2 and Hab3 as dust-free as possible.

When the time came to move in, he planned to relocate the MVDA in here and run flexitubes to the airlocks, so they wouldn't have to track dust in at all.

Dr. Hofstadter sat in the first room off the trunk corridor, behind a large swoopy-looking transparent carbon-fiber desk with embedded screens and a bulging underside.

"So this is where my new desk went," he said.

Joe shrugged. It was true. The desk had originally been intended for Dr. Hofstadter as a replacement for his old computer, which had broken. Actually, Joe had had Kat break it, under cover of routine maintenance, because he didn't like what Dr. Hofstadter was doing with it. The new one was better. It was, in fact, a Quantix Computing Productivity System. The bulge under the desk was an honest-to-God quantum computer, capable of smashing with insouciant ease through pretty much any commercially available encryption.

"It's amazing how much stuff gets damaged in transit," Joe said.

"Clearly," Dr. Hofstadter said. Everything else in here had also been intended for ILI's use, including the chairs that Drs. Hofstadter and Nataraj were sitting in, the naturalistic area lights, and the ECLSS that filled Hab2 with sweet, richly oxygenated air. Dr. Hofstadter tapped one of the embedded screens of the Quantix. "But bumpy landings don't explain the presence, on top of this hill, of a Ka-band antenna."

He had found the antenna selector in the comms software suite.

"How'd he get into the Quantix?" Kat said angrily.

"Biometric recognition." Joe sighed. "It was supposed to be his, so his fingerprints are in the system as the admin. We would have had to wipe the whole thing to get rid of them, and you didn't want to do that, remember?"

"Heck no," Kat said. "There's a hundred thousand dollars'

worth of software on there. You don't need it, anyway," she added to Dr. Hofstadter.

"Yes, I do," the ILI field director said.

"What for?"

Joe winced. He hadn't told Kat exactly why he'd asked her to break Dr. Hofstadter's old computer, because he himself was implicated to some extent. He looked at Priya Nataraj, wondering if she knew. The doctor sat with her arms folded, staring at the wall. She did not look happy, not that she ever did. What was she doing here, anyway? It seemed strange she would be Dr. Hofstadter's first choice for moral support. She was an Indian national.

"Government business," Dr. Hofstadter said, typing.

"Oh yeah? What are you trying to do?" Kat sneered. "Hack the Chinese comms sats?"

Joe couldn't see the screens from where he stood. He went around the desk to see better. Dr. Hofstadter cringed at his approach but kept typing. Joe stood behind his shoulder.

The screen showed a launch trajectory that originated near the moon's equator, broke lunar orbit, and sailed across the moon-Earth gulf into LEO, where it performed several loops around Earth before deviating from its orbit to intersect with another launch trajectory, this one originating from Earth. In fact, from Cape Canaveral.

The diagram was the result of calculations performed by Joe himself earlier in the year. Dr. Hofstadter had asked him to work out the orbital mechanics.

Kat elbowed past him to see. "Is that your stuff, Joe?"

"I did the calcs... He promised in exchange that he wouldn't say anything about the tunnels. *Didn't you*, Dave?" Joe yelled at the seated man in front of him.

"No more I have," Dr. Hofstadter said. "You have my word on that."

Kat was still frowning at the screen. "What *is* that?"

"It's a projectile from Five Stones' Little Sling," Joe said. "Good old Dave hacked its guidance circuitry and nudged it off course so it collided with Tranquility 12."

"America thanks you for your help," Dr. Hofstadter said.

"Wow, that was you?" Kat said to Joe. "I knew the space-debris story was bullshit."

"It was *him*," Joe said, a sense of rage heating up. He hadn't wanted Kat to know about his involvement in the Tranquility 12 disaster. He'd been afraid she'd be horrified. He hadn't told Yuta Nakajima about it, either. He made out it was all Dr. Hofstadter, knowing full well it was a distinction without a difference.

The distinction didn't matter to Kat, either. "You threw a stone at a rocket and hit it, from *this* distance?" she marveled. "The math must've been insane."

"Diabolical," Joe said.

Priya Nataraj spoke up, her voice harsh, toneless. "Six people died on that rocket... But six thousand people died in the water riots in New Delhi last year. *Sixty* thousand farmers in India have committed suicide because of climate-related crop failure. We cannot leave the solution to climate change in the hands of private capital, even if there is a slight amount of collateral damage."

"Hey, it's cool," Kat said. "You had to protect your investment." She winked at Joe. India's investment in ILI—and the investments of the USA, Europe and Japan—would soon be *theirs*.

So would the Big Sling.

If Dr. Hofstadter didn't throw a monkey wrench in the works.

"What are you doing with those calcs?" Joe said.

"Washington asked for a copy of the files," Dr. Hofstadter

said. The humidistat clicked and the fans came on, roaring. The breeze blew Dr. Hofstadter's hair away from his bald spot.

"Who *do* you work for, anyway?" Joe had never quite figured this out.

Dr. Hofstadter took orders from some US government agency, and it wasn't NASA. Rather, it wasn't *only* NASA. From reading Dr. Hofstadter's emails, his contact person was someone who used the alias of "Harrison McNally," but that didn't tell Joe anything. The emails were frustratingly light on specifics. In fact, Joe might never have guessed what it was all about if Dr. Hofstadter hadn't needed him to work out the orbital mechanics. "Is it the DoD? Or the CIA?"

"Neither," Dr. Hofstadter said.

"Oh, don't give me that," Joe said. He slung a quick glance at Priya. She didn't seem shocked. That was odd. Surely Dr. Hofstadter hadn't told *her* he moonlighted for the US government? He wondered for an instant if they might be sleeping together, but dismissed the thought as soon as it occurred. Nothing in their body language implied it. Besides, Dr. Hofstadter was already married... to the moon.

It was the fate of science to get leveraged for profit and power. Dr. Hofstadter should have made his peace with that by now. There was something weird about his demeanor, something Joe had seen in him often recently. A sort of controlled desperation. Maybe he was nearing his snapping point. Maybe Joe would be able to win him over, at long last.

Joe went to get a drink from the cooler in the hall. Returning, he took a turn around the room. "Why don't you just tell them where they can stick it? They can't touch you as long as you're up here. On the moon, we're *free*."

The orbital trajectory of the Little Sling's projectile glimmered in miniature, doubled, on the lenses of Dr. Hofstadter's reading glasses. His eyes were invisible behind the lenses.

"The moon is not a new frontier to colonize, as you seem to think."

"What is it, then?" Joe said agreeably. He took a swig of his reconstituted grapefruit juice.

"It belongs to all of us," Priya said.

"I thought you didn't even like the moon," Joe said.

"One doesn't have to like it," she said, "to recognize its importance to all humanity."

"The moon is not a quarry," Dr. Hofstadter said. Joe recognized the line from his Nobel Prize acceptance speech. "It isn't a piggybank we can smash in case of emergency. It is an inestimably precious part of our shared human inheritance. Priya agrees with me. Emilie and Riku agree with me." He named the leaders of the European and Japanese science contingents, respectively. "The Big Sling must not be built."

"Come again?" Joe said.

"The moment the Big Sling goes into operation," Dr. Hofstadter said weightily, "the era of lunar exploration will be over, and the era of lunar desecration will begin."

"They're already almost finished," Joe said.

"Regrettably, yes... I know."

Joe ran his fingers over the aluminum wall. Cold, smooth. Inert. He leaned over the desk, forcing Dr. Hofstadter to tip his head back to look up at him. Using his physicality to imbue his words with menace, Joe said, "If you do anything stupid, it won't be Washington you've got to worry about."

Dr. Hofstadter started to speak and then stopped. His Adam's apple bobbed. "Surely you agree we can't let the moon be carved up for profit."

"It'll never happen," Joe said.

"It will," Dr. Hofstadter said. "A devastation I will not be a party to." He typed as he spoke.

Joe glanced at the screen. "What have you done?"

"As you noted, up here, we're free."

Joe realized with a shock that he was behind the curve. Dr. Hofstadter wasn't nearing his snapping point. He'd already reached it. He wasn't thinking about going rogue. *He already had.*

With a controlled movement, Joe reached across him to the intercom built into the desk. "Wez, Dr. Hofstadter and Dr. Nataraj are leaving now."

"Roger that," Wez crackled.

Kat saw the pair out, with a certain amount of shoving and swearing. While she was doing that, Joe sat down in his chair, unpleasantly warm from Dr. Hofstadter's haunches. He looked at what Dr. Hofstadter had been doing while he was talking... and before Joe and Kat got here.

"Well?" Kat said, returning.

"Look what he's done. I guess Five Stones' security was no match for the Quantix." Joe gave the desk a hard bang with the flat of his hand.

"That—ohhh no. Maybe we can knock it off course." Kat elbowed him aside to reach the keyboard.

"Already tried. He used up all the fucking propellant." Joe stood, overturning his chair, and headed for the airlock.

48

Nick sat outside, monitoring the braiding machine. His foot still ached if he stood for too long, so he sat on the ground, propped against the black pile of the sling arm. The pile was now taller than he was, and half the length of a soccer field. The braid was a tube slightly over a meter in diameter at the tip, widening as it grew. It would be able to deliver payloads massing up to 1,500 kilograms.

Spiffy the robot bounced from spool to spool, tirelessly turning them to give the machine more slack.

Nick got up to coil the ever-growing braid out of the way.

The ground twitched under his feet.

Moonquake?

A piece of metal fell gently through the beam of his headlamp.

He stooped to pick it up.

Then it was raining metal, plastic, and stone. Big pieces, little pieces and dust. The fragments fell and bounced in utter silence.

Nick stared stupidly at the fragment in his glove. It glinted like a razor blade.

Fenella died of a suit breach. Her life had boiled away in the vacuum.

Nick dived at the pile of braid. He tried to burrow between the lengths, to hide from the deadly hail, but the braid was too heavy to shift. He got his head and shoulders in, while Maddy screamed, "We're hit! Something *hit the hab*!"

"Close the pressure doors," Kurtis bellowed.

"I am! I have!"

Nick felt an impact on the back of his leg. He twisted, turning his upper body between the heavy lengths of braid to see if his suit had been sliced open by the falling debris.

Spiffy squatted over him, straddling his legs. Shielding him.

"Charlie?" he blurted.

"This is Rachel," the familiar crisp voice said. "The hab's been struck by a meteor. We're looking at the satellite images now, but it's dark. Can't see much. Everyone, check in, please."

"Here," Maddy said, breathless. "I'm in the personnel module. I was in the lab when the—the meteor hit. The shock wave knocked me off my feet. I got up and ran. Shit was being sucked backwards all around me. I closed the pressure door at the end of the module. I-I only just made it. Then I closed the pressure door at the end of this module. I'm in the kitchen now. Is pressurization holding in the junction?"

"I'm not sure," Rachel said. "We've lost telemetry from the hab. The comms were obviously in the module that's been affected. I'm speaking to you now via Spiffy."

The robot's bland, Cyclops-eyed visage ceased to be an avatar of Charlie and became a representative of Mission Control.

"I'm here," Nick said.

"Yes, I can see you," Rachel said.

"Here," Kurtis said. "I'm on the summit. Can't see shit. Coming down now."

"Here," Lee said. "I'm in the greenhouse. Did you do this? Did Aaron tell you to wipe me out? Sorry to inform you, you missed. Pressurization is holding in here. Only a couple of trays fell over."

"It's not clear exactly what the impactor was," Rachel said. "Obviously, we had nothing to do with it, and your unfounded accusations are the opposite of helpful, Lee, so if you have nothing else to say, shut up. Nick, you're outside. Please confirm that your suit is undamaged."

Spiffy moved aside so Nick could stand. "My suit's OK." Debris littered the ground. Amazingly, the braiding machine was still turning. "Where's Theo?"

"Theo, check in, please," Rachel said.

"He was in the hab," Kurtis said.

"He was about to come out and relieve me," Nick said.

Nick started running. The closer he got to the hab, the more debris strewed his path. He kicked a shard of tinted glass that looked familiar.

"The rover..." He skidded to a halt.

The vehicle airlock was gone.

Where it once stood, a fresh, shallow crater gaped in the lunar rock.

The end of the work module had sagged into it. The kinetic force of the impact peeled the steel end of the cylinder open like a tin can. The contents of the workshop spilled into the crater. Gas escaped from the wreckage in thin white jets.

Nick's helmet lamp swung, picking out slices of destruction, but couldn't find the rover.

It had been parked at the vehicle airlock...

Eventually his stunned brain connected the concept of *rover* with what he saw: a four-wheeled chassis, dashboard still attached, lying on its side a little way off.

"Theo? You there?"

After many minutes of searching, they found Theo's helmet twenty meters away, with his head still in it.

49

Joe and Kat caught up with Drs. Hofstadter and Nataraj partway back to base. Joe tied tow cables around their necks, and Kat tied the other ends to the rover. They drove on, a little faster than walking pace, forcing Dave and Priya to jog after the rover.

"Got satellite images coming in now," Joe said, sitting in the rover's cabin. "The optics aren't worth shit this time of day, but look at the radar and thermal imaging... the whole north end of their hab is spread across the crater."

There was no response from Dr. Hofstadter. He probably didn't have enough spare lung capacity to talk, after breathing dust all these years.

"Good news is, there's two people moving around outside. So at least two of them escaped."

"There could be more survivors inside the hab," Kat said. "Depends where they were at the time of impact. How big was the projectile?"

"How big it is matters less than how fast it hits," Joe said.

"I know, but if it was a standard Little Sling basalt delivery—"

"It was." He recalled the awful details he'd read on the Hab2 computer screen. "Good old Dave found a payload the Little Sling just launched into lunar orbit. He adapted my calculations to shove it *out* of slingshot orbit and point it at Amundsen Crater. We've got a hollow basalt sphere, likely mass about fifty kilograms, falling from a height of hundreds of kilometers. That gives it a striking velocity almost equal to lunar escape velocity: roughly Mach 7."

"Yowza," Kat said.

She fiddled with the radio settings. The satellite images were coming in via a relay from the Ka-band antenna.

"Hey, looks like we can get audio. I guess they have some kind of emergency backup."

Nick Morrison's voice filled the cabin, as clear as if he were in there with them. "I think I found something—"

Joe and Kat listened in silence to the choppy conversation between Nick, Kurtis Dean, and Rachel Hamilton, relating the discovery of Theodor Johansson's head.

"I can't even imagine..." Kat said.

"You did that," Joe said to Dr. Hofstadter. "Hear me, Dave? You killed that man. How do you feel about that?"

Breathless, indistinct, the croaking reply came: "Fuck the government!"

Joe laughed until tears welled up. "Oh, Dave. Check out that twenties radicalism. 'Fuck the government'—right. That's the kind of thing you doomers used to write on social media. Then a big research grant came along, and you sold out to the Department of Defense, or whoever the fuck it is. You're guilty twice over, Dave." He touched the accelerator. "Run faster."

Joe had to slow down again before they reached base, because Dave and Priya kept falling to their knees and getting dragged. He didn't want to hole their suits. God knows suits and spares were at a premium.

Back at the landers, he docked the rover with the MVDA. "You go in," he said to Kat. "Sit on that channel. Try to find out how many survivors there are, what their life-support status is."

"You think we should drive up and offer to help?" Kat, irrepressible, waggled her eyebrows.

"I'm thinking about it," Joe said.

"Got it."

She slithered through the docking hatch. Joe climbed into his suit, exited the rover, and untied the two scientists. He gave Priya a slap on the back. She stumbled away, sobbing wordlessly. Joe took hold of Dr. Hofstadter's arm. "You're coming with me."

He dragged the geophysicist straight to the reactor.

"No, please!" Dr. Hofstadter said, like they all did.

"You didn't give Theodor Johansson a chance to say no. He didn't have any chance at all."

The radiator vanes floated in sunlight like a gigantic, wide-open pair of scissors. Joe hauled Dr. Hofstadter to the airlock in the bottom of the truss, opened it, and went in with him. Dr. Hofstadter struggled.

"You're a filthy murderer," Joe said.

"I'll tell Luxembourg what you're doing! I-I'll tell Washington!"

"Go right ahead," Joe said. "Then I'll tell them what *you* just did."

The inner end of the chamber opened. The familiar bassy throb of the Stirling pistons seeped through Joe's suit. Dr. Hofstadter's mouth gaped in a cry of panic. Joe gave him a shove onto the catwalk and backed away before the rising tide of terror surfaced the memory of watching Dr. Hofstadter click EXECUTE to shoot down Tranquility 12.

Fuck the government.

Good old Dave wasn't wrong about that.

Joe went back to his office, where several people had gathered. They eavesdropped, while drinking coffee and eating blueberry muffins, on the aftermath of the impact, as conveyed by the chatter among the surviving Five Stones crew. It seemed Theo was the only casualty. Maddy Huxley and Lee Yang were safe in the hab. However, the destruction of the vehicle airlock and the rover also destroyed both of the spacesuits in the charging assembly—Maddy's and Lee's. The crew now had only two suits for four people.

"And the other two won't be able to wear the ones they've got," said Andy, the ArxaSys Lunar spacesuit repair expert. "They're custom-fitted. Maddy Huxley can't weigh more than fifty kilos soaking wet. And looking at this publicity shot of the crew, Lee Yang's a little squirt of a guy. Nick Morrison and Kurtis Dean are both taller; Kurtis is built like a brick shithouse."

"So, Lee and Maddy won't be able to wear either of their suits," Kat said.

"Well, they could put them on," Andy said. "They just wouldn't be able to do any work in them. Either way, that's two people with no suits."

"Basically, they're stuck in the hab," Joe said.

"That's what it looks like."

"At least they're in the personnel module, which has a working airlock," Trig said. "Their vehicle airlock was on the end that got destroyed."

"Along with their rover." Joe checked the time since he incarcerated Dr. Hofstadter. Thirty minutes.

"That's not even the worst part," Kat said. "Their ECLSS was in there, among other stuff. Oxygen isn't getting replenished."

"Except by the plants," Joe said. "You did leave them *some* plants."

"Not many. What do you think? We head up there and offer a helping hand?"

Everyone grinned, looking at Joe.

"Not yet," he said after a long moment. "They can hold on for a while. And they still haven't finished the Big Sling."

"Hell," Kat said. "They're not gonna be working on *that*."

"I think they will be." Joe checked the time again. Thirty-five minutes.

"He's got a point, Kat. Could be risky sticking our necks out right now," Trig noted.

"Exactly. I want to sit tight for a while and see what the blowback is gonna be." Joe got up. "I'll be back."

He'd never left anyone in the reactor room longer than forty-five minutes. Fifty minutes had passed by the time he got the airlock open.

Dr. Hofstadter lay on the floor beside the cap of the reactor, stripped to his long-johns and one sock. His face was bloody. He'd been banging it on the aluminum floor.

Joe cursed. And kept cursing while he forced Dr. Hofstadter back into his suit—a clumsy, frustrating job, as he didn't dare take off his own suit. Fighting against fear, loneliness, and guilt, he dragged the older man up the ramp to the catwalk and out.

Dr. Hofstadter moaned continually. His blood smeared the inside of his faceplate. Hauling him away from the reactor, Joe finally made out what he was saying: "Put me back in."

"*What?*"

"Put me back in!"

Joe wondered if the old guy had lost his mind for good.

"Better to kill one person... than to kill the moon."

"Oh, is *that* how you're justifying it?" Joe said. "What a solipsistic dweeb you are. And it isn't just one person. The projectile destroyed their life-support machinery, so you may have killed *five* people."

He received no answer. Dr. Hofstadter had passed out.

Joe delivered him to Priya in the ILI hab and went back to monitor the Ka-band.

50

They were dropped off outside the Memorial Amphitheater in Arlington National Cemetery, and crossed the road: Charlie, Yuta, and Aaron, fighting the soupy heat in shorts and T-shirts. Baseball caps with LED visors to thwart facial recognition. They were recognized despite the effort to remain anonymous. A man trotted across the crosswalk and caught up with them in front of the *Columbia* Memorial.

"Listen, I hope I'm not intruding," said Sean Radek, the CEO of SpaceZ.

Aaron scowled. "How did you know we were gonna be here?"

"Asked your PA," Sean said.

His bodyguard stood at a distance, attracting nervous glances from the chaperons of day-tripping schoolchildren.

"I was sorry to hear about the latest thing," Sean said.

"The latest thing," Charlie echoed, in a mood halfway between cynical bafflement and despair.

An impactor had struck the Five Stones hab. At first, they thought it was a meteor. Until the latest payload from the Little Sling turned out to be missing. Putting the pieces together, someone had hacked the payload, despite the expensive security upgrade Aaron bought after the last time. The hab was half-ruined. Another crew member was dead. *The latest thing.*

"Was it... *them?*" Sean moved his head in the direction of the Korean War Memorial. The direction of Washington, DC.

"I can't say anything about that," Aaron said, in a tone unusually lacking in bravado, "because I don't know. I kinda doubt it though. If we can't finish the Big Sling, guess who's screwed? Not just us."

"We're screwed anyway," Yuta said in a low voice. He'd been virtually silent during their trip up. Charlie caught him drawing pictures of weird creatures, half-man, half-machine, on the airplane cocktail napkins.

Sean sighed. "What I came to say—this stupid lawsuit. Let's settle it." He spread his hands. "There's nothing in it for you because you can't win. We can and will prove we weren't at fault in the T-13 incident. And there's nothing in it for us, either. You don't even have enough cash to pay our legal fees. So I'm willing to settle out of court."

Aaron cocked his head. "Why, because you're such a nice guy?"

Sean nodded, a smirk tugging at the corners of his mouth.

"Bullshit," Aaron said without humor. "We actually have a meeting." He glanced at his smartwatch. Charlie looked at her phone. The guy was late. "Gimme a call when I'm back in Florida."

"Listen, I want us to work together," Sean said. "I still believe in the Big Sling. You're close to completion, right? I still believe your crew can do it. And I'm still willing to buy your capacity. We're facing in the same direction, with the same vision. First the moon. Then Mars. The future of humanity—"

"Isn't gonna happen," Aaron interrupted, his face pain-racked. "We already did a deal!" He spun around, scanning

Memorial Drive and the tour groups milling on the other side of the street. "With *them*."

Two men and a woman in business suits were getting out of an SUV with tinted windows.

"Uh-*huh*," Sean said.

"Now you know," Aaron said.

"Why would you—"

"They offered me money!" Aaron's voice was so agonized, Charlie cringed.

"For your launch capacity."

Aaron nodded.

Charlie thought, *Sean's guessed. He must have guessed. It's so obvious—*

In reality, it hadn't been obvious to her. Not until they told her about the secret heart of the deal, the reason they never should have done it.

"It's done and dusted, Sean," Aaron said. "I can't back out now even if I wanted to."

"No," said Bill Lundgren, ambling up to them, breezy in a seersucker shirt that skimmed his paunch. "You'd better not, Aaron. Better not even think about it."

"Hey, Bill," Charlie and Yuta mumbled.

Bill, the VC who'd thrown Five Stones a lifeline during their darkest days; Bill, who made a dirty fortune shorting stocks after the Little Sling launched; Bill, who descended from the heights of the venture capital industry to roost on Five Stones' board of directors, claiming he wanted to dedicate the rest of his career to achieving the dream of large-scale lunar ISRU... Bill, who had so many connections in DC. To people who never appeared on television and never gave out their real names.

It was through Bill the deal had been proposed to Five Stones, and Bill who encouraged Aaron to accept it.

And it was Bill smiling now, shoulder to shoulder with the

older of the men from the SUV. Their congenial expressions matched like a set of Halloween masks.

The other man and the woman had taken up positions nearby, one near the USS *Maine* Memorial, the other between the box hedges on this side of the street.

The older man from the SUV—Charlie knew him as Harrison McNally—said to Sean, "You'd better go."

"Yes, sir," Sean said, backing away. His bodyguard fell into step with him, watching the closer of the two AR-eyed operatives. She stared back at them, fingers playing over her concealed weapon.

Charlie thought of her own weapon, the Beretta she'd gotten from Rachel. It was at home in the same safe where she kept her important papers. She hadn't even considered bringing it today. For which she was glad, and at the same time, disgusted with herself for being a coward.

She turned away and pretended to look at the *Columbia* Memorial, and then she really did look at it, while McNally engaged Aaron in ersatz small talk. She looked at the *Challenger* Memorial and the Crew Dragon Memorial, too. Three monuments shaped like gravestones, with inset bronze plaques bearing names and faces. *In Grateful and Loving Memory.*

People shuffled behind her, chatting loudly, scarcely pausing to look at these tributes to brave men and women who died for the dream of space. There should be a fourth memorial here: Tranquility 12. Charlie knew it would never be built. As far as the world concerned, the crew of Tranquility 12 died in the pursuit of profit by an upstart NewSpace company. Along with Fenella Khan and Theodor Johansson.

The dream of space had motivated Charlie ever since she was tall enough to peer through her mother's backyard telescope. Far from failing in the wake of the disasters that beset

Five Stones, it burned brighter than ever. And the burning was painful now.

She felt something she'd never expected to feel: *guilt*. Because she wasn't up there on the moon, risking her own life alongside Nick, Lee, Maddy, and Kurtis. Instead, she was standing in Arlington National Cemetery, listening to a man from the government carve Aaron's dignity away in conversational splinters. The heat was soupy. The smell of new-mown grass arose from the graves.

"Well?" McNally said at last. "You wanted to meet with me?"

"We were wondering—" Aaron said.

"Our *people*!" Yuta interrupted, almost shouting. "You have to help! We don't have any money!"

McNally clicked his tongue. "What happened to the money we gave you?"

"The down payment?" Aaron said. "Spent it on Tranquility 13. You know that."

"If you don't help, they're going to *die*!" Yuta lurched at McNally. The operative on the other side of the hedge feature lifted her head as quickly as a snake. Aaron grabbed Yuta's arm.

"Mr. Nakajima," McNally said, "you're begging the question."

"You have to help!"

"You're assuming that I—that we—give a shit."

McNally kept smiling. Bill chuckled ruefully.

Yuta looked from one to the other, allowing Aaron to haul him out of punching range. He jerked away and stomped past Charlie. He stood facing the *Challenger* Memorial, head down.

"They don't care," Charlie said to him, pitching her voice for Bill and McNally to hear. "They genuinely don't care if our people die. They would even prefer it if they did, because it makes NewSpace look bad."

Yuta spun back around to McNally, whose name was as fake as his smile. "What about your guy at ILI? You could make him help them! He could do *something*!"

"Who?" McNally said, pouting in real or affected confusion.

"Dr. David Hofstadter," Yuta said.

"Where did you hear that name?"

"From—"

"No one," Charlie said.

"From someone we know up there," Yuta finished.

Charlie held her breath. Yuta was talking about Joe, the ArxaSys Lunar guy who'd arm-twisted them into growing cannabis. Yuta had asked Joe if he knew anything about the Tranquility 12 disaster. Joe confirmed he did. He even knew who did it, and he would tell them in exchange for the cannabis plants. Turned out that the famous Dr. David Hofstadter was working for McNally's people. He hacked the Little Sling on their orders. Charlie was pretty sure Joe wasn't supposed to know any of that. And nor were they.

McNally stared at Yuta. Then he sighed and shook his head, a touch theatrically. "Poor old Dave. He's been up there too long. He's gone a little..." He raised one palm, parallel to the ground, and twirled it like a spacecraft going into a tumble.

"A little what?" Yuta said. "A little criminal? A little without any basic morality? A little like *you*?"

"You know these genius types," McNally said, his gaze steely. "Just because they know a lot about one thing, they think they're competent to make judgment calls about everything."

Yuta reddened and turned back to the *Challenger* Memorial. Tears glinted in the corners of his eyes.

"Sounds like you might want to replace him," Aaron said. "You need someone reliable up there to safeguard your investments."

"That's the truth," McNally said.

"Was it you this time, too?" Aaron demanded, point blank. Charlie let out a gasp. She hadn't expected him to confront McNally like this. "Did you drop that payload on our hab?"

"No," McNally said.

"*Why?*"

"Don't be a goddamn idiot," McNally said. "We neither anticipated nor sanctioned this. We're as upset as you are."

"The issue is comms security," Bill murmured. "These days, with quantum computing, no encryption is good enough."

"And who's got quantum computers except the government?" Aaron said, no longer expecting a response. "You'll be glad to know we've shut down the Little Sling. Should have done it before, but we needed the revenue stream."

"Get the Big Sling finished, and you'll never have to worry about money again," McNally said

"Did your guy on the moon hack Tranquility 13, too?" Sean Radek had approached them again, unnoticed by Charlie. A few paces distant, his bodyguard faced the female operative, holding her off. Sean shoved past Aaron. "Did he put a time bomb in the subsystems control software?"

"I thought I told this punk to go away," McNally said to Bill.

"You did, Harry," Bill said.

"He came back," McNally observed.

"Because he's smart," Aaron said wearily. "He knows that if you got us, he's probably gonna be next."

"There was a time bomb in there," Sean said rapidly, with nerdish conviction. "A real clever piece of malware, designed to shut off the cryocooling system and disable the vent valves as soon as the spacecraft landed. We didn't detect it previous to launch, which means it wasn't *in* there at launch. It was injected into the control interface at some point during the flight or on the spacecraft's approach to the moon. That points to your guy."

McNally shook his head. "Dave Hofstadter may be a world authority on cold traps, but he wouldn't recognize malware if it up and bit him on the ass." Bill laughed.

Sean persisted. "Does he have a computer person working for him? Don't tell me you didn't put a world-class hacker up there to guard against Chinese and Russian cyberattacks."

"Quit trying to shift the blame," McNally said. His joviality had vanished. "Your software is shit. Period."

"We have the best spacecraft control systems in the world." Sean pointed to the Crew Dragon Memorial. "Our predecessor company sweated blood to build our inheritance of flight-tested, self-improving AI, which we have continued to iterate—"

"Then look at your own people," Bill said. "It's usually an insider. People will do anything for money."

"Not everyone is as cynical as you," Charlie blurted.

A small girl stood on a stepladder in a Connecticut back-yard, gazing in wonder at the moon caught in a circle of glass. Harriet's hand rested on her shoulder: *Maybe your children will get a chance to travel there.* Before her brain betrayed her, Harriet had been an astrophysics professor. Charlie saw herself as carrying on her mother's legacy of disinterested valor.

"For us, money is just something you have to have in order to do things. Which is exactly how you got us. You couldn't convince us to sell out, so your guy on the moon hacked the Little Sling to destroy T-12, so we would have no choice except to sign your deal. We lost everything in ten seconds. We couldn't carry on without an immediate cash infusion." She stared at Bill, who'd come up with that cash, with strings trailing behind it to infinity.

"Maybe we shouldn't have signed. Maybe we should have given up, called it a day, sold the company for parts. Doesn't really matter though, does it? Someone *else* would have done it, now that we've proved it can be done." Her lips curled back in distaste. She was shaking. "You killed six people to force our hand! Now another person is dead! How many more people are you going to kill, for *power*?"

"Charlie," Aaron said.

Head high, she turned and walked away. After a few steps she lost her nerve and started running. The second operative, stationed beneath the memorial to the sailors of the USS *Maine*, left his post and kept pace with her, jogging along the tree-shaded paths, waiting for her to get out of breath and slow down.

51

Halfway back to Florida, Charlie surfaced from gloomy contemplation of the clouds outside the window. Yuta was listening to music. Aaron was pestering the cabin attendant for another mini-bottle of wine.

"Switch with me," she said. She made Aaron change places with her: shuffle, slither, stoop. She sat between them, boxing Yuta in against the window. She pulled his headphones off.

"Wha—Hey! What is it?"

"Where are those drawings you did this morning?"

"I threw them away." Yuta sunk into his seat, but Charlie wouldn't let him withdraw.

"What were they of?"

"Just stupid sketches."

"You were drawing exosuits."

"Just thinking about it."

"I've been thinking about it, too."

He shrugged. "It was your idea in the first place."

"And it might just work."

Aaron leaned across, blasting Charlie with winey breath.

"Hey! That's an idea! I knew you guys would think of something—"

Charlie pushed him, hard. "You—just—shut up." She angled her body so she faced Yuta, her back to Aaron. "Let's do a quick and dirty schematic..."

———

In the dark, beneath the floating blue jellybean of Earth, Nick dug through the rubble of the work module. The ECLSS was a write-off, but Nick was hoping to find one or more of the backup oxygen tanks intact. He jerked on a crumpled stringer; the whole structure swayed around him.

Spiffy took hold of the stringer and bent it out of the way.

"Drag that stuff out from under there," Rachel said.

Nick no longer trusted the robot. He silently strained at the wreckage, careful not to get underneath the stringer.

"Well?" Kurtis said over the radio.

Dragging the smashed ECLSS clear, Nick panted, "How about some fucking help?"

"If you're beat, I'll do it."

"No, it's fine," Nick gasped. He'd been trying to goad Kurtis into leaving the braiding machine, which Kurtis stubbornly continued to monitor. He heaved again. A pipe came away in his hand.

"There," Rachel said. "That's the primary backup tank."

It had split open. The astounding force of the impact continued to reverberate, limned all over again by each piece of steel crumpled like paper, each lump of junk that used to be a high-tech machine.

Nick pawed through the debris some more. The secondary backup tank was also a dead loss. Some of the piping might be salvageable, he just couldn't be bothered right now. He climbed out of the crater. Spiffy cleared the rim in a single bound.

"Your next option is the oxygen plant," Rachel said. "It may be possible to get it up and running—"

"I know, I know," Nick said, trudging around the hab.

Theo had complained throughout their mission about the lack of resources allotted to the oxygen plant. Nick ended up helping him build that bamboo frame for the solar concentrator array. They hadn't yet finished assembling the thing, and now Theo was dead. Nick would have to spend hours getting up to speed on the assembly procedures. There really wasn't any particular hurry. The reduction furnace wouldn't be usable until lunar dawn, in any case.

He went in through the personnel airlock. He had to crank it manually, struggling against the resistance of the inert hydraulics, since the hab had lost power.

Every time the airlock was used, they lost fifteen cubic liters of oxygen to the vacuum. Dust came in, too. Nick was beyond worrying about that. Coughing, he removed the oxygen cylinder from his suit's life-support backpack and placed it in the oxygen concentrator. The little machine had its own battery. It sucked oxygen out of the ambient atmosphere to refill the cylinder.

Leaving the air in the hab slightly worse.

He'd done the math.

Assuming a 22% oxygen content, the greenhouse and the personnel module held roughly 45,000 cubic liters of oxygen.

While that sounded like a lot, a moderately active adult needs about 550 cubic liters of oxygen a day.

There were four of them.

The math gave them twenty days to live.

Of course, in reality, they wouldn't last that long. They'd die from carbon dioxide poisoning once the CO_2 content of the air rose above 5%.

The math got tricky there, because the plants sucked a certain amount of CO_2 out of the air and exhaled a certain amount of oxygen, both factors impossible to precisely measure now that the atmospheric sensor data processing computer was a smear of metal and plastic in the crater. Nick's best guess was that they had nine days before CO_2 toxicity kicked in.

They would die at dawn.

He walked through the dark, cold personnel module. Emergency chemlight pads glowed green on the wall. The floor chilled his socked feet. On the moon, things heat up fast but cool down slowly. In the twenty-four hours since the disaster, the hab had cooled by about two degrees. Assuming a steady rate of cooling, they wouldn't freeze to death before they suffocated.

The plants, though...

Nick cranked the greenhouse pressure door. He closed it behind him before too much of the comparatively warm air could escape. In here, the grow lights created a semblance of normality. They were running the lights, space heaters, and a couple of standing fans off Greenfinger's integrated fuel cell. The gardening robot had been dismembered so the garden might live—for a little while longer, anyway.

Nick felt a bamboo leaf. It was ominously brittle.

Lee slumped over the workbench with his head pillowed on his arms. He'd reacted with heroic presence of mind in the moments after the impact, shutting down the plumbing in the greenhouse, and had then worked for hours to reroute the graywater loop so precious H_2O wouldn't be lost to the vacuum. After that burst of activity, he'd withdrawn into himself. Nick laid a hand on his back. It rose and fell. Just sleeping.

Maddy scuffled between the bamboo plants. "What's happening?" She plucked at Nick's arms. "What are you doing in here?"

"Sit down," Nick said. "Stop yelling. The less you talk, the less you move, the less oxygen you use."

"Why aren't you working on the oxygen plant?" She swayed in front of him like a daffodil in the breeze.

"I have to eat."

No more tortillas. No more hamburgers. Nick scooped soy cereal into a dirty bowl, added water, and shoveled the mixture into his mouth with his fingers.

"I feel trapped," Maddy said, sitting on the floor with her arms around her knees. "So trapped."

Nick understood. He could at least go outside. She was literally trapped in the hab without a spacesuit. There was nothing to say that would help.

He ate as much of the soy cereal as he could force down, then leaned back against the wall. He closed his eyes. In the darkness, he saw mosquito coils burning on the verandah of the farmhouse, and heard his father saying to his mother, *I think they're coming tonight.*

Don't let them in, Will.

They only want to talk.

"Guys? Nick? You there?"

The memories drifted away like smoke from the mosquito coils.

"Who's that?" Maddy said, lifting her head.

"Charlie," Nick said.

"Yeah, it's me," Charlie said, from the intercom. "How are you doing?"

Lee opened one eye. "Can't complain. A little carbon dioxide in the air. A little dust. It just gives you a tickle in the throat. Getting a bit cold in here, but I hear it's nice and warm where we're going. Tell Aaron before I die, the last thing I'm gonna do is delete my regolith analysis code."

Kurtis, outside, said, "Zip it, Yang."

"You zip it, knucklehead," Lee yelled.

"I'm calling because I may have a solution of sorts for you," Charlie said before tensions rose any higher. "Don't get your hopes up. It may not work. But if it does, you'll at least all be able to work outside, and maybe move the oxygen plant to the top of the central peak, which would give you a chance of getting production underway."

"Let's hear it," Maddy said, sitting up.

"What I have for you right now is an experimental spacesuit concept that we refer to as an exosuit. This is something I came up with a couple of years back. It's *very* experimental, but Yuta and I are building a prototype right now, and we think you could duplicate our work with the materials you have on hand. I'm sending you some blueprints. This is basically a human-operated macrobot. It doesn't need a power source, because you are the power source. It doesn't need to be custom-fitted, because you're inside a space that's relatively capacious compared to the volume of a spacesuit."

"OK, go on," Maddy said.

Charlie's voice picked up. "I catch a lot of flak whenever I say this, but spacesuits are an obsolete technology. They're confining and hard to move around in. The glove is like a mitt that doubles as a hand-grip exerciser. Every movement costs significant effort. You guys know this and have probably wondered more than once why we're still using these Apollo-era pressure suits.

"The short answer is there are gaps telepresence just can't fill. That's why you guys are there. The longer answer is that research into skinsuits, supposedly the next generation of space-suits, has been going on for decades, soaking up millions and millions of dollars, and they just keep failing. There are a lot of hard problems there. My thought was, why not go *backwards*? Cruder is Better. Let's stop trying to fit the spacesuit to the astronaut, and instead make a robot the astronaut can sit inside and manipulate by moving his or her arms and legs."

"Oh, holy almighty rising star." Lee cackled, jabbing a finger weakly at the screen of his laptop. "She wants us to build *mechas*."

Nick got up and looked at the screen. Charlie had sent a concept sketch and a couple of detailed diagrams. The sketch showed a grotesque, apelike robot with a bubble head and a barrel chest, short thighs with long shins, short upper arms and long forearms that ended in claws.

"Yeah, we're trying not to use the M-word," Charlie said. "Just look at the blueprints. The hub, the body, is a chopped-off cylinder. You have plenty of those in the quarry. The head is the helmet of a pressure suit. You have two pressure suits that are too damaged to wear, but—"

"No, we don't," Nick said. "Lee's and Maddy's suits were *vaporized*. The helmets are not intact, let me tell you."

"I wasn't talking about those. I meant Theo's and Fenella's." There was a short silence. Charlie went on, "For the skin, I sent up some sheets of Kevlar with a synthetic rubber lining. I believe you're currently using those for curtains. Take them down and cut them to shape. For the insulation layer, you can use the insulation from the work module, which is basalt fiberglass. You'll also need a vaporproof inner layer. We think you could use the foam that the advance cargo was packed in inside the Dailirs. It's out in the shed. Melt it down with the acetylene torch and re-form it into polyethylene, and there you have it. You'll just have to do a lot of sewing."

No one smiled.

"The grippers and the joints can come from the Bobs. I'll instruct Spiffy to dismantle them—"

Nick coughed. "Excuse me. The skeleton. Your notation here says 'basalt bones.' We don't have any basalt rods like this.

We can't cast any basalt until dawn. And we'll all be dead by then."

"Right... I forgot to alter that. I was in a hurry. I know you don't have basalt rods, but you do have something else. You've been using it to build things all along—furniture, crutches, spaceframes—*Bamboo*."

"Not anymore, we don't," Nick said. "My whole harvest got pulverized. It was in storage in the work module."

"Um, yes, you do," Charlie said. "At least, I was told you've still got a lot of it growing in the greenhouse."

Nick looked around at the tall bamboo thickets shivering in the wind from the fan. The only positive factor in the oxygen/CO_2 equation on which their lives hung.

"Forget it," Kurtis said from outside. "We ain't got time for all that. And anyway, Nick stole the shears."

52

Kurtis squatted by the braiding machine, as still as a monk at prayer. Nick approached silently. He waited for Kurtis to notice him. Kurtis didn't move.

Nick gathered up a coil of braid, staggering under its weight, and lugged it over to the pile. The low mountain of braid extended farther than his headlamp beam could reach.

"I had the shears in my room," he said. "I've put them back."

"Don't put 'em where Lee can get them," Kurtis said.

"This exosuit thing. Why not give it a try? It might work."

"It's just a distraction. Something for Maddy and Lee to do to give them hope."

"They can't do it without us," Nick said.

"They'll have to do it without me," Kurtis said. "I'm busy."

"We gotta be up to twenty klicks by now."

Far above them, the summit of the central peak floated like an iceberg on the sea of darkness, already lit by dawn. Kurtis said, "When I finish with this, I'm going to commence the winching operation. We gotta get the whole arm up to the top and thread it through the hub. Attach the counterweight, and hook up the Stirling engines. I'm gonna need your help with all of that."

"If we get it done, then what?"

"Then they send the rocket. That's all they're waiting for. This moon mecha thing is just a distraction."

"They're not gonna send a rocket."

"You gotta have faith, Morrison."

Nick went to the shed. He gathered up a giant load of the foam packaging material. It was all in one piece, so he could easily drag it. He looked for Theo's helmet. It wasn't there. He went back to the braiding machine. "Have you seen..."

Kurtis had Theo's helmet lying on the ground beside him.

Nick went closer. Theo's head was still in it.

"Quit shining that light in my eyes," Kurtis said.

"I need that," Nick said.

"Shut the fuck up and go away!" Kurtis exploded. "All you care about is saving your own lily-white ass."

Nick squatted down, so his headlamp shone on the ground, and Theo's helmet, between them. "Listen. I know I haven't been the greatest person to work with. I... I got my issues. But can you... can we work together? We need..." He trailed off, exasperated with himself.

Kurtis raised his head. From behind his blank, scratched-up faceplate came a raw tone of voice Nick had never heard from him before. "What are you *talking* about? You ain't got issues. *I* got issues. I always gotta be right; never make mistakes. And when I do, it's other people who pay for them." Kurtis got up and turned the spools to give the braiding machine more slack. He sat down again. "I thought I could get it right this time. Ain't no Chicaps on the moon, right? What could go wrong?" He patted Theo's helmet.

"Stop beating yourself up," Nick said. "I miss him, too. Theo was..."

Now that Theo was dead, Nick knew he'd been their peace-keeper. He defused conflicts with his gentle humor. Despite his annoying klutziness, he'd maintained a steady temperament. He'd been a kind of anchor for them all.

"He was a good guy," Nick said, unable to put anything more into words, in case he started crying.

"Yeah. He was a good guy."

"Let's bury him."

Kurtis was silent for a long moment. "All right. The braid'll be done in another twenty minutes. Then we'll do it."

When the braid was complete, they turned off the machine. After removing Theo's head from his helmet, they put the head in a body bag, folded it up small, and buried it under a light covering of regolith in the outdoor shed.

Then they cut some of the insulation out of the damaged work module, as much as they could reach. They took that and Theo's helmet into the hab.

"You need to remove the electronics from both helmets," Charlie said. "Find the oxygen regulators. We're going to incorporate those into a simple system like scuba divers use."

"Roger," Kurtis said. "What about the foam packaging? You want someone to get started on that?"

"Yeah. Do you have the acetylene torch? Use it on the bottom of the container holding the foam, and don't go too hot or it will burn. I would do it in the personnel module. Make sure you have a fan nearby to get rid of the fumes. When it melts, you'll pour it onto a flat surface, shovel the fiberglass on top of it, and then sew it behind the Kevlar."

"I'll get started cutting up the foam," Maddy said. She left the greenhouse, taking one of the fans with her.

Kurtis spread the insulation out on the floor. The smell of burnt gunpowder rose from the dirty, ragged sheet of fiberglass.

He measured and drew lines, singing softly: "Oh Susanna, don't you cry for me..."

Nick sized up the bamboo stems with his eyes. He knelt and chopped. The newly sharpened shears went through the stems like butter.

Lee worked on the helmets. Nick, deep in the bamboo forest, heard him saying something, and Kurtis responding irritably. He backed into the central aisle, dragging an armload of bushy stems. "What did you say, Lee?"

"Come take a look at this."

Nick went over to the workbench. Lee had Theo's and Fenella's helmets upended on the bench, side by side. He'd pried the covers off the internal electronics.

"See this?" He lifted a component out of Fenella's helmet with his pliers. "It's not the same."

"Not the same as what?"

"As Theo's. This device isn't in Theo's helmet. Only in Fenella's."

"What is it?"

"That's what I'm going to find out."

It was a silver square with two or three small circuit boards dangling off it. Nick said, "Is that a single-board computer?"

Lee looked up at him. "And how do you know that?"

Long, slow afternoons in Remy the cracker king's mom's trailer. The guys yelping at their screens amidst clouds of THC vapor, while Nick patiently disassembled smartphones and removed components that looked a lot like the ones dangling off that device. Like 6G modems.

The 6G loophole was ten years dead. So was warshipping.

But technology for use in space always lagged about ten years behind consumer tech...

"I never knew you worked with computers," Lee said.

"I don't anymore," Nick said. "You said this was in Fenella's helmet? Not Theo's?"

"Quit running your yaps," Kurtis said from the floor. His tone was easy but cool. "If we're going to do this, let's do it."

Lee said, "I was only—"

"You were only wasting time like always. Do what you were fucking told, or let someone else do it."

Lee bowed his head, his shoulders rigid.

Nick backed away and began to chop the leaves off his lengths of bamboo. They would cure in no time in the increasingly cold and dry air.

53

With his upper body inside the first exosuit, his legs sticking out of the collar, Nick connected the oxygen cylinder, which was mounted on brackets inside the body of the suit, to the regulator in the helmet. He backed out. The exosuit lay deflated on the floor of the pressure module.

The crew spent the last day and a half melting, cutting, sewing, epoxying, and welding. Now they all gazed down at what they'd built.

It looked more like a giant's rag doll than a mecha from a science fiction movie. But it wasn't going to get any more done than this, and the air was getting worse all the time.

Nick broke the silence. "Well, someone's got to try it out."

"I will," Maddy and Kurtis said simultaneously.

Kurtis shook his head at Maddy with a tender half smile and sat down to work his legs into the suit. "I did the sewing. If the seams pop, I got only myself to blame."

Nick passed Kurtis the helmet. Kurtis screwed it on while huddling inside the suit. Nick had cut a hole out of the lid of the dust canister that formed the body of the suit, and welded the helmet onto the lid, adding handles on the inside, so Kurtis just had to turn the handles to close the lid and seal himself in. His head popped up into the bubble.

"Well, here I go," he said through the radio transmitter in the helmet.

The suit was too tall for him to stand up inside the hab; using the direct-drive claws on the ends of his arms, he hauled himself to the airlock.

"Be careful," Charlie said over the radio. "Oh God, guys, I have, like, no fingernails left. I'm biting my toenails now."

Nick rolled his eyes.

Maddy closed the airlock behind Kurtis. Moments later they heard him say, "Well, I'm out."

"Aaand, any leaks?" Nick said.

"That's a negative, so far. Suit's kinda sticking to my legs. Hard to stand up."

"Add more oxygen," Nick said. "Just open the regulator a bit."

"Got it. Standing up now."

"Wow!" Charlie's delighted shout overloaded the intercom speaker and generated an electronic squeal. "I can see you!" She watched Kurtis through Spiffy's eyes. The three inside the hab could see nothing on the dead, gray screen beside the intercom. "You're walking around! It works! It *works*! Holy hell, Yuta, come here and look at this! He's outside and moving around!"

"You look like a circus performer, Kurtis," Yuta said.

"I feel like one of them fairytale giants," Kurtis said. "Covering seven leagues at every stride. Man, this is great. Feels like I'm not wearing a suit at all, it's so easy to move. I could get so much done in this. Long as it doesn't need five fingers and a thumb." He laughed boyishly.

"Well, I was thinking about that," Charlie said. "The glove is probably where we have to make a concession to complexity.

Decent force-feedback haptics in datagloves is the way to go. But that's in the future."

Nick's jaw tightened. He sat down and knitted his hands together between his knees.

"I'm gonna see if I can climb in this," Kurtis said. "Long as I can grip the ropes, I should be able to get all the way to the top."

Nick started to his feet. "No! Don't do that."

"Yeah," Charlie said nervously. "I think you'd better not push your luck too far. Stay close to the hab."

"If I stay close to the hab, how'm I gonna get any work done? We're gonna move the oxygen plant up to the peak, right? I gotta find out if it's possible to even get up there in one of these suits." Breathless gasps punctuated Kurtis's voice. "And as long as I'm going up, I might as well take the sling arm."

"Don't," Nick said, and lunged for his own spacesuit. Maddy blocked his way and they wrestled for a moment.

"He needs to do it," she whispered. "Can't you see?"

"I'm at the bottom of the cliff," Kurtis said. "I've activated the winch and it's hauling the end of the sling arm. I'm climbing alongside the winch, holding onto it, and allowing it to take some of my weight. No problems so far."

"What'll I do when I run out of toenails?" Charlie said.

Nick snatched up his tools and returned to the greenhouse —no longer a greenhouse: without the bamboo, it was just another empty tin can with slightly better air and light. He donned his work goggles, powered up the oxy-acetylene torch, and arranged his supplies in front of the standing fan. It would blow the fumes away from him, but the particles and gases would stay in the hab. Nothing he could do about that.

"Kurtis isn't gonna make it," Lee said, flopping down at the workbench. He laughed. "This way I don't have to kill him. So: a win."

Nick switched on the torch and began to cut a hole in the second canister lid to attach the helmet for the second exosuit.

———

"Well, I'm up," Kurtis said.

Nick let out a long breath. "Now you have to come down."

"Not until I get this sling arm threaded through the hub."

———

"*Please* come down now," Maddy said. "You've only got four hours of oxygen left."

"I still need to attach the counterweight."

The counterweight was a one-tonne block of stone carved out of the peak by Kurtis, Nick, and Maddy a month ago. To attach it to the sling arm, Kurtis would have to lift it up and tie the sling arm around it like he was wrapping a parcel, and finish off by inserting masonry screws into the predrilled holes in the counterweight for hasps to hold the braid in place.

"You can't do all that with *claws*," Maddy said.

"Yes, I can," Kurtis said.

"The Camptown ladies sing this song," Lee sang very quietly. "Doo dah, doo dah. Kurtis Dean is never wrong, oh, doo dah day."

———

"I'm sorry, guys, I have to bow out," Charlie said, audibly stifling a yawn. "I haven't slept in two days, and I've hardly seen my kid for a week."

"Bye," Nick said, head bowed over the Kevlar he was cutting.

He never went back to see his mother and aunt before he left for the moon. The last time he'd seen them was after he returned from training in Hawaii. He spent a day and a half in Alandale. It was supposed to be three days, but he left early after an argument with Lydia. Filling up the front door, she'd yelled after him, *What do you think your father would say about this crazy bullshit space company?* Nick had responded with a single monosyllable: *Bye.*

Lee and Maddy lay on the floor under the fan, huddled in their separate sleeping bags.

Over the radio, Kurtis said, "I wasn't really a good fit in the Rangers, you know."

"Why not?" Nick said. Measure. Cut. Measure.

"I was trying to be someone I wasn't. I gotta be my own man, see?"

"I know what you mean," Nick said. "What happened?"

"Back then? The thing that sticks out for me now, it was during the Mato Grosso campaign. We were ordered to occupy this little village in the jungle. The intel said it was all friendlies, but I *knew* the intel sucks. Those satellites can't see inside people's hearts. They don't know if the old lady selling cachaca is also hiding an AK under the counter. I should have done a thorough recon before we went in. It's just... I was tired and mosquito-bit, and our drone swarm was down on account of the ants—"

"Whoa, wait, the what?"

"Ants. These big, red mutant motherfuckers. They ate the insulation off the drones' circuitry. They were always doing it." Kurtis chuckled. He sounded very far away. "This is why I believe in Cruder is Better. Our networked, AI-facilitated, five million dollar field-reconnaissance drone swarm got bricked by fucking *ants*."

Nick laughed.

"Right? You gotta either laugh or cry. I laughed, and we went in. And the place was crawling with fucking Chicaps. I lost three men inside five minutes... then I cried."

"I can see why you decided to come to the moon," Nick said.

"Yeah?"

"At least there aren't any ants up here."

"Ain't that the truth," Kurtis said. "You know what, though? I *miss* it."

"Brazil?"

"Oh, hell no. Well, actually, all of it. Nature, you know? I'm up here with nothing in between me and this black sky, and I would give my left nut to hear a bird singing."

"For me it's the sea," Nick said.

"Uh huh—Fuck!"

"Everything all right out there?"

"Yeah, yeah. This goddamn counterweight..."

The shears chewed through the Kevlar and caught. Nick got up and went to get the whetstone to sharpen them again.

———

Eleven hours and forty minutes after he left, Kurtis crawled back out of the airlock. Dust dribbled off his exosuit's misshapen limbs. Nick grasped his helmet and twisted it, adding his efforts to Kurtis's twisting from inside. It came away. Kurtis's sweat-slicked, seal-like head thrust forth. He gasped for air. "I did it."

"You did it," Nick agreed, repressing a grin. "Get out of that contraption, you crazy motherfucker."

Maddy grasped Kurtis under the arms. She helped him clamber out of the exosuit.

"Water," he said.

"Never put me through that again," Maddy said.

"I did it for you," Kurtis said.

Maddy's face crumpled. Stretching up on her tiptoes, she kissed him. Kurtis swept her into a passionate hug.

"We're gonna get off this rock, lady."

Lee stood halfway down the module, watching.

Kurtis poured water down his throat. Nick inspected the seams of the exosuit and the interior liner as best he could using a flashlight. They seemed to have held up.

"I'm almost finished with Lee's suit," he said, changing out the oxygen cylinder. "It went faster the second time. I figure we get some rest; then we can all head out and start moving the oxygen plant to the peak."

No one answered.

He backed out of the suit.

Lee stood skull-faced in the glow of the chemlights, his sleeping bag draped over his shoulders like a poncho, facing Kurtis.

"What's wrong, Lee?" Nick said.

"What's up?" Kurtis said uneasily.

"Now you're gonna kill us all, huh?" Lee said in a voice so dark and choked, it sounded like he was talking in his sleep.

"What's this paranoid-ass bullshit?" Kurtis said.

Maddy stepped between them. "Kurtis, he's got this crazy idea that Aaron gave you orders to kill us all as soon as the Big Sling is complete."

"It ain't complete yet," Kurtis said.

"No, but all you have to do is hook up the heat batteries and connect the Stirling engines to the turntable," Lee said. "That's two more days' work at the most... The thing is, we don't have two more days. CO_2 is up to three and a half percent. If we use our remaining oxygen to fill four cylinders, we'll come back to air that's too toxic to breathe. *For four people.* But *one* person could survive until dawn. Then they just have to sit here running the oxygen plant and wait for their rescue flight."

"Hell, if you think I'm going anywhere without my girl." Kurtis pulled Maddy into the curve of his arm.

"You aren't denying it?" Lee's voice rose.

"Of course I'm denying it!" Kurtis said. "That sounds more like *your* diabolical plan for survival."

"Like I'd wait around for a rescue flight. Five Stones isn't going to save you, Kurtis. They've sold out to the government, and the government doesn't give a shit about any of us."

Nick remembered showing Lee the ILI-printed circuit board. He tried to guess what Lee had put together from that, but he couldn't concentrate, caught up in the horror of the moment.

"Why you so sure they're evil?" Kurtis said.

"They're a *corporation*. Corporations are evil. 'Don't Be Evil'—remember that? It was a joke from day one. Corporate capitalism has killed the planet, and now it's killing us."

"Corporate capitalism isn't the problem," Nick said. "The problem is people."

Lee shot him a glance and shrugged his sleeping bag off his shoulders. "Right. People like you." He had Kurtis's Glock in his hand.

The gunshot reverberated in the hollow steel module.

Maddy dived to the floor.

Nick crouched with his arms over his head.

His father shouted, *Please! No—*

A second gunshot hammered his eardrums.

Kurtis dropped heavily to his knees.

Stay where you are! Don't make a goddamn sound, Nicholas!

Kurtis fell facedown.

Nick could see out from under the table through the hole in the tablecloth where his grandfather had once dropped a lit cigarette. The kitchen door was half open. The long black muzzle of a gun edged around it, gripped in a lean, brown hand. They were coming in. Coming to kill him, too.

Maddy crawled to Kurtis's body. She struggled to roll him over, screaming and sobbing.

Blood spread out from under him, glistening red in the cone of the flashlight Nick had dropped.

"He's dead," Maddy shrieked. "He's *dead*."

She sprang up and sprinted away along the module. Lee put out a half-hearted hand to stop her. She brushed past him. Lee stood like a statue, staring at Kurtis's body. The gun in his right hand drooped to point at the floor.

Nick stood up. "Give me that."

Lee said nothing.

Nick stepped around the pool of blood and inched up to Lee, trying to catch his eyes. Lee wouldn't look at him. Nick took the Glock from his limp fingers.

The greenhouse door wheezed and thumped. Maddy came running back. "You killed the best person on this crew," she said hoarsely, gasping. "You fucking murderer."

Steel glinted in her hand.

Lee turned to face her.

Maddy swung the shears, open in a slashing motion.

Lee let out an inhuman scream of anguish and clutched his stomach.

Maddy took a quick step forward and drove the shears home with an upward twisting motion.

Lee stumbled backward, hit the wall, and fell sideways to the floor. He pawed weakly at the handles of the shears sticking out of his torso.

Nick swung his left arm across Maddy's throat, getting her in a headlock. The Glock was alive in his right hand, as dirty as the moon, the trigger waiting to be pulled.

"I did it," Maddy sobbed. "I did it."

Nick hurled the Glock in the direction of the airlock. He pushed Maddy away from him in the other direction. He knelt and jerked the shears out of Lee's body. The blades scraped on bone.

Dark blood gushed out of Lee's mouth. He died.

54

"Here," Nick said. He pulled Maddy's DIY pipe and some leaves out of her stash and wrapped her trembling hands around them. "Smoke that. It'll calm you down."

Almost before she finished the pipe, she drifted into a sniffling, twitching doze.

Nick turned the intercom back on.

Rachel yapped at him, asking pointless questions.

"Kurtis and Lee are dead," Nick said. He pulled Kurtis's spacesuit onto his lap and began to cut the sleeves off. The shears left traces of Lee's blood on the fabric. "Bullet could've gone through the wall. It didn't, so that's good."

Rachel asked more questions.

"Yes. No. I don't know," Nick said.

Then it was Aaron on the radio. "How far did Kurtis get? Did he complete the installation of the sling arm?"

"I think so. Why?" Nick said.

"It's really important."

Nick forced the blades of the shears together. His hands ached. "Fuck you."

He got up and turned the intercom off.

Then he went back to work.

Since Kurtis didn't need his spacesuit anymore, Nick decided to use its gloves for the second exosuit. The additional flexibility would compensate for the reduction of volume.

He sewed the gloves to the Kevlar sandwich garment he'd made, and then began to sand the rim of the canister lid, where he would epoxy the garment to it.

Maddy made little whimpering noises in her sleep.

Nick could see his breath. Thin puffs of fog.

The lights flickered and dimmed.

Then they went out.

The fan slowed to a stop, admitting a profound silence into the room.

Nick hurried into his spacesuit. He rushed outside and found Spiffy crouching in the darkness outside the hab. He faced the iconic kangaroo-legged robot. "Hands in the air," he said. "Lie down."

Spiffy made humanlike gestures—an attempt to communicate. Nick had turned the volume of his helmet radio all the way down, so he couldn't hear whatever she was trying to say.

"I said get down!"

Nick was holding a socket wrench. He swung it at the robot's face, knocking it backward. He pounced on top of it and bore it to the ground. Though the robot was twice as strong as he was, it did not resist. Nick rolled it over and opened its housing. He coughed inside his helmet, over and over, like a sputtering engine. He removed the robot's fuel cell.

Spiffy went inert.

Coughing, sobbing, Nick lugged the fuel cell indoors. He hooked it up to the improvised power cables in place of the one that had run dry.

The lights came back on.

The fan started up again.

Maddy's lips were tinged blue.

Nick opened the fuel cell's O2 valve and released a blast of oxygen into the room. Then he cursed himself for wasting it.

"Wake up, Maddy. Wake up."

She was confused, wobbly. He pulled her over to the newly completed exosuit and induced her to crawl inside it. He opened the regulator and sealed her in. Then he clambered back into his own suit. His fingers seemed clumsy. It took forever to seal the rear entry port—a tricky thing to do by yourself at the best of times. At last, the *Seal Verified* indicator lit up his HUD. He sucked in several lungfuls of good, canned air.

"From now on," he said over the radio, "we only come out of the suits to eat and drink."

"Copy that," Maddy said.

"And, I guess, to pee."

"Ha. Yeah."

"We can top off our cylinders directly from the fuel cell. But I think we should abandon this module and move into the personnel module. A smaller volume of air means a higher oxygen concentration. I'm going to run the compressor to suck up whatever O2 we've still got in here."

Dead leaves littered the floor. Nick trudged to the workbench, treading on fragments of bamboo and scraps of plastic. It felt surreal to be wearing a spacesuit indoors. He opened Lee's laptop with stiff, gloved fingers.

He had an email.

Actually, this was Lee's account. The email had been cc'ed to all of them, including the dead ones.

I started this thing to save the planet.

The email was from Aaron.

But what percentage is there in that for the vested interests? Like they're EVER going to let someone like me steal even a fraction of their power. I admit it. I was naïve. Idealistic. Wrong. I shouldn't even have tried. For the last several years, I've been fighting against forces that you can't even imagine. Now they've won. I'm exhausted. EXHAUSTED. There's nothing more I can do. So, I guess this is goodbye.

Best regards,
Aaron Slater
Chief Visionary Officer
Five Stones Inc.

"Aaron's washed his hands of us," Nick said to Maddy.

"I think he's possessed by a demon," Maddy said. "Or he *was* possessed by a demon. It wanted to go to the moon, so it glommed onto us and followed us up here."

Nick closed the laptop and unplugged it. His nerves twitched with the urge to throw it across the room. He stopped himself. He still might need to look things up in the technical manuals.

55

Joe, Kat, and Trig sat around the computer in Joe's office. Joe clicked replay.

"*Hands in the air,*" Nick Morrison snarled. "*Lie down.*"

"*Nick, please.*" It was a woman's voice. "*Let me try to help—*"

"*I said get down!*"

"*Don't! No! Oh, God—*"

The transmission ended.

"What do you think that was?" Joe said.

"He killed someone," Trig said. The big man's face was dough-pale. Even Kat looked shaken, sitting hunched over, twisting a lock of hair around her finger.

"Yeah, maybe," Joe said.

They'd listened to the entire chaotic sequence in the hab, followed by a long stretch of silence, followed by this cryptic exchange. And then more silence. For the last eight hours, the channel had been dead, save for small bursts of data traffic.

Joe roused himself from his reverie. He looked into his mug of cold coffee and put it down. "Well, we know for sure that

Kurtis Dean and Lee Yang are dead, anyway. That leaves one survivor, two at the most."

"Nick," Kat said.

"Yeah," Joe said. "I knew if anyone survived, it would be him."

"But he can't survive long," Trig said. "Just the oxygen situation is bad enough. The hab's probably lost power..."

"Yeah."

Joe clicked up the camera feed from the Five Stones satellite and compared it with the feed from ILI's own comms satellite. The top of the central peak of Amundsen crater was already bathed in daylight. The hub of the Big Sling cast a conical shadow across the equipment littered around it. The length of the shadow indicated the hub was 5.5 meters tall. It stood on a stone turntable. Next to it sat a block of basalt. On the other side of the turntable was a pile of something dark, which was probably the sling arm, coiled up in readiness for deployment.

"Looks pretty much finished," Joe said.

"Nothing left to do except spin it up," Kat said.

"We can do that ourselves," Trig said.

Joe shut down the feed. "Saddle up, folks. It's time to go rescue the survivors."

Uncurling from her hunched posture, Kat stretched and smiled. "I'll prep the rover."

"Actually, we'd better take both rovers," Joe said. "Tell Maria to provision them for a five-day sortie."

"Will do." Kat left the office.

"You'll stay here," Joe said to Trig. "You're in charge while I'm gone."

"Understood," Trig said seriously.

A tremor of unease cut through Joe at the thought of leaving Trig in command, given the volatility of the situation following his punishment of Dr. Hofstadter. But who else was there? And he had to go himself. He couldn't risk another disaster like Kat and Trig's unauthorized raid on the Five Stones greenhouse.

"If anything happens while we're gone, anything at all, call me," he said.

"You got it," Trig said. "Who else are you going to take?"

"Wez, I think. And Evan. Two per rover should be enough."

Left alone, Joe arranged his chessmen on the board. He set up a position from a game he recently lost to the computer. As white, he'd played the Ruy Lopez and castled quickly, but the computer devastated his position by picking off his light-squared bishop. He tried to see how he could have forestalled the attack.

He hadn't expected to have to make his big move this early. Aaron Slater had forced his hand, and Joe would never forgive him for that.

But he could still pull it off.

The next Artemis shuttle wasn't scheduled to arrive for two weeks. That was long enough to play a strong opening and then castle, making his position impregnable.

There it was, the mistake. He should have moved his queen out sooner to defend the bishop.

He replayed the exchange. This time, black ended up on the defensive. Joe mentally ran through the rest of the moves. With this advantage, he would be able to fight the computer to a draw, at least. Good enough.

He put the chessmen away and packed a few things for the trip. Before leaving, he used Dr. Hofstadter's stolen password to check his email, to see if there were any new risk factors he needed to know about.

Dr. Hofstadter had an email from the man who went by the name of Harrison McNally.

Joe read through the clipped paragraphs instructing Dr.

Hofstadter to order the ArxaSys Lunar contractors to take control of the Big Sling immediately. He couldn't help smirking.

"Way ahead of you, chump," he murmured.

He thought for a moment. It was clear McNally didn't know Dr. Hofstadter had gone rogue. He might *suspect* him of destroying the Five Stones hab—who else could it have been, after all?—but he had no proof, and crucially, he had no one else up here to order around. All he could do was hope Dr. Hofstadter would do as he was commanded.

Dr. Hofstadter, unsurprisingly, hadn't answered the email. Poor old McNally must be tearing his hair out.

Joe decided to set his mind at ease. He composed an emollient reply, promising he would do as ordered. Impersonating Dr. Hofstadter over email was a risk he'd never taken before, out of concern that Dr. Hofstadter himself would notice. That no longer mattered. Good old Dave wasn't going to be around much longer, anyway.

He signed off with a Hofstadter-esque "Very best wishes," hit send, and rose to go. Then he sat back down and checked his own email, just in case.

Dear Joe,

Writing in a hurry. Things are totally crazy here, but I have to let you know that the Charlie situation is about to go critical. She told me she's planning to go public. She's going to tell the whole world about the deal, including the real reason for it. We're talking scorched earth. Sodom and Gomorrah time. I hope I can talk her out of it, but if she goes through with it, that's going to shine a huge spotlight on ILI. It could ruin everything! What should I do?

Joe's first instinct was to throw something. He suppressed it and read the email again, more slowly.

He smiled.

He wrote: *Thanks for letting me know. Wow, that sure doesn't sound good.*

For McNally.

Joe couldn't care less what lengths Charlie Fitzgerald's conscience drove her to.

But publicity would be a disaster for McNally and his shadowy organization. If Joe could prevent Charlie from going to the media... McNally would owe him big-time.

And as soon as Joe took control of the Big Sling, the real game would begin. McNally would be furious as soon as he discovered what Joe had done—so would everyone, from the president on down—but a slippery swamp creature like this McNally undoubtedly was, might just decide it was better to work with Joe than against him. Especially if Joe could point to the way he helped them out by taking care of the Charlie situation.

I think you're right, he wrote. *We have to stop her. In this situation, extreme measures would be justified. Obviously, I'm not asking you to do anything yourself. But is there anyone you could reach out to? Maybe for a price? I can send you more $$$ if you don't have enough left from the last time. Let me know. I'm going to be on the road, but I'll check my email regularly. If this is time sensitive, and it sounds like it is, just move ahead with whatever you decide to do. I trust your judgment.*

Love, Joe

After sending the email, he shut down his computer and clattered down the ladder.

Wez and Evan were waiting for him, as were the other off-duty contractors. Everyone had been briefed by Trig. Joe basked in their affection and support.

He and Kat went down to the MVDA and checked the supplies Maria had packed into their rover. Joe's thoughts doubled back for a moment to Florida. Charlie Fitzgerald had no idea what was about to hit her. Sure, Joe didn't either, but he knew it wouldn't be pleasant.

He mentally appended a gloating P.S. to his Hofstadter-impersonating email. *Behold! From the moon, I can stretch out my hand and touch Earth.*

Click, click—kaboom.

56

Nick collected the tools he would need and put them into Kurtis's rucksack, along with Lee's laptop. He went into his own room and pawed through his belongings until he found the other thing he was looking for. He put that in, too.

"Are you going out?" Maddy said.

She was slumped in her exosuit on the floor of the kitchen, as far as possible from the two corpses at the other end of the personnel module.

"Yeah." Nick stepped over her giant, bamboo-boned, Kevlar-skinned legs to reach Spiffy's fuel cell and the air compressor. He'd prefilled all the spare oxygen cylinders they had. He put three of them in the rucksack, leaving Maddy three.

"Why?" Maddy said.

"You might kill me next," Nick said, lifting the gallon thermos, which he'd filled with water. He tipped it and the water didn't move. It was ice. He took the oxy-acetylene torch and directed split-second blasts at the thermos until the water melted. Then, as fast as he could, he unsealed his suit, shrugged it down to his waist, and drank the whole gallon. The air was so bad that by the time he got back into his suit, his head was spinning.

"Later," he said, trudging to the airlock.

Maddy dragged herself after him with her fat, Kurtis-sized hands. "I'm sorry! I'm sorry, Nick! Don't leave me here!"

Nick's headlamp found Lee's body on the floor where he died. His blood had spread and joined with the pool of blood from Kurtis's body. They lay together in a frozen red lake that stretched from wall to wall. Nick had wanted to put them outside, but it proved too difficult to break them out of the red ice. His boots skidded. He stumbled to his knees and caught himself on Kurtis's exosuit. It lay in front of the airlock like a grotesque empty pupa. He swallowed hard.

"Where are you going?" Maddy wailed.

Nick picked himself up. "Going to finish the job."

"The Big Sling?"

"Yep."

"Why?" When Nick didn't answer, her voice grew quiet. "What should I do?"

"Whatever you like."

He went out.

"I'll come with you," Maddy said over the radio, with desperate brightness. "I'll work on the oxygen plant."

Nick was passing the oxygen plant. "No point." He'd come out earlier with the intention of working on it himself. Now his headlamp flashed over shards of broken glass and splintered bamboo scaffolding. Kurtis must have seen this, too, before his last climb to the summit. Probably hadn't said anything so as not to destroy their hopes. Nick no longer cared about that. "Some of the debris from the impact must've hit the solar array. The parabolic mirrors are totaled. Just stay where you are, and... and pray, I guess."

Maddy started to cry.

Nick turned the volume down so he wouldn't have to hear her.

He found his way to the cliff. The winch cradle lay on the ground where Kurtis left it when he came down the last time. Nick stepped into it, took a firm grip on the cables, and pulled the lever. The winch was powered by a solar array up top; it never ran out of power. Sedately swaying, it lifted him up.

Nick had rarely visited the summit. Installation and assembly up here had mostly been Kurtis and Maddy's job. Nick had helped them raise the hub to its upright position and carve the counterweight—hadn't been back since.

He stepped off the winch and squinted in the sunlight.

The sun drenched a plateau about the size of your average suburban lot. Steep slopes fell away on every side. The hub stood in the middle of the plateau with its base sunk into a large stone turntable. On top of the turntable on one side lay the counterweight. On the other side, Kurtis had coiled the entire twenty-kilometer length of the sling arm. The coil reached as high as the top of the hub itself. The whole thing looked to Nick like a stone-age monument, marking the graves of Lee, Kurtis, Theo, and Fenella.

And maybe, before long, Nick and Maddy, too.

There was one last hope for survival.

He hadn't shared it with Maddy because it was such a slim hope, maybe no more than wishful thinking, and because he could hardly stand to talk to her, anyway.

Nick stared into the sky. The sun painted the expanse black. There were no stars, let alone anything closer, but he knew that somewhere up there was the Deep Space Gateway.

If he could complete the Big Sling and get it turning, maybe they'd see it and realize that someone must still be here, alive.

Alive, but not for much longer.

He set to work.

In a straight line heading across the summit from the hub of the sling, Kurtis and Maddy had built ten heat batteries. These consisted of pits dug in pairs, above which six-hundred-kilogram bags of crushed regolith were suspended from the ends of basalt beams mounted on pivots. One bag of each pair hung in the sunlight, heated up by now to 150 degrees Celsius or more. The other bag of each pair was down in the shade of its pit, nearly as cold as the ambient temperature of space. Each bag had a flexible conduit, premade components containing liquid oxygen, embedded inside.

The transfer of the working fluid from each hot bag to each cold one would power Stirling engines. The gear boxes, worm wheels, and crankshafts lay partially assembled on the ground. Nick completed the remaining assembly tasks, following the diagrams on Lee's laptop. He crawled underneath the turntable to hook up the main crankshaft. Lastly, he connected the conduits of the heat batteries to the engine assemblies and flipped the switch.

That was all there was to do.

His HUD told him that seven hours had passed since he started work. He was down to twenty-nine hours of air.

He sat down and drank some water from his suit's reservoir.

Nothing happened.

Maybe he'd made a mistake somewhere.

The shadow of the hub sprawled across the gravel-flecked surface of the plateau. Nick stared at it in a mood of torpid exhaustion. In a while, he would review the diagrams to see if he could find the problem. He sucked in another mouthful of water, holding it in his mouth before swallowing. His mouth was a miniature Atlantic; this was all the water in the world. Waves swilled around his teeth. The last drops trickled down his throat.

The shadow of the hub wobbled slightly from side to side.

Nick whipped around.

The turntable was moving.

It had taken a while for the engines to overcome the static rolling friction of a three-hundred-tonne mass. That was all.

The hub turned slowly.

Nick held his breath.

The counterweight sat on one side of the turntable, the sling arm on the other side, but the two masses weren't yet equal. There had been some concern that oscillations would build up and overbalance the hub, or destroy the turntable's bearings.

The hub turned faster, rocking from side to side.

Faster. Faster.

A loop of braid rose off the top of the pile, pulled outward by centrifugal force. It flailed in the vacuum, growing longer by the instant. It whipped over Nick's head. Now the hub was rotating several times per minute. Kurtis had bound each loop up with a tension-activated auto-release binding, so as the speed increased, the loops would unfurl one after another. Meter by meter, kilometer by kilometer, the pile of loops shrank, and the whipping sling arm grew longer and sank lower. Nick crouched on the ground, watching the last feet of the pile fly off the turntable.

The end of the sling arm zipped over his head so fast he hardly saw it.

The hub rocked—rocked back—trembled—and settled back onto its base with a thud that jarred Nick's teeth.

The counterweight lifted into the vacuum. The sling arm slid through the eye on top of the hub, letting the counterweight fly out, until both masses were precisely balanced.

The sling arm blurred over Nick's head in a mathematically straight line. It appeared parallel to the ground from here, though it actually dipped slightly over its length. That wasn't a problem. Thanks to the elevation of the central peak, the end of the arm would still be high above the floor of the crater.

Strangely, now that he completed the job, Nick's fantasies of rescue by an Artemis shuttle faded into sickly will-o'-the-wisps. He sat down again with his back to the hub, gazing at the distant rim of the crater. The sling arm blurring overhead created a strobing effect that made the sun appear to flicker, as if it were a ceiling fixture running out of power.

Aaron's done a deal with ILI, Kat had said. *They've bought up the Big Sling's entire launch capacity.*

Charlie had used an ILI component in the Woombat.

And Lee, moments before he died, said, *Aaron's sold out to the government.*

Sold out to the government.

Had he been talking about ILI or something else? Did the deal with ILI have some hidden meaning?

Anyway, NASA had a stake in ILI, and NASA was also the primary operator of the Deep Space Gateway. They should be interested now that the Big Sling was up and running.

That was it, the basis on which his hopes rested.

There really wasn't much there.

He'd just been stringing himself along. No one was coming to rescue them.

More likely, they were sitting up there waiting for him and Maddy to die.

Yet he stayed where he was, not knowing what else to do.

On the night his father died, Nick and his mother waited for hours for the police to arrive. At two in the morning, a couple of patrol cars parked on the flowerbeds in front of the farmhouse, and an unshaven police captain had sauntered in. He asked the usual questions while his underlings explored the house.

Meanwhile, Nick had gone on sitting under the kitchen table, hugging their mastiff, Millicent. From time to time he made furtive sorties to climb on the counter and look through the window to the verandah, hoping his father's body would have gone away. Every time, it was still there. His father's bare feet stuck out from under the end of a sheet. One of his flip-flops had fallen off.

The police captain's voice trilled from the sitting room. "Well, Mrs. Morrison, do you have any idea of the motivation that might have caused these men to commit this crime?"

Lydia cut across him, her Afrikaner accent sharper than usual. "They want our land." There was a thud. Nick cringed under the table. His mother's voice moved closer. "I don't care anymore! If they want it, they can have it!"

A convulsion in Nick's chest brought forth a laugh. "If you want it, you can have it," he gasped.

The Big Sling spun.

Nothing else moved.

Nick bowed his head inside his helmet, arms wrapped around his shins, shaking.

57

Charlie sat in her great room at home, in front of the computer she bought to replace the one stolen during Tropical Storm Molly. She was putting the finishing touches on a document entitled *For Those Who Need to Know*. Outside the French windows, giant land crabs scuttled through the scruffy grass. Weeds had sprung up after the flood, and she had no spare cash to have the lawn done.

Her phone buzzed.

Fear paralyzed her for a second. Ryder Stillman? She'd blown him off amidst the crisis on the moon.

Aaron.

Pick up! Call me!

She called him, steeling herself to pretend nothing was amiss. Dead people on the moon. Total chaos at the office. And she was just taking a personal day to spend time with Anna. Could she make him believe it?

She didn't have to try. He was practically in tears. Around him, the whole office was celebrating. "They've done it. The Big Sling is operational. It's right there on the satellite feed. This is incredible!"

"Oh, good," Charlie said. "McNally will be delighted."

"The SEC already called. They're going to let Bill and me settle the case with a token fine."

"Of course they are."

"Have you seen our stock price? We're saved!"

"What about our surviving crew? Will *they* be saved?"

"I don't know. I don't know what's going on up there."

"Then, for Christ's sake, try to find out!" Charlie yelled. She hung up on him.

"Mom?" Anna stood in the doorway. "Are we going?"

"In a *minute*. Stop bothering me!" Charlie bit her lip. "Sorry, baby. Let me just print this out."

She stood over the printer, lifting out single-spaced, heavily footnoted sheets of A4. She'd included screenshots and photos of documents that proved the existence of the deal. She couldn't prove its dreadful implications for humanity. But no journalist worth his or her salt should doubt them.

Her own guilt breathed up from the pages.

She'd gone along with the deal all the way, thinking Aaron knew best, that it was worth it. *Anything* was worth it to reach the moon.

She knew better now.

The moon was too far away.

All the illusions that she could reach it were shattered.

She'd given the crew the best she had—her robots, her exosuit concept, her single-minded dedication—none of it was enough.

Fenella died anyway. Theo died anyway. Kurtis and Lee died anyway. If Nick and Maddy weren't dead yet, they would be within another day—it was a mathematical certainty.

All that remained was to tell the truth and hopefully achieve some kind of justice here on Earth.

Folding the pages into her bag, she caught sight of herself in the gold-framed mirror they'd brought from her childhood home in Connecticut. She was wearing denim shorts and an Einstein T-shirt. She looked haggard, plain, and had aged ten years in the last ten days.

"Darling?" Harriet peeked in. "Where are you going?"

Charlie had told her several times already. "I'm taking Anna to the manatee sanctuary, Mom. We'll grab lunch afterward. Would you like anything from Flamingos?"

They drove across the causeway in the little red Chery. Anna bounced around in the passenger seat. A day out with her mother was a rare treat. Charlie felt a pang of guilt at the thought of how much she'd neglected Anna recently.

At the A1A, she automatically signaled right, to head for the office. The car saved her, pulling the wheel left. "Dumb machine," Charlie said, slapping the steering wheel. "Thanks anyway."

"Mom, could I drive this car?"

Charlie had occasionally let Anna "drive" their old car. It had been equipped with state-of-the-art AI, so all you had to do was sit in the driver's seat and pretend. "No, honey, this car is too stupid. But I tell you what, let's ride on the Segways at the manatee park."

There weren't actually any wild manatees left in the Banana River. Warming waters and frequent hurricanes had killed them all. The Manatee Sanctuary Park preserved its purpose by keeping several of the docile creatures in a tank. It was one of Anna's favorite places.

She squirmed when Charlie turned off the A1A onto Center Street. "Mom! This stupid car is going the wrong way!"

"No, it isn't," Charlie said. "I have to make one quick stop before we go to the park. It'll only take a few minutes."

Anna groaned and switched on her tablet.

Tropical Storm Molly had devastated this stretch of the

shore. Cheap apartment buildings had subsided, become unstable, and been abandoned to the rats, including the human variety. Charlie swept a wary eye over the glassless windows on either side of the street as she parked on the pocket-handkerchief of asphalt behind Center Street Park.

"Anna, stay in the car. I'll be right back." She left the engine on for the air-conditioning, and got out.

She didn't know any journalists well. Didn't know whom she could trust. She'd asked Rachel if she knew anyone. Once Rachel understood how important it was, she'd dug around in her contacts and come up with a name that sounded good to Charlie: Asafa Fang, of the *New York Times*. Mr. Fang, a technology reporter, agreed to come to Florida to meet Charlie. She was afraid he would want a long sit-down. That's why she specified Center Street Park as a meeting place. It was so unsavory, she'd have an excuse to just stuff her papers into his hands and go.

Flood debris still littered the small gazebo, mixed with used syringes, cigarette ends, and Coke cans. Charlie walked around the gazebo, through waist-height palms sprouting from old roots. The river shimmered in the sun and the damp ground smelled of sewage.

Although it was far from an idyllic spot, this was the closest Charlie had come to nature in a long time, and all the green around her, the give of earth under her feet, freed her thoughts from the tightly wound spiral of necessity that brought her here. She imagined an alternate world in which she'd not betrayed Nick Morrison. Where he returned, pale and weak at first. After getting his strength back, he would want to get out into nature. She imagined them coming back here together, walking along the shore, laughing about how crazy it had all been. Anna would walk between them, holding both of their hands.

Her eyes prickled. She rubbed them with the back of her wrist.

Where *was* Asafa Fang? There was another car in the parking lot, a top-of-the-line SUV. It had to be his.

"Hey, Charlie."

She turned.

A beefy white man in his forties, wearing a Clemson Tigers shirt, walked out of the gazebo and stopped, too close to her. He was smiling, but it wasn't a pleasant smile.

"You *are* Charlie Fitzgerald, right?" He gestured to the Five Stones logo T-shirt she was wearing so that Asafa Fang could recognize her.

This man definitely was not a Chinese-American *New York Times* journalist.

"What is it?" Charlie said.

"You got the docs in there?" He nodded at her shoulder bag.

It held her papers and also the Beretta. In the Center Street area, she thought it a wise precaution.

"Sorry, but who are you?"

"Guess you don't recognize me. No reason you should." He jerked a thumb back at the SUV in the parking lot. "I bought that with some of the money you sent me. Appreciate it. Also bought a new boat, a thirty-footer. I'm on my way to make the down payment on a new house. Thinking I'll move inland, away from the floods."

Charlie said hoarsely, "Ryder... Stillman?"

She took a step backward. Weeds tangled her legs.

"You heard from my buddy, Nick, recently? I heard he's not doing too good up there. I'm not surprised. He never could commit. Got himself mixed up in all kinds of things, but when the going got rocky, he would just fade."

"How do you know..." Charlie trailed off and reached into

her bag. "I'll give you the documents. I'll give you everything I have."

"Yeah, I heard you're fixing to go public," Ryder said. "That's a bad idea, Charlie."

And suddenly, so fast she couldn't see how he'd done it, he was pointing a pistol at her in a two-handed grip. His eyes behind the gun were as cold as a hunter's. The gun's muzzle was a third eye, the coldest of all. A great chill encased her body despite the day's wet heat.

"I'll give you more money." Her voice sounded high and far away.

"You told me you didn't have any money left."

"I-I could find some—twenty thousand—fifty thousand—"

"Keep it. I already got paid a hundred K for this." He gestured with the pistol. "Turn around. Walk down to the shore."

Charlie couldn't move.

"I said *walk!*"

In the parking lot, an engine started up, accompanied by a cacophony of turning chimes and horn blasts. Ryder and Charlie both turned to look.

The red Chery accelerated toward them, climbing the curb, heading for the gazebo.

"Hey, stop!" Ryder shouted.

The ice casing on Charlie's body fractured. Her hand closed on the Beretta inside her bag. She dragged it out. Without any conscious memory of the videos she'd watched or the tips she'd read, without any conscious thought at all, she aimed at Ryder and pulled the trigger. She kept on pulling the trigger until the bullets were gone.

The noise startled a pair of herons off the riverbank. They flew away, thin legs dangling.

Somewhere a car alarm whooped.

Ryder lay in the weeds, weeping and snarling, clutching his knee.

The Chery stalled with its bumper crumpled against the gazebo steps. Its engine died.

Charlie sprinted to the car. Anna climbed out of the driver's seat. "I guess I couldn't drive it, after all."

"Oh, baby, sweetheart, are you all right?"

"I wanted to hit *him*. He was pointing a gun at you!"

"I—oh, God." Charlie started to run back to where she'd left Ryder.

"Did you kill him, Mom?" Anna shouted, catching up with her.

Charlie hadn't killed Ryder. She was a tyro with no aim. Nearly all her rounds must have gone wild, even at point-blank range. One hit him, by accident, in the knee. A frightening amount of blood was coursing down his shin.

"Anna, call 911." She threw Anna her phone.

Ryder cried and cursed. Charlie found the gun he dropped in the weeds. She put it into her bag. It would prove to the police that she fired in self-defense. They would find out everything. They would find out about the blackmail. It didn't matter anymore. Now that the Big Sling was operational, the company was safe... and Charlie was damned. She wouldn't even care if she got arrested, if it weren't for Anna.

She stood over Ryder. "How did you know I was going to be here?"

He swore at her.

"Don't look, sweetheart," Charlie said to Anna. She kicked Ryder's injured knee. He screamed.

"Wow, Mom," Anna cried.

"Who told you I was coming here?"

Ryder called her a fucking bitch. Charlie's face burned.

"Who paid you to kill me?" she shouted.

Sirens dopplered nearby. The police were coming. Ryder smiled spitefully. "You're gonna love this. It was your best friend."

"I don't have a best friend."

"Rachel Hamilton."

58

The collision with the gazebo had busted the Chery's radiator. Charlie and Anna rode in the back of a cop car to the Brevard County sheriff's office, less than a mile away from Center Street. It had a well-tended lawn out front, and posters on the walls about saving the turtles.

"We'll need you to talk to the DA when she gets here," the sheriff said to Charlie.

"How long?"

"Could be a while. Can't say."

It turned out there was already a warrant out for Ryder Stillman's arrest in Georgia. He'd been carried off in an ambulance, handcuffed to a police officer. Charlie could still hear him cursing her: *Psycho bitch! You're gonna fuck it up for everyone!*

He'd threatened to go to the media with his stolen documents on the insider-trading thing. Except he'd showed up with the intent to kill her to *stop* her from revealing the truth about the deal. It did not add up.

"I get a phone call, right?"

"Ms. Fitzgerald, you're not under arrest."

"Then, can I make a phone call?"

Corporate counsel Cameron arrived within half an hour. He dropped the names of high-profile defense lawyers, handed out business cards, and extracted Charlie and Anna from the sheriff's office with a promise to return for an interview at the DA's convenience. Ten minutes later they were in his car.

"Thanks, Cameron," Charlie said. "Can you drop me off at the office, and then take Anna home for me?" She twisted around and reached out to stroke her daughter's pale, tense face. "Baby, I won't be long."

"I want to be with you!"

"I'm coming home soon, and then we'll be together, OK? You'll be safe with Gran."

"The sheriff said he'd send an officer to sit outside your house," Cameron noted. "Just in case."

"Good."

"Do you think I could drive a cop car?" Anna said.

———

Charlie crossed the lobby of the Five Stones office building at a run. She waited impatiently for the elevator.

Up on the fourteenth floor, the morning's excitement had died down. Charlie looked through the internal window of Mission Control. Rachel wasn't there.

"Do you know where she went?" she asked Jason.

"Didn't come in today. Tried calling her about the Big Sling but she didn't pick up." Jason shrugged. "Weird."

Yuta came out of his office, barefoot, with his T-shirt on inside out. "Cameron told me what happened. Are you OK?"

"I'm fine. I need to find Rachel."

"What *did* happen?"

"A career criminal from South Carolina tried to shoot me." The events hadn't fully sunk in yet. And when it did, there'd be hell to pay emotionally. She had to make use of the momentum she had going right now. "I didn't tell the cops this, but he said Rachel paid him to do it."

She said it on a wry note—she couldn't believe it. Yuta's exclamation turned heads across the office. "*Rachel?*"

"I mean, I don't think it's her. It must be someone else—I *need* to talk to her."

"She said she might have to go away," Yuta mumbled. "Seems like her mother is sick."

"She said that? To you?" As far as Charlie knew, Yuta and Rachel never had a conversation on any subject more personal than satellite radio protocols.

Yuta went into his office and came back with his Tevas on. "I'll come and look for her with you."

Yuta had an electric VW van with enough space in the back for a yoga mat. During their dark days, he had called it home at one point. Charlie cleared wrappers, Starbucks cups, sketchpads, Japanese comics, and industry magazines off the passenger seat. "How come your car is such a mess, when your apartment is this pristine modern art installation?"

"Maybe I'm messy inside and it has to come out somewhere."

On the way to Rachel's house, he confessed that he'd been sleeping with her for the last nine months.

"Well, let me just pick my jaw up off the floor." Yuta didn't smile. Charlie had never been sure he understood English idioms as well as he seemed to. "You? Are sleeping? With Rachel?"

"This is why we never told anyone," Yuta said. "I hate dealing with people's reactions. Stupid questions. I just want things to be simple."

"I... Yeah. I can understand that."

Yuta accelerated onto the causeway. Charlie noticed he was rubbing his stomach as if it hurt.

"You decided to totally compartmentalize it," she said. "I'm not judging you, but you know, if you have to lie to your best friends... then maybe it isn't simple. Maybe it's something else."

"I don't have any best friends."

The words echoed precisely what Charlie said to Ryder Stillman in the weeds on the riverbank. "Of course you do. Me and Aaron." As she spoke, she remembered her phone call with Aaron this morning.

"That fucking asshole," Yuta said. "He's personally responsible for murdering twelve people. I'll never forgive him."

Charlie told him about her decision to go public. How she'd written up everything she knew about the deal, and asked Rachel for her advice on finding a trustworthy journalist.

"So... she knew." She faced the central fact she'd tried to rationalize away. "She was the *only* person who knew what I was planning to do."

"I can't believe she would do a thing like this."

"I can't, either. Let's hope there's some explanation."

Yuta pulled up in front of Rachel's house. Her car wasn't in the drive. "She's gone."

"Let's just look around."

"I never came here," Yuta said, staring at the pretty little ranch-style house. "She always wanted to come to my place. I asked her, like a joke, does she have something to hide?"

Charlie touched his arm as he opened the door. "Inside out," she said gently. "Your T-shirt."

"Oh." Yuta stripped it off and put it back on right-side out. "Thanks."

They rang the bell and tried the front door. Locked. The sliding glass door behind the patio stood six inches open. They shrugged at one another and went in.

Everything was gone. Rachel's glass working kit and tools, the coordinated pillows and throw rugs, the electronics. In her bedroom, they found the closet empty.

"She took all of her six thousand pairs of shoes," Charlie said.

Beside the stripped bed stood two large suitcases and a dog carrier large enough for Rachel's labradoodle. It was empty.

Yuta read the address labels on the suitcases. "That's strange. Is this her mother's address? I thought she's from Chicago."

The address was in Tel Aviv, in Israel.

The front door slammed.

The labradoodle barked. Claws clicked on the floor in the hall.

"Yuta!" Rachel called out. She must have seen the VW van outside. "Are you here?"

Yuta went to meet her in the living room, followed by Charlie.

"Guess you decided to leave the country," he said.

Rachel's shocked face looked like a random jumble of bones covered by makeup. For once, she was wearing comfortable running shoes. "What happened?" she rasped.

"I don't know," Charlie said. She looked for a weapon in Rachel's hands, but there was nothing. Just the end of the dog's leash. "You tell me."

"I was all set to go, and then Biankini ran away. I had to chase her for blocks."

"Biankini," Yuta said. "Quite an unusual name. I looked it up, you know... It's the name of a settlement in Israel, near where the Dead Sea was."

"Why would you look up something like that?" Rachel said.

"I wanted to know everything about you. I guess I didn't know very much after all."

"I'm going to miss my flight," Rachel said.

"Why are you going to Israel?" Yuta said.

"That's where my parents live. My mom *is* sick. She's diabetic."

"Oh, come on!" Charlie exploded. "You're fleeing the country! I'm calling the cops!" She took out her phone, but Yuta grabbed her hand.

"I think she's going to tell us why she did it," he said. "There must be some explanation."

Rachel tottered to the couch and sat down. Biankini flopped at her feet. "I didn't want to kill anyone."

Charlie tensed. Yuta's fingers tightened on her wrist.

"I was only trying to help my brother."

Charlie and Yuta exchanged confused glances.

"Is this the same brother who works in law enforcement?" Charlie said. She'd turned the Beretta over to the police.

"Well, not exactly," Rachel said. "He used to work for the Israeli Space Agency. I guess that kind of counts?" She tittered. "He knows all kinds of people. He's a genius, actually."

"A genius," Charlie echoed.

"When I was little, we had to move to Tel Aviv. It was a nightmare. My father—I guess the move was hard on him, too—anyway, he used to—to hit us." Rachel started to cry. "Joe stood up for me. He protected me. I would do anything for him. Anything."

59

Nick had twenty-four hours of air left. It seemed like a nice round number.

Time to go down.

He guessed he could just sit here until he died, watching the Big Sling flickering across the sun. But the vibrations were getting to him. The rotation of the turntable and the pistons in the Stirling engines—although inaudible in the vacuum—made the plateau thrum perceptibly.

The crew were warned about this. Regularly spaced vibrations could induce infrasound, a phenomenon mostly felt on Earth near large wind farms. In a vacuum, there was no sound of any type, but there was a possibility that the vibrations of the Big Sling could generate infrasound waves inside a pressure suit. Those could induce, as well as nausea and headaches, weird psychological effects, such as fits of grief, regret, and fear.

Nick felt all those things while lying on the ground, and not much better after standing up. It was probably just him.

He had one more thing to do before he left.

He picked an open space near the turntable and laid down Kurtis's rucksack. Out of it he took Lee's laptop and set that next to the rucksack. Next, he took out something of Theo's: the hardcopy Bible the geologist often used to read. Nick flipped through it. Norwegian and English were printed side by side. A passage in red caught his eye: *And whatever you ask in prayer, you will receive, if you have faith.*

Huh, Nick thought. He couldn't bear to read any further. He laid the Bible next to the rucksack and laptop.

One more relic remained: Fenella's holocube. Nick turned it to the sun and pressed the button with his gloved finger to watch the slideshow one last time.

Carefree young climbers laughed and fooled around in the sunlight of Earth. Nick gazed at the scenes, mesmerized again by what he never really had. Maybe he once did... He'd just thrown it away.

There. That flicker of recognition. There it was again.

He paused the slideshow.

A dark-haired young man stood with his arm around a younger Fenella's shoulders, in front of an overhanging ochre crag. The shadows behind them were as stark as the moon's. They looked so happy.

Wasn't that... Joe Massad?

It couldn't be. If he'd known Fenella, he would have mentioned it when they were talking, wouldn't he?

It was probably just a coincidental likeness.

Nick had no will to ponder it. He set the holocube next to the rucksack, laptop, and Bible. He transferred his spare oxygen cylinders to the other satchel he brought up. For a minute he gazed at the makeshift shrine. All that was missing now was Maddy's DIY marijuana pipe. And Nick? What would he leave of himself?

A puddle of water, to represent all the rivers, waterholes, beaches, and harbors he loved. Even though it would boil away in the vacuum, that would be fitting, too.

He remembered his first day at SubSea Solutions in Charleston. He'd been pitched straight into a harbor job, raising a yacht that had sunk in the last big storm. Jeff, the owner of the company, greeted him on the wharf. *Got your fins and drysuit? All righty then. Ryder'll take you out to the dive location.*

Seagulls keening. The seaweedy smell of the harbor. The dive boat rocking on the chop. And Ryder standing on the deck, grinning like a pirate, while the ancient compressor's two-stroke engine clanked. Instead of saying hello, Ryder offered Nick a beer. Nick had liked him immediately.

Thirty feet below the surface, Ryder pulled him down the sunken yacht's gangway and, with gestures, indicated he should search the cabin while Ryder went through the wheelhouse. They'd found three hundred grams of fentanyl in waterproof packaging; it had been a drug-running boat. After the yacht was raised, Ryder returned the drugs to the relieved owner. The gold eagles Nick found in the cabin they split between them. The bigger thefts, from flooded houses and businesses, came later.

Nick wished Ryder was here now. Sure, he was a weapons-grade cockroach. But if anyone would know how to survive on the moon, with no air, no power, and no wheels, it would be him.

Nick smiled, tears in his eyes, shaking his head.

He wrapped his despair around himself like a blanket and went down.

Riding in the cradle of the winch, scraping over the craggy middle zone of the slope, pushing off from the rocks, he saw lights on the floor of the crater, to the southwest of the peak.

Two sets of two lights.

Moving in a straight, purposeful line.

He blinked.

The winch descended past a jagged buttress, and the lights —if they'd really existed—were hidden by the mountain.

When Nick reached the top of the last cliff, there was no longer any doubt. The lights were closer. They were heading for the Five Stones base camp. The rear set of lights—headlamps—illuminated the tail of the rover in front.

Nick fumbled frantically with the wrist controls of his suit radio.

"Hello! Hello!"

"Who's that?"

"Nick Morrison."

"Nick," said, unmistakably, the voice of Joe Massad. "You mean to tell me you're not dead *yet?*"

"Not quite," Nick said, laughing. He drank the rest of his water as he swayed down the cliff.

By the time he reached the ground, the rovers had parked in the construction zone. Two spacesuits detached from each rover. They bounded here and there, headlamps flashing over the ground. Nick walked toward the hab, listening to their terse commentary. They were on the ground channel, so Mission Control couldn't hear any of it.

"The furnace looks usable," a man said.

"Yeah, definitely leave that," said another. "What about the earthmover?"

"Haven't found it yet."

"Probably out in the quarry," Nick said.

"I found the construction robot," said Kat's voice. "This'll make up for all those parts we gave them."

She trudged past Nick, dragging the powerless corpse of Spiffy in the direction of the nearer ILI rover.

"Need some help with that?" Nick said.

"Nope," she said.

"Where's Joe?"

"Over there."

RHETT C. BRUNO & FELIX R. SAVAGE

Joe stood at the edge of the crater. Nick stopped on the other side.

"What a mess," Joe said. "I want you to know I had nothing to do with this."

"Yeah, but you hacked Tranquility 13, didn't you?" Nick said.

A single-board computer hidden away in Fenella's helmet, attached to a 6G modem. Nick hadn't said anything at the time, but he guessed what that was: a warshipping package. To successfully penetrate a secure digital network, you needed to put your package in physical proximity to its RF signals. The package had been in Fenella's helmet, and Fenella had known Joe. The proof was in the holocube and right here in front of him. Joe rocked on his heels, his toes over the edge of the crater.

"I'm not blaming you, man," Nick said. "You took care of business. Did what you had to do to protect your interests. Pretty neat hack: put the malware physically on board, with instructions to turn itself on *after* the final checks. I guess you got a login from somewhere."

Joe barked a laugh. "I'm astonished, that's all. I didn't think anyone would figure *that* out."

"I was into warshipping in high school," Nick said.

"No kidding? I knew some guys who were into that."

"Almost went to jail for it. Got my sentence reduced for being underage."

"That's nothing," Kat said from somewhere out of eyeshot. "I was ransom-botting Fortune 500 companies when *I* was in high school. And I never got caught."

"She's the one who wrote the hack," Joe said. "I just facilitated it."

"How? You're up here, they're... down there."

"Yeah, but my sister's the flight director for Five Stones."

"*Rachel?*" It was Nick's turn to be astonished.

"She's not at Five Stones anymore, actually," Joe said. "She quit. Sadly, our mother is ill and she needed to go home to Tel Aviv."

"Oh, snap," Nick said.

"Right? And in a further happy coincidence, our last prime minister tore up our extradition treaty with the US."

"Fenella had a picture of you guys together," Nick said. "On a mountain. I think it might have been in Israel."

"Yeah, we dated for a while."

"Rachel was so jealous of Fenella," Kat said. "Luckily, she doesn't know about me. And if she finds out, I'm a quarter million miles away, which is probably safer for my health."

Nick felt a chill. He gestured up at the sunlit peak of the mountain. "That's where Fenella fell from."

"It could be the package interfered with her suit telemetry," Joe said indifferently.

Another chill, stronger. He hunched his shoulders. Joe started to walk away to the other end of the hab. Nick hurried around the crater to catch up with him. "Why?"

60

Joe pointed up to the top of the central peak. "In chess, the king is the key to the whole game. When you capture the enemy's king, the game is over." Nick could see the reflection of Earth's distant blob in Joe's faceplate, split by the epoxied crack. "The Big Sling is the enemy's king."

Aaron sold out to the government.

"Are you working for the feds?" Nick blurted.

Joe let out another of those short barks of laughter.

"*Are* you?"

"Only one working for the feds around here was Dr. Hofstadter."

"Dr. Hofstadter!"

"You met him, remember?"

"Yeah—yeah. I remember." Nick shook his head in amazement. "Did he approve this expedition?"

"Are you kidding? He doesn't even know we're here." Joe turned. "Hey, Evan! Careful with that."

Nick walked in silence for a minute. "Was this your plan all along? Kill us and take over?"

"Hey, it wasn't me who destroyed your hab. It wasn't me

who shot down Tranquility 12. I gave you supplies, remember? You'd *already* be dead if it wasn't for me."

"Right, right... All right," Nick said.

Joe's tone became a degree or two friendlier. "As far as I've been able to work it out, their game plan was something like this: NASA has a stake in ILI, only, that's not enough. They want more. They want the glory days of *Apollo* back. They want the moon all to themselves."

"This is *NASA* we're talking about?" Nick laughed despite himself, remembering the cracked tiles around the pool in the Neutral Buoyancy Lab, the century-old equipment at KSC. "They couldn't organize a clambake."

"Which is exactly what drives McNally and his pals crazy."

"Who the hell is McNally?"

"Defense intelligence. Maybe Space Force." Joe shrugged. "When the tide of an empire withdraws, it leaves a lot of ugly, deep-sea creatures stranded on the shore, gasping desperately for power."

Nick shuddered.

"NASA doesn't really like lunar ISRU. They see it as a distraction from pure science. The deep-sea creatures basically forced the mass driver down their throats. Then the Big Sling came along. Cruder and *better*! McNally and his pals tried to force Five Stones to sell out. When Aaron wouldn't play ball, they shot down Tranquility 12."

"Couldn't you have stopped them?"

"I didn't try," Joe said brutally. "Listen, I didn't want the Big Sling to go ahead. They get everything they want, but I'm going to be left sitting on top of an eight-billion-dollar pile of junk? We spent all those years building the mass driver; now we're going to be leapfrogged by a startup? Fuck that."

"What changed your mind?"

"Simple. You did."

"Huh?"

"We thought when Tranquility 13's cryocooling failed, they would abort the mission. If you'd already disembarked when they found the problem, they'd at least come back and take you off in a couple of weeks. There's no way you could build the Big Sling with half your cargo missing. Right?"

"Wrong," Nick said.

"See! That's what I'm saying. You didn't give up. You kept on working on the damn thing, and I'm over there watching, thinking, let them finish it. *Help* them finish it. And then..." Joe bounced one fisted glove lightly off the other. "*Checkmate.*"

They were near the personnel airlock.

"This hab is a piece of shit, isn't it? No rad shielding to speak of."

"It's just as good as yours," Nick said. "At least it used to be."

"Nope," Joe said to the others. "We don't need it." He turned back to Nick. "You saw the landers, but that's just the beginning. We've built an underground hab. My people are finishing construction on that as we speak. We're going to be the first moon colonists. I mean, we kind of already are; we're just making it official."

"Are they seriously going to let you do that?"

"They'll have to," Joe said. "Won't have any choice since *we* have the Big Sling."

Nick's thoughts whirled at the implications.

"He still doesn't get it," Kat said from somewhere else in the construction zone.

"Yeah. It's amazing how naïve these NewSpace people can be," Joe said. "All right, Nick. Aaron told you this was a lunar launcher, right? In his defense, that's probably what he really thought it was. He's looking at Mars. He's imagining the future. Thinking about oxygen deliveries and space-based solar arrays."

Joe swept a glove toward the top of the central peak. "It's not a fucking lunar launcher! It's a weapon."

"Is there... a way to calculate the TNT-equivalent of a tonne and a half of lunar rock dropped onto Washington, DC?" Nick asked.

"Sure there is. If it's just a lump of rock, you'll lose a lot of it to ablative friction on the way down. But you can be sure McNally and company were planning to use high-density rods with some kind of heat shielding. And it's reasonable to assume such a rod could achieve an in-atmosphere velocity of Mach 12. That gives us twelve billion joules of kinetic energy on impact—three tonnes of TNT-equivalent.

"Even the lump of rock, assuming it had some onboard guidance to achieve the optimal angle of attack, could deliver about two tonnes of explosive force—enough to raze a city block or two. The mass driver was going to be capable of launching payloads five times that size. But if the question is 'can a projectile thrown from the Big Sling take out any spacecraft, any space-based asset in existence,' the answer is yes, obviously."

"Can't they do that already?"

"Oh, sure. You've got your fake debris, your ground-based interceptors. They think some Chinese satellites are actually energy weapons in disguise. There's never been a real battle in space, simply because any space-based weapon is vulnerable to being shot down." Joe gestured at the Big Sling again. "Not this baby."

"Huh... Guess it's like an unsinkable aircraft carrier," Nick said.

"Exactly."

"With a sustainable biosphere for the gunners, so they couldn't be starved out."

"You got it."

"I wonder what the Chinese and the Russians think about that."

"Oh, they saw the risk immediately. There's just nothing they could do about it without starting a war. Aaron placated them by promising to hold open and fair capacity auctions once the Big Sling was operational." Joe glanced to where the Big Sling continued to turn on the summit. "It'll keep on turning by itself, right?"

"Long as the sun keeps shining."

"Excellent. You'll have to take us up there and show us how it works. The payload-launching mechanism, that in place too?"

"Yeah. Everything's all ready to go," Nick said.

"What I'd do now, if I *was* working for the government, is kill you," Joe said. "Then I would launch projectiles at the Chinese and Russian moon bases. That would give them total control of the moon, lunar orbit, and LEO... Everything."

"Wild," Nick said tonelessly.

"As it is, I think my first target will be Tehran," Joe said. "Followed by the White House."

Kat trudged past with one of the other ArxaSys Lunar contractors. She was carrying a cylinder with one pointed end, three legs sticking out from the other end. Nick watched them open the hatch of the personnel airlock. Then he turned back to Joe.

"You're kidding, right?"

"About what?"

"Blowing up the government."

"Absolutely not," Joe said. "I'd do Tel Aviv, too, but, you know, my family is there."

Kat and the other contractor backed out of the airlock chamber, unreeling a cable attached to a small box.

"I can't let you do that," Nick said.

"Come on, Nick. I thought you wanted to save the planet," Joe said.

"I didn't build a weapon. My friends didn't die to build a *weapon.*"

"Sorry, but they did. Anyway, it's not up to you. The Big Sling is ours now. You can either stay here and help Kat and Evan get up to speed, or you can come back with me and Wez. Your choice."

The ground vibrated slightly. Orange light flashed out of the airlock chamber. Debris flew out in slow ballistic trajectories over the crouching Kat's and Evan's heads.

Nick ran to the airlock.

Kat got there ahead of him. Amidst dispersing smoke, she leaned on the scorched, twisted inner hatch. It swept aside the crumpled mass of Kurtis's exosuit. The rush of escaping air—unbreathable, at this point, but still at nearly one full atmosphere of pressure—plucked up the corpses of Lee and Kurtis and tossed them into new sprawled positions. Around them, the frozen lake of blood began to sublimate into the vacuum.

Kat shoved Nick aside in her hurry to get out. "I'm *not* going in there."

Evan poked his helmet in. Crimson fog rose from the floor, partially veiling the faces of the corpses. He in turn retreated. "Dead people."

"There could have been someone alive in there!" Nick shouted.

"Well, there isn't anymore," Joe said. "Hang on. Someone's pinging me from base."

Joe fell silent and gestured with both hands—talking on a different channel—then went still.

When he spoke again, his voice had changed. "Trouble at home," he said, and Nick's helmet became a bubble of silence.

The ArxaSys Lunar contractors were talking on a scrambled channel he couldn't receive.

Nick peered down the length of the personnel module, over the flattened partitions. If Maddy had been in her exosuit when they blew the airlock, she might still be alive. Nothing moved. He was torn between investigating the module and allaying the contractors' suspicions. He scanned the floor near at hand for anything he could use as a weapon. Nothing.

"All right," Joe said abruptly. "Stay in touch."

Nick backed out of the airlock. Joe and Kat were jogging away in the direction of the rovers.

Wez said to Nick, "They're going home. We're staying here."

"What happened?" Nick said.

"None of your business," Wez said. "And in case it's not clear, if you do anything stupid..." He held up a length of steel pipe. "You die."

61

"I knew Trig would screw up," Kat said.

"I shouldn't have left Dave alive," Joe said.

Dr. Hofstadter had demanded access to the ILI "lifeboat," the Artemis lander that remained on-site and fueled up, ready to launch. Trig made the mistake of going into the ILI hab complex to talk it over with him, taking two other contractors, Jésus and Sam. The discussion turned ugly.

Joe had *known* Dr. Hofstadter's time in the reactor room unbalanced him. Trig said Dr. Hofstadter himself had thrown the first punch. What happened next was unclear. Seemed one of the scientists pulled a knife, and Jésus, a sweet-natured boy from California, bled out on the floor of the chemistry lab. Trig, outnumbered, was forced to leave the body behind.

At that point he'd called Joe in a panic.

"He should have called me earlier," Joe muttered. "Shouldn't have even gone over there." He'd most likely have done the same thing.

"I just hope he doesn't do anything else stupid before we get back," Kat said.

"All he has to do is sit tight," Joe said.

As soon as he heard the news, Joe told Trig to cut ILI's comms. This amounted to an open declaration of war on ILI. A move he hadn't wanted to do until he was ready to get rid of the scientists. Everything was moving too fast...

...*Except* the rover.

Damn thing was crawling over the floor of Amundsen Crater like an insect in a jar. He drummed his fists lightly on the steering wheel.

"Look on the bright side," Kat said. "We've got the Big Sling. That means we've already won."

"Yeah," Joe said. He called Wez again.

———

Wez cocked his head. "He wants us to go inside." They were all sitting on the ground outside the hab.

"To do what?" Evan said.

"Just check it out."

"Fuck that," Evan said. "I'm not stepping over dead people."

"Dude, what are you, superstitious? Fine, whatever, I'll go in." Wez handed his length of pipe to Evan. "Don't let him get away."

"Seriously, *where* would I go?" Nick said.

He'd mentally mapped out the route to the remaining rover. It represented shelter, food, water, air. *Life*. Except there was no chance of making it that far, much less getting inside, as long as they were watching him.

Wez stooped into the airlock. "Fucking hell."

"Just step over them," Evan said.

Nick sat facing the dark. His teeth gritted, fists bunched between his knees. Long shivers of regret and weariness travelled through his body like a fever.

Dust and gravel bounced into his headlamp beam.

A six-legged metal beast leapt out of the darkness, straight at Evan.

The Woombat.

The electromagnetic dust collection device formerly attached to the front of its body had been replaced by a six-inch conical drill bit.

Evan was knocked flat, held down by the Woombat's forelegs on his chest. It shouted in Charlie's voice, "Run, Nick! Run!"

Evan yelled and swore, trying to get up. He threw the robot off and it pounced on him again. They struggled. The drill bit tore into the plumped-up fabric of Evan's suit, just below the collar of his helmet.

Air escaped in a visible jet that faded in the vacuum, along with the sound of Evan's screaming.

Nick shoved the Woombat aside and shook the man. He was limp. His suit had crumpled, the way Fenella's had, leaving the true outline of his body visible. Evan looked very small.

"*Run!*"

Nick dropped Evan's body. He picked up the length of pipe and ducked into the airlock. His headlamp threw the shadow of his own arm and the upraised pipe ahead of him, monstrously large.

A gleaming bubble moved out of the shadows near the end of the module. Maddy was crawling toward him in her exosuit.

"Nick?"

"Yeah, yeah. It's me."

"I killed the other one," she said. "He didn't see me moving until it was too late. I shot him with Kurtis's gun." She laughed thickly. "Can we get out of here now?"

Nick's arm trembled. He flung the pipe down.

Maddy's laugh turned into a cough. She collapsed.

"Maddy!"

The exosuit lay still. The sound of violent retching came over the radio.

Nick fell to his knees and rolled her over. He aimed his helmet lamp at an indirect angle that allowed him to see, dimly, through the gold coating of her faceplate. Her face was down low in the exosuit, only her forehead and a spray of blue-tipped hair showed above the collar. Dark stuff clung to her forehead. There was also something dark smeared on the inside of the glass.

"Maddy, what's wrong?"

She shook inside the suit, her head twisting from side to side as she vomited. "Been puking—for hours. Shitting—my guts out, too."

"That sounds like food poisoning."

"*Air* poisoning."

"Ah, fuck! The dust," Nick said.

"Yeah. Dust sticking—to the inside—of this damn container. Been breathing it—couple of days now. Symptoms match—iron toxicity." She broke off and vomited again.

"Hold on. Hold on, Maddy. I'm going to get you to their rover." He lifted and dragged the exosuit, his arms wrapped around the canister. He backed toward the airlock.

"Nick—the—devil. Nick. Remember. He wants us—all." More retching.

"Stop with that kind of talk," Nick said.

"Feel—bad."

"You're going to be fine." His boot hit Lee's frozen-solid leg and he stumbled, dropping the exosuit.

It bounced on the floor and lay still.

"Maddy!"

Behind the gold veil of the helmet bubble, her face was as still as a marble Madonna's. Her hair floated like seaweed in the puddle of vomit where her cheek rested. The radio roared soft silence.

Nick fumbled with the exosuit, rolling it over so Maddy's face lay against the inside of the faceplate. He waited for her breath to fog the glass.

Nothing.

He stumbled into the open, his breath laboring.

The Woombat lay on the ground like a dog. "What happened to Maddy?" Charlie said.

Nick—the devil—Nick. Remember. He wants us—all.

"Iron poisoning," Nick said.

Maddy had been vomiting and suffering diarrhea for hours. Days. She'd said nothing to him because he'd frozen her out to punish her for the deaths of Lee and Kurtis. And so she died, too. They'd all died.

He searched the ground for the satchel Wez and Evan had taken from him. In his peripheral vision, Earth floated like a child's balloon above the crater rim.

The Woombat butted his leg. "Nick."

"What?"

"You have to save yourself."

"You're always *so full* of helpful advice," Nick said. He found the satchel and picked it up.

"You have to stop them," Charlie said, far away. "You have to stop them, Nick. There's no one else."

"Stop them from doing what?"

The signal lag gave the conversation a detached, surreal quality.

"Rachel told me what Joe's planning," Charlie said. "They're going to steal the moon!"

"Steal it from who? It wasn't yours to begin with. It wasn't ours, either. To be honest, I don't see why anyone fucking wants it."

Distant headlamps twinkled in the darkness.

"What's that?"

"Gulliver. I'm sending him to help you."

"I've had enough of your help," Nick said.

He went back into the hab. Lee and Kurtis stared at him with blank, frost-white eyes. Maddy lay beyond them, curled up like a child in the Kevlar and steel blanket of her exosuit. Her words about a devil bounced around in his mind. Or *the* devil. *I don't know why anyone fucking wants the moon.*

The devil did—hitchhiked all the way here with them from Earth. *Wants us all*, and he wanted the moon, too. Nick didn't believe in that kind of bullshit. But now he wished he'd brought that Bible he left on the summit down with him. It was getting harder and harder to breathe.

His helmet beam fell on another shape, this one in a space-suit, sprawled at the end of the module. His heart skipped a beat. The figure wasn't moving. Must be Wez, whom Maddy shot. *The devil—stop that.* The moon—

Nick cautiously approached Wez and stooped to make sure he was really dead. There was a shiny abraded place on the chest of his suit. The round hadn't penetrated the Kevlar, but a bullet fired at point-blank range was still a terrific blow to the chest. Didn't baseball players sometimes die of fastballs to the chest? Wez's face behind his faceplate wore an expression of unspeakable horror. *Cardiac arrest.* That must be it. *He died of cardiac arrest—*

Nick stumbled into the kitchen. After a few minutes of searching, he found Kurtis's Glock. He put it into his satchel and ran headlong out of the hab, into the lunar night.

62

"Nick, Aaron here. Listen, I've been a total dickhead. I apologize. I'm going to lose the company. I'll probably have to go on the run—just, never mind that. You're the only one who can stop them. Go to ILI. I already emailed Dr. Hofstadter—"

"According to Joe, he's working for the feds." Nick sat on the ground, getting his breath back, watching the hab in case something moved.

"We're getting conflicting information about that. Either way, this Joe guy is clearly the real problem. Like I said, I emailed Dr. Hofstadter, but I don't think he got the email. You have to go and warn them before it's too late. I'll pay you—"

"Take your money and shove it up your ass," Nick interrupted. "I'm not working for you anymore." He turned off the radio.

Silence filled his helmet, like the inside of a seashell.

Cautiously, he returned to the hab. This time he only went as far as the airlock and gathered up Kurtis's exosuit. Carrying it, he walked toward the ILI rover. At a short distance from the rover, he put the exosuit down and took the Glock out of his spacesuit's thigh pocket. The trigger guard was a custom job, extended to allow a gloved finger access to the trigger. He walked around in front of the rover.

On top of its roof was a satellite dish, plus a couple of other antennas. He raised the Glock and sighted on the satellite dish.

The rover's headlamps clicked on. It started to roll toward him.

Just as he'd feared, it could be operated remotely. Had he gotten into the rover, they'd probably have vented the atmosphere or killed him by turning off the CO_2 scrubbing.

Blinded by the headlamps, Nick fired.

The rover gathered speed—an impression of living malevolence. It was going to run him down.

He stood his ground and fired again.

Nick sprang aside as the rover coasted to a stop. The headlamps were still on. He aimed his helmet lamp at the roof. The dish had two holes torn through it; the receiver in the middle was broken off.

He climbed the external ladder to the roof. He stamped on the remaining antennas until they were bent out of shape, destroying their ability to operate remotely. Nick jumped back to the ground.

He swung the sample return hatch open. Fragments of vacuum-frozen leaves littered the bottom of the chamber. He stuffed the exosuit and gun into the hatch, closed it, and climbed onto the step and sealed his suit to the suitlock.

The cabin was spacious, warm, and noisy with fans. It held a driver's couch, a work area with a table, and two racks of bunks built into the wall. Nick stretched his wobbly limbs, glorying in the breathable air and the freedom to move around without his suit. Tears tracked his cheeks. His hair stood away from his skull, stiff with sweat and grease. When he looked in the mirror in the little toilet cubicle, strands of hair at the front glittered white.

He ransacked the storage lockers—rations, beverages, chocolate, protein bars, and loaves of not-too-stale bread. He tore huge hunks off a loaf with his teeth, barely stopping to chew. He drank fortified orange juice and reconstituted milk.

When his stomach was full, he familiarized himself with the controls. They were similar to the Five Stones rover's controls, with a few differences, such as a steering wheel instead of a yoke. He tested the comms just to make sure they were really out.

Satisfied, he fell onto a bunk and slept for several hours. No dreams disturbed him.

When he woke up, every muscle of his body ached. He found some ibuprofen tablets and swallowed those. There was even analgesic cream he applied to his hands. His marathon stint on top of the central peak had cost him two fingernails on his right hand, one on his left. Both hands were so stiff and sore, he had to pincer things between his palms rather than gripping them normally.

He ate instant oatmeal, warmed up in the rover's microwave, and then set off across the floor of the crater, following the tracks the other ILI rover left in the dust a few hours ago.

"*Shosholoza,*" he hummed under his breath. "*Shosholoza, shosholoza. Wen' uyabaleka, kulezo ntaba, stimela siphume South Africa...*" Running away, on this train from South Africa. Running away...

The Five Stones site shrank behind him and vanished into the dark.

Now he had a new problem. He strained forward over the steering wheel, squinting through the rover's small, slit windshield. There were three large dashboard screens, none of which was any help. One showed a fixed view to the rear. Another was blank—Nick must've accidentally shot out the forward-facing camera. The worst of it was that the main navigational screen was also dead. With no antennas, the rover not only had no comms, it had no satellite-based navigation. Nick had to follow the tracks ahead of him so as not to get lost in the expanse of the crater floor, but they were mixed up, overlapping, hard to see.

He slowed down, afraid of losing the trail.

Pinpoints of light appeared on the rear camera feed. They grew.

Gulliver bounced past. The earthmover's roller attachment had been removed to make it faster and nimbler. It tucked in ahead of the rover and settled down to a steady eight kph.

Nick slammed on the brakes.

Ahead, Gulliver stopped, as if waiting for him.

"What's the deal, Charlie?" Nick yelled. "I told you I'm not working for you anymore!"

Without comms, he couldn't really talk to her.

He didn't even know if it really *was* her.

Without Gulliver's help, he couldn't reach the southern rim of the crater, let alone ILI.

Nick drove the aching heels of his hands against his temples. *Nick—the devil—Nick. Remember.* He remembered, but he also remembered Charlie's eyes, brown and green and gold in the sun. How she looked standing by the side of the pool in the Neutral Buoyancy Lab. Clumsily asking her out.

God, what a loser—yet she hadn't shot him down in a mean way. She'd just blushed. And afterward she had done everything in her power to keep him alive.

Blink if you're there, Charlie. Twice for yes, once for no...

Gulliver's taillights blinked twice, as if urging him to hurry up.

Nick sobbed out a laugh. "You're going to be sorry," he said. He touched the throttle. The rover moved on.

————

Three a.m. in Florida. The whole Five Stones building was dark, except for the Mission Control room.

Four a.m. Yuta did yoga stretches on the floor.

Five a.m. Aaron procured more coffee for them all. He sat down beside Charlie, who was staring at the black-and-white satellite feed. Gulliver was a computer-generated dot inching around Faustini Crater. The ILI rover was an optical speck behind it.

"The feds'll probably come first thing in the morning," Aaron said.

McNally had demanded yesterday that the Five Stones comms apparatus be turned over to his organization. Aaron pleaded technical difficulties, but that wouldn't stall them for long.

"And when they come, you hold them off as long as possible," Charlie said.

Six a.m. "Get some rest," Yuta said. Aaron was snoring on the floor, using Yuta's yoga mat as a pillow.

Seven a.m. Dawn paled the lights in the mission control room. Sunlight glared on Charlie's screens. She scowled, got up, and stepped over the sleeping men to pull the blinds. Then she sat back down and went back to guiding Gulliver through the intercrater highlands.

————

Nick jerked awake for the twentieth time. The rover was drifting along a sunlit ridge with the stygian depths of Shackleton Crater on one side. Ahead, Gulliver had stopped. The earthmover's taillights were dark. It must have finally run out of power.

That was all right. He knew where he was now.

63

"Try Wez again," Joe said.

Kat bent over the comms. She shook her head. "Something's happened."

"I should have killed Nick," Joe said. "Thought he was coming around to my point of view."

"Trig?" Kat was on the radio with base again. "We're going to be there in about five minutes. Give me an update."

Joe pushed the rover up the last hill, heading for the peak of eternal light. The solar installation looked wrong. Shadows lay on the panels. It hadn't been turned to track the angle of the sun for the last twelve hours.

"We're all in the landers," Trig said breathlessly. "The counterattack didn't work out. We had to fall back." Joe heard shouting in the background.

"Where are they?"

"Outside. They've got us trapped in here. What should we do?"

"Sit tight." Joe pushed the rover's speed into the red. They bounced past the oxygen plant. No one was working outside.

The shadow of the peak of eternal light stretched farther at this time of day. Its black tip reached all the way to the ILI hab complex. Beyond that, figures in ILI spacesuits clustered around the MVDA. Joe immediately saw what Trig meant. All the suits had been taken from the MVDA's suit charging assembly. The men and women trapped in the landers had no way of getting out.

Trig had been an idiot not to post a guard outside. But everyone had wanted to participate in the punitive expedition to the ILI hab complex to avenge the death of Jésus. That ended in an inconclusive retreat with several casualties on both sides.

"They're messing with the MVDA," Kat said as the rover careered toward the landers.

The ILI suits seemed to be helping two of their number to climb up to the suitlocks.

"Trig, you got hostiles coming in," Kat said. "Send someone down to the MVDA to shank them when they get out of their suits."

"On it," Trig said. "Maria's down there already. I'll go down now."

It was a pretty stupid move on Dr. Hofstadter's part, Joe thought. He had to know his infiltrators wouldn't survive the vulnerable moment of climbing out of their suits backward. Maybe the plan was to claim they just wanted to talk.

He drove the rover straight at the people around the MVDA.

In the vacuum, there was no sound to warn them of its coming. They looked around when the shadow of the rover touched them. By then it was too late. The duckbilled prow bore two people down to the ground. The wheels bumped over them. Joe set his teeth and threw the rover into reverse. The wheels bumped again. Kat bounced in her seat, screaming in excitement. Joe spun the wheel and gunned the rover away from the landers, chasing down the survivors.

———

Nick eased the rover around the peak of eternal light and idled the engine, scanning the plateau below.

The Artemis shuttle stood in the landing zone.

The reactor's radiator vanes still spread their shadows across the Mylar apron at the base of the truss.

Closer at hand, the ILI hab complex and the repurposed landers sprawled at the edge of the hill's shadow. No one moved outside. It all seemed eerily quiet.

He drove closer.

Near the MVDA, several spacesuits lay on the ground.

Nick circled the rover at a distance, close enough to see they weren't moving. There were seven of them altogether. They looked kind of crushed, with X-shaped marks on their backs.

Nick drove back to the ILI airlock and parked near it.

He was tempted to head straight for the Artemis shuttle. Couldn't be that easy. There would be boarding procedures, most likely passwords, maybe biometric security. Even if the shuttle's launch procedures were entirely controlled by the DSG crew in cislunar orbit, he would need to convince them to launch it. The Big Sling hadn't convinced them. That meant he needed the support of someone in authority.

He hurriedly drank some milk and ate a protein bar. Then he got out.

In the sunlight, the primitive-looking regolith shields of the habs looked as if they'd been frozen in liquid nitrogen, as if a touch could crumble them.

Nick opened the sample return hatch and retrieved the exosuit and gun. He'd cleaned the dust off the Glock's firing mechanism en route. The magazine still held four rounds.

Carrying the exosuit and gun, he bounded to the airlock and tried the lever.

The hatch opened.

Dr. Hofstadter met him in the vestibule. "I received Aaron Slater's email," he said. "It was a case of horse and barn door, I'm afraid. I was already aware of the situation and had taken steps to rectify it. Unfortunately, those were largely unsuccessful. And now they've cut our comms."

Most of the stored spacesuits had gone. Nick figured they were lying in the sun, with dead people inside. "It's bad, huh?"

"Very bad," Dr. Hofstadter said. "Come in, come in."

Nick followed him into the maze of the ILI hab complex. Despite the monotonously roaring fans and clanking pipes, there was an atmosphere of deadly quiet. No conversation. No one running on the treadmills. No one poring over scientific instruments.

"Where is everyone?"

"Gone. Gone," Dr. Hofstadter said. He stepped over something that partially blocked one of the narrow pressure doors that joined the inflatables—the body of a young man with longish dark hair and a skimpy beard. Blood discolored the chest area of his ArxaSys Lunar fleece. Dust dimmed his eyeballs.

"Who's this?"

"One of them," Dr. Hofstadter said, without giving the corpse a glance.

A little way on they passed the body of another contractor, this one a woman, with her face bashed in by a blunt object.

Nick swallowed bile. He was now beginning to notice the smell, a sweetish nauseating taint that reminded him of mud left behind by contaminated floodwaters. The fans circulated it around and around in the stale warm air of the complex. They passed the partition that blocked off the medical clinic. Nick stopped and looked around the screen.

Each of the cots in the clinic held an injured person. Nick recognized Ajay the radio astronomer, Cynthia the seismologist, and one of the Italians. They twitched in drugged sleep. Dr. Priya Nataraj sat in her chair, slumped forward with her head on her keyboard. The way her left arm dangled down and the purplish discoloration of the fingers told Nick she was dead. Had been for a while.

"Priya killed herself," Dr. Hofstadter said, behind him. "I suppose it must have been especially hard on her, as a doctor."

Nick was still holding his exosuit, with the gun concealed under its folds. He turned, a little too quickly, and staggered back. "Yes, I guess so."

Dr. Hofstadter's green eyes looked more intense than ever. The Nobel laureate was peering out through a filter of extreme paranoia and despair. That was understandable. Whether or not he really had been working for the government, he'd failed catastrophically.

He gave Nick a quick up-and-down stare, as if judging his will to go on. "Well, come on, hurry up. By the way, your foot seems to have healed."

"Yeah, it's uh, it's better," Nick said.

"Good, good. Priya was very good at what she did."

They were now in a module Nick hadn't previously visited. A sort of combination kitchen and pantry, except the shelves were nearly empty.

"They used to keep us short," Dr. Hofstadter said. "Joe called it a just-in-time distribution system. In fact, it was a way of keeping control over our entire food supply. He used the implicit threat of starvation to force me to go along with his whims."

"Why didn't you ever say anything?"

Dr. Hofstadter flashed him a hawkish glance. "Pride."

A pressure door sealed off the end of the module. An intercom hung beside it. Dr. Hofstadter put his face up close to the screen. "Look who I've got here, you rat-faced psychopath."

The intercom whistled. "Rat-faced?" Joe said, sounding amused.

A moment later the pressure door unsealed with a wheeze. Nick caught a momentary whiff of a new smell, something like musty grass cuttings. He grabbed the lever and pulled the door open. Joe stood in the flexitube tunnel on the other side. The frozen grimace stitched to his face would resemble a smile only if you knew nothing about human beings.

"You got here fast."

"It's a good rover," Nick said. "Would be better with a working sat dish."

"What did you do to Wez and Evan?"

"Robot killed Evan, though I'm pretty sure it was an accident. Maddy Huxley killed Wez. That wasn't."

"Wez never was careful enough about who he pissed off," Joe said. Then he lost interest in Nick, looking past him at Dr. Hofstadter. His grimace crumpled into a snarl. Nick realized that Dr. Hofstadter had made *him* open the door in case Joe came out swinging. "How can you live with yourself, Dave?"

"I had to do something," Dr. Hofstadter said. "I can't allow the moon to be turned into a pawn in geopolitical power games."

"It already is, you idiot."

"What did he do?" Nick said.

"He's the one who dropped a basalt football on your hab at Mach 12," Joe said.

Nick looked at Dr. Hofstadter in shock. The geophysicist cringed near the fridge. "You're as bad as the rest of them."

"Have you ever been to the Apollo 11 landing site?" Dr. Hofstadter said. "It ought to be required for everyone planning to work on the moon. The descent stage of the lunar lander is still there. Attached to one of its legs is a plaque that reads *We Came In Peace For All Mankind*. It's signed by Armstrong, Aldrin, and Collins."

"And Richard Nixon," Joe said.

"We came in peace," Dr. Hofstadter said. "We have to keep that ideal alive. Stop the spiral of violence. If it can't be stopped on the moon, it can't be stopped anywhere."

"Oh, shut up, you fucking Nazi," Joe said.

"You've set lunar exploration back by decades!" Dr. Hofstadter shouted.

"Your mistake is thinking I care," Joe said. "The moon is mine. No one's getting here or leaving without my permission."

"Guess you're not going to give me the keys to the Artemis shuttle," Nick said.

"You're in the way. Move." Joe reached past Nick's chest to pull the pressure door shut.

Nick shoved his arm away.

Joe stepped forward to push him out of the door's arc.

From far away in the maze of inflatables came a sound like something large and soft falling over.

Nick felt a tickle of wind on his face, blowing out of the tunnel where Joe was, or more accurately, *being sucked* out of it. He remembered Kat and Evan backing away from the Five Stones hab, unreeling a length of fuse from their blasting machine.

He thrust the heavy bundle of exosuit into Joe's face. The steel canister made contact with Joe's head. Joe stumbled backward, then threw himself past Nick again, shouting, "The door! *Get the door!*"

Nick shoved his right hand under the bundle of exosuit and transferred the Glock into it. He fired, one-handed, at Joe's body. He didn't see where the bullet went. Joe reacted with a violent thrust of both arms against Nick's chest, knocking him off-balance, back against the door. He sprang away into the flexitube tunnel and leapt up the ladder at its end.

Nick dropped the exosuit and gun in the tunnel and seized

the lever with both hands. The flow of air past him was stronger now, ruffling his hair. He braced his feet against the bottom of the pressure door's heavy steel frame and heaved.

Dr. Hofstadter thrust himself into the gap on all fours. His mouth worked wetly, shouting. Nick couldn't hear him over the thin howl of the escaping wind and the roaring in his ears. He kicked Dr. Hofstadter in the face and pulled the door shut. There was an improvised deadbolt on this side, a steel bar that could be slid through hasps to prevent the lever's being worked; Nick dropped it into place.

His ears popped. A portion of the air in the landers had escaped through the door, leaving the pressure lower than normal. But his memories of deep dives assured him that his brain was getting enough oxygen to function, at least for now. He picked his stuff up and went looking for Joe.

64

"I blew the airlock," Kat yelled over the intercom.

Joe was too out of breath to answer. He ran past the bodies of his people lying where they'd fallen, their faces tinged purple. Molly. Sam. Miguel. Andy. Oleg. Amanda. Noah. Bethany. He knew each of them inside and out—their little personality quirks, their backgrounds, whom they were sleeping with, what they could have brought as individuals to the first true colony on the moon.

Amanda had been three months pregnant. Her baby would have been the first moon child.

At least good old Dave had by now died the cruel but unfortunately quick death of suffocation.

Atmosphere alerts shrilled from every console. There was a very faint smell of musty hay. Joe ran faster. Nick Morrison wouldn't be far behind. Nick didn't know the layout of the landers like Joe did, but there was no evading him in here, either. And Nick had a gun.

Joe ran down the steps to the MVDA. On the floor, Trig and Maria lay in tormented postures, dead hands clawing at their throats. Joe stepped over them and slapped the intercom. "Meet you outside."

"Copy." Kat's voice sounded strained.

Joe climbed into the rover and sealed the vehicle docking hatch behind him. He was safe now. Safe... With Nick still running around in the landers. He needed to lure him into the open.

He backed the rover away from the MVDA, into the sunlight.

———

Nick bounded through the landers, gun in hand. His gaze darted here and there, ricocheting from one corpse after another. Ten, fifteen—he stopped counting.

"What *happened* in here?" he screamed.

"Good old Dave," Joe said over the intercom, his voice bouncing in stereo from both behind Nick and ahead of him. "Used ILI's world-class chemistry lab to mix up a batch of phosgene and filled the life-support backpacks of two suits with it... Sealed them to our suitlocks.

"It's deadly but goes away quick. So the bastard, just to make sure, put tanks inside the suits with their regulators set to about twenty hPa above ambient pressure so the stuff would keep hissing out. I expect everyone died inside a few minutes. By the time I got inside, the atmospheric hydrators had decontaminated the air. All the hydrochloric acid will have corroded them, though—they'll have to be replaced. The alarms, you know."

"Where are you?" Nick stopped in the middle of the break room. He spun around. Dead contractors stared into the eyes of God.

"Outside," Joe said.

Nick descended the steps to the MVDA, flinching from the sight of Trig and the stocky Latina woman he'd met before, lying dead on the floor. He eyed the row of suitlocks. Two of them indicated there was a suit charging on the outside. Those would be the ones Dr. Hofstadter used as phosgene delivery mechanisms. Nick had left his own suit at the ILI airlock. It was now out of reach, beyond the vacuum that filled the ILI hab complex. Tempting as it was, he wasn't touching either of these suits. At the very least, they had no real air in their tankage.

He looked down at the exosuit bundled in his arms.

He dropped it, unfolded it, and climbed in.

It was still possible to manipulate the trigger of the Glock using the exosuit's direct-drive claws, holding it in one of them and depressing the trigger with the other. It was just a simple squeezing motion, after all.

The vehicle docking hatch could double as an airlock for transferring cargo in and out of the landers.

He folded himself into the chamber and watched the pressure dial drop toward zero.

———

"Where are you, Kat?" Joe expected to see her running for the rover.

"Over here. Near the reactor."

Movement caught his eye: a glove, stiffly waving. Kat was lying on the ground.

"Suit's fucked," she said.

"Breached?"

"Nope. Joints finally locked up. I can't bend my legs. Too much time in the fucking... *dust*."

Those fucking knee joints. Those assholes never sent

replacement parts. The cloud of dust from the shaped charge couldn't have helped, either.

"I'm coming." Joe parked near her. One hundred fifty meters away, something fell out of the MVDA docking hatch.

"Can you get to the rover?" Joe asked Kat, watching it.

"I can't *move*, Joe!"

The thing that had fallen out of the MVDA unfolded. It stood, taller than any human being. Barrel body, bubble head, and stilt-like tapered legs. It took a tottering step, and another.

"That's an unusual-looking contraption," Joe said. "Looks like a kid's first attempt at drawing a mecha."

"We're trying not to use the M-word," Nick said.

"The Artemis shuttle's that way."

Even if Nick reached the Artemis, he couldn't launch it. The only person who could do that was Joe himself. Just another of their little security measures: Kat had inserted a password verification routine into the protocols, which shook hands with the ArxaSys AI before launch. And Nick didn't know that. Joe expected him to head for the Artemis, into the open ground beyond the nuclear reactor, where he could easily be overtaken and run down.

He did not.

The spindly-legged alien mecha strode toward the rover.

Toward Kat lying vulnerable on the ground.

"Help!" she screamed, pulling herself nearer the rover with her arms. "Joe! Help!"

Joe cursed. He scrambled into his suit. The seal verification process had never taken so long. Suspended helplessly from the suitlock, he caught sight through his faceplate of Nick's gun held in the alien mecha's claws.

Seal verified. Joe dropped down to the ground. He ran to Kat and hauled her upright. Once she was on her feet, she was able to move in awkward strides, swinging her legs without bending her knees.

The alien mecha broke into a run.

It was *fast*.

Its elongated legs covered several meters at each bound. There must be stilts in there, maybe made of flexible aluminum, for that extra snap of springiness every time it pushed off. Joe saw in an instant that he and Kat wouldn't have time to enter the rover before it reached them and put a bullet in each of their suits. It would get them while they stood helplessly in the suit port.

"I just want to talk," Nick panted.

"There's nothing left to talk about," Joe said. Dragging Kat with him, he started to run. Where to? He didn't know at first, but the geometry of the pursuit left only one terrible possibility.

The reactor.

———

I could get so much done in this thing, Kurtis had said. Nick now understood where he'd been coming from. This was the first exosuit they made, and probably the better one. He felt like he was walking on springs—a giant striding across the lunar terrain in seven-league boots.

At the same time, there was a certain comfort in the weight of the thing—it forced him to use the same muscles he used to walk on Earth. He fleetingly imagined a future moon colony where workers in exosuits, like this one, only better made, traversed quarries and construction sites in comfort.

No more needing to grit their teeth and strain every time they bent their limbs. Bones protected by the compensatory effort of moving around something that weighed five times as much as a human being. Eating lunch inside the operator cabin, trading banter over the radio, leaving their "rides" to charge overnight in stables attached to secure, spacious underground habitats. It all unfurled in his mind's eye in a flash, and then it was forgotten as he chased Joe and Kat.

They were heading for the nuclear reactor. He stopped and shot at them. Missed. The claws gave him poor control, and the pause allowed them to widen the distance.

They got there ten seconds ahead of him. Joe unlocked the airlock hatch, threw Kat inside, jumped in after her, and banged the hatch shut. When Nick got there, the hatch refused to move.

"It's locked from the inside," Joe said. "Don't bother."

"What's in there, anyway?" Nick said.

65

Joe's mind may as well have been full of wet towels, each one slapping him with a fresh shock of humiliation and grief. He reminded himself it wasn't real, none of it. He was still in the game. All that mattered was his position and his next move.

"Here's what we do." He helped Kat out of her spacesuit. She was crying. "We wait for him to go away. Load up the rover with supplies, head back to Amundsen, and launch our first strike. *Kaboom*, we're in business."

Kat shook her head. "We need him to tell us how to launch the payloads," she said through her tears. "We don't know jack about the launch system. And the guidance electronics for the payloads could be anywhere."

"All right." Joe was sure they could figure it out, but he was willing to go along with her in this state. "Then we let him in. When he comes out of the chamber, he'll be disoriented. That's when we hit him. Grab the gun..."

They were huddling on the catwalk. The air was stale, warm and filled with the rumbling of the Stirling engines. Down on the floor of the reactor room, and on the stairs leading up to the catwalk, scientists lay dead. There were five in all.

Five spacesuits lay separately. None of the corpses were fully clothed. One wore nothing but a brassiere and a single sock.

Joe's mind automatically put names to them: Patrick Mahoney, BSc, knowledge engineer; Kristina Polonski, PhD, organic chemist; Sajid Ali, robotics specialist; Milo Ferrara, PhD, astronomer; and Patricia Reiss, also an astronomer. Trig must have captured them during the counterattack on the ILI hab complex and stuffed them in here. No one had remembered to let them out.

Milo appeared to have cut his own throat with a pair of wire cutters. It looked as if Patricia was missing an eye.

Joe was about to throw up. Suddenly calm, he bowed his head, averting the nausea by force of will. "All right, Kat? All right?"

She didn't answer. He looked up. She was pulling her thermal shirt off.

Joe reached out. She smacked his hands away. "I told you never," she shouted, "*never* bring me back in here again. I can't stay in here! It's too dangerous. They're going to get me!" She gestured down at the corpses. "They're coming for me! Look!"

Such was her vehemence that Joe actually did look. By the time he verified for himself that the corpses weren't moving, Kat had jumped to her feet and slapped the button that opened the airlock.

"Kat!" Joe grabbed her leg.

She wrenched free. "Nuh uh! You're not keeping me in here this time. I'm gone, Joe. I'm gone." She jumped backward into the chamber. The hatch started to close.

Joe threw himself into the opening. He braced his back against the curved seal and his feet against the edge of the hatch. It ground toward him, bending his knees. Kat had her thumb pressed hard on the close button. She called him a mother-fucking murderer. The hatch kept shutting.

He tumbled out of the narrowing gap, back onto the catwalk.

Before the hatch closed, he got a last glimpse of Kat pulling her long johns off.

———

Nick leaned against the base of the reactor truss, holding the gun in one claw. He gazed at the stiff metal earthworm of the mass driver receding into the distance, mentally peopling the scene with human beings, buggies, and payloads being prepared for launch.

"Talk to me, Joe," he said.

In the stillness and silence, his mind was finding it hard to hold onto things. His thoughts drifted back to Earth. When he worked at SubSea Solutions, he spent a lot of time volunteering. Part of that was helping Ryder Stillman steal stuff, but they did real work, too. They rescued people stranded by storms, and helped them rebuild. Some of Nick's best memories were of days spent drywalling or roofing in the nippy winter sunlight of the Carolinas. Even Ryder, he thought, enjoyed it—the satisfaction of building a thing that worked, the taste of that first cold beer at lunchtime, the smiles of those they helped. Nothing felt quite as good as helping people. Made up for the other stuff they did.

Nick came to the moon for selfish reasons. Now, emotionally shattered and physically exhausted, there was a new openness in his heart, like the slackness of tired hands falling open. The Artemis shuttle, sitting fatly behind its berm, looked too far away to get to. And anyway, why did he need to get there? *Why do people still live someplace like this?* he'd often wondered. Now he knew. It was because they were already there. The answer wasn't running away. It was something simpler: rebuild.

"Come *on*, dude," he said. "You can't hide in there all day."

The airlock opened.

Nick whirled around, tangling his legs up, almost falling over.

A slender, pale figure burst out of the chamber. So unprepared was Nick for this sight that it took him a second to realize he was looking at a woman with no spacesuit on. She didn't even have any *clothes* on.

"Hey! No!"

Katniss Reyes's long red hair floated in the vacuum. Her hands grasped at nothing. Her mouth opened wide. She fell and convulsed on the regolith. Bloody sputum misted from her mouth.

Nick levered himself down awkwardly; the exosuit wasn't good at kneeling. He pushed at Kat with his claws. It was like pushing a beanbag. Soft. Dead. Her face looked like she had seen the devil in the vacuum.

Nick stood up, groaning incoherently.

"Hey." The voice was just about recognizable as Joe's. "Still want to talk?"

Nick coughed, fighting a surge of nausea. When he could speak without the risk of throwing up, he said, "What about?"

"Anything you like. Come on in."

———

"Fuck no," Nick said. "Your girlfriend's lying out here dead, with no fucking clothes on."

"She got a little crazy," Joe said.

"A little?"

"She did five years in a federal penitentiary before ArxaSys Lunar recruited her. She didn't have an easy time of it inside. Always thought it messed up her head."

Nick leaned against the base of the truss again. He stared at Kat's body. So pale, it almost looked like part of the lunar landscape, except for her red, red hair. "What messed up *your* head?"

There was a long silence. Just when Nick was starting to think Joe had gone away, he said, "I grew up on the shore of the Dead Sea. 'Cept there's no more sea there. It's just dead. That is a *direct* consequence of the incompetence, greed, and pride of the global elites."

"I believe you."

"When I first came here, I fell in love with the moon. It reminded me—still reminds me—of home." Joe made a choking noise that could have been either a laugh or a sob. "Because it's *dead...*"

Nick coughed again. Leaned heavily against the truss. "Bro, I'm breathing iron here. I don't feel good." He ran his claw over the metal, trying to find something to hold onto.

"Go back to the landers," Joe said.

"I can't be around all those dead people."

"Where did Kat go?"

"Nowhere." Nick looked at her again. "She's *dead*."

When Joe spoke again, his voice was soft. "Calm down."

"I'm fine."

"It's gonna be all right."

The pale curves of Kat's body. The cyanotic corpses in the landers. Fenella, Theo, Kurtis, Lee, and Maddy. Dead eyes staring. One flip-flop off. Blood seeping from underneath a bedsheet. The smell of burnt gunpowder, wafting across the years. *Remember—Nick—the devil. Remember—*Nick squeezed the bamboo handles of his claws until pain flared in his knuckles.

"Nick? You there?"

"Here..." Nick said through his teeth.

"It's natural. Seeing dead people like this, I mean. It's enough to make anyone freak out."

Nick let out a laugh that turned into a cough. "First time I saw a dead person, I was ten."

"How did that happen?"

"It was my father."

"Shit..."

"Yeah... I'm from South Africa, you know."

"Problems there, huh?"

"Always have been, always will be. My parents thought things were getting better. We had this farm in the Western Cape. My dad's chardonnay used to win prizes... His chief assistant was a guy named Midas Ngidi. I grew up with Midas. He lived in the township next to our farm. My dad trusted him like a brother.

"Was the township politicians who weren't happy. They looked at the crowding over there, at all our slopes covered with grapevines, and they figured something wasn't right. So, with no one telling them no, they started to invade our land. Put up shacks, moved people in. My father went down there and argued with them. Didn't make a bit of difference. They went round and round about it, everyone getting more and more pissed off."

"Sounds like a West Bank kind of situation."

"They said it wasn't our land to begin with, and my mom said it wasn't their land to begin with, either. *That* didn't help. And Midas... that piece of shit... he was there all the time, pretending to be a friend to us." Nick coughed, remembering Midas's sandaled feet tramping through the turned earth, the soft resonance of his voice. *What do you see?*

I see the devil, Midas. I see the devil in a handful of dust.

"One night they were going to come up to the farmhouse and talk. My parents had wine and cheese ready; was going to

422

be this civilized discussion. They knocked and the dog ran to see who was there. She always did that. I—I went after her and opened the door. There were five guys out there. Four I'd never seen before. Turned out later the politicians hired them from Johannesburg. These were the kind of guys who hang burning tires around people's necks. And the fifth one... Midas—he said —he said—*It's me; let me in...*" Nick's voice was wobbling. "So I did. I let them in."

"And they shot your dad?"

"Straight to the heart. They threatened my mom that they'd shoot her, too, if we didn't leave the farm. I hid under the kitchen table until they were gone. Hid the whole time the police were there. Until they took the body away."

"Hell, I would have *run.*"

"Pretty much what I've been doing all my life." Nick wriggled his left arm out of the exosuit's sleeve and worked it up inside the canister to wipe his eyes.

He'd been running away, putting distance between himself and the rest of the human race. But it was cold out here and getting harder to breathe. Dead Kat screamed silently at him to go inside before it was too late.

"They've ruined the farm. The vineyards are gone. We had fifty hectares of conservation land. They've ruined that, too. Shot the leopards, scared off the antelope. Do you know where tortoises go in the winter?"

"No idea, man."

"Trick question. They don't go anywhere, because there ain't any left."

After a few minutes, Joe said, "You sound like you're coughing pretty bad."

"I—huh!—yeah..."

"I'm unlocking the hatch. Come on in."

———

Come on in.

It's me.

Let me in.

Nick stooped into the airlock chamber. He sealed the outer hatch and slumped onto the floor. He twisted the handles of the canister lid, popped it off, scrambled out of the exosuit and gulped clean air.

The other end of the chamber began to open.

Nick glanced at the Glock, which he'd dropped on the floor, and mentally shrugged.

Warm incandescent light streamed into the chamber. There was a throbbing noise. Joe stood silhouetted in the circular opening. He held something that looked like a pair of wire cutters.

Nick tried to say something, but it was lost in the surge of unreasoning terror flooding through him, destroying his fragile resolve to trust this man.

"You fell for it," Joe said. "Idiot."

66

Joe ducked into the chamber, swinging the wire cutters at Nick's face.

Nick flinched and lost his balance. He stumbled over the discarded exosuit. The wire cutters pulled an echoing screech from the metal wall of the chamber. Nick's right hand, extended to break his fall, brushed the Glock.

Joe was a blur in bloodstained long johns. He struck with the wire cutters. The heavy metal head of the tool glanced off Nick's left shoulder, numbing it. The pain came an instant later, only Nick now had the Glock in his hand. He squeezed the trigger. The bullet clipped the edge of the inner hatch and ricocheted out of the chamber. Joe plunged out of the chamber and Nick followed.

Joe was waiting just to the side of the hatch. Peripheral vision caught the wire cutters blurring for Nick's head. He dodged sideways and fell heavily against a waist-height guardrail. They were on a catwalk running around the periphery of a circular room like a deep pit. The wire cutters cracked down on his wrist. The gun fell and skittered off the edge of the catwalk. He hardly noticed. His clothes were suffocating him. He needed to get them off.

"Sucker," Joe said, stepping back, letting the wire cutters droop. His eyes were oddly soft. His smile a scream.

Nick tore his sweat-soaked thermal shirt off over his head. His chest was heaving. Tears fell. His sobs seemed to be ripped out from the bottom of his soul. "What's wrong with me?"

"The vibrations from the Stirling engines," Joe said. "We lined the walls with aluminum. It amplifies the vibrations. Had no idea it was going to do that. The guy who was project manager before me—he ran out of here butt naked. Like Kat. Everyone said it was suicide." He gestured down at the floor of the room. "They killed themselves, too. But it wasn't suicide. It's this place."

Nick rubbed his eyes. "It's an infrasound trap."

"Got it in one."

There was nothing actually wrong with him.

He gripped onto that fact like it was an oxygen regulator.

Nothing actually wrong with him.

He spun and ran for the stairs leading to the floor. Joe clattered after him, nightmarishly close. Halfway down, he had to leap over a corpse. They were no longer objects of horror, only pity. He bounded toward the bank of consoles on the far side of the room. Where there were engines, there was a switch somewhere that would turn them off.

"No! Stop!" Joe shouted.

"I have to turn it off!"

"No! You'll kill the power to the landers—to everything!"

Nick wheeled, his back to the consoles. Joe was floundering toward him, zigzagging around the corpses. "There's still the Artemis shuttle," he said.

"How long have you been on the moon?" Joe said.

"Too long," Nick said, with a chuckle that was more than half a sob.

"That's right."

"What do you mean?"

"You're never going home."

Joe charged, his grip tight on the wire cutters.

Nick ducked the wire cutters and grappled him. Joe brought a knee up. Nick seized it and pulled him off balance. In the lunar gravity the fight was oddly balletic. Punches carried less force; throws were Olympian. They tussled back and forth, banging their elbows and heads on the housings of the Stirling engines, skidding in the blood.

"I'm gonna turn it off," Nick gritted. If he killed the power to everything, Joe would be helpless. He wouldn't be able to steal the moon.

"I'll just kill you and turn it back on again!" Joe swung at his head, the blow slow and clumsy. Tired as he was, Nick ducked with ease. He kicked at Joe's legs, sending him stumbling. Then he broke away and dived for the reactor console.

"I don't care," Nick gasped. "Do what you have to do, and I'll do what I have to do." There were so many buttons and levers. Which one would shut the reactor down? There. The one that said SCRAM. That had to be it.

"That's not the right move, Nick! You don't throw the game in a stalemate. You play it out."

Nick glanced around. Joe was pointing the Glock at him. That strange smile was back on his face, twisting his scar into a livid question mark. There was an inhuman glint in his eyes.

"Maddy was wrong," Nick muttered. "The devil didn't follow us to the moon. He was already here."

He stabbed the SCRAM button.

The soft throbbing noise died away. The whooshing of liquid through pipes bubbled down to nothing.

The lights went out.

In the dark, the keyed-up madness of grief and fear drained out of Nick's body. He laughed aloud, lighthearted, almost giddy.

Emergency lights came on, green and dim. Nick startled. Joe stood a few paces away, aiming the Glock loosely at his stomach.

Nick sighed a deep, soft sigh of resignation. "Oh well... Go on, then." Locking his gaze with Joe's, he opened his arms in a gesture of welcome, like his father had done when Midas stepped onto the verandah.

Joe's smile wavered. "Tell them—" Joe abruptly shook his head. "Tell them all to go to hell. I'll be waiting there for them." He raised the gun to his own head and pulled the trigger.

Click.

67

Nick bent over the aeroponics trays in the ArxaSys Lunar greenhouse, adjusting the hoses that fed the moisture chambers. He talked to the plants, a quiet soothing stream of baby language, the same way his father used to talk to their chardonnay vines.

The plants in the greenhouse had quite the shock when he'd turned off the power. At least the landers hadn't had a chance to cool down too much before the reactor came back online, and now the salad greens were flourishing. So were the marrows and the wheat. The tomatoes and berries looked a bit sad. Nick gave them more nutrient solution to cheer them up, and told them he would be back soon.

As he walked through the rippling knee-height sea of green, he stripped a ripe head of wheat between his fingers, rubbed the grains between his palms to husk them, and ate them. Then he climbed down the ladder.

On his way out he visited Joe.

The Glock had misfired. Joe's suicide attempt ended with a click. Nick had wrested the gun away from him and used it as a club to knock him out. While Joe was unconscious, Nick scavenged a spacesuit from one of the dead men in the reactor room. Patrick Mahoney had been the same height as Nick, and no thinner than he was now. When Joe woke up, they restarted the reactor. Then they put on their suits and hurriedly left the reactor room.

Now Joe lay in the bed he'd shared with Kat. His tired eyes, slitted by the swelling from his broken nose, watched Nick move around the room, placing drinks and painkillers within reach.

"Do you want your chess set?" Nick asked.

"No... I've kind of lost interest."

"Well, do you want a book or something?"

"We don't have any."

"I was tidying up their stuff," Nick said. He'd carried the bodies of the dead contractors outside. There was no time to bury them, but he made a stab at tidying up the mundane, heartbreaking clutter they left behind. "I found a Quran, a how-to about building a home distillery, a copy of *War and Peace*, and three Bibles. Want any of those?"

A spasm crossed Joe's face. "I'll pass."

"So good to see you showing an interest in life," Nick said.

Joe made a small curving motion of his lips. "Maybe when you come back, we can have a game of chess."

"I don't know the rules."

"Don't worry... I'll teach you."

"*If* I get back," Nick said.

He went down to the MVDA. The single undamaged rover, resupplied with rations and oxygen, waited at the docking hatch. Nick undocked it and drove away, past the ILI hab complex. The entrance tunnel was a heap of rubble. Exposed rags of fabric had already started to fade under the bombardment of cosmic rays.

He slept most of the way to Amundsen Crater, letting the rover navigate for him by satellite. The past hours had seen several cyberattacks on the ILI comms satellite, but dead Kat's code was holding.

———

Dawn had come to the Five Stones base camp. The Big Sling's arm flickered around overhead, as regular as an atomic clock. Nick parked near the basalt furnace. He got into Patrick Mahoney's suit and went into the shed. On one of the storage racks, he found the kit he was looking for: small thrusters, and the canisters of cold gas that would power them. There were also a number of large, hollow titanium molds.

The last time the Five Stones crew used the furnace, they'd been too busy to dump the melt before night fell, so there was a lump of solid basalt in the crucible. The sun heated it up. Nick positioned the mold and opened the magma taps. He cast two hollow half spheres; sealed together, they massed 1.5 tonnes. He fixed the thrusters and gas canisters into their holes. Then he dragged the massive sphere over to the winch.

On the way, he passed Spiffy lying on her face with her guts out.

Are you there, Charlie? Blink twice for yes, once for no.

Spiffy did not react.

Nick smiled bleakly. He bowed his back, heaving on the tow cable.

The sphere barely fitted onto the winch cradle. Nick had to sit on top of it. Legs dangling, he watched the base camp shrink beneath him. From above, the ruined hab looked like garbage. It wasn't a fitting tomb for the four who died inside. He'd need to think of a better monument.

On the top of the peak, he walked over to his little shrine. The rucksack's camouflage pattern had started to fade; the holocube and the laptop had stopped working. The gold lettering on the cover of the Bible was also faded. Nick opened it up again with clumsy gloved fingers. The words inside were still legible.

He read: *My heart is blighted and withered like grass; I forget to eat my food. In my distress I groan aloud and am reduced to skin and bones. I am like a desert owl, like an owl among the ruins. But you, LORD, sit enthroned forever; your renown endures through all generations.*

Nick smiled. He started to put the Bible back. After a moment's thought, he put it into his satchel. Then he went to prepare the spring-loader.

The Big Sling's payload-insertion system was mounted on a larger version of the H-frame they used to fling dust into the furnace. Nick tried it out with a small rock first. He dropped it into the tube, which was two meters across. The other end of the tube was a plunger powered by a memory-metal spring.

Spiffy used to operate the spring-loader for the furnace. It was simple enough for Nick to flip the switch on the attached solar engine, which activated the spring by heating the fluid in the cylinder inside. That made the spring rapidly lengthen. Nick eyed the funnel at the top of the Big Sling's hub and angled the tube just right.

The plunger shot up the tube. The rock shot out. Holding his breath, he watched it whizz through the vacuum. If it hit the Big Sling's whirling arm, that would be a disaster.

He'd timed it right and judged his aim well, too. The rock dropped into the funnel. From there, it fell down into the hollow top of the hub and into the gap in the arm. Nick saw a minute quiver in the arm as the rock rolled and slid out along its length, moving faster and faster. By the time it reached the arm's tip, it would be moving at several hundred kilometers per hour—well over lunar escape velocity.

Sometime in the next few days, that rock might enter Earth's atmosphere and harmlessly burn up. Maybe it would speed away into space, never to be seen again. It had no on-board guidance, unlike a real payload.

He rolled, nudged, and kicked his basalt sphere into the tube.

Then he took out the ruggedized tablet he brought from ILI.

It connected with the ILI satellite via the rover.

He placed a call.

They must have been watching him from the satellite, because they picked up almost immediately.

"Hello," Nick said. "I want to talk to Harrison McNally."

They pretended not to know who that was.

"Get him. *Now*."

A few minutes later, McNally came on the radio. Video and everything. He was a nice-looking elderly man sitting in an office. His image could have been used for politician clip art. "Who the fuck are you?"

"My name's Nick Morrison," Nick said, "and I'm the only one left alive."

They'd agreed to pretend that Joe was dead, as well. Heck, he might really be dead by now. If he was still feeling suicidal, there were plenty of sharp things in the landers. Enough Tylenol would do it.

"So, the Big Sling is mine now." That was no lie. "I don't need to tell you what that means. I own the moon. I own everything."

McNally's fuzzy video face blurred and shifted; a flaw in the reception lengthened his jaw so that his mouth yawned and his eyes stretched. The effect was demonic. Nick shivered in his suit.

"Here's what I want," he said. "You're going to renounce any claim you might think you have to the Big Sling. It's going to be used for its original intended purpose of delivering lunar resources for space-based manufacturing and spacecraft reactant supply. To ensure that happens, you're going to work with Five Stones to send up a new crew, who will be approved by China and Russia, as well as all the nations involved in ILI. These people will bring with them all they need to rebuild and equip the habitat here in Amundsen Crater.

"They will also bring five steel crosses carved with the names of Fenella Khan, Theodor Johansson, Kurtis Dean, Madeline Huxley, and Lee Yang. I want those crosses to be big enough to see from space." Nick swallowed and went on. "The international crew will remain here to oversee the operation of the Big Sling. When the mass driver is completed, it will be managed under the same open and transparent format.

"While you're arranging for all that, you'll issue an official statement disclaiming any government interest in the Big Sling, and initiate discussions leading to an international treaty that guarantees private companies from all nations total freedom to operate on the moon without undue government interference. You'll also commit, right now, to stop going after Aaron Slater and his colleagues." Nick thought for a minute. "That's all."

"That's *all*, huh? Tell me, what makes you think you can give orders to us? Who *are* you? A commercial diver. Juvenile arrest record. Known associate of violent criminals—"

"This," Nick interrupted. "I've got a tonne and a half in the tube right now. I don't know exactly where your house is, but I bet I could find out. And if I can't, I'll just drop it on the Senate. After that, maybe I'll go for the Federal Reserve. Then, I think, the Parliament buildings in Cape Town." His palms were sweating, his heart racing, yet his voice was calm.

"Sit tight," McNally said. "I'm sending some guys down

from DSG. They'll put a hole in you and your half-baked utopian ideas."

"Want to find out how many payloads I can launch before they get here?"

There was a long, long pause.

"All right!" McNally said. "All right. Damn you."

"I'm glad you've decided to do the smart thing," Nick said. He threw the switch on the spring-loader, and put down the tablet to aim the payload at the funnel. This time, the recoil from the plunger nearly knocked him over.

"Morrison? Morrison! What are you doing?"

"Just making it real for you," Nick said. "Watch for a big kaboom in a few days. You won't know exactly where it'll hit until it arrives." He'd programmed the guidance chips to aim for the middle of the Atlantic. "The suspense will give you a taste of what you tried to do to everyone else on Earth."

"Goddamn," McNally said. His face stretched again. It looked like he might be laughing. "Is there anything *else* you want?"

"Actually, yeah," Nick said. "Call my mother and aunt, and tell them I'm all right."

"Done."

Nick hesitated. "As long as we're speaking... Can you put me through to Five Stones?"

———

He descended from the central peak and radioed Joe the preagreed code word that meant it was going well so far: *Hailsong*. Then he cast another payload, just in case he needed it.

Nick was resting in the rover, eating reconstituted clam chowder, when the comms screen lit up.

"Nick?"

Her voice filled the rover like sunshine. Her face on the screen was haggard. Her smile healed his soul.

"Charlie."

"You made it," she said.

"So far, so good," Nick said.

"When are you coming home?"

"I don't know."

"I'm in jail," she said. "The Woombat killed a man—guess you saw. It was an accident, but they're holding me responsible."

"You were only trying to do the right thing," Nick said.

"I hope they see it that way... Anna's staying with my mother, so... She'll be fine. She's a tough girl. Yuta stops by every day. Aaron's vanished. No one knows where he is. Maybe he'll pop up in a few years with a plan for Mars ISRU." She laughed wryly, and Nick's heart brimmed over with a clean, reckless feeling. *On the moon,* he remembered Joe saying once, *even losers can dance.*

"I took your safe," he said. "It was Ryder who opened it. But I was there, too. I should have told you... I'm sorry."

"I already know about that," she said. "Ryder's in jail, too. *He's* not coming out for a long time."

Nick smiled.

"I had a visit from McNally today," she said. "He offered me a deal. A reduced, suspended sentence if I join this fancy international committee they're setting up. I gather you had something to do with that."

"Are you going to take it?"

"I think so, as long as they don't want me to go to the moon. I could do ground support. I can't leave Anna."

"Well..." Nick hesitated. "Guess I'll come back to Earth at some point. Don't know when, though."

"I'll be waiting," she said.

Nick didn't know what to say. He was too happy. He kissed his fingers and smeared them lightly on the screen. She reached out on her end.

Their fingertips touched through the screen.

————

Eight Continent will continue in MOON 2.0!

THANK YOU FOR READING THE EIGHTH CONTINENT!

We hope you enjoyed it as much as we enjoyed bringing it to you. We just wanted to take a moment to encourage you to review the book. Follow this link: **The Eighth Continent** to be directed to the book's Amazon product page to leave your review.

Every review helps further the author's reach and, ultimately, helps them continue writing fantastic books for us all to enjoy.

––––––––

You can also join our non-spam mailing list by visiting www.subscribepage.com/AethonReadersGroup and never miss out on future releases. You'll also receive three full books completely Free as our thanks to you.

Facebook | Instagram | Twitter | Website

Want to discuss our books with other readers and even the

authors? Join our Discord server today and be a part of the Aethon community.

Also in series:

Eighth Continent
THE EIGHTH CONTINENT
MOON 2.0
LUNAR SUPREMACY

Check out the series here:
(tap or scan)

Looking for more great Science Fiction?

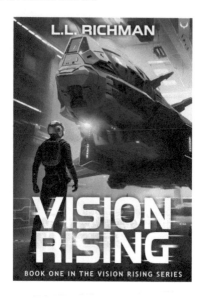

A lone soldier is gifted the power to save humanity. When a training exercise at a classified research facility goes awry, Joe Kovacs loses much more than his eyesight. He loses his career. He can't lead one of the military's top spec-ops teams if he can't see. A decision with consequences. Joe's only shot at getting his life back lies in the hands of an anonymous 'shadow' scientist. The offer is risky, an experimental implant that may or may not work. He jumps at the chance, but quickly learns the device does more than restore his sight. Much more. There's no going back. Joe begins seeing strange flashes. Ghosts of images, overlaid atop his own vision. Actions he could have taken but didn't. Worse, the visions are increasing in scope and frequency. Believing he's going mad, he confronts the scientist, only to discover the implant's shocking origin. Nothing is as it seems, and all the possible futures Joe can now see point to a system-wide conspiracy that will shift the balance of power for hundreds of years. Joe's visions hold the key to stopping it... if he can learn to control them in time. **Don't miss this exciting new Military Science Fiction Series that will make you not only question just what it means to be human, but also if there is ever a "right" side. It's perfect for fans of Halo, Rick Partlow (Drop Trooper), Jeffery H. Haskell (Grimm's War), and Joshua Dalzelle (Black Fleet Saga).**

Get Vision Rising Now!

A colony cut-off. A mysterious alien wormhole. A Captain with nothing to lose... Contact with Earth has been lost for generations and mysterious waves of disappearing colonists have been shaking the five moons of the Archimedes System for decades. When suddenly a wormhole appears in the middle of the system, the Union Navy faces an ancient danger from the darkness of deep space. A merciless war erupts, and Jeremy Brandt, Captain of the UNS Concordia, is sent through the wormhole to confront the mysterious enemy. **Pick up your copy of this new Military Science Fiction adventure from bestseller Joshua T. Calvert. Aliens, War, and a Captain who will stop at nothing to defend his people, this is Sci-Fi the way it's meant to be!**

Get Behemoth Now!

For all our Sci-Fi books, visit our website.

AFTERWORD

The basic concept of using a "sling of David" to launch a projectile is as old as written history. The idea of using a slingshot to launch projectiles off the moon is a bit newer. As far as we know, it was first proposed in 1990 by Robert Zubrin and David Baker (Baker, D., Zubrin, R., "Lunar and Mars Mission Architecture Utilizing Tether-Launched LLOX," AIAA Paper 90-2109, 26th Joint Propulsion Conference, Orlando, FL, July 16–18, 1990). Geoffrey A. Landis of NASA offered a new iteration of the idea in 2005 ("Analysis of a Lunar Launcher," Journal of the British Interplanetary Society, September 2005). Felix first encountered the concept in the work of Michael Turner, a fellow Tokyo-based space enthusiast ("Space Colonization For Real: A Moon for the Tokugawa," May 2017).

The Zubrin lunar launcher would have a rigid arm, like Five Stones' Little Sling, but Michael proposes a flexible arm and a hub situated on a crater central peak. Assuming a sling arm twenty kilometers—no, not meters—long, and a rotation speed of three rpms, a payload ejected from the tip could travel fast enough to reach Earth. The idea of using inertia to deploy the sling arm is my own. Glossing over the construction issues that gave the Five Stones crew so much grief, that leaves the choice of construction material. Here, we went with Michael's idea: basalt. In the absence of hundreds of kilometers of carbon nanotubes, basalt is a pretty great choice. It's strong, flexible when woven, and best of all, cheaply available on the moon itself.

The greatest obstacle to doing anything in space, of course, is the cost of getting stuff up there. That's the whole rationale for lunar ISRU. Use the stuff that's already up there! It's free! However, you still have to put people or robots on the moon to extract the resources. In 2019, we've yet to prove that this would be economically worthwhile. Science fiction writers have fallen back on various "killer apps" to justify sending people to the moon, such as the ever-popular helium-3. We chose something more mundane: oxygen. Even without the demand from manned space stations, on-orbit refueling of rockets and satellites could be a market worth billions of dollars within ten years (see Watts, Griffis and McOuat Ltd., "Conceptual Economic Study for Lunar Water Mining," August 2019). Basalt could be used in orbital construction facilities to manufacture heat shields and a wide range of satellite components.

The economic case for the moon, however, is inseparably bound up with human and geopolitical factors. Our love of adventure drives us to take risks, even the life-threatening risks of living and working in a hostile vacuum, not only for profit, but *just because*. As Fenella Khan says, we want to go to the moon "because it's there." We feel the same way. Nothing could be more natural to us than to push the limits of the possible and pioneer the Eighth Continent.

Unfortunately, one aspect of lunar exploration that's received less attention is geopolitical risk factors. What happens when the "space race" is won by people with bad intentions? This book suggests some of the strategic risks that any such launch system as the Big Sling would entail. Solutions are hard to envision, but will have to involve a global reexamination of space law, which at the time of writing, is a hot mess.

Other technologies depicted in this book either already exist, or could be bunged together from parts, just as the Five Stones crew built their "exosuits" from bamboo, Kevlar, and insulation. Exosuits would be a desirable solution to the space-suit problem (another concept we borrowed from Michael Turner). In real life, the frames would probably be premade from light, strong metal, but wood might actually be preferable in some use cases, or for in-situ repairs. Once we have a permanent lunar base, it would be economically efficient to grow our own repair materials. Green growing things are also a great comfort to human beings, as ISS astronauts involved with space cultivation experiments attest.

Some readers may wonder about the infrasound effects experienced by people trapped in the reactor room. Infrasound has been established as a health hazard by the WHO, and people who live near wind turbines have frequently testified to its unpleasant effects. More disturbingly, British researchers, Vic Tandy and Tony Lawrence, have linked high levels of infrasound to ghostly sightings (Tandy and Lawrence, "The Ghost in the Machine," Journal of the Society for Psychical Research, April 1998).

Efforts to develop infrasonic weapons have continued intermittently since the Cold War. But infrasound also occurs in nature, when strong winds can set up resonances with topological features. One such incident was probably responsible for the deaths of nine hikers in 1959, as detailed in Donnie Eichar's gripping book of investigative journalism, *Dead Mountain*. My depiction of the reactor room and its victims is based on the real-life fates of the "Dyatlov Nine." May God have mercy on their souls, and on all those who have died on journeys of exploration.